SUMMER OF SECOND CHANCES

A MOONWATER LAKE BOOK

ANDREA HURST

Story Editor – Stephanie Mesa

Developmental Editor – Cate Perry

Copy Editor – Audrey Mackaman

Proofreader – Diane Lander-Simon

Interior Design – Sean Fletcher

Cover Art by – Alan Ayers

Cover Design - Cherie Chapman

In memory of my own Mrs. Warrens, Lepska Warren, and Burt Siskin,
who both believed in me when I did not believe in myself.

Grief is just love with nowhere to go.

~Jamie Anderson

The Legend of Moonwater Lake:

Countless years ago, legend said a lover's kiss as the full moon reflects across the lake will connect two souls forever.

"*Y*ou're shaking," he said.

Shelby squeezed his frail hand. "Thank you for doing this."

His smile warmed the nervous chill rushing through her body. "I wouldn't miss this for the world." He offered her his steadfast arm. "Are you ready?"

She clutched her bouquet of tea roses and pale blue hydrangeas and took a deep breath to still her racing heart. The sweet notes of Pachelbel's "Canon in D" from the string quartet signaled her entrance. Another dream in Shelby's life was coming true. "Even rocky roads can lead to rainbows," Mrs. Warren had said, and she was right.

They stepped out onto the rose-petal-lined steps leading to the private dock overlooking the lake. Water and sky were a perfect cornflower blue and early summer sunrays filtered through the ancient oak trees that shaded the chairs filled with guests. A sliver of moon lingered in the sky, a sign of new beginnings.

So many smiling faces watched as she glided by in a twinkling blush and white lace gown. Around her neck, her "something old" was a cherished pearl necklace from her grandmother. As Shelby approached the front row of seats, her blissfully smiling grandmother blew a kiss, and her mother wiped a happy tear from her cheek. Three generations of women celebrating this day together. That was more than a dream come true; it was a miracle.

Once Shelby reached the raised platform, her escort took his seat in the front row next to Alice. On the stage, under the floral altar, the groom's eyes met hers. Everything else faded away as she took the final steps to meet him. Shelby handed her bouquet to her maid of honor. Now face to face with her fiancé in his gray suit and pale blue tie, without a doubt in her heart or mind, she was ready to commit to this man forever.

From the platform, a familiar dog bark punctuated the air with approval. Shelby glanced over at Scarlett, her grandmother's adorable doxie-poodle, in the arms of the best man. Around the dog's neck was a floral collar similar to Shelby's bouquet with silk bows. Their wedding rings rested on a satin pillow on Scarlett's back. The dog's auburn curls had faded, her face now threaded with white. Yet if it hadn't been for sweet Scarlett when Shelby had reluctantly come to Moonwater Lake those ten years ago, she may not be standing here as a bride at all.

CHAPTER 1

TEN YEARS AGO

*S*helby stared at the computer screen. She'd read the same line three times and was no closer to prepping for her high school English final than when she'd first sat down. Keeping her A average was crucial. It would make all the difference as to whether she would receive a college scholarship. She lifted her thick hair off her neck, allowing the slight whisper of A/C to cool her. The Las Vegas climate was brutal, and it didn't help that the only place to study was the tiny kitchen table.

Her mother, Dana, oblivious to Shelby's attempts at concentration in their cramped apartment, washed and clanked dishes in the sink. And she was humming. It was unlike her mother to hum, much less have a smile on her face, unless there was a new man in her life. It was probably that guy who had taken Dana to dinner a few times and had been nonstop calling ever since.

The man, she thought his name was Gus, had brought flowers and candy when he'd picked her mother up the other night. After he'd driven Dana home, Shelby had heard them through her bedroom wall and had to pull the pillow over her head to get any sleep. Some nights her mother wouldn't come home at all. And even though Shelby would be worried and a little uneasy, at least it was quiet in the house. Gus had tried to start a conversation with Shelby that morning. Asked her what she was doing in school, pretended to be interested, but she thought he was just making talk, trying to impress her mother.

Dana, finished with her task, stood hovering at Shelby's side, her too strong perfume filling the air. "When's the semester over again?" she asked.

Shelby's stomach clenched. Dana always had an ulterior motive. She tried on a few possibilities, feeling worse by the minute. Maybe the rent was due again and Dana didn't have the money to pay it? Or, worst case scenario, they were moving again. Shelby hoped not. She'd finally gotten used to this school, and she had summer plans to finish lifeguard training. And Nick from her English class was going to be in class too. Of course that wasn't the only reason she was taking the training, but perhaps "sweet sixteen and never been kissed" would finally not be true by summer's end.

"When did you say your last day of school was?"

Shelby sighed. "I told you, it's next Monday, June 4th. My last final is tomorrow. Why?"

"Oh," her mother said. "Well, I might have a surprise coming for you. Very soon."

Shelby highly doubted it was a surprise she would be happy about. That giddy smile Dana was wearing now usually meant her mother was supposedly falling in love. Again. That word, again, like a mantra in Shelby's life.

Striking a pose, her mother asked, "Do you like my new top? Gus is coming to take me out tonight. You remember him. He's so dreamy."

Shelby stared at her mother, shaking her head.

Her mother bristled. "This one is different."

"Right," Shelby said. She looked down at her own faded, too-tight shirt, bought from the thrift shop in the former town they'd lived in. And if it got any hotter in their apartment from trying to save money by not turning up the air conditioning, Shelby would melt. With Dana, there was always another man, another job, another scheme. Something that was going to make their life better. As soon as she heard her mother's cell phone ring, and the sugary voice Dana answered with, Shelby knew exactly where this was heading.

Shelby retreated to her bedroom and closed the door. Not that it would make a difference in this closet-sized place with cardboard-thin walls. At least the room was hers. It was only 8:00 p.m. After her mother went out for her date, Shelby would try again to study. And turn the A/C up so her brain wouldn't vaporize in the process.

THANKS to her mother not coming home until after 2:00 a.m. the night before, Shelby breezed through the test the next day in school. Mostly that's what she was good at, school. Studying, figuring out what the teachers wanted and giving it to them. It was the one place where if she studied hard and applied herself, things would work out in the form of a top grade.

Shelby sat with Maddie in the corner of the lunchroom, picking at the peanut butter sandwich she'd made herself before leaving home. She didn't have many friends. Maddie was new and in her sophomore English class. They hung out sometimes at lunch, but conversation was limited. Shelby and Dana were never in one place long enough for Shelby to make a good friend, and so she usually kept her distance.

Shelby scanned the beige-on-beige room. They were serving tacos today and it made her mouth water as kids walked by carrying trays filled with real food. As usual, the established cliques had already claimed their tables along the windows.

She noticed Nick, with his broad shoulders and cool hairstyle, sitting with a group of friends, and the longing started again. Before she could stop herself from staring, he looked over and caught her gaze. With a wide smile and noticeable wave, he acknowledged her presence. His friends at the table turned to see where Nick's attention was focused. But after spotting it was only Shelby, they fell back into their own conversation. Nick shrugged and turned to join them.

"He was looking right at you," Maddie said.

Shelby wanted to be invisible. "I know," she whispered. "Don't stare at him. It's no big deal."

"But it is," Maddie said. "He's on the football team. And maybe he likes you."

"I don't think so. Nick and I are in the same lifeguard training course at the pool, that's all."

Maddie was quiet. "I guess," she said, "but I think he does."

Shelby looked down at her wrinkled, out-of-style outfit of jeans and a dated t-shirt she'd managed to find clean today. A guy like Nick hung out with the popular girls with the nice clothes and fancy cars. She glanced back over at the table where Nick and his pals were. Their raucous laughter echoed throughout the room. She hoped they weren't laughing at her. She could feel her face getting hot when Nick stole a quick glance back at her.

One of the cheerleaders, with long, silky, auburn hair, sat down next to Nick at his table. Her hand reached across his back as she slid in next to him and rested her head on his shoulder.

"I know you're wrong, Maddie." The room felt like it was closing in on her and Shelby found it hard to breathe. She scrunched up what was left of her sandwich and stuffed it into the paper bag. "I'm done and out of here," she said standing. She waited for Maddie to reply but the girl just stared up at her. After a few awkward moments, Shelby turned to leave. "I guess I'll see you later." She couldn't get out of there fast enough.

Nick's smile dawdled in her memory as she stood in the hall

by her next class letting herself cool off. The way his silky hair fell across his forehead, his soft-looking lips. If only. Shelby stepped inside the classroom. Her favorite teacher, Mrs. Warren, was at her desk and waved for Shelby to come in and join her. It always surprised Shelby how short the teacher was in stature, because her presence in class was bold and brilliant.

"You're here early," Mrs. Warren said as Shelby approached her desk.

"I guess so."

"How have all your finals gone?"

"So far, so good. I think." Shelby let her shoulders drop as the safety of being in this room with her philosophy teacher relaxed her.

"I'm sure you aced them as usual. With that sharp mind of yours, you'll be able to accomplish anything you set out to."

Shelby let those words sink in. "Do you really think so?"

Mrs. Warren's steel blue eyes seemed to look right through her. "I know so."

And when she said it, Shelby believed it. But then she remembered her mother's surprise. "I think we're moving again," she said.

"I see. And you're not happy about that?"

What could Shelby say? She was devastated. She wanted to spend her junior year at this school and take every class Mrs. Warren taught. And maybe this summer in lifeguard training she would finally have her first boyfriend. Her mind wandered to Nick. He was a year ahead of her and might ask her to his senior prom, and in a few years she'd get a scholarship to college, she'd move into her own place, and her life would not be controlled by her mother's whims.

Mrs. Warren was still waiting for an answer. Shelby could feel her throat constricting. "I don't want to leave, but I don't have a choice."

Mrs. Warren's voice softened. "You always have a choice, Shelby. Sometimes they are just not great ones. But you need to remember, you deserve to be happy. We all do."

Before Shelby could comment, a couple of giggling girls piled into the classroom.

She wanted to tell Mrs. Warren just how much she meant to her, how she had opened Shelby's eyes to see her own potential. But the classroom was filling up and the bell had just rung. She had to take her seat.

"Thank you, Mrs. Warren," Shelby said.

Mrs. Warren looked straight at her. "Don't forget what I said."

Shelby met those piercing blue eyes she would never forget. "I won't. Or you."

AFTER SCHOOL, some of Shelby's classmates were going out for ice cream, and for once they asked her to join. She really wanted to. To be happy, to be normal with the other kids. But her mother, who was usually not home until after 4:00 p.m., had insisted Shelby come right home from school today. She took the bus and got off close to the apartment. Walking the last two blocks was sweltering, even in the shade. When she reached her apartment complex, Shelby saw her mother's latest boyfriend, Gus, getting out of his silver Ford pickup. A shiny camper was fitted over the back of the truck bed. Her mother had mentioned what he did for a living, but Shelby couldn't remember. She never listened that closely, since he probably wouldn't be around for long. Maybe he was on his way out, too.

Shelby hesitated long enough to watch Gus walk up the steps and knock on their door. Dana opened it and threw her arms around him, before pulling him inside the apartment. Usually her mother was at work this time of day. Shelby looked around the parking lot for their faded old '97 Toyota. The car Shelby had hoped would be hers for her sixteenth birthday, that had passed uneventfully last week, was not to be seen. A familiar sense of panic washed over her as she thought about what the real surprise might be.

All Shelby wanted was to go home, take a cool shower, and a long nap in her own room. But that was not possible now. She walked over to their downstairs neighbor's apartment, where she could hear GiGi yipping behind the door, but no one answered. The neighbor sometimes paid Shelby to pet-sit the little white Chihuahua when she was working a late shift.

"Hi, GiGi," Shelby called through the door. "How's my little girl?"

The dog moved from the door to the window and cast aside the drapes to see Shelby. Her little nose pushed against the window as she continued to bark.

Shelby leaned over and kissed the dog through the window. "Love you, little sweetie."

The one time Dana had let Shelby get a dog a few years ago, it had gone back to the shelter when they'd moved. It had broken Shelby's heart to have to say goodbye. But at least it was a no-kill shelter and they'd promised to find Suzy a good home. Shelby had cried for days, but her mother had said, "Oh, it's just a dog. We can always get another one when we get settled." And of course, there was never another one. At their last place, Shelby had befriended a stray tabby she'd named Tiger. He'd hung out behind their apartment and she'd left food for him when she could. He'd purr and rub against her. She'd made sure one of the neighbors agreed to feed him before they moved that time.

Shelby decided to just go upstairs and face what was happening. She rattled the doorknob to announce her presence before opening the door. Voices drifted over from the sofa.

"Come on in," her mother said.

After dropping her backpack on the kitchen table, Shelby joined them in the living room. Her mother's freshly bleached blonde hair tumbled loose around her bare shoulders, exposed by a strapless sundress. Her makeup was even heavier than usual. There was a half empty wine bottle on the table and Gus had just arrived. It was only three o'clock in the afternoon; obviously her mother had started celebrating early.

"Come join us," Dana said. She patted the worn couch next to her.

"What's the occasion?" Shelby forced herself to ask.

"Well…Gus has asked me to go on a trip with him this summer. We're going to drive cross country. He got a brand-new, fancy camper that even has air conditioning."

For a moment, Shelby imagined all three of them packed in that camper. It was a worse nightmare than this apartment.

"We're going to see the sights," her mother continued. "All the way to Florida where Gus's family lives." Dana rested her head on Gus's shoulder. "Right, honey?"

Gus put his arm around Dana's shoulder. "Anywhere you want," he said. "The beaches in Miami are warm enough to swim in. You'll love it."

In his bright Hawaiian shirt and shorts, he looked like he was already headed for the beach. With his thinning hair and being at least ten years older than her mom, he was no Prince Charming, but to Dana he obviously was. Shelby hoped he was a nice guy at least.

"Oh, that sounds exciting," Shelby choked out.

Shelby thought about Disney World. She'd always wanted to go since she was a kid. But when she glanced up, her mother was giving her the sympathetic I-have-something-to-tell-you- that-you-won't-like kind of look.

Dana's eyes flashed back at Gus for support. Shelby recognized the expression on her mother's face when she turned back around. The guilty, pleading look that meant Shelby had to be the adult again.

"You're going to be very excited to hear," her mother said. "You'll be spending the summer with your Grandma Alice at Moonwater Lake. You know how much you love it there, and she's got a cute dog you can play with."

Dana took a breath, staring expectantly at Shelby. When Shelby did not reply, she continued. "You know your grandmother's been so lonely since Grandpa died. We're going to drop you off there, and you'll have the whole summer. No school, just swimming."

Shelby stared at them. So far Gus had been silent. They both looked to her, obviously hoping for approval. All she could think was that she was being dumped at her grandma's so her mother could have another adventure. They would lose their apartment and probably never come back. And Nick...she'd have to say goodbye to him on Monday.

"When are we going?" Shelby asked.

"We were thinking of leaving tomorrow, so you'd better hurry up and pack your stuff."

"But my last day of school is Monday. Can't we at least wait until then?"

Gus finally spoke up. "If we leave tomorrow, the pressure will be off your mother to have to come up with another month's rent."

"And I already sold the car," Dana said.

So that's where it went, Shelby thought. And that money was probably already spent on her mother's vacation clothes, by the look of Dana's new outfit.

"I'll make sure we get you safe and sound to your grandmother's," Gus said. "I look forward to meeting Alice and seeing the lake."

"You don't know anything about my grandmother or the lake or what I might want."

"I'm sorry, I don't," Gus said. "But I would like to."

For a moment Shelby thought maybe this man would be nice to her mother. Maybe he would last. Maybe her mother would keep humming and being happy. But it was so unlikely, Shelby doubted their relationship would even last the whole summer. Or if Dana would show up at some point at her grandmother's and announce where they were moving next. What choice did Shelby have? Mrs. Warren's words came floating back to her. *We always have a choice.* And the consequences? Shelby needed time to consider this. But her mother was leaving her precious little of that. She had to get away from them and think. Fast.

Shelby stood up. "Okay then," she said, trying to keep her voice even. "I'll go pack."

"You do that," Dana said. "Gus is going to take me shopping for a few things for our trip. We'll bring dinner back."

Once in her room, Shelby shut the door and dropped down on her bed. It wouldn't be her bed much longer. The place came furnished. The only thing that was hers was the ratty suitcase. She could hear GiGi barking downstairs. It was probably the sound of Gus's truck pulling out that disturbed the dog. If only Shelby could just tell them to go and she would stay. She'd find a place to live, a job, maybe dog sitting on one of those online sites. She could do it. But how? The walls felt like they were closing in and sucking out all the oxygen with them.

She jumped off the bed and pulled the old suitcase out from under it. She'd packed so many times and knew exactly what could fit in the case and her backpack. She stuffed her clothes in and a few other items. Her out-of-date, donated laptop went in her backpack. She looked around the bedroom. There were very few personal belongings. From the top of her bed, Shelby took the pink and white furry blanket her grandmother had made her when she was little. Grandma Alice had always thought of her and given her little gifts. Shelby squeezed it against her heart, taking in the lingering, faint scent of her grandmother's house. Carefully she rolled it up and placed it in her pack.

On top of her brown painted dresser was a framed picture of a rocky path winding through a garden with a rainbow at the end. She had painted it in art class. She almost tossed the picture in the trash. Mrs. Warren had inspired her the day she'd painted this, but as far as Shelby could tell, all she'd seen so far were the rocks. She held the picture in the air and felt the same hope stir in her chest that had inspired her to paint it. Before she changed her mind, she tucked it in the top of the suitcase. There was no time to say goodbye to anyone. She put on her Dollar Store sunglasses, hefted the backpack over her shoulder, picked up the suitcase by the handle, and shut the front door behind her.

Dana and Gus were nowhere in sight, so the coast was clear. She could hear GiGi barking as she hurried down the stairs. "Bye, little girl," she said to the dog as she passed. She blew her a kiss.

A few blocks down, Shelby took the first side street heading south to get off the main road. The afternoon sun beat on her head and shoulders. She would need a hat. And food, soon. And a place to sleep. The twenty dollars she had saved from dog sitting wasn't going to get her very far. And where was she going? But she kept walking, one foot in front of the other, for about a mile, until dizziness made her hesitate. She looked for shelter amidst the fake puddles of water she knew to be a mirage.

Shelby found a minute patch of shade under an elm tree near a curb and sat down, suitcase at her side. Her t-shirt clung to her back and sweat dripped down her brow. "Just where are you going?" she asked herself. And then the tears started. She didn't even have a Kleenex with her, or a simple bottle of water. Running away took planning.

All that talk about choices. Now all she had were choices, but none of them made any sense. She had nowhere to go. She wiped her tears with her arm and imagined Mrs. Warren telling her she was a smart girl and would figure this out. Shelby considered calling her grandmother and laughed at the absurdity of the idea. That was exactly where Dana and Gus were taking her anyway. She would be safe there. Suddenly the idea of being with her Grandma Alice seemed like a reprieve. At least she wouldn't have to be present when everything fell apart for her mother again, this time with Gus.

After a few moments of rest, suitcase in hand, Shelby stood up and started walking back the way she'd come. Hopefully, Dana and Gus wouldn't see her and she could sneak back in before they returned. As she approached the apartment stairs with the flimsy metal railings, she spotted her neighbor out walking GiGi.

"Going somewhere?" the neighbor asked, glancing at the suitcase.

"Actually, we're moving," Shelby said. She leaned down and petted the dog one more time. "I'll miss GiGi."

"And we will miss you. GiGi adores you."

The woman truly looked sad that she was leaving. Shelby could feel tears building. "I'm glad we got to say goodbye."

With a last glance at the dog, Shelby hurried up the stairs and into the apartment. The first thing she did was crank up the A/C. They were leaving anyway, so what did it matter? She curled up on the sofa and waited for her mother to return. Maybe Moon-water Lake would be fun. She could swim in the clear water and get a little part-time job. She hadn't seen her grandmother in over a year, not since Grandpa Stan died and they'd gone back briefly for the funeral. Grandmother Alice had looked so sad and lonely. Shelby hated that Dana had insisted on leaving right after the funeral. They'd really had nowhere to be. Alice had always been there when they needed her. She deserved better.

There was her grandmother's puppy, Scarlett, to keep her company. A few months before Grandpa Stan died, he'd surprised her grandmother with the curly doxie-poodle mix. A woman had been sitting outside a grocery store with the pups in a box and he couldn't resist. Shelby remembered from their brief visit to Moonwater Lake that year that the puppy was a real cuddler. She imagined playing with it, taking it for walks. It was all in how you viewed things, she reminded herself. She would see this as a summer vacation at the lake, and maybe even enjoy it. She was used to starting over and making the most of things, and this would be no different.

CHAPTER 2

They had been driving for what seemed like hours since Dana had dragged Shelby out of bed at four o'clock that morning. Even at dawn, her mother had on full makeup and a low-cut shirt with white shorts. Her wavy blonde hair fell over her shoulders. Half asleep, Shelby had thrown on old jeans and joined them in the car. Finally, they were going to stop for some food. Shelby was curled up in the back seat of Gus's truck, wrapped in her furry blanket. Her stomach had been growling for hours, but Dana was insistent they make the over-600-mile drive to Moonwater Lake in northern California before dinnertime today.

"Wake up, sleepyhead," Dana said. "We're going to drive through this fast food place."

Gus chimed in, "Get whatever you want. It's on me."

"Can't we go in?" Shelby asked. "I have to use the bathroom."

Gus looked at Dana for an answer.

"We're already in the line. And it will be faster if we just eat in the car. You can run into the bathroom before we take off. You'd better order plenty, because I'm not sure we're going to stop again before we get there."

Great, Shelby thought. Perhaps she'd better not order a drink either. She had no idea what the big hurry was and didn't want to ask. Dana had instructed her that morning to be on her best behavior with Gus around. As if she wasn't already doing that. Certainly Dana had been her most charming self with the man.

After ordering, Gus parked under a shade tree, rolled the windows down, and they ate their fast food brunch. Shelby had ordered extra hash browns for later even though they would be cold, two egg sandwiches, and an apple pie. It was nothing like what Grandma Alice made, but it would do for now. She heard Gus say they were somewhere around Barstow and were making good time. She wished she had her own cell phone so she could put on some ear buds and listen to music. Dana had tossed their burner phone after Gus had bought Dana a new cell phone for the trip. Instead, she tugged a book out of her backpack and settled in for the rest of the drive. Her grandmother would be waiting when she arrived, and there would be a home-cooked dinner that night.

THE NEXT TIME Shelby opened her eyes, the sun was shining bright and Gus was parking the truck in front of her grandmother's white house with matching green louvered shutters. Shelby loved the cottage-style home with small dormer windows in the upstairs attic. Towering oak and willow trees shaded the yard, and the red-blooming hibiscus bush had a few early blossoms. Standing on the porch behind the white railing was her grandmother, in a floral shirt and tan slacks. She waved to them and walked down the faded brick path toward the street.

"You made it," Alice said.

Before Dana exited the car, she commented to Gus, "Let's just stay for a few minutes. We still have an over-three-hour drive ahead of us."

"Are you sure?" he said. "I'm happy to meet your mother."

Dana shrugged. Shelby watched as her mother reconsidered her statement to Gus. Usually Dana would have snapped and said, "Of course I'm sure!" Maybe Gus's relaxed demeanor was rubbing off on her.

"And she will want to meet you, too," Dana said. She gave Gus a flirty look and continued. "But we don't want to be late for our romantic dinner in Lake Tahoe."

His smile said it all. He was falling hard for Dana, and Shelby knew that one way or another, her mother would get her way.

Once permission was granted, Shelby exited the car, carrying her small suitcase, and flew into her grandmother's comforting arms. The suitcase fell to moist green grass, something Shelby had not seen in a while. Barking at the screen door was Scarlett, Alice's curly-haired little dog.

"So good to see you, sweetheart," Alice said. "Let me look at you. Taller and prettier by the minute."

Shelby could feel herself blush. She scrambled for something to say back. Alice had dark circles under her eyes, and her clothes hung loosely on her body. "Thanks, Gram."

Dana walked over and introduced Gus.

He extended his right hand. "It's so nice to meet you, Alice." With his other hand he offered her the box of fresh strawberries they'd hastily picked up at a fruit stand along the way. "Dana mentioned that you like these."

Alice raised a brow and made eye contact with Dana. "Did she, now? Well thank you, Gus. Why don't you all come in? I've made some iced tea and you can rest a bit before you're off."

Even before Alice opened the screen door, the familiar scent of butter and cinnamon permeated the air. The minute they stepped in, Scarlett charged Shelby and jumped into the air in excitement. Shelby picked up the shiny-haired red dog for a hug. "You are so cute," she said. The dog licked her face and then squirmed out of her arms and back to the floor.

Gus bent over and gave the dog a scratch behind its ears. "What breed is this? She's the color of an Irish Setter."

"That little troublemaker is part dachshund, part poodle, and all love." Alice pointed to the fluffy dog bed in the living room. "Scarlett, bed." The dog's eyes pleaded for a moment. Seeing no reprieve, she strode over and plopped on her bed.

Shelby glanced at the wall of family photos, noticing the familiar wedding picture of her grandma in a long, lacy wedding gown and Grandpa Stan in a dark suit. Grandpa's hair was a little long back then. Most of Shelby's memories were of him in overalls working in their apple orchard she used to visit as a child.

Alice led them to the dining room, where the table was set with glasses filled with ice topped with a sprig of mint. In the center was a large pitcher of deep amber-colored tea and a plate of her grandmother's fresh-baked cookies.

"Help yourself," Alice said. "Sugar cookies with raspberry frosting."

Gus pulled a chair out for Dana.

Polite conversation followed, mostly led by Dana's description of their cross-country trip ahead. Shelby tuned out and let the delicious taste of the buttery cookie calm her nerves. The white shiplap ceiling brightened the room and set off the brick fireplace that Grandma's recliner nestled near. Grandpa's old books still filled the shelves, and Alice's blue-and-white-patterned dishes the china cabinet. It looked just like it had before Grandpa died, but somehow it still felt sad. She wondered if Dana missed her father at all, since she'd never spoken of him after they'd left the funeral. And he was one of the kindliest men Shelby had ever met.

"Shelby," her mother said. "Are you listening to me?"

For a moment Shelby was disoriented.

"Did you get everything out of the car? We have to go now."

"Yes, everything," Shelby answered.

Before they rose to leave, Alice asked, "About when do you

plan to return to pick up Shelby? I'd love to have her here all summer."

Dana shrugged. "Sometime before the summer ends." She looked over at Gus and smiled sweetly. "Speaking of returning, we'd better get going. We have a lot more driving to do today."

Gus stood and pushed in his chair. "Right," he said. "We don't want to be driving those mountain roads in the dark."

"Of course not," Alice said as she rose to walk him to the door. "It was nice to meet you."

"Same here, ma'am," he said.

Shelby followed them to the door, hoping the goodbye would be fast.

Her mother's hand was already on the doorknob when Gus stopped her and turned to Shelby. "I hope you'll have a wonderful summer here with your grandmother."

Shelby looked him right in the eyes and saw nothing but sincerity. "Thanks. You have a good trip, too."

Dana took his arm and opened the door. "You two enjoy your summer at the lake. We'll call and check in."

Before Shelby could respond, the couple were out the door. Alice and Shelby walked out on the porch and waved goodbye as the camper truck drove off.

Alice started down the front steps toward where Shelby had left her suitcase on the grass. "Let's get you settled in your room."

Shelby hurried over to pick it up. She didn't want her grandmother having to do anything extra for her. "Same room in the front of the house?" she asked as they walked in.

Alice nodded. "It's all ready for you. Why don't you go get settled in?"

Shelby yawned. "Do I have time for a quick nap?"

"Of course. Take all the time you need. Dinner isn't for a few hours. I'm making one of your favorites, honey-baked chicken."

The thought of a home-cooked meal that didn't come out of a box or can was comforting. Shelby took her things to her room down the hall. Scarlett followed at her heels and jumped on the bed. Pale blue walls with white trim gave the room a beachy vacation feel. The large window facing the front yard caught morning sun and had a peek-a-boo view of the lake. Before that huge modern home across the street had been built, the room had had an unobstructed view. But the town of Moonwater Lake had changed over the years. Been discovered, her grandpa had said.

Shelby placed her suitcase on the wingback chair and slipped off her shoes to feel the cool wood floor. There was plenty of time to unpack later. She took a few steps to the window and pushed the sheer curtain aside. Out in the cul-de-sac, two boys were tossing basketballs in a hoop. At least there were some young people around, and not just tourists.

The older teenage boy had his shirt off, displaying his toned, suntanned back as he moved with ease around the street. Golden-brown, sunlit hair tousled across his face. He darted onto her grandmother's lawn to retrieve the ball and caught her watching from the window. She was rewarded with a dazzling smile that shot through her body like lightning.

Tossing back the curtain, she hurried away from the window. Perhaps summer at Moonwater Lake wouldn't be so bad after all!

CHAPTER 3

The room was so neat and tidy that Shelby decided to unpack the few things she had brought and put her suitcase away. It didn't take long. She hung up a couple shirts and put the rest in the white dresser with the antique handles. She placed her framed painting of a rainbow on the nightstand facing the bed. There was a small desk in the corner where she put her worn computer and some books.

She couldn't remember ever having a nice big bedroom like this all to herself. Maybe when Keith, her father, was still alive before the motorcycle accident, she wondered. Dana had shown her pictures of a bright yellow house with a picket fence where they had lived when Shelby was little. Her mother looked so young and happy in those pictures. Her dad, whom she had only vague memories of, was handsome, with dark, curly hair touching his shoulders. What would her life have been like if he had lived? She'd fantasized on that many times, but the reality was he had died.

Shelby dropped on to the bed and rolled on her side, the familiar furry blanket at her feet. Scarlett snuggled up under her arm and placed her head on Shelby's shoulder. "You sweet girl,"

Shelby said. "You and I are going to be great friends this summer."

The dog's tail thumped the bed in a rhythmic beat. "Woof, woof," Scarlett barked, staring into Shelby's eyes.

"What do you want, little one?" Shelby asked. "A snack? A walk?"

At the word "walk," the dog stood up in bed with a very hopeful look on her face. Shelby figured Scarlett hadn't had many walks lately, if at all. On the way up, Dana had mentioned that since Grandpa died, Alice was not getting out much, and that maybe Shelby could cheer her up. First of all, what was Dana, Alice's own daughter, doing to help with that? Nothing. Was Shelby the appointed fix-all-the-adults person?

But now that she had seen the sadness in her grandmother's eyes, Shelby really hoped she could help bring back her smile. Scarlett nudged her hand with another low bark. "Okay, okay. Perhaps we can manage a short walk before dinner," Shelby said.

Scarlett jumped off the bed and stood waiting for Shelby to do the same.

"I guess I'm not going to be napping much today." Shelby opened the bedroom door and the dog raced out toward the front door, where her leash was hung on a hook.

"That was a short nap," her grandmother said. She looked half asleep herself in her recliner in the living room.

"Did we wake you?" Shelby asked.

Her grandmother shook her head. "Just dozing."

Shelby looked over at Scarlett, who was waiting not so patiently at the door. "I think the dog would like to go for a walk. Why don't you join us?"

Alice's gaze dropped to her lap. "I'm afraid I've not taken her out much lately." When she looked up, tears glistened in her eyes. "I just can't seem to find the energy since Grandpa Stan died."

"No worries. I'd love to walk her. My legs are stiff from the drive anyway."

"Thank you, dear. I'm so glad you're here."

"Me too," Shelby said and realized she meant it.

"I'll get dinner started soon. It'll be a bit late tonight, but ready when you get back. You've got time. The sun doesn't set until after eight these days."

Despite Scarlett's squirming, Shelby clipped on the dog's harness and waved to her grandmother as she left. A container of doggy bags was attached, so she was prepared.

Once down the porch steps, Shelby turned left on the path that led down toward the lake. Puffy, pink clouds hung in the sky, reflecting like cotton candy on the water. A few fishing boats were making their way back before dusk, but otherwise the lake and sandy area were calm and mostly empty of people. Rather than choose the path toward town, Shelby took the wooden staircase that led down to the beach area.

When they reached the sand, Scarlett tugged toward the water and Shelby let her take the lead. With no one in sight, Shelby removed the leash and let the dog chase the water line, splashing her little paws in and out. The dog needed to play. So did Shelby. She kicked off her shoes and chased the pup along the shallow water's edge. "I've got you," she said, pretending to catch Scarlett.

The dog raced away, barking playfully before losing her footing and somersaulting into the sand. She hastily righted herself and shook the wet sand off.

"You are too funny," Shelby said. The sound of her own laugh surprised her; it had been a while.

Sadness will do that to you, she thought as she sat down on the sand to watch the sun begin to set. She'd seen her mother alternate between deep sadness and elation so many times, Shelby wondered if either side was real. To balance her mother, Shelby tried to stay level, but mostly that meant flat. Not happy, not sad, just careful. The reflection of the sunlit clouds on the water now reminded her of orange sherbet, perhaps mixed with some black cherry. Tomorrow she would go down to Redd's, the great ice cream place in town. After all, it was summer. She would swim in the lake, walk the dog, and try some new flavors of her favorite treat.

Scarlett leapt into Shelby's lap with her cold, muddy feet. "You ready to go home now, little one?"

Shelby hooked the leash back on, stood, and brushed off the sand. Her stomach growled and she remembered a welcoming dinner would be waiting for her. They hopped up the wooden steps and walked over to a grassy area overlooking the lake. She wanted to make sure Scarlett had a chance to go one more time before heading home. As they walked along, Shelby noticed a slumped elderly man with a beagle sitting on one of the benches. They walked quietly behind him, but Shelby couldn't help but notice he seemed to be talking to someone next to him. Except there was no one sitting there. The words, "I wish you were here…" drifted in the air. Shelby pretended she did not hear and hurried past him. So much sadness everywhere, she thought.

She forced a smile back on her face. She had a whole summer before her, a wonderful place to live with her grandmother, and a dog to love. She could get a part-time job and make a friend. Maybe she was right where she was supposed to be, and everything would work out. At least now she could hope.

CHAPTER 4

The dog's snoring woke Theo up. Wally was better than an alarm clock.

Another day.

He looked around the bedroom he'd shared with his wife, Jean, of almost fifty years. Every cell of his body ached. The weight on his chest made it hard to breathe. Without Jean's warm body next to his at night, he could barely sleep. The old beagle would snuggle close, just the two of them, and for a moment everything would be all right. But the loneliness crept in the minute he opened his eyes and found the space beside him was empty.

"Give it time," his son Cameron had said. It was well over a year now and time was not a healer for him. He knew he was kidding only himself if he believed this would get better.

The dog stirred and Theo knew he had to drag himself out of bed and put some clothes on. These dark moods had to lift sometime. It was summer and the sky was crystal blue reflecting off cool, clear water. At least he could leash up his old boy and go for a walk. Theo tried to keep to a routine for the dog, something he could hold on to. Wally's safety kennel was in the corner of the room if Theo needed to go out for a few hours. But he hadn't needed to use it for a long time.

Theo sat down in the brown leather recliner and put on his walking shoes. Wally used to jump in the air to go for a walk, but now he patiently waited by the door. Once outside, they trudged along the path adjacent to the lake, passing through familiar oaks and pines that he and his wife had admired so many times together. They had retired here over ten years ago and been active in the community. The townspeople were kind to him that summer after Jean passed, but the casseroles in his kitchen had been mostly left untouched. He stopped answering his door; he could not force a smile one more time. And then the summer folk left, the air chilled, and eventually it was just him, his dog, and his grief.

He wanted to sit down, but knew he needed to walk. Or at least the dog did. He watched Wally waddle up ahead, his gait slow.

"What a pair we make, two old men," Theo said.

The beagle's golden-brown muzzle was almost pure white now, and Theo couldn't believe Wally had turned down his favorite treats for days. When Jean had held the treat in her hands, Wally danced in the air, the room echoing with barks. But since she'd died, neither of them was doing much dancing. At first Wally had spent most of his day lying beside Theo on the bed or in the recliner. He'd never left his side. Now he mostly slept in his favorite spot on the couch where he used to snuggle with Jean, occasionally opening his eyes to make sure Theo was nearby.

Tired already after only a few blocks, Theo gave in and sat down on the wooden bench overlooking the west side of the lake. He and Jean had sat there almost daily. It was still morning, so only a few joggers were out and a couple of people walking dogs. A fishing boat caught his attention as it left the pier, probably heading out for bass.

On the sandy beach down below, Theo watched Logan the lifeguard setting up for the day, getting ready for the beachgoers who would soon overtake the sand. He was glad to see him back again with his family this summer.

"Such a fine young man," he said to the dog. "His whole life is in front of him." Theo remembered working as a lifeguard at a local pool when he was in college. Mostly he'd liked the job in hopes of meeting girls.

Yes, he was talking out loud to the dog now. There was no one else to talk to. Theo's life was behind him. There wasn't a part of his body that didn't remind him of that daily, especially his heart.

"Jean," he whispered. This was their spot. If she could still hear him, it would be here. "I'm walking the dog, like you asked. But I'm getting a bit worried about the old boy."

Theo could almost hear her answering him. "You two just need to get out more. Remember, you promised me."

Theo lowered his head. He was not sure how much longer he could keep that promise. Some mornings it was only the thought of Wally needing to go out that forced him out of bed. If the dog… "Don't go there," he told himself.

A young girl's voice cut through his foggy brain.

"Scarlett, come back here," she said.

A red-haired, little poodle ran up to Wally, nudged him, and wanted to play. Theo remembered seeing that dog now and then, but not so much lately. Wally allowed a polite sniff and proceeded to do the same to the perky dog.

"I'm sorry if she's bothering you," the girl said. "When she saw your dog, she just pulled the leash right out of my hand."

Theo blocked the sun from his eyes with his hand. The teenage girl looked sweet, with her soft eyes and flowing, brown hair.

"That's okay. Wally doesn't seem to mind."

"Cute dog," she said.

Theo watched Wally flop to the ground and ignore the young pup. "Wally has not been his usual self lately."

The girl's eyebrows knit together. "Oh, what's wrong with him?"

"Old age, like me," Theo said.

The teenager chuckled. "Is that all? I don't think that will stop Scarlett."

Theo glanced down and saw that the two dogs were sniffing each other again, both their tails wagging.

"Maybe Wally just needs a friend," he said. "I haven't seen that old dog perk up like that in a long time."

"They might just be lonely," she said. "My grandma's dog doesn't get out much since Grandpa died. Everybody needs friends."

Wise words from such a young girl, Theo thought. The dogs were playing together in earnest now and his heart warmed at the sight. He took a close look at this young girl. He didn't remember seeing her before. Her doe eyes showed a deep sadness that he could recognize. "So, do you have friends here?" he asked, nodding toward the lake.

She shrugged. "I've only been here a few days. I'm just visiting and I haven't made any yet."

"Why is that? You're young. I used to have a lot of friends when I was your age. It was so easy then."

"Maybe so, but…well, my mom moves a lot, and I've gone to many different schools. I never really get time to make friends."

"Oh," Theo said, looking back down at the ground. A bit of a lost soul, he thought, and his heart went out to her. The two dogs were prancing around, and Wally looked almost back to his old self.

"Maybe we could walk together sometime," she asked. "The dogs seem happy."

"They sure do." Theo could feel the start of a smile. He

weighed the thought of having to be responsible to show up and meet another person against his recent reclusiveness.

The girl gave Theo a bright smile. "By the way, I'm Shelby and this is my grandma's dog, Scarlett."

A bicyclist sped by, catching Wally and Scarlett's attention. Both dogs yanked their leashes, trying to follow the rider.

"Wow," Theo said, holding the dog back. He turned back to Shelby. "I'm Theo and of course this is Wally. Nice to meet you, Shelby."

Theo, now energized by the young lady's attention, and Wally with Scarlett's, was ready to go.

"Shall we walk these two?" he said.

Scarlett led the way down the path from the park to the lake then circled back up a few blocks later. Wally trotted right along beside her. Theo, not used to expending all this energy, picked up his pace to keep up with them.

"I'm here for the summer," Shelby said. "My grandma lives off Second Street. Alice Meyer. Maybe you know her."

"The name's familiar. I seem to remember a Stan Meyer," he said. "Didn't he volunteer for the Arts Council?"

"That was my grandpa. He died a year ago. Scarlett hasn't been out that much since, so I have the job of dog walking her for the summer. I'll probably look for more work soon if all the summer jobs aren't already taken."

Theo thought for a minute. As the former director of a nonprofit that dealt with foster and homeless teens, he'd seen kids like Shelby before. Some were already roaming the streets, others trapped in a home with no real parent or protection. All she needed was a little support and direction. She obviously had a good head on her shoulders.

"A dog walker is a very good profession," he said. "Any previous experience?"

Shelby's face lit up. "Hey, thanks for the idea. I might just do that. And yes, I used to help my Grandpa Stan out with their dogs when they still lived on the farm."

"A good fit then," Theo said. "I could help spread the word around if you'd like." Theo's step lightened as they continued down the path. The dogs stopped every few feet to smell the grass and mark their territory when needed. Wally's sense of smell still seemed quite intact.

Theo found himself nodding "good morning" to people, noticing the birdsong and the way the sun bounced off the water. It felt good to help someone else. Maybe he could still be useful somehow. They circled the last block before town and then turned around to start back.

"You're the first person I've met here since my mom dropped me off," Shelby said.

"Well, I'm sure you'll meet lots of people this summer. Another week or two, the beach will be packed with tourists and young people too. It's not just us old-timers."

Shelby laughed. "At least you're out walking. My grandmother hardly leaves the house."

Theo thought about the girl's dilemma. New in town, a grieving grandma, no friends. His mind spun with ideas and he was glad his brain cells were still firing. When they reached the lake, they stood for a few moments watching a squadron of white pelicans floating out on the surface.

"They are pretty spectacular," Shelby said. "I love when they all take to the sky together."

"My wife, Jean, used to love them too," Theo said. "She's been gone over a year now."

"I'm so sorry," Shelby said.

Theo nodded. So was he. The sun rose and set over the lake. Tourists came and went. Life went on.

The morning sun was fierce, so they decided not to go out on the sand. Instead they took the turn back up the other side of the path that let out near Misty Meadow Lane. After a few blocks,

Shelby stopped when they reached the corner of Second Street. "I'll be turning here," she said. "Scarlett and I will look for you tomorrow, and Wally."

Theo watched Shelby almost skip up the street, her long brown hair trailing down her back. The pretty young thing would probably have a great summer here. Meet some nice kids her age. He'd been about her age, fifteen or sixteen, when he'd first spotted Jean that summer at the local pool. Her auburn curls had circled an angelic face with eyes of fire and skin of alabaster. It had been love at first sight. Of course, he would never let Jean catch him gaping at her, as if she ever cared. Miraculously she had, though. And after Jean's first smile in his direction, Theo had been a goner. He wiped the sweat from his brow and wished he'd worn a hat. But he'd had no idea he would be out here so long today.

Wally wagged his tail as he watched the twosome gallop up the hill. "Shelby will probably forget us old boys soon when the young ones arrive," he said to the dog.

The dog whined and gave a tug to follow.

"Maybe we'll see them tomorrow."

After a few moments, Theo journeyed back to his special bench at the park. He took a seat to rest awhile before heading back to his empty house. Wally's tail thumped in the grass.

"Jean," he said, "we met a new friend today. A real sweet girl. You would like her."

Theo gazed out at the clear water, smooth and tranquil, not a cloud in the sky. Instinctively he reached out for Jean's hand to share the beauty, but the empty bench sent a wave of grief derailing his very breath. He'd seen the lake in a devastating winter storm and that memory would never completely fade. He shuddered as his breath returned.

Wally stood and offered Theo his paw. The dog's chocolate brown eyes were overflowing with love as Theo lifted him up onto his lap. "You're a good boy. All I have left."

Wally kissed his face, then jumped down and gave a little pull.

"You ready to go?" Theo said, rising slowly.

A light breeze brushed through his hair, carrying with it the scent of wild sage. It was not like him to wallow in self-pity. After all he'd seen in his career, he truly had a blessed life. Jean would want him to go on, and he would try.

"Okay, let's finish this walk and meet the new day, as Jean would say."

CHAPTER 5

*S*helby brought Scarlett in and slipped off her leash. "You're free again." The dog's nails tap danced across the wood floors and Shelby reminded herself to see if they needed trimming. Scarlett's coat could probably use a grooming for the summer.

The pup jumped in the air and made some twirls before running to the kitchen to her bowl of water. Shelby could hear the dog lapping it up.

"Good morning, honey," her grandma said, standing in the kitchen still in her robe and slippers. At least Alice was out of bed, and from the luscious-smelling breakfast on the table, she had been baking too.

Shelby took a seat at the polished oak dining table, scooping up a still warm blueberry muffin off the platter and some fruit salad.

After feeding Scarlett, Alice joined her, a mug of coffee in her hand. "There's orange juice in the pitcher. Just let me know if you'd like anything else."

She watched her grandmother sip her drink. Even the sweet, moist muffins hadn't tempted Alice to eat breakfast.

"How was your walk?" Alice asked. "I bet Scarlett was thrilled to get outside."

Between bites, Shelby answered. "It was good. I met a new friend. An older man named Theo, and his beagle Wally."

Her grandma paused. "I remember that dog. Your grandpa and I used to see that couple we knew from the Art Center out walking him." Her voice dropped. "I heard his wife died recently."

"He did seem a bit sad, but he was pretty nice. And the dogs got along splendidly."

Sunlight streamed through the living room windows, brightening up the room. Shelby had only been there a few days, but already she felt the calmness of being with her grandmother in these familiar surroundings. She loved the floral wallpaper behind the china cabinet, the blue-checkered curtains in the kitchen, and the white farmhouse-style cabinets Grandpa Stan had installed.

"Oh, and by the way," Shelby said, "Theo gave me a new idea for making money this summer."

Grandma Alice put down her coffee. "You really don't need to worry about that while you're here."

Shelby did not want to be a financial burden on her grandmother. And if she could save some money of her own, she'd have more choices. Especially if her mother's relationship fell apart and she wanted Shelby back. "I really want to work," Shelby said. "His idea is perfect for me."

"Oh really? Tell me."

"I could be a dog walker. While people are working or on vacation, I could walk their dogs."

"That's wonderful," Alice said. "I'll be your first customer. I bet we can think of several more. In fact, Mindy, who lives a few streets over, just had surgery. We can let her know you're available."

Seeing the enthusiasm from her grandmother made the whole idea seem even better. "I'll have to come up with a name.

And what should I charge? No charge to you, Grandma, of course."

"Let me think on it," Alice said. "You could put up a flyer on the grocery store bulletin board, too."

"Perfect, I will. Thanks." The dog walking business was sounding better by the minute. She'd never had her own money before.

Alice started to clear off the table with Scarlett at her heels, hoping for a scrap to fall. "My friend, Eleanor, is stopping by later in the week to catch me up on town gossip. She's the former mayor and will have lots of ideas for you."

After washing up and drying her hands, Alice returned to her recliner in the living room.

Shelby followed and curled up on the tufted couch beside it. She picked up the squirmy dog and hugged her. "You are a handful." Scarlett reminded her of a stuffed animal she'd had as a child that had mysteriously disappeared after one of their moves. When asked, Dana had said it was scruffy and probably got lost.

They sat in silence for a while with only the distant ticking from the kitchen clock. Alice stared out the window and seemed lost in thought. Shelby's stomach clenched. The behavior reminded her of how Dana acted when she was depressed. Grandma Alice had never been like this before. All of Shelby's memories were of Alice barely sitting still, baking, gardening, out with friends, or volunteering to help others.

"It's such a pretty day out," Alice said, looking over at Shelby. "You don't have to sit here with me. Why don't you take the afternoon off and go for a swim?"

Shelby sat up. "Will you come too?"

Alice shook her head. "We're fine here, Scarlett and I."

"Maybe next time?" Shelby asked.

Alice nodded. "Maybe."

Shelby went to her room and pulled her swimsuit from a drawer. "I guess it will have to do," she sighed. It was her chlorine-faded one piece she'd worn for lifeguard training. Originally it had been a bright blue, but it was bordering on gray now.

She pulled it on and looked in the full-length mirror behind the door.

"Ugh," she said. Perhaps she would put a t-shirt over it and leave it on at the beach.

Sunglasses in hand, Shelby walked into the living room to ask her grandmother for a beach towel. Alice was standing by the door with a colorful towel, a bottle of sunscreen, and a folding beach chair in hand.

"You are prepared," Shelby said with a laugh. "See you later."

Supplies in hand, Shelby walked down the front path, admiring the colorful flower beds.

"Don't stay too long," her grandmother said from the porch. "It's your first time in the sun."

Shelby turned and smiled. "I'll be home soon. Are you sure you don't want to come with me?"

Alice shook her head. "Maybe another time. You go now and have a good swim."

Shelby turned to walk the few blocks to the public beach. The walkway directly across the street was private and belonged to the DeLucas, who, according to her grandmother, had built the massive waterfront home a few years ago but were mostly here only in the summer. The boys playing in the cul-de-sac probably lived there because she'd never seen them before on her other visits.

When she reached the beach, the sand was warm and soothing under her bare feet. The crowds were not too thick yet in early June, but there were plenty of people swimming, kids running around in the sand, and a few rowboats out fishing in the lake. She picked a spot a bit down from the lifeguard station and put out her chair with her towel beside her.

The freshwater lake sparkled in the sun, inviting her to plunge in. She should have brought a book from her grandmother's library. She glanced around. No eyes were on her. Her t-shirt stuck to her skin and she wanted desperately to jump in and cool off. Deciding to be brave, she removed her t-shirt and lay back on to the chair. Eyes closed, she pretended her pale white skin and ratty bathing suit did not bother her at all. Shelby was just drifting off when she felt a spray of sand across her legs. When she opened her eyes, three teenage girls were traipsing by. She heard the tall, thin blonde say in a snooty tone, "Nice fashion statement there." The other girls snickered and threw quick glances back at Shelby.

Shelby brushed the sand off her legs and glared after them. This whole beach to walk and they had to bother her. High school girls were the same everywhere, she guessed. Especially the mean ones. She watched them walk toward the lifeguard, who was standing near the edge of the water. When he turned to face them, Shelby recognized his face. He was the exceptionally cute boy she'd seen playing basketball the other day.

She heard the girls yell, "Hi, Logan," and figured that must be his name. She watched the girls in their fancy bathing suits gather around him, giggling, and the slender blonde put her head on his shoulder. Taken, was the clear message. Shelby sighed. He was probably some popular jock type anyway.

She yanked her t-shirt back on in case they passed back her way. She really wanted to go for a swim, but not with them watching. In fact, she just wanted to pack up and go home and never come back. Did a bathing suit really make that much difference? Was she going to let this stop her from going in the water? Anger tried to override her fear, but it wasn't winning. She was used to hiding, being alone. What made her think this summer was going to be anything different? Besides, she'd rather spend her time with dogs any day than with entitled people like those.

Giving in, she folded up her chair, shook out her towel, and headed back to the house. Happily, her grandmother was outside on the porch reclining in one of the white wicker chairs. Scarlett was in her lap and perked up when she spotted Shelby.

"Back so soon?" Alice called out.

Shelby stiffened. "I guess I'm just not used to the sun yet." She brushed past her grandmother and headed into her room. Towel and chair landed on the floor. She ripped off her bathing suit and tossed it in the trash, slipped on a nightshirt, then flung herself into bed. What made her think she could fit in here any better than the last place she'd lived?

Alice stuck her head in the door. "Everything okay?" Scarlett scampered into the room and leapt up on to Shelby's bed.

Shelby looked up at her sweet grandmother and remembered how Alice had always been the one to care the most about her. Almost like a second—or, in this case, first—mother. "I'm fine. Just tired," she said.

Shelby noticed Alice eye the trash can where her discarded bathing suit was draped across the edge. "I'm here if you want to talk," she said.

"Thanks," Shelby said.

Her grandmother hesitated at the door. "Oh, and by the way, Mindy is interested in your dog walking services. She said she'd confirm tomorrow."

"Thanks for contacting her," Shelby said, pushing herself up in bed.

Alice stood silent for a moment, as if waiting for Shelby to say something. When that didn't happen, she gently shut the bedroom door behind her as she left.

Alone in the room, Scarlett and Shelby curled up together. Maybe she was just tired. Tomorrow she would focus on starting her new summer business. She could buy any bathing suit she wanted once her business got started. Shelby kissed Scarlett's glossy curls on the top of her head. Snuggled together, they drifted off to sleep.

CHAPTER 6

*I*t was early morning. From his living room window, Theo saw the mist hovering above the lake as sunrays danced across the surface of the water. He knew Wally needed to go out, so he'd better dress and get going. Perhaps they'd walk along the lake today, let Wally run in the sand the way he used to do when he was a puppy. Meeting that girl Shelby and little Scarlett had gotten Theo thinking. Perhaps he could help her out a little with her business idea. She seemed a bit lost and alone and he could relate. Maybe he could... Theo stopped himself. There were other people, young people, and soon she would be gone anyway at the end of summer. Maybe he shouldn't get involved.

This gut-wrenching loneliness was the worst thing he'd ever been through. He'd never truly understood grief before. How could you understand pain like this unless you'd felt it yourself? And after summer, how could he go through another dark, cold winter without Jean?

Wally seemed eager to go out. At least try, he told himself. He could almost hear Jean say, "Put on a smile."

After finishing his morning coffee, Theo grabbed a light jacket and headed down the path to the lake with Wally. A few hawks hunting for breakfast screeched as they flew across the lake, then off to some unknown destination. Once on the sand, Theo noticed there was no one nearby, so he set the dog free. He knew his beagle was well behaved, would kiss rather than bite, and if anyone complained, he'd put the leash back on. Theo had his trusty doggie bag with him in case of any accidents, so he wasn't concerned on that front either. Wally waddled down to the water, moving pretty fast for an old dog. He jumped in, feet first, and waded out a bit before shaking the water off his coat.

Theo observed the flux of early morning fishing boats starting out for the day. In the distance he saw the lifeguard setting up. It was that nice boy Logan whose parents had built a summer home up here. They'd talked a few times and he'd liked the boy. Maybe he and Wally would wander over, see how Logan was doing.

"Come on, Wally," he said.

Logan, in red shorts and a t-shirt, was setting up for the day. He waved and reached his arms out toward Wally.

Wally tore right for him, Theo trailing behind. In the last couple days, Wally had been a lot more active. Come to think of it, ever since they'd met that girl Shelby, they both had a little more pep in their step.

"Morning," Theo said. "How's the summer treating you so far?"

Logan smiled. "Just started, but already we've got so many tourists. Haven't been any near drownings yet."

Theo laughed. "Well, I'm sure if anybody's in distress you'll be right out there helping them."

Logan sat on the base of the ramp leading up to the lifeguard station. His tube of sunblock and red rescue buoy were at his side. Wally scampered up to him and started licking his face.

"Hey there, boy," Logan said. "You're perky this morning."

"For a thirteen-year-old dog, he's been livelier the last few days, so I'm feeling a little more hopeful." Theo thought about

Shelby and realized she lived across from the DeLucas' house. "I don't know if you realize it yet, but you have a new neighbor. I met her yesterday. Her name is Shelby. She's staying with her grandmother, Alice, right across from you."

"Yeah, I noticed," Logan said. "My mom said something about it, too." He petted Wally, scratching behind his ears. "You're lucky to have a dog. My dad won't let us. My little brother and I would love to rescue one."

"You can come by and pet Wally anytime," Theo said. "Maybe your dad will change his mind?"

A shadow crossed Logan's face. "There's very little chance of that."

Theo thought about how they all had their disappointments and challenges, even a smart, handsome, young boy like this. The sun was already beating down and he was grateful he'd remembered to wear his canvas hat.

"You just never know," Theo found himself saying, trying to give the young man hope, something he himself did not have a lot of right now. "C'mon, Wally, let's get going on our walk. You take care, Logan. We'll be back to visit you again soon."

"Have a good day!" Logan called after them.

Theo continued down the sandy lake shore. Maybe it was time for him to take some of his own advice. He thought about his friend Trevor's offer to volunteer at the Veterans Center. Trevor had asked him about it a few times now, but Theo hadn't really wanted to get involved with anything, much less make a commitment when most days he could barely get out of bed. Trevor had confided in Theo some of the horrific experiences he had been through when deployed and trying to adjust to being home again. If that young man could still volunteer, Theo could certainly consider it. Trevor had just graduated from college and married his sweetheart when the unthinkable happened on 9/11. He'd signed up and been stationed in Afghanistan. But he'd come back with a severe case of PTSD and to discover his wife had left him.

Theo remembered when Trevor had first moved to the lake. He'd kept to himself, a recluse, but eventually he'd started coming out when he got Buddy, his service dog. One day on a walk they'd finally met at what he now called, "Jean's bench." The two men had hit it off right away. Theo's wife had been pretty sick back then, so Theo had been happy to have someone to confide in and Trevor had seemed happy with the arrangement as well.

They strolled along the path. Theo turned uphill toward the tree-lined ridge. "Let's stop in and see if Trevor's home," he said to the dog.

Wally all but galloped up the steps when they reached Trevor's rustic wood cabin. He loved Buddy, Trevor's golden retriever. Theo knocked on the door and waited.

"Greetings," Trevor said when he opened the door, a coffee cup in his hand. He was dressed in his usual cotton t-shirt and faded jeans. His hair was tousled, face unshaven. Theo worried he might be intruding.

Buddy, tail wagging, greeted Wally with a welcome sniff.

Trevor waved them in and gave Buddy a hand signal that it was okay to play. He was not wearing his service vest today. Wally sniffed the kitchen floor in hopes of finding a scrap, with Buddy close behind.

"And how are you both doing today?" Trevor said, smoothing his hair back and slipping his glasses on.

"We're doing just fine," Theo said.

Trevor smiled. "I'm glad to hear it." He took a seat by the river rock fireplace and motioned for Theo to do the same. "Something new and exciting in your life you came to tell me about?"

"Not really," Theo said. "We're just starting to get out a little more. I think the summer weather is helping."

Trevor rose and retrieved his coffee cup from the table. "I just made a pot of fresh coffee. Would you like some?"

Theo nodded. He usually stopped with one cup in the morning, but today he could splurge. He watched Trevor navigate the small but well-stocked kitchen. Mason jars of grains and beans were lined up on barnwood shelves, and pots hung from a rack below them.

The dogs stood at the French doors that faced the tall trees and lake. "Shall I let them out?" Theo asked.

"Sure, go ahead."

Theo opened the door and watched Wally tag behind Buddy down the stairs to the grassy fenced backyard. He knew that Trevor enjoyed the secluded peace and quiet and "space," as he'd put it.

"Here you go," said Trevor. "Black, right?"

Theo followed Trevor out on the deck. They sat on the redwood chairs that afforded them a panoramic view of the lake. Bird calls were plentiful here in the trees, and the sweet smell of pine lingered in the air. Theo thought it would be a wonderful spot to take some photos. He circled back to the idea of volunteering. He'd been an amateur photographer for years, even taught classes before they'd retired to the lake. The veterans might enjoy the hobby too.

"I've been thinking about the Veterans Center," Theo said. "Can you tell me more about the volunteering you spoke of?"

"Be happy to. There are several men and women, all ages, who are interested in doing some kind of creative outdoor activities. I thought you could offer a photography class, you know, taking shots of birds, local flora and fauna, the water at sunset."

Theo nodded. It might boost his own confidence to be useful again. "I think I could do that. We could start small. Talk a bit about cameras and shooting angles. Even if they don't have a camera, they could use a cell phone."

"The center can probably pick up some used cameras too," Trevor said. "Get them donated."

"That's a splendid idea," Theo said. "Why don't I come down

and check it out in a few days?" The thought of starting something new made him anxious, or was it excitement?

"Sure," Trevor said, looking a little surprised. "I'm there almost every afternoon, so just stop by. And if you want, I'm giving a little talk about my journey with a service dog next Tuesday. You could join us."

"Sounds interesting," Theo said. "I'll put it on my busy social calendar."

"Be sure to bring Wally. He'll be popular there."

"That reminds me," Theo said. "There is a new young girl here for the summer, Shelby. She's a teenager and living with her grandmother, Alice Meyer."

"I remember Alice. Didn't she just lose her husband last year?"

Theo nodded. "Shelby is trying to start a little dog walking business. If you think of anyone who could use her services, let me know."

"How do you know she's good with dogs?"

Theo gave him his best smile. "She is. I'll introduce you. Then you can decide."

"Fair enough."

Theo noticed the sun was getting higher in the sky and the morning would soon slip away. He walked over to the railing and watched the dogs play in the shade of the old growth trees. He knew Trevor still worked at home running websites for large nonprofits. He didn't want to take up too much of his time, so he called Wally to him.

The dogs tramped up the steps and toward the glass door. Trevor opened it and the dogs sped in.

Theo put his mug on the tile counter. "Thanks for the coffee." He put Wally's leash back on. The dog looked longingly back at Buddy. Theo ruffled his fur. "We'll come back and play soon."

"Where are you two off to now?" Trevor asked.

"We're going to finish our walk, go home, maybe take our morning nap."

"Really? I thought most naps were in the afternoon."

Theo laughed. "When you get to our age, sometimes there's more than one nap each day."

"Whatever you say," Trevor said. "I'm really happy to see you. Come by any time. And don't forget about our ice cream meetup at Redd's coming up."

"I won't. Wally won't let me!"

Theo waved as he closed the gate behind him. They continued down the path toward the bench Theo and Jean had donated to the park. As he approached, the sunlight was just hitting the weathered wood through the trees. Theo sat down and closed his eyes, letting the sun trickle across his face and warm his shoulders.

"Good morning, Jean," he said. "We're having a pretty good day, Wally and me. We've been to the beach, we've talked to two young men, and guess what? I'm thinking of volunteering."

He sat and listened inside for the reply. He could almost hear Jean laughing and saying, "It's about time."

His mind drifted, imagining himself walking with Jean along the path hand in hand. He could hear her delighted giggle as a squirrel scampered up a tree. He was jolted out of his thoughts by Wally's excited barking. He turned his head, and there was Shelby walking with her grandmother's little dog, Scarlett. He hadn't seen her for a few days.

"Uh-huh," he said to Wally, "your friend is here."

CHAPTER 7

*R*eturning from her morning walk with Scarlett, Shelby turned into her cul-de-sac and noticed her cute neighbor, the lifeguard, shooting hoops again. He was in red shorts and slide sandals, probably taking a quick break before going to work. She really didn't want to walk by him after he'd probably heard those girls at the beach diss her, but she couldn't avoid him. She hurried toward her house, and just as she got in range, he turned and tossed her the ball.

Shelby caught it with her free hand and just stood there looking at him.

"Want to play?" he asked.

He was asking her? She tossed the ball back. "Can't right now," she said and turned to walk inside with the dog.

"Hey," he called. "Don't let those girls bother you. I don't."

Shelby cringed. So he had heard. "Thanks," she said, making quick eye contact before rushing into the house.

Her grandmother, lounging on the couch, gazed out the front window. No lights were on and the house was quiet. It worried Shelby how her grandmother seemed so sad and never wanted to go anywhere. She understood, of course, because she'd felt that way herself before. Particularly after another move. At least Alice was up and dressed today.

"Hi," her grandmother said. "How was the walk?"

"Brisk," Shelby said. "We ran into Theo and his cute beagle again." She pointed at Scarlett. "You should see the two of them together. Those dogs really love each other."

Alice called Scarlett to her lap. "Do you have a new friend?" she asked her before turning back to Shelby. "I'm so glad you're taking her out with you in the morning. The poor girl was getting a bit stir-crazy."

"What about you, Grandma? Don't you want to get out some too?"

Shelby watched as her grandmother's face slackened before she hastily changed the subject. "Remember, you have your first meeting with Mindy today. Poor thing, that surgery has really slowed her down."

"I'm excited to meet her."

Shelby hugged her grandmother; the familiar scent of gardenia Alice wore lingering in the air. When Alice looked up, Shelby saw a bit of a spark returning to her grandmother's eyes.

"My first client," Shelby said. "It's definitely time to brain-storm a name for my company. What do you think? Do you have any ideas? Something like Shelby's Dog Walking Service?"

Her grandmother laughed. "That will work, for sure. Maybe you could come up with one of those little fliers with the tear sheets. We could put it up on the bulletin board in town and at the market."

"Absolutely," Shelby said. "I can make one on my computer. Do you have a printer?"

"We do, but I'm not sure how to use it. Are you good with computers?" Alice asked, looking hopeful.

"Pretty good," Shelby said. "Why? Do you need help?"

Alice nodded. "Your grandpa used to handle all the bills and other computer things. I'm afraid I'm a bit slow with all of that."

"No problem. Just let me know when you want to sit down and I'll show you how everything works."

"One problem solved." Alice breathed a sigh of relief. "Now let me tell you about Mindy. She has a summer home here but most of the time she lives in San Jose, where she has a big job."

"Probably in tech," Shelby said.

"I think that's it," Alice said. "A couple summers ago, I used to see her running around the lake and we met and became friends. But recently she tore something in her ankle and now she has to stay off her feet. She and her dog, Karma, came up here for recovery, but she's having trouble. Karma's an active dog and needs regular exercise."

Shelby pulled her legs up under her to get comfortable. "I can't wait to meet Karma. Does she want me to come up today?"

"She does," Alice said.

"I'm on it. And what are your plans for the day?"

Alice released Scarlett from her lap, who as usual went to check out her bowls in the kitchen. "I'll probably read a little, take a nap."

It was such a nice-looking day and Shelby hated to see Alice this way. She used to be out and about, in her garden and smiling all the time. "Maybe we should plan a little outing or something?"

Her grandmother looked up. "Ever since your grandfather died, I just don't seem to have any energy. And the more I stay home, the harder it gets to leave."

Shelby squeezed her grandmother's hand. "Believe me, I understand. I miss Grandpa, too. I'd really like it if we could take a walk sometime together, get some fresh air. The blue sky and sunshine will make you feel better. And if I can help you in any way with the house, cooking, or going to the market, let me know."

"You are a sweet girl," Alice said. "I'll tell you if I need anything. As far as going for a walk, maybe soon. Now let's talk about you. Tell me all about what you've been doing this year before your mother brought you here."

Shelby thought for a moment just how much she wanted to share with her grandmother. She did not want to upset her more than she already was. "I was taking lifeguard training and hoping to work at the pool this summer. I really liked it."

"That's good to hear. For now, you can walk dogs, swim in the lake, and perhaps go back to lifeguarding in the fall. And school?"

"I've kept my grade point average high and done extracurricular activities when I can." Shelby didn't say when they did not cost anything or she was in one place long enough to do it. "I've been getting information on scholarships. If I keep my grades up and do well on my testing, I think I have a good chance of getting one so I can go to college."

"You always were such a smart girl," Alice said. "Maybe you'll even be the valedictorian."

Shelby shrugged. "Probably not. I don't even know where I'll be going to school in the fall."

Alice gave her a sympathetic look. "So how do you feel about your mom's new boyfriend and this trip to Florida?"

Shelby stared at the wood floor and the familiar braided rug. She wondered if she should give an honest answer and risk upsetting her grandmother. "Truthfully," she said, "I don't want to think about it. What if Dana likes Florida and wants to stay? Another broiling place where I have to start over, make new friends, and watch my mother with another man who may or may not stay."

Alice sat up straight in her chair and took a deep breath. "I understand. Meanwhile, let's focus on having an enjoyable summer."

"Thanks, Grandma." It was nice to have someone on her side after feeling adrift for so long. And she was finally going to make her own money, too. "Speaking of that, I'd better go meet Mindy now."

Alice walked with Shelby out to the front porch and pointed toward town. "Mindy's place is just a few blocks up. You turn left and you'll see a white house with red rocking chairs on the porch. Can't miss it. Just go up the steps and knock on the door. She's expecting you."

SHELBY WALKED the few blocks over to Mindy's and, as instructed, knocked on the red door.

"Come on in," Mindy said. "You must be Shelby." A petite woman with beautiful, long, dark hair stood balanced on one crutch with a heavy-looking cast on her left leg. "Have a seat."

Mindy looked to be around thirty, pretty and self-assured. Her warm, brown eyes made Shelby feel at ease. The cottage was tastefully decorated in bold colors and natural wood. A massive desk under the far window had two computers on it. Mindy turned and faced the black and white dog who was in a perfect sit. The dog quietly whimpered in excitement but waited for Mindy's command.

"Karma, release," Mindy said.

The medium-sized dog perked up its ears and came tearing over to Shelby. She petted the dog's coarse, wavy fur. "She's a beauty. What breed?"

"She's mostly border collie and who knows what else?" Mindy said as she carefully sat in a soft chair and put her foot up. "I rescued Karma a couple years ago. Still a puppy really. She's just over three years old."

Shelby scratched behind Karma's silky ears. The dog licked her hand then rolled over to have her belly petted. "And so adorable."

"We used to do a lot of running in the park and she's used to a high level of activity. Her new circumstances are making her restless and bored."

"I bet," Shelby said. Mindy's workout capris and sleeveless top revealed a toned body that was used to regular exercise.

Mindy got right down to business. "So, tell me a little about your experience with dogs."

"Well, I just started walking dogs here in town. But I used to help on my grandparents' farm with all of their dogs when I'd spend the summer there. I also did pet sitting for a neighbor back in Las Vegas. Now I walk my grandmother's doxie-poo, Scarlett, every day."

"Dogs are pretty special," Mindy said. "Not everyone understands that."

Karma dropped to the floor and laid her head on Shelby's feet. "She does have an interesting name," Shelby said.

Mindy's smile lit up the room. "In my Indian culture," she said, "we have certain beliefs. I used to have this colleague at work who would constantly complain what bad luck it was the day he got his dog. He left her alone all day and she chewed and barked, disturbing the neighbors."

Shelby grimaced, hoping the story did not have a tragic ending.

Mindy continued. "A few weeks before Christmas, I asked him if he ever walked the dog or played with it. He said no, and he was going to take her to the pound that weekend."

"Oh no," Shelby said.

Mindy's voice got fierce. "I was not going to let that happen, so that night I went to his house and offered to take her. He handed her over without reservation. Karma has been my best friend ever since. What was bad luck for him was good karma for me. Hence the name."

Karma stirred at the sound of her name and looked up at Shelby. "You are one lucky pooch," she said. "I'd be happy to start walking her anytime."

"When are you available?" Mindy asked.

"I can start tomorrow with long walks, short walks, once a day, twice a day…"

Mindy laughed. "Why don't we start with three days a week for now? What's a good time for you?"

"Probably mornings," Shelby said. "It's cooler."

"That works. Do you know what you'll be charging yet?"

Shelby shrugged. "I haven't thought about it. You're my first paying client."

Mindy squinted, as though in deep thought. "I believe the standard dog walking charge is fifteen dollars an hour if that works for you?"

"Oh, that would be awesome," Shelby said. "How about I offer you a weekly discount plan of forty dollars for three hour-long walks a week?"

"Done. Let's start tomorrow." Mindy lifted her bandaged leg. "This darn thing. I miss running too."

Shelby looked at the woman in front of her. Her long hair was pulled back in a ponytail. She hadn't told her how she'd injured herself and Shelby did not want to pry.

"I'm sure you'll feel better soon. In the meantime, I can keep Karma happy and play with her anytime you want."

"That will help. I'm really pleased to meet you, Shelby. And I hope to see a lot more of you." Mindy got up on her crutches and walked Shelby to the door.

Karma followed, her tail wagging. At the door the dog made a low whine and looked up at Shelby with expectant brown eyes.

"Look, she's already wanting to go with you."

"Good dog," Shelby said, petting her soft ears. "I'll see you tomorrow."

She galloped down the steps and walked the few blocks home, humming to herself. Her first client and more money than she'd ever made. She would easily be able to buy a new bathing suit, maybe get her hair cut, and save some too.

CHAPTER 8

Of all ·times for Dana to call, Shelby thought as her grandmother handed over her cell phone and whispered, "It's your mother." She was trying to leave so she could be on time to Mindy's for her first day walking Karma.

"I can't really talk right now," Shelby said. She wished she had her own cell phone so she could walk and talk. "I'm on my way to work."

Her mother skipped right over Shelby's words. "We made it to Florida. What a trip. We saw the Alamo in Texas, and so many other places. You won't believe the Overseas Highway we took from Miami to Key West. I saw my first alligator too!"

Shelby held the phone away from her ear, exasperated that she was going to be late on her first day at the job. It was that familiar feeling of being sucked into a tidal wave, and no matter how she tried to pull herself out, it seemed impossible to break free of her mother's wake. Breathe, she told herself, and leave now. "I have to go," she said and hit end call and raced out the door.

Breathless from the run, she made it with barely a minute to spare and took a moment before knocking to compose herself.

Mindy answered with Karma at her side. "Good morning. I know someone who is very excited to get outside today," she said, smiling at her dog.

Karma wriggled in excitement as Shelby hooked up her harness. Leash in hand, Shelby stepped out the front door. Karma hesitated and kept looking back at Mindy as if wondering why she wasn't coming.

"Go on, girl," Mindy said.

Karma sprinted down the sidewalk, her head high. Her pace quickened when they reached the lake path. She missed regular swim practice and could use this exercise as well. Karma was a magnificent dog that moved with grace and speed. Yet when she tried to chase a squirrel or bird, Shelby would give her a quick correction with the leash the way Mindy showed her, and this dog would obey every time. Even though the dog was well trained, Shelby had assured Mindy that Karma would be on leash at all times. Safer that way.

They trotted along for about a mile and were both lightly panting. The heavily traveled dirt pathway that wove around Moonwater Lake was often shaded by the thick, gnarled branches of the towering oak trees. The sun filtered in and out as the temperature rose. It was going to be a hot one today. Shelby decided to take a trail down to the water for a breather. The dog followed eagerly.

After a quick splash they sat down on the sand. Karma stretched, arching her back, her eyes glued on everything that moved, from the mallard ducks floating on the surface to the red-tailed hawk circling overhead. That dog missed nothing. She thrived on being outside. But she obviously loved her owner as well and wanted to be by her side. Mindy had looked so sad when they'd left. Shelby hoped she'd feel better soon.

After a few minutes, the dog rose and began pacing.

"All right, let's go," Shelby said.

They upped their speed and continued around the lake path.

As they rounded the last bend that headed back toward the swimming beach, she could see the lifeguard station in the distance. Maybe she could get a quick glimpse at Logan again. He'd never look at her, but at least she could admire him from a distance. They walked on the sand for a while to reach the steps leading home. As she got closer, Shelby recognized the girls who had given her a hard time the other day. They were laid out on their towels planted right in full view of the cute lifeguard. They didn't even bother to look up when she passed by. And honestly, she didn't care. Shelby had her first paying client, and she was feeling good. She attempted a covert glance at Logan and, to her surprise, caught him looking at her too with a kind of goofy smile on his face. She turned and hastened her step.

"Let's go into town," she said to Karma. "I think we both deserve a treat after that workout." Shelby had heard that Redd's ice cream place had a new owner. She'd been meaning to go, and this was as good a time as any. She had fond of memories going for a cone several years back with her Grandpa Stan.

Mindy had told her to keep the dog out as long as she wanted, so there was no hurry. She was sure that Karma could get a little something there, too. Maybe they even had dog treats, like the coffee shop they used to visit back in Las Vegas that made puppuccinos.

As they approached the old town area, hanging baskets of flowers in riotous colors lined the street. Shelby located the faded blue cottage, with a striped awning over the window. Out in front, a hand-painted candy apple red sign with white lettering said Redd's Ice Cream. Redd had been the old owner's last name. His daughter and her husband owned it now, according to her grandmother. From over a block away, the tempting aroma of fresh-baked waffle cones floated in the air. Outside, in front of the shop, were white metal tables and chairs with umbrellas over them, and a couple wooden benches. Sugar cones with colorful flavored ice cream dripping down the sides were being enjoyed by children and adults alike. At another table, Shelby saw Theo sipping an iced drink. Wally was settled next to him on the sidewalk. The younger man with glasses sitting beside him was finishing the last bites of his cone. At his feet was a golden retriever with a vest on. Maybe he was a service dog. He sure was a very pretty one.

Karma gave a yank when she saw the other dogs. "Halt," Shelby said. Karma slowed down, tail wagging furiously as they moved forward. Wally perked up and exchanged sniffs with Karma. But the service dog stayed in place, looking up to his master for instruction.

"Good morning," Theo said. "Now, whose dog is this?"

Shelby was happy to say, "This is Karma. Her owner, Mindy, is my first dog walking client."

"Not sure I know her," Theo said.

"Mindy's here for a month or so while she's recovering from an injury."

"Well, congratulations on getting your business up and running," Theo said. He reached over and gave Karma a pet. "By the way, I'd like to introduce you to someone. Trevor, this is Shelby, Alice's granddaughter. I think I mentioned her to you."

He reached out a hand to shake Shelby's. "And this is my dog, Buddy. We're both happy to meet you."

"Nice to meet you, too. You have a beautiful dog," Shelby said.

"He's a beauty, all right, and a wonderful pal. He doesn't get out much except with me. I know he'd probably love to go for a run with some other dogs sometime."

"Is he a service dog?"

Trevor shrugged. "He's classified as an emotional support dog. The vest helps so I can bring him with me anywhere I go. But I do let him play with others like a regular dog once in a while."

"Walk? Did I hear dog walk?" A woman with bright red hair, looking to be in her twenties, wearing jeans and a checkered apron, stepped out the front door. "Theo, who is this young lady you haven't introduced me to?"

Theo smiled. "I'd like to introduce you to Shelby and her first dog walking client, named Karma."

The woman's smile was contagious. "Greetings," she said. "I'm Steph, one of the owners of the shop. And that lazy dog over by the door is our Oscar."

Oscar was an adorable corgi with big solemn eyes and short little legs. Shelby particularly liked his little plaid bow tie.

"He loves ice cream way too much," Steph said. "He doesn't get near enough exercise, so we're hoping we can be client number two."

"I'd be very happy to walk this sweet little guy." Shelby couldn't resist petting him. He rolled over for her and looked quite content as she rubbed his belly.

"Josh and I don't have much free time in the summer. There's usually a line out the door. We just hired Emily for summer help. You stopped here just at the right time between rushes."

"Oh," said Shelby. "You must be Redd's daughter." Her hair was the same strawberry blonde color as her father's.

Steph laughed. "That's me. My husband, the one with the dark ginger-colored hair, is Josh. We own the shop now. Come on in. Anything you want is on the house as a welcome. You can leave Karma out here. There are plenty of dog-tying poles, and I'm sure Theo would be glad to watch him. There're dog treats inside to bring back." At the sound of the word "treats," Karma thumped her tail against old wooden slats.

Theo grasped the dog's leash. "I'll keep a close eye on the dog."

Shelby walked inside and was hit with a comforting blast of air conditioning. Behind the old-fashioned soda counter was a young man with a short beard. He also had red hair, but darker than Steph's.

"I'd like you to meet my husband, Josh," Steph said. "This is Shelby. She's here for the summer, and she does dog walking."

"Welcome," Josh said. "And this is Emily," he said, pointing to the girl next to him scooping ice cream.

Emily looked to be around Shelby's age and was lucky to get such a fun summer job. But Shelby was happy with her new business. She could be outside and set her own schedule.

Josh pointed to the flavors on the antique menu board behind the counter. "Can I get you some ice cream? What's your favorite? We've got moose tracks, apple pie à la mode, and everything from chocolate mint to strawberry sorbet. Double scoops for our first-timers, on us."

Shelby walked to the counter and looked at all the scrumptious flavors in the tubs. She had a hard time making up her mind. "I'll have chocolate peanut butter and salted caramel, please."

"Good choices," said Steph. "Cone or cup?"

"Well..."

"Let me guess," said Josh. "Everybody wants one of our famous waffle cones. You can smell them three blocks away."

"I sure did," Shelby said. "Thanks!"

Once outside with her piled-high ice cream cone and three bone-shaped dog treats, Shelby joined the two men at the outdoor table. She handed each dog a treat, which were quickly gobbled up. A line started forming at the door of the shop. It was certainly a popular place and she could see why. Ice cream began to drip down the side of her cone, so she licked up the edges that were starting to melt.

Theo took a sip of his iced coffee. "Have you been down to the beach much?"

Shelby thought about her last unpleasant outing to the beach. She had not gone back since except for the brief time this morning. "Not yet," she said.

"Trevor lives right off Lakeside Drive in a remodeled summer cabin. You might see it through the trees from the path when you walk. He also volunteers at the local Veterans Center."

"That's right," Trevor said. "In fact, you should bring one of the dogs over to the center some time. It's always helpful for the vets to have a friendly canine nearby."

"That would be fun," Shelby said. "I'll bring my grandma's dog, Scarlett. She's a bouncy bundle of joy, and she loves everyone."

"She sounds perfect," Trevor said. "We're just down the road."

Shelby saw Theo nudge Trevor.

"And…" Trevor hesitated. "Bring a flyer or something. Maybe some of the guys could use a dog walker."

"I'd love to! Just say when."

Shelby was making fast work of the cone. The creamy mixture was cool and comforting. People wandered in and out of the shop. Children stopped to pet Oscar. Some asked to pet Karma, but Shelby wasn't comfortable allowing that without Mindy there.

After a while Karma started to get restless, so Shelby rose to leave. "Good to meet you, Trevor. Tell the Redds I said goodbye if you see them." They were so busy inside, Shelby did not want to disturb the owners. She turned to Theo. "And guess what! It looks like I will be walking Oscar, too."

"Business is building fast," Theo said.

After throwing her napkins away in the trash can, Shelby departed to take Karma home. When she got to the house, she knocked before opening the door. The border collie flung herself through and leapt onto the couch next to Mindy.

"Here's my sweet girl," Mindy said. Karma immediately lay down next to her. "Finally she's tired. You two were gone awhile."

Shelby sat on a chair opposite her. "We ran the one-mile trail by the lake. And then we went down to the water for a break. Next we went for a treat at Redd's Ice Cream Parlor, and Karma had a couple of treats herself. I hope that's okay."

"Oh, sure," said Mindy. "Sounds like you had a wonderful first day. I wish I could have gone with you."

"Maybe soon," Shelby said. "Let me know if I can do anything else to help you out, too."

Mindy adjusted her leg on the pillow where it rested on her ottoman. "That is very kind of you. It's hard for me being tied down like this, but at least my job's letting me work remote for now."

"What kind of work do you do?"

Mindy pointed to her laptop on the end table beside her. "I'm a computer analyst for a company in Silicon Valley. Usually I can only escape up here for weekends, and I much prefer Moonwater Lake to the busy city."

"I've lived all over with my mom," said Shelby. "I know what you mean about big cities. Recently, we were in Las Vegas."

"Not the friendliest city. Are you living here permanently now?" she asked.

Shelby shrugged. "We've never lived anywhere permanently. My mom is traveling with her boyfriend while I stay here for the summer."

"Parents can definitely be difficult sometimes," Mindy said. "Mine are very traditional. They want me back in Palo Alto closer to the family. They think it's crazy I'm recovering up here. Last year I redecorated the cottage and made the place my own. It's quiet, peaceful, and beautiful. And the local grocery store delivers."

Shelby liked the way Mindy had designed the house. Filtered sunlight from the windows flickered across the dark wood floors, setting off the mocha colored walls and colorful furniture. "How long have you been coming here?" Shelby asked.

"Before my life became all about going to an Ivy League college, obtaining a high paying job, and meeting the right man, my parents would take us up here to the lake. It's only a few hours' drive from the Bay Area. Some of my best memories as a kid were here."

Shelby wasn't surprised to hear how different Mindy's childhood had been from her own. She tried to imagine what it would've been like to have a wonderful family that took vacations together and cared about their daughter's future. "My mom brought me here a few times to see my grandparents, but we never stayed long."

"Well now you have all summer to have fun," Mindy said.

Shelby hoped so. "Please let me know anything I can do," she said, getting to her feet. "My grandma drives if you need us for an appointment or something." Maybe Alice would be up to leaving the house if Mindy needed them. It could be just the thing to motivate her grandmother. She loved helping people too.

"Thanks a lot. I'll keep that in mind. You go ahead and enjoy your day. Back on Monday, I hope?"

"Sure thing," Shelby said. She gave Karma one last pet and closed the door behind her. On her walk home she thought about how she would be making real money now for the first time ever. If she saved most of it, her dream of going to college in a couple of years could become a reality.

Out on the lake she admired the multitude of boats, showing off their colored sails for June's Race Week. Temperatures were rising, and a cool swim would feel great. She'd love to go down to the beach, but she really hated the thought of those girls. And the awful bathing suit that she'd thrown away left her no choice now but to go home and do something else. She skipped up the front steps and entered the living room. Her grandmother was still sitting in the same recliner with Scarlett curled up next to her.

"How did it go?" Alice asked.

Shelby took a chair opposite her grandmother. "It was great. Karma is an energetic girl! After our walk we went into town for ice cream and I met Steph and Josh, the new owners of Redd's."

"Oh, they're such lovely people, "Alice said. "And I do enjoy their ice cream. Maybe I'll walk down there with you one night. They're open late on weekends."

"Would you? How about tomorrow?" Shelby said. She really

wanted to see her grandmother get out and was up for anything that would encourage her, especially ice cream. "I want to try one of their specialty ice cream sodas. They look amazing."

"Soon," Alice said. She lay back in the chair and her eyes drifted shut.

"There are so many dogs in town," Shelby said, hoping to keep Alice's attention. "Steph and Josh's corgi, Oscar, is adorable and they hired me to walk him. I now have two clients. And...I met Trevor and his service Buddy. He's going to tell the veterans in town about my business, too."

"Congratulations," Alice said, a smile lighting up her face. "I remember Buddy. A golden retriever, right?"

Shelby nodded.

"Your grandpa knew them," Alice said. "A very productive day for you. We should celebrate. How about I cook a special dinner tonight?"

"I can help," Shelby said. Then with a wry smile she said, "And maybe after dinner we can go for ice cream."

revor was going to be speaking at the Lakeside Veterans Center today at 9:00 a.m. sharp. Theo was determined to go and show support for Trevor, and maybe sign up as a volunteer to teach a photography class. Wally was welcome to attend, so after their morning walk and a light breakfast, the twosome headed into town. The LVC, or Lakeside Veterans Center, was located in an old refurbished brick house about five blocks up from the lake on the outskirts of the main downtown.

As they approached, Theo noticed a few young men and women standing off in the freshly mowed yard having a smoke. Who could blame them? he thought. The kind of stress vets went through was unimaginable to him. Jean's death had totally devastated Theo. Jean had lived a full, long life, never long enough but with plenty of time to say goodbye in each other's arms. For these people who served in war-torn areas, battlefield trauma was an unspeakable and unresolved horror. Theo would never truly understand the depth of what these men and women had to live with.

He opened the screen door and walked into a small reception area. The old wood paneling looked like it was the original from when the house was first built, with the faded linoleum floor to match. But it was spotless and the person behind the counter was friendly. Toward the back was a large multi-purpose room, where people stood and bits of their laughter and conversation drifted toward him.

"Well, who do we have here?" said the man minding the desk. He knelt down to pet Wally. "You are a handsome boy," he said, scratching Wally behind the ears. "I had a beagle growing up, nothing like them."

Theo introduced himself and the dog and let the man know they were here for Trevor's talk.

"I'm Marc, at your service," he said with a smile. "Follow me and I'll take you back where we're meeting today."

Theo followed Marc through the main meeting area comprised of old couches and various mismatched chairs. Ceiling fans circulated the already warming air. There were posters on the wall of serene settings, from mountain ranges to seascapes, some with encouraging sayings. Theo felt his shoulders relax as they moved through the space. He hadn't ventured out to try anything new in a long time.

There were several wooden chairs lined up and arranged to face a small raised platform. Most were filled, with about twenty men and women of all ages. A few in uniform, the rest casually dressed. Trevor stood on a low stage with Buddy, wearing his vest, at his side. He had on a nicely ironed plaid button-down shirt. It was the first time Theo could remember seeing him in anything but a t-shirt. His brown hair was cut neatly as always, and his glasses were in place. Looking around, Theo noticed a few people probably still dealing with injuries resulting from combat. But other people's scars were not visible to the human eye. Theo knew all about that. He'd talked to Trevor enough to get a basic understanding of PTSD, and it was as deadly a disease as they came.

"You made it," Trevor said as he waved hello. He motioned for Theo to come up to where there was a vacant seat up front.

"Come on, boy," Theo said to Wally. Theo hesitated to sit so far from the exit, just in case he might feel like leaving, but he dismissed it and took a seat in the front row. Wally sat at his feet and promptly dropped into a nap. That dog could sleep anywhere.

After waiting for the crowd to settle, an announcer said, "Welcome, everyone. Today our speaker is our very own Trevor Lucero. He is going to share his journey with you how he found and ultimately bonded with his service dog Buddy."

In response to his name, Buddy lifted his head and did a crisp bark. The whole room broke out laughing and the quiet tension dissolved.

Trevor walked to the microphone, Buddy at his heels. "As you can tell, Buddy and I are happy to be here. In fact, if it wasn't for this dog, I'm not sure I would ever have made it out of my cabin and down to this center to begin with."

A few people nodded in understanding. Theo remembered when Trevor had first moved here about four years ago. He'd seen him once in the market and in the office supply store. The young man always had his head down, and Theo's wife, Jean, had been concerned about him.

"We should stop over, bring him a casserole or something," she would say. Theo smiled remembering Jean's generous heart. And so they had, and because of that meeting Theo and Wally were sitting here now.

Trevor continued. "I tried counseling and medication, but I needed something more. Sometimes just going to the market threw me into full on panic attack. All that changed after I heard about Double Rescue for Vets. The people at DRV understood everything I was going through. The isolating and chronic depression that had drained the color out of every day of my life since returning from Afghanistan. Many of you know exactly what I mean."

He paused while a wave of acknowledgement moved through the crowd.

"One of the wounds of war is the way many veterans suffer in silence. Centers like this change lives and help us recover."

Theo had never completely realized the extent of what Trevor had been going through until now. He looked around the room at the men and women who had served their country. The very least he could do was volunteer here and help them find some joy through a new hobby.

Buddy nudged up against Trevor's leg, and he bent down to pet him. "Buddy knows what I need before I do half the time."

A hand went up in the audience. "How did you find DRV?"

"I was lucky enough to find a flyer here at the vet center when it first opened. We all met in a much smaller place back then, just a room in the back of a church. But I was afraid I couldn't afford a dog," Trevor continued. "Then I learned that through generous individuals, community fundraising, and corporate sponsorship, DRV is able to rescue dogs from shelters and then rescue us vets by training them as service dogs to help with our specialized needs."

There was a smattering of applause and thumbs up throughout the crowd. Theo looked down at Wally. What would he have done without his canine best friend after Jean died? He could feel a tear at the corner of his eye and wiped it away. Furry angels, that was what Jean had called dogs.

A woman stood up with a question. "I've heard a therapy dog and service dog are different. Can you take Buddy with you anywhere you go?"

"Good question," Trevor said. "Buddy, thanks to the ADI certification, is a service dog and I can take him anywhere I go. Having Buddy at my side helped me feel safe enough to leave the house, confident enough to start my own web design business, and eventually come down to LVC and volunteer myself. Now before I take any more questions, I am going to show you some of the things Buddy is trained to do with me."

Buddy stood alert, waiting. Trevor pulled a chair to the middle of the stage and sat down with a sideways view to the audience.

"My lap," Trevor said.

Theo watched Buddy lift both paws onto Trevor's lap and give him some dog kisses.

A big "Awwww" sounded from the crowd.

Then Trevor laid on the stage and pretended to have trouble getting up. "Brace," he said.

Buddy promptly scooted in close and locked all four of his legs tightly. Trevor was able to brace himself on the dog's back and stand up.

This time the crowd cheered and a few members clapped.

"These are not just tricks," Trevor said. "There are many more and some not only help us physically, but get us through another day." He petted Buddy's head and released the dog from duty with a hand signal. Buddy sat and looked out at the audience as if waiting for questions.

The beautiful golden in his service dog vest was a true hero in Theo's eyes, just like the man beside him.

"Questions?" Trevor asked.

Several hands flew in the air and Trevor pointed to them one by one.

"How long does it take to get a dog once you are approved?"

"It can be a while, but it is worth the sixteen to eighteen month waiting list. When the dog is ready, DRV flies you out and houses you for twenty-one days to train onsite and in public with the dog. I was really nervous we wouldn't bond, but one look at each other and I knew he was the dog for me. Next?"

"It seems like a rough life for a dog," an older gentleman said.

Trevor smiled. "Let me put it this way. Buddy sleeps in my bed, claims the couch, and chases squirrels in the backyard like the best of them."

The man continued. "But do they ever get to play with other dogs? I know we're allowed to pet Buddy sometimes, so how does that work?"

"Good question," Trevor said. "The dogs wear their vests when they're working. The vest carries a water bottle on each side for man and beast, waste bags, a pop-up water bowl, sunblock, and a pack of Kleenex...for those kinds of days. I can say 'make a friend' and Buddy can leave my side to greet other people. But if Buddy wants to go play with one of his friends, like Wally there in the front row, I take off the vest to signal play-time." Trevor called Buddy over next to him and held up his hand and waved. Buddy mimicked him with his paw held high. "That is a trick I taught him for when we occasionally give speeches."

Laughter filled the room.

"Our official talk time is over now, but we'd be happy for any of you to come up after, greet Buddy, and ask any individual questions you may have. Thanks for coming today."

Everyone stood and applauded, and it filled Theo's heart to see the big smile on Trevor's face. Theo had always believed in paying it forward and it was time to put some action behind that belief. After meeting a few of the people and waving goodbye to Trevor, Theo and Wally walked right up to the front desk, pocketed a brochure, and filled out a form to volunteer.

On their way home, Theo felt particularly energized. He had an even greater respect for the husband and wife counseling team that had raised funds to open LVC. He looked down at his faithful canine companion trotting alongside him. The relationship between man and dog went far beyond explaining. He'd heard them called man's and woman's best friend, and Theo agreed. He couldn't wait to tell Jean about his wonderful experience today. Why had he waited so long to listen to Trevor and stop by? It was one of the most impressive and inspiring places he'd ever been. And the fact that he could be a part of helping those vets through teaching photography brought him great joy. Maybe he still had something to give after all.

When he reached the park bench, Wally circled the grass looking for the perfect spot to plop down and nod off. Theo wished he could fall asleep as unfettered as the dog. The lake reflected the turquoise sky and white pelicans soaring in the distance. He closed his eyes and took a deep breath, letting the fresh air fill his lungs the way the visit had filled his heart.

"Jean," he whispered, "I miss you more than ever." He stopped a moment, letting the self-chastisement pass on through. He should have gone sooner, he should have stopped wallowing in the grief and gotten out there, and on and on. The regrets running through his mind spun endlessly. They were useless and just a way to feel bad again. Jean would never stand for it. He sat up straight and addressed her again.

"Today I met some wonderful fellas and ladies and learned all about service dogs as well. I plan to get myself involved and help every way I can. I wish you were here," he said. "But I guess in some way you are, otherwise I'm just talking to myself!"

He chuckled and Wally roused.

Theo leaned over and petted the dog. "Love you, boy."

The sun was starting to steal the shade from the tree overlooking the bench. But a slight breeze blew up from the lake and with it the sweet smell of wild flowering lavender growing on the low bank before them. He pulled out the LVC brochure and looked it over. Some of the endorsements spoke of how being understood by others relieved the feeling that you were the only one grappling with tough challenges. Theo considered his own grieving process. He had purposely stayed isolated and not wanted to talk to anyone. Perhaps he should look into a grief and loss group himself. Or at least talk to a friend.

Theo stood and Wally followed reluctantly. "Let's get going before it gets too hot. We could both use a cold drink."

As they turned to go home, Shelby came into view walking the Redds' dog, Oscar. Wally's thick, dark, white-tipped tail vigorously wagged back and forth.

"Okay, boy, let's go say hello."

"Hi, guys," Shelby said as she approached.

Theo noticed the girl had some color in her face now. And her eyes had lost their sad edges. The dogs greeted each other like old friends with their "sniffing ritual," as Theo liked to call it. The greeting presented quite a challenge to keep their leashes from twisting up together.

Shelby laughed as they struggled to untangle the two dogs. Her smile never failed to brighten his day.

"I see you are out on a professional booking," Theo said. "You seem to be getting pretty busy."

"I sure am," Shelby said. "I now have three dogs I walk, including Scarlett, of course. I can't thank you enough for giving me this great idea."

"Well I may have suggested this, but you are quite the young entrepreneur to put this all together."

"Are you headed home?" Shelby asked.

Theo nodded. "We just visited at the Lakeside Vets Center and I will be volunteering there soon. Wally was quite the hit with the folks too." Theo thought a moment. "I saw the flyer Trevor put up about your dog walking service at the center too. Before you know it, you are going to be all booked up."

"I will have a full pack soon," she said with a smile. "I wish the town had a dog park where they could all play together safely off leash sometimes. But for now, I'll be taking lots of walks!"

Theo considered the idea of a dog park. "That would be nice," he said. "Just a small one where we could all get together."

Oscar barked at a person going by on their bike and let Shelby know he was ready to get moving. "I'd better get this dog back to Redd's," she said. "Great to see you both."

Theo watched as they headed toward town. The girl was a natural with dogs. If only he could help her with that dog park idea. A gust of wind blew over him, and it felt like Jean playfully ruffling his hair. Maybe he could help her out with that idea. He would think on it.

CHAPTER 10

*S*omeone was licking her face. Shelby lifted her hand and felt a furry face with a wet nose just above her.

"Good morning, Scarlett," she said. She yawned and wondered if she could just turn over and go back to sleep.

Scarlett stared her down and gave a loud woof. When that didn't work, she cocked her head and woofed again.

"Okay, I get it. You want to go for a walk."

Shelby had been spending more time walking her clients' dogs this week and Scarlett was letting her know it was her turn. She threw on some shorts and an old t-shirt and would shower when she got home. All was quiet in the living room, her grandmother still asleep, so Shelby shut the door gently behind them as they headed out toward the lake. She strode down the deserted street to the steps leading to the lake path and began to jog. She was determined to wear this young dog out today. When the lake came into view, Shelby stopped for a moment to take in the beauty. It was worth getting up this early to see the golden sun spilling into the puffy clouds above and turning them shades of canary yellow and rose that were mirrored back on the water's surface. Patches of blue covered the rest of the sky like a painted background setting.

To get a better view, she walked up the low bluff ahead, Scarlett anxious to explore the territory. When they reached the top, Shelby leaned against a giant oak and watched as the scene before her came alive with early morning birds and a lone fishing boat gliding across the still water. A noise below caught her attention. Keeping Scarlett close, Shelby leaned slightly over the edge to see what had caused it. She was quite surprised to see a young girl about her age, perched on a ledge, sketching the sunrise. She had captured the scene perfectly with what looked like colored pencils.

"That is gorgeous," Shelby said.

The blonde girl, the pretty one she'd seen at the lake, turned sharply to see where the comment had come from. Her face morphed from surprise to anger as she glared up at Shelby.

"Sorry, didn't mean to disturb you," Shelby said. "You're an amazing artist."

For a moment the girl smiled and let the compliment set in. Then she looked down at her work and slammed the sketchbook closed. "I was just finishing," she said as she picked up her art supplies and stomped off.

Shelby watched her disappear back into the trees. Not the friendliest person she'd met so far. Scarlett gave a tug, reminding her their jog was not finished yet. They raced around the path, the wind moving through her long hair and chasing the lingering clouds away. By the time they reached the stairs to return home, the lake and sky were a perfect cornflower blue.

As soon as she got home, Shelby wanted to pull off her sweaty clothes and shower. She contemplated going to the beach later and wearing shorts and a t-shirt. Maybe bring a book. She could always say she was working on her tan. Alice was not in the living room or kitchen. The silence was so unlike the grandmother Shelby remembered from a few short years ago, who would be filling the house with the smell of fresh-baked cookies or outside gardening.

"Grandma, are you home?"

"In the bedroom," her grandmother called out, her voice laced with sleep.

When they entered the darkened room, Scarlett jumped up on the bed with Alice. "It's beautiful out. How about I open the blinds?" Shelby asked.

Her grandmother covered her eyes with her arm. "I just had a bit of a headache, nothing to worry about." She pushed herself up in bed. "Sure, go ahead and open them. I love watching the bird feeder out the window."

As Shelby opened the blinds facing out to the grassy back-yard, she wracked her brain for some way to help her grand-mother feel better. She was used to being a caretaker, but mostly for her mother, whose grief clung to them both year after year like clothes out of the dryer too soon.

Outside, the sun filtered through the large oak tree, spilling light over the standing bird feeder. A vibrant blue jay was picking at the seed while a little sparrow waited its turn.

"It's pretty out," her grandmother said, propping herself up in bed.

Shelby nodded. "Getting a little warm."

"Why don't you go for a swim? You're living at one of the clearest lakes in the U.S. You might as well swim. You love the water."

Shelby avoided eye contact. "Oh, I don't know. I'm kind of tired."

Her grandmother patted the bed for Shelby to sit beside her. "What's going on?" she asked. "I've never seen you like this. Swimming's your favorite thing. You've got time. Why don't you go? Meet some kids your own age."

Shelby flinched.

"Is there something wrong? Tell me, sweetheart."

Shelby really didn't want to upset her grandmother, and she certainly didn't want to tell her how bad she felt. "I don't know. It seems like wherever I go I just don't fit in."

"I see." Alice pushed aside her covers and slid her legs over the side of the bed so they were now sitting side by side.

A lump formed in Shelby's throat and she leaned her head on Alice's shoulder. Her grandmother held her close and spoke softly, her voice filled with kindness.

"When I was young, fitting in seemed like the most important thing in the world. I think many young people feel the same way you do," Alice said.

"Do you think so?" Shelby asked. "Some of the kids at the beach seem very confident in themselves."

"You'll find out that many people put on false fronts to cover what they really feel inside. But young people can be pretty mean sometimes. Eventually I figured out it's just good to be yourself, and then the people you fit with will come to you."

Shelby took a deep breath. Now it was her grandmother comforting her. "That's good advice. I'll give it a try. I still wish you'd come out with me sometime."

"I'm not much for the beach," Alice said. "I can't risk getting sunburned anymore, and the sand gets everywhere. Besides, you need to meet some young people, not drag me along."

"I'll go soon," Shelby said.

Her grandmother gave her a probing look. "Are you going to tell me the real reason why you aren't going swimming?"

"Actually," Shelby said, avoiding eye contact, "I threw my bathing suit away."

"What?"

Shelby looked up. "It was old, and faded, and ugly."

Alice laughed. "And you don't own a second one?"

"No, I barely had that one. It's not exactly like Mom takes me shopping very often. And it was from the last thrift store purchase. It was already used."

Alice frowned. "You were taking lifeguard lessons. You should have had at least two bathing suits."

"Well, you know how my mom is."

"Yes, I do." Arms crossed, Alice got up and began pacing the room, her long nightgown trailing behind her. "That makes me upset."

Shelby knew her grandmother would refrain from saying anything bad about Dana. She'd overheard her mother and grandmother fighting several times. She knew Dana had run off and gotten married at eighteen, hardly speaking to her parents since. Except to ask for money. Shelby remembered those calls. But her grandmother always tried to be kind whenever they visited, and Shelby had nothing but good memories of the time she and her grandparents spent alone together.

Alice stood before her and reached out her hand. Her eyes were bright and skin flushed, and she looked like her old self in that moment. Shelby rose and took her grandmother's hand.

"We need to go to the mall and buy you some new bathing suits," Alice said."And for that matter, your clothes are a little tight. We need a girls' shopping trip."

"Really, Grandma? Would you be willing to go? I have some of my own money, already. Mindy paid me for a week."

"It's time I got out of this house," Alice said. "How about this for a deal? I'll buy the first bathing suit. You can buy the second, but you'll let me treat you to some new clothes too."

Shelby felt her heart race with excitement. "You'll really take me?"

"I'll really take you," said Alice.

"Okay, when?"

Her grandmother looked a little nervous at first when the reality of it sank in. Alice stood up tall, took a deep breath, and said, "Well, it seems there's no time like the present. I think we should go get in the car. The mall's only half an hour away. There are some nice shops and cafes there, and we can even have a treat to reward ourselves for a job well done."

"Are you sure?" Shelby asked.

"Absolutely, yes," Alice said. "As soon as I take a shower and get some clothes on."

Shelby threw her arms around her grandmother.

Scarlett didn't know what was going on, but she knew it was big, so she started barking and twirling in circles.

"No, this time you're staying home, little one," Alice said. "It's too hot to leave you in the car and you had your morning walk." She turned to Shelby. "All right, you go get ready and so will I."

THE OUTDOOR MALL was a small but well-designed one-story collection of stores meandering around a flowering courtyard. Shelby couldn't be happier. Most stores had outside awnings so people could window shop in the hot weather.

They ambled by first to see which store looked promising. "This one is having a summer sale, how perfect," Alice said. "Let's go find you some new clothes."

"Love to."

Her grandmother smiled at her. "When was the last time you had anything new?"

Shelby thought about it and could not remember. She shrugged her shoulders.

Alice frowned. "Well it's about time then."

They walked into a boutique called Judy's Closet that had some really cute floral dresses in the window display. A song by Katy Perry was playing in the background. Shelby liked everything she saw and didn't know where to start, until she saw a two-piece, pale yellow bathing suit with little white flowers. She pulled out her size and held it up to show her grandmother.

Alice gave her a thumbs up. "Pick out a few more to try on."

"How about this one?" Alice asked, holding up a pair of distressed shorts and one of the sundresses from the window.

Alice was browsing through a table of suits and pulled out a bright turquoise tankini with a pink and white striped bottom.

"Love it," Shelby said.

The salesgirl brought them into a dressing room with everything they had picked out. Shelby hummed along to the music as she made her decision where to start. She chose the one her grandmother had picked out first. She loved the way the top tied around her neck, showing off her shoulders, and the colors worked so well together. Shelby peered out, making sure no one else was around, then stepped forward and modeled it for Alice.

"It's adorable," her grandmother said. "Put it in the 'yes' pile."

Next she tried on the blue suit with horizontal stripes of colors. It had an opening and showed off a little of her pale-colored midriff. It was not as tan as her arms and legs, but that would be remedied soon. Shelby couldn't believe her reflection in the mirror. She was a cute girl and...her mind flashed to Logan. Even in this suit there was still that blonde girl who was probably his girlfriend. Oh well, it didn't matter. She would have two new bathing suits and couldn't wait to go back to the lake.

At the counter, Shelby paid for one of the bathing suits as promised.

Alice bought her one of the others, some shirts and shorts that actually fit, a sundress and hat, and a new pair of sandals. She handed the bag to Shelby. "Here you go. You will be the best dressed girl in town."

Outside in the courtyard, Shelby hugged her grandmother. "It made me feel good to buy one for myself, too."

"You worked hard for it," Alice said. "I'm very proud of you."

"You are the best, Grandma."

"Oh dear," her grandmother said, wiping away a tear. "I'm so pleased we can be together."

"Me too," Shelby said, feeling tears well up.

"And look what we have here," Alice said.

Shelby turned and they were standing in front of a cell phone store.

"With your new dog walking business, you need to have a cell phone. It's only practical. Let's stop in and get you one on my plan."

"Even after all the clothes?"

"Come on," Alice said. "It makes me happy to see you happy."

The store was offering a special on a small silver phone if they signed up today. Now Shelby would have her own number to give out to clients and to anyone she wanted. She'd be able to do some texting. Maybe, just for now, she might not give her number to her mother. They left with the new phone in Shelby's bag to activate when they got home.

"I'm exhausted," Alice said. "Let's go find a coffee shop to sit down and celebrate. Not to mention get off my feet for a while."

Along the brick promenade they spotted people sitting outside under red and white striped umbrellas with the Lake Brew Coffee logo on them. Shelby ordered a tall iced hibiscus tea blended drink, and her grandmother a cup of coffee. Their special for the day was lemon bars and Alice ordered a couple of those to share. They found a seat at one of the petite tables on the outside patio and watched the people go by.

"It's the first time I've been out in a while, and it feels good," Alice said. "I really haven't been myself since your grandpa died."

"I know how much you miss him," Shelby said. "He was the best grandpa anyone could ever have." Shelby was happy to see her grandmother had put on linen pants and a nice blouse, and a touch of makeup like she used to. Her eyes looked sad, but her energy seemed to be returning.

Alice sipped her coffee, staring into space. "I really do miss him." She looked up at Shelby. "I just don't know what to do with myself with him gone. We were together so long." She patted

Shelby's hand. "But you're here with me now, and we will have a wonderful summer together."

Shelby felt a glow inside. She had to thank her mother. Whether Dana knew it or not, this summer with her grandmother was the best thing that could have happened to them both.

Shelby sipped the icy, sweet drink. It was nice to be out among people, hear them talking, dig into a lemon bar and let her worries go. "Why don't you come out with me one day when I take Scarlett for a walk? Get some fresh air, see some people."

Alice smiled. "I'll think about it." She paused. "You are right though, and I certainly could use the exercise."

"You always liked helping people," Shelby said. "I told you about that nice man, Theo. I think he's going to volunteer at the vets center and do some photography lessons. Maybe you could volunteer somewhere, too."

"I remember seeing his work. Wasn't he a photographer? His shots were often displayed at the arts and crafts festival. He's talented, and they are lucky to have him. But I don't know what I can offer."

"You bake a mean cookie," Shelby said. "And you used to work as a nurse. You're good with people. You could volunteer at the hospital."

"I've had enough of hospitals after your grandpa's illness," said Alice. "Maybe something a little lighthearted, something a little more fun. Baking classes might work."

"I'm sure we can find something." Shelby made a mental note to come up with more ideas. Watching her grandmother enjoy herself during their shopping trip made Shelby more determined than ever to keep that direction going.

"Now, what about you?" Alice asked. "You only have two years of high school left. Have you thought about your plans for college?"

Shelby sighed. "First off, I don't know where I'll be finishing high school. I wouldn't mind staying here for it."

"The former mayor, my friend, Eleanor, knows all about the school, and truthfully the whole town!" Alice thought a moment. "We could also talk to Joann. She was an English teacher there and said it has a top-notch curriculum."

"I don't think my mom would let me stay. Although, I don't know when and if she's even coming back."

"Of course your mother's coming back. We never know when, though."

They both laughed.

"I'm so glad I came," said Shelby. "This is already my best summer ever."

"Me too," Alice said. "Now, let's get you home. Put on one of those cute bathing suits, and you march right down to the beach."

As if they had radar that homed in on Shelby in her vulnerable moments, the teenage girls from the beach appeared, dripping with shopping bags. Except for Emily, who she recognized from Redd's Ice Cream Parlor, the girls were all made up and wearing perfect little outfits. They snickered as they walked by, seeing Shelby sitting with her grandmother.

Shelby sighed. "I can't escape those girls anywhere." She'd even tried to be nice to one of them that morning.

"Those girls?" Alice asked, watching them saunter by.

"This is not the first time they've acted like this to me. Remember that movie? Maybe you saw *Mean Girls*."

"Oh, yes," Alice said. "I recognize the tall, pretty blonde one. Her name is Madison. She always has a posse of girlfriends with her."

Shelby nodded in assent.

"I've heard about them from Eleanor," Alice said. "She complains that her niece who lives here, Emily, is not the same girl when she hangs out with Madison every summer."

"So, they don't live here all year?"

Alice shook her head and Shelby was relieved. "They have one of those architectural homes right on the lake," Alice said. "They don't interact much with the locals. Their friends tend to arrive by boat or fly in. Madison seems like an unhappy girl. She never looks up or says hello."

Shelby hadn't thought about Madison's personality reflecting her own unhappiness. "Yeah. Well, she sure knows Logan."

"Logan across the street?" Alice said.

"He's the lifeguard down at the lake."

"Oh, that's right," Alice said. "What about him?"

"Madison and Logan seem to have a thing."

"Well you'd think that boy would have better taste," Alice said, her eyes amused.

Shelby squelched a laugh. "Oh, Grandma."

"You don't let those girls bully you," Alice said. "You're the prettiest of them all."

A voice from behind them said, "Mirror, mirror on the wall, who's the fairest of them all?"

Shelby turned to see a tall, elegant white-haired woman carrying two large shopping bags from the fanciest department store within a hundred miles.

Her grandmother stood. "Eleanor," she said. "Come join us. This is my granddaughter, Shelby, who I mentioned to you the other day."

Eleanor extended a perfectly manicured hand to Shelby. "Well, hello," she said. "I remember you from the funeral. You looked so young then, and now look at you, a little over a year later and a lovely young woman. With those long legs and glossy hair, you could be a model."

A warm flush moved up Shelby's face. "Nice to meet you too," she said.

Eleanor, in a cream-colored sheath dress, laid her shopping bags in one chair and pulled another up to join them at the table. "My feet are killing me," she said. "I had to shop for two events.

One at my husband's golf course and the other with the city council. Now I need a gallon of iced tea."

"It's on me," Alice said, pushing her chair back. "Black or green?"

"Black, please, and no sweetener." As Alice walked away, Eleanor turned to Shelby. "Your grandmother tells me you're going to be here for the summer and have started a little business. Good for you. Tell me more about your dog walking service."

"Well," Shelby said, "I've just started and already have a few customers and others interested."

"That's because it is a very needed service here at the lake. Smart girl. In fact, I hate leaving my little puffballs Dixie and Ruby alone when I'm gone so much." Eleanor lifted up her sleek white iPhone from her matching purse and presented pictures of her dogs to Shelby. "Aren't they just the sweetest things ever?"

Shelby couldn't help but smile at the two perfectly groomed, pure white Pomeranians with black button eyes and noses, smiling into the camera. "Adorable," Shelby said. "Very huggable."

A smile lit up Eleanor's face. "Perhaps you could come by sometime soon and meet them? I'd like to book some times with you before you get too busy."

"That would be great. I'll check my calendar at home and let you know a day."

Eleanor frowned. "Don't you keep a calendar in your phone like all the young people these days?"

Inside Shelby cringed. But before she could answer, her grandmother cut in.

"Here's your drink," she said, placing it on the table. "For now, Shelby is keeping a paper calendar at my house," Alice explained. "Just until we can get her new cell phone connected on my service."

Eleanor took a few sips of her tea and then launched right into catching Alice up on the local gossip on health issues, relationships, and other various topics. She mentioned she'd driven her niece Emily and her friends to the mall too, but they had promptly taken off. Shelby tuned out from their conversation after a while. She didn't know any of the people. She thought about walking down to the lake later today in her new bathing suit. Her thoughts floated to Logan and she sighed aloud.

"You must be tired after all this shopping," Alice said to Eleanor.

Eleanor looked at her watch and then rose to leave. "Tired, but no time. I'd better get going now, too. The girls are all alone at home and need their walk. Now if I can just find my niece and her friends," she sighed. Eleanor gathered her shopping bags, waved, and rushed off.

"That woman makes me tired just watching her," Alice said. "I wish I had that kind of energy."

"We had a great day out of the house, and that's a good start," Shelby said. "Let's do something like this again soon."

"Deal," Alice said. "Now I need to get back and take a nap. Maybe tomorrow you can go to the lake." She winked at Shelby. "Perhaps sit by the lifeguard station and then have a swim in one of those new bathing suits."

CHAPTER 11

*S*helby had waited a few days after the shopping trip before having the confidence to go back to the lake. She decided to be brave and picked a spot on the sand not far from the lifeguard station. She adjusted the backrest on her beach chair, leaned back, and pulled out a book. Today she was escaping into the world of fantasy in another time and place. She glanced down at her new bathing suit with the small ruffled top and smiled. If Madison and her posse showed up today, they'd have nothing to make fun of with Shelby. She'd been sure to cover herself in suntan lotion before leaving the house. Now she would work on that nice, even tan.

The sun beat down in its afternoon intensity, lulling her into wanting to swim or nap. After reading a few more pages, her eyes wandered along the shore. A ways down from her, she spotted Logan, red buoy in hand, scanning the water for swimmers in distress. If her mother hadn't moved her from their last home, Shelby might be doing the same job herself right now.

Peeking over the top of her book, she surveyed his perfect V-shaped swimmer's body. Tall, broad shoulders, his back tapering down to his narrow waist. And how good he looked in the red swim trunks, his body silhouetted against the turquoise lake. Luckily her sunglasses hid her admiring gaze. Suddenly he turned her way, as if he was aware of someone staring. She quickly focused into her book and froze. Her cheeks were aflame, and it was not from the sun. She let her eyes glance over the book and saw Logan turn back the other way and continue his walk down the shore until he was almost out of sight.

Shelby tried to go back to reading, but it was no use. She tossed it on her towel, with her sunglasses beside it, and walked to the edge of the lake. The cool, clear water rippled over her feet, tempting her to dive in, but the children splashing and yelling as they played made her seek a quieter spot. She strolled down the beach, confident in her new bathing suit. She noticed a few admiring gazes, so different than what she was used to. Leaving the noisy swimmers behind, she found a quiet spot and stared out over the horizon.

Shelby glanced back to make sure she hadn't gone outside the designated swimming area marked by the buoys. In the distance she saw the lifeguard station and Logan sitting in his chair surrounded by his fan club. She could hear the giggles echoing toward her, and the familiar feeling of being left out seeped into her chest. She shook it off and, eyes closed, waded deeper into the welcoming water where the sounds and images would not travel. The soothing water hit waist level and sent a chill through her body. She caught her breath as a strong wake from a passing speedboat almost made her lose her footing. She righted herself and waited for it to subside.

A faint cry caught her attention. Immediately, her lifeguard training kicked in. Her eyes flew open and searched the surface of the lake, trying to locate the sound.

"Help," a voice gasped behind her.

Turning around sharply, about twenty feet away in deeper water, Shelby saw a woman's head bobbing up and down. Her arms flailed in the air as she gasped for help. Shelby swam quickly toward her, eyes fixed on the gray-haired woman's position. Just as Shelby reached the spot, the woman dropped out of sight.

Shelby dove, kicking her legs to go deeper, eyes searching under the water. She spotted the unconscious woman floating limply. There was no time to spare. Shelby grabbed the woman from behind, put her right hand over her right shoulder, and brought the limp woman back to the surface. Using the scissor kick as she had been instructed, she swam briskly to shore, making sure the woman's head was always above water. The woman began to cough and Shelby hoped she'd gotten to her in time. When they reached shallow water, Shelby stood and supported the woman's body as they walked to shore.

On the beach, a small crowd had gathered, watching her efforts. Shelby yelled, "Someone call 911."

She sat the woman on the sand and told everyone to step back. The woman leaned over and spit out water as she coughed again. Relief flooded Shelby and she almost passed out herself from the adrenaline drop.

Logan, his face pale, rushed in beside her. "I'll handle the situation now," he said. Shelby took a step back as Logan began questioning the woman. "How are you feeling? Are you on any medication?"

The woman broke out crying.

A siren wailed in the distance. Shelby stood close, her whole body shaking. The woman reached out to her. "Thank you," she said between tears. "I used to be such a good swimmer."

An elderly man scrambled over beside them and took the woman in his arms. "Adele, what were you thinking?"

She laid her head on his shoulder. "I'm so sorry. I didn't realize how far I drifted. That was really dumb."

He shook his head. "All that matters is that you are okay." He looked up at the lifeguard. "Thank you for saving my wife's life."

Logan pointed to Shelby. "You can thank her," he said. "They were almost out of my sight range, so it took me a little while to get here."

"Thank you, little lady," the man said.

The paramedics came running down the beach with a stretcher and loaded Adele on it. "We'll take it from here," they said.

Shelby could hear them asking the woman more questions, but Adele did seem stable and that was the best outcome possible.

They watched as the paramedics whisked Adele away. Logan asked the crowd to please disperse and watched while they drifted away. He turned to Shelby. "I'd like you to come back to my station with me now."

She nodded and followed him silently down the beach. His face was unreadable, and Shelby wondered if she was in some kind of trouble.

When they reached his station, Logan thanked the other life-guard for covering while he was handling the incident. Madison rushed up to Logan and tried to hug him, but he stepped back.

"You were amazing, Logan," Madison said.

"Not me," Logan said, nodding toward Shelby. "Got to go, I have to fill out a report."

Madison glared at him then turned to Shelby. Even after the adrenaline and euphoria of saving a woman's life, Shelby felt the daggers hit their mark, deep in the recesses of her gut. With a flick of her hair, Madison motioned for her friends to follow as she stomped off.

Finally, Logan turned to Shelby.

"I don't know what you were doing way down there outside the limit area, but I will forever be grateful you were there and knew what to do."

Shelby looked into his golden-brown eyes and knew his words were sincere.

"I took," she faltered, "some lifeguard training."

"It was obvious," he said. "By the time I spotted Adele, she would have drowned if you weren't there. It was my fault for letting anything distract me from my job. It won't happen again."

Shelby found herself trying to comfort him. "We both drifted out of your territory. It was partly our fault."

"No excuse," he said. "If you hadn't been there…"

"But I was," she said.

He reached out his hand to her. "I'm Logan. You're my new neighbor, Shelby, right?"

She almost said "I know" but stopped herself. His handshake was strong and put her off balance in a good sort of way. "Shelby."

"Nice to formally meet you, Shelby."

His color was returning now. Their eyes met and the intensity of the moment seemed to stop time. Shelby caught her breath and tried to respond. "Me too. I mean, you too."

His smile lit his face and dimples graced his cheeks. Shelby's heart pounded as the adrenaline letdown encompassed her like a rogue wave. She swooned, a bit dizzy, and he reached out to catch her.

"Sit down," he said. "I can't believe I didn't ask you if you're all right."

After plopping on the sand near the lifeguard station, Shelby took deep breaths, trying to slow down the spinning. She really didn't want him to see her like this, and his warm hand on her shoulder was not helping her accelerated heart rate.

"I'm okay," she said, trying to stand. He gently pulled her up. The close proximity of his body made her sway again.

"That was very brave," he whispered.

All Shelby could do was nod and stare numbly toward the lake.

"Can I get you some water or something?" he asked.

She shook her head. "I'm fine. I'll go home and rest."

Logan scanned over his shoulder at his station, where the

other lifeguard was still waiting for him. "If you're feeling okay, I'd better get back to work now."

She didn't want to become a distraction herself now. "Of course. Sorry to delay you."

"Don't be," he said. "In fact, how about I take you for an ice cream after I get off work today? You earned it."

Shelby took a few steps back. "Sure...yes." She was acting like an idiot. "I've got to go now."

"The beach closes at five," he said as she turned to leave. "Meet me here?"

Shelby tried to act casual, but her voice sounded ten octaves higher when she agreed. On her way to get her belongings off the beach, Shelby spotted Madison and her friends again. Emily from Redd's was with them, and she gave Shelby a thumbs up and smiled. But one of the other girls stepped forward, hands on her hips. "Oh look, it's the hero," she said sarcastically.

Shelby shrugged her shoulders and smiled. "Gee, thanks."

Laughing to herself, she walked home, her mind racing with all the things she needed to do before the beach closed. Wash her hair, figure out what to wear, tell her grandmother, and learn how to breathe again.

AT 4:55 PRECISELY, Shelby took one last glance in the full-length mirror. She'd washed her thick waves and let them drape over her shoulders as they dried. It was still close to eighty degrees outside, so she wore her new denim shorts with a crisp white t-shirt and her sparkly white Sketchers. She'd considered the sundress, but it seemed a bit dressy for ice cream. Her heart did a flip as she headed for the door.

"This is no big deal," she told herself. "You're sixteen years old —well, just barely—and he is only being nice." She remembered how it felt to have his hand on her shoulder and his concerned eyes focused on her. "Deep breath," she told herself.

Her grandmother held the front door open. The smile on Alice's face reassured Shelby that all was going to be fine. "You look lovely. Remember to have fun," she said. "And don't forget these."

Shelby took the sunglasses she'd almost forgotten, then hugged her grandmother. "You are the best."

She traipsed down the two steps and followed the path leading to the sand. In the distance the lake glistened. Gulls caught the breeze, filling the air with their piercing calls. The beach was mostly deserted, and the "closed" sign was turned forward at the lifeguard stand. She watched Logan slip into his flip-flops, pick up his gym bag, turn, and wave in her direction.

She felt weighted to the sand as he approached. He was probably a few years older than her. Confidence radiated off him, and yet he seemed kind. Was he for real?

"Are you ready for the best ice cream around?" he said.

His close proximity set off her treacherous heart, betraying her again by pounding so loudly she was sure he could hear it. "I am," Shelby said. She wished her reply was more clever, but just getting her voice to work around him was hard enough. It was like she'd never been around a boy before. Which she had. Some. Mostly from a distance.

"Have you been to Redd's since his daughter took over?" he asked.

"Just once," she said.

Logan motioned for her to walk in front of him and up to the path toward town. "After you."

A gentleman, she thought.

"The place is better than ever," he said. "Those waffle cones are amazing. And they added new flavors, too."

She kept pace with him as they continued along the grassy path that Shelby followed every day with her dog walking clients.

To their right, the lowering sun shifted the lake reflections to the colors of jewels. A white pelican with black-tipped wings dove into the water, rewarded with a fish for dinner.

"Thousands of pairs of white pelicans nest in and around the lake every year," Logan said. "They make an awesome sight."

Only inches from her, Shelby was intensely aware of his presence. Was this her first real date? Did it count? She looked up shyly at his striking, carved profile, and it took her breath away. He didn't seem aware of how handsome he was, or didn't act like it anyway, like some of the boys she had known.

A few blocks from town near the public plaza, the traffic picked up and the sidewalks were full of people walking their dogs, exploring the town with family and friends.

"So tell me where you learned water rescue like that," he asked.

"I took lifeguard training at our local swimming club back in Las Vegas. I didn't expect to get to use it this summer."

"Makes sense now," he said. "Did you move here with Alice, or just visiting?"

Shelby hoped he hadn't seen her peeking out the window at him and his brother that one time. Or maybe twice. "She's my grandma. I guess I'm here for the summer. My mom is on an extended vacation. You?"

"Same sort of thing. We usually come just for the summer, while my dad works in the city. I'm not sure how long my mother will stay this time."

The tone of his voice indicated that it was not an easy answer for him either. Nothing in her life was simple. Or maybe it was very simple. If and when her mother came back, she would have to leave. But that was in the future and right now she was where she wanted to be, on her way to an ice cream shop with a very cool boy.

"With my lifeguard job," he continued, "I plan to stay all summer at the lake until I leave for college in September."

"Oh, of course," she said. That sounded stupid even to her own ears. He was soon to be a college boy and she was only going to be a junior in the fall. At least she had just turned sixteen, so he couldn't be that much older. But he probably saw her as a kid still. A sigh escaped her lips.

Logan stopped and gave her a concerned look. "Something wrong?"

Shelby's face felt aflame. She waved her hand to dismiss any worries. "I'm fine." More than fine, she thought, staring back at him. But of course she didn't say that.

Logan's eyes searched her face, looking for something. Thank goodness he couldn't read minds. At least, she hoped not. "You can tell me if we need to sit down, or something."

His concern made her knees buckle. Logan reached out and supported her by the side of her arm. "Steady," he said.

How could she be steady if he kept touching her? She took a small step back and tried to laugh it off. "I think an ice cream will fix everything."

"Ice cream it is then," he said.

The irresistible scent of homemade waffle cones wafted through the air as they approached Redd's Ice Cream Parlor.

"Not fair," Logan said. He pointed to a back window of the shop. "They have a fan blowing out of their kitchen right toward us."

Shelby smiled. "And the problem is?"

He laughed and held the red Dutch door open for Shelby to enter. The inside was packed even more than a few days ago when she'd met Steph and Josh. The old-fashioned tin ceiling had been repainted, and white globe lights hung from the ceiling with fans circulating the air. The soda fountain had a sparkly granite top where patrons sat on metal stools with red leather seats. The line to order a cone reached almost to the door.

They studied the flavors posted on the wall above the glass cases. "Got any favorites?" Shelby asked.

"I usually get three scoops. Depends on how the job went that day at the lake. Sometimes I like the fruity flavors. But on nerve-wracking days like today, I definitely lean toward the chocolate and caramel."

"I can relate." Shelby laughed. "Cup or cone?"

"Today is a celebration, so a chocolate-dipped waffle cone. Get whatever you like," he said. "It's on me."

Some young kids walked by with their parents, cones piled three scoops high in pinks, blues, and other colored flavors coated in sprinkles. Shelby wanted the double chocolate chip cookie dough but did not want to worry about chocolate running down her chin or little chips getting caught in her teeth. Emily waited for their order behind the counter.

"You go first," she said.

"I'll have the dipped waffle cone with caramel crunch, raspberry cheesecake, and chocolate chip cookie dough," he said.

"That's a unique combination," Shelby said.

He shrugged. "I couldn't make up my mind, so I got them all."

Shelby placed an order for the strawberry swirl, but just one scoop in a cup.

"That's the best you can do?" Logan asked.

Suddenly Shelby was embarrassed. Had she chosen the wrong thing?

He started laughing. "Just kidding, whatever you like. But how about a topping of some kind?"

Shelby eyed the toppings in the case. "Fresh strawberries, please."

"Coming right up," Emily said. "And, Shelby, I'm sorry about those girls today. You were awesome."

"She sure was," Logan echoed.

Steph brought some milkshakes to a table and waved over to Shelby and Logan as she whisked by.

Once their order was filled, they sat outside on the deck overlooking the lake. The evening breeze rippled across the water and through Shelby's hair. There were still a few boats and a kayak gliding through the water. Shelby ate her ice cream in small bites and enjoyed the relaxed quiet between them. After a few minutes she wracked her brain for something to say.

"What are you going to major in at college?" she asked.

"Wildlife biology and ecology," Logan said. "This planet could use some relief from the corporate world. My dad thinks I should go to law school like him, but that's the furthest thing from my mind. How about you?"

For a moment, Shelby considered lying about her age, but that was crazy. "I don't apply for a year or so," she said, "but I'm thinking about psychology or social work."

"Both admiral professions," he said.

"My mother thinks I should go to a tech school, get a trade. But I want more." Shelby looked at him, wondering what his opinion was.

"Good for you," he said. "Follow your heart."

Shelby watched Logan lick off the sides of his cone where it was melting over. His lips looked so kissable. She jerked her head quickly back, her face warm. What was happening to her? She took a quick bite of her ice cream. Feeling his eyes on her, she looked up.

He pointed to the side of her lip and nodded toward her. Oh no. She reached for a napkin and wiped her mouth.

"Wrong side," he said with a grin.

She dabbed the other and was tempted to throw the rest of the dessert away. She was not really tasting it anyway. Her thoughts were on him. She let her eyes wander to other tables and

saw a woman with a gray-streaked bob haircut sit down a few feet away. Shelby remembered seeing her before out walking along the path. The woman was always stopping to pet other people's pups. A couple times the woman had asked if she could hug Scarlett, and said she was a friend of Shelby's grandmother. Scarlett loved her, but Shelby couldn't remember her name.

Steph wandered out, followed by Oscar, his short little legs trying to keep up while his nose to the ground searched for crumbs. They gray-haired woman called Oscar over and lifted the dog up on her lap. She spoke sweetly to him then plopped a kiss on the dog's head before putting him back on the deck.

"You spoil him, Joann," Steph said to the woman with a big smile.

Shelby remembered now. Her name was Joann and she used to teach at the high school.

As soon as Oscar noticed Shelby, he came running over to her. Steph followed.

"Are you two enjoying your ice cream?"

"The best ever," Logan said, finishing his last bite.

Shelby nodded in agreement and petted Oscar's white-tipped nose. "He's got lots of admirers."

Steph nodded. "Oscar adores Joann, always has, and the feeling is mutual. He was best buds with her dog, Roxie, that passed two months ago." Steph sighed. "Poor Joann. She had that dog over sixteen years, and she was everything to her."

"That's so sad," Shelby said.

Logan joined the conversation. "I've seen her walking the beach in the early morning staring out at the lake. I remember last summer, her and the dog hobbling around in the sand. Sometimes Joann would just carry her down to the water, and they'd curl up together on the shore."

Oscar wandered back to Joann and rested his head across her feet. Dogs could sense where they were needed, Shelby thought.

"Joann has lived here a long time," Steph said. "When I was in high school, the kids all loved her. And she did so much for the school until she retired a few years ago. She lived alone, but always seemed quite happy. But, you never saw her without that dog."

"I'd like to meet her," Shelby said. "Officially."

"Oh, of course," said Steph, "Come on."

She looked over at Logan. "Do you mind?"

"I'll come too. I'd like to say hi."

They followed Steph. Oscar had rolled over to get a good tummy rub, and Joann was obliging.

"Joann, I'd like you to meet our local dog walker, Shelby."

Joann looked up and smiled. "I've seen you out walking. You have the most wonderful job in the world."

"I think so too," Shelby said.

"I love being around dogs." "What could be better?" Logan said.

Joann's expression darkened, obviously remembering her dog. Shelby's heart went out to her. "Perhaps you'd like to walk the dogs with me some days?" Shelby asked.

"Oh yes!" Joann said.

Shelby watched the woman's face brighten up before her. "We usually start on the path along the lake near Second Street and make our way to town and back. Just look for us anytime."

"Thank you, dear," she said. "You made my day." With that, Joann rose to leave. "I'll see you tomorrow," she said, waving as she left.

Shelby and Logan watched Steph hurry back inside to help customers. Oscar retired to a shady spot near the door.

"That was kind of you to offer her a chance to walk with you and the dogs," Logan said.

She looked up at him. It seemed such a natural thing for her to do, but it was nice to be noticed by this cute boy. "I was happy to do it."

Logan stared at her like he was trying to figure something out. Then he shook his head, his slightly crooked, adorable smile emerging. "Some people are just good people," he said.

Dusk was setting in and Alice was probably starting dinner at home. Shelby felt awkward suggesting they leave, and really didn't want to.

As if he read her mind, Logan said, "Shall we start back?"

Shelby nodded. "Thanks again for the ice cream."

"Anytime," he said. She hoped he meant it.

They walked back along the lake path. The water's surface was darkening by the minute as the sun dropped out of sight. A few people were wading along the shore, but mostly the beach was deserted.

"The moon will be peeking over the hills soon," Logan said.

Shelby stopped for a moment, enjoying the panoramic view. "It is so beautiful here. A lot nicer than Las Vegas."

Logan laughed. "Not much water there, I imagine."

"There was a lake not too far from where we lived, but it was pretty barren."

"Have you ever seen the full moon over the lake at night?" he asked.

Shelby thought about the few times she'd spent with her grandmother here and couldn't remember ever seeing that. "I don't think so."

"Legend says the lake was named after an enormous full moon that lit up the entire lake, many years ago."

"Really?" she said.

He turned to face her directly. A shiver coursed through her body, and it was not from the chilling evening.

"That's what I've heard," he said. "Our deck in back of our house is a great place to view it. The next full moon is in a week. Want to come over and see it?"

"Sure," she said, her voice sounding an octave higher than normal.

"Cool. Shall we head back now? I'll walk you home."

Shelby laughed. "All the way across the cul-de-sac?"

"All the way."

CHAPTER 12

Theo was not looking forward to his Skype call with his son, Cameron, today. He loved Cam, but he hated being treated like a feeble old man who had to be dealt with. His son had a good heart, he was just busy, impatient, and a bit intolerant of other's feelings sometimes. Jean had always told Theo it stemmed from Cam's hidden insecurities, but sometimes he just wanted to take that boy and shake him. He had to admit, though, his son had checked on him almost every week since Jean died.

He sat down at his computer and turned on the screen so he could answer when the call came through. Cam was sitting at his desk in his high-rise office and Theo could see the Seattle skyline out the wall of windows behind his son.

"Good morning, Dad." His cell phone was in his hand and it looked like his son was texting as they spoke.

Theo nodded.

Cam looked up. "Are you there?"

Theo wanted to say, "If you were looking at me, you would know." Instead he grunted. He was particularly grumpy today. Edgy. Not his usual immobile self at all. Having some energy all of a sudden made him restless.

"Have you thought any more about our discussion last week about selling your house?"

"Why would I want to do that?" Theo said. He knew he was being difficult, and he had thought a little about it but it had only made him sadder.

Cam's sigh grated on his nerves. "Dad, what do you need with that big house anymore? It's too much for you."

Theo thought about his spacious home and yard. Again the dog park popped into his mind. "Maybe it's not," Theo said. "I have some ideas that might work out."

"Like what?" Cam seemed very distressed. "Last week you could barely get out of bed, today you have ideas?"

Theo chuckled to himself, imagining what Cam might have imagined his ideas were. He was going to keep them to himself for now.

"How are you and Judy doing?" Theo asked, trying to change the subject.

His son glanced down at his phone again and back to the screen. "Fine. We worry about you. You were so down last week, I was thinking of coming out and getting you myself."

Cam cared, that was clear, but the thought of being whisked out of his home rattled him. Yes, he had been depressed since Jean's death, but he was fully cognizant of what was going on around him and still had a good brain. "I can take care of myself just fine. I'm feeling a bit better and so is Wally."

Cam looked skeptical. "Glad to hear it. We can discuss more about future plans next week."

In that moment, Theo knew he was facing a crossroads in his life. He had a choice to make and he wanted it to be his alone. Did he want to come back to life or run away from it? The weight of grief clung to his chest like an anchor pulling him to sea. With little effort he could let go and the waves would overtake him. Or he could do something with his life and the time he had left.

"I've got a meeting, got to run," Cam said. "But I wanted to wish you a Happy Father's Day."

"Thanks, son."

Always running, Theo thought. He hoped his son was happy with the fast-paced life he lived. No grandkids yet. But, he needed to respect his son's choices too, if he expected Cam to respect his. His son probably wanted his dad to be happy.

"Love you, son," he said.

"You too. Bye, Dad."

Theo let out a sigh as the screen went blank. Jean would want him to try harder to have a better relationship with their son. But he wasn't sure how that could be accomplished at this point. He was not going to move into a conveniently located—for Cam and Judy—high-priced care facility where he would lose not only some of his freedom, but his beloved Moonwater Lake home and all the memories it held. He looked down at Wally nestled at his feet. His faithful companion.

He'd been so close to giving up hope recently, giving up and just letting Cam handle everything. No wonder his son had been worried. But now Theo had other things calling him to pay attention, wake up, and reach out.

"Wally," he said. "What would you think about having some visitors around here again?"

The dog looked up with his big brown eyes, sleepy but attentive.

"Treat?" Theo said. Hounds never refused.

That got Wally up and he followed him into the kitchen. He tossed the pup one of his favorite cookies and heated water for a second cup of coffee for himself. Ideas raced through his mind and he searched for paper and a pen to write them down. Jean always said he was good at putting together a plan. He might be a bit rusty, but he was going to give it his best.

CHAPTER 13

Oscar rambled along next to Shelby on the sidewalk as they headed back into town to Redd's. As they turned the last corner, Oscar's nub tail wagged and his pace quickened.

"Hold on, Mr. Oscar," Shelby corrected him.

Reluctantly he obeyed.

As soon as they reached the store, Oscar sprawled out in the shade under the tree bordering the front door. Shelby freed the dog from the leash. A sigh escaped from his mouth, indicating he was finished moving for the day.

A lady walked by with a frisky black puppy that tried to pounce on Oscar. The sedentary corgi remained in a reclining pose, opening one weary eye.

"He's such a lazy dog," Steph said from the door. She put her hands on the hips of her ice-cream-splattered apron. "Oscar, the least you could do is get up and say hello." Steph ruffled his big ears. "You see why I need to hire you to get this dog up and walking? How about twice a week when you can?"

"That would be great," Shelby said, adding another spot on her calendar in her head. "I was just talking to Theo about how nice it would be if there was a dog park in town where they could run and play."

"We could use one for sure," Steph said. A few customers drifted in and Steph turned to go inside. "Emily's working today, so why don't you come around to the back patio and I'll bring out a cold drink so we can settle on a schedule?"

To Shelby's dismay, at one of the tables she saw Madison with a classily dressed woman, who was probably her mother, and a little boy. The woman was wiping ice cream off the boy's face with a napkin and it looked like they were just leaving. "And don't think after all we spent on private schools for you, Madison, you can run off to some art school." The woman's raised voice had heads turning and Shelby was embarrassed for Madison. She moved quickly to a seat away from them, careful not to make eye contact and make matters worse.

Shelby chose a table in the shade with a clear view of the lake. She glanced back and made sure Madison's family had left and then settled back in her chair. The thermometer on the wall was pushing over ninety degrees and it wasn't even noon yet. She wiped her brow and was glad she'd worn her hair up today. Heat shimmered off the surface of the lake. In lifeguard school she'd learned the sun's beams reached only the upper layer of a water body. The lake would remain cool and very swimmable this afternoon when she was off. She'd purposefully not scheduled any clients on Wednesday afternoon, knowing it was one of Logan's workdays. Shelby hadn't seen him since they'd met for ice cream. Her stomach fluttered as she imagined their next encounter. Should she sit near his station, or was that too obvious? But if she sat far away, would he think she wasn't interested in him? Was he?

"You look deep in thought," Steph said. She sat down beside her and placed two glass mugs on the table. "Never too early for ice cream," she said with a smile.

Shelby pulled the glass over, eyeing the foam rolling over the side, and took a sip from the red and white striped straw. "This is great."

"One of our bestsellers. An ice-cold, old-fashioned root beer float."

Shelby stared out at the swimming beach where people were starting to arrive. Families with kids were spreading blankets and putting up colorful umbrellas. Her breath caught.

"Something on your mind?" Steph asked.

Steph seemed easy to talk to and probably much closer to her age than most of the people she'd met here. Shelby took a chance.

"Yes, it's…"

"A boy?" Steph finished for her.

Making sure Emily was not in ear reach, Shelby nodded, affirming Steph's guess.

"I see." Steph sipped her drink for a moment, obviously in thought. "Did you know I met my husband, Josh, at the lake a few years ago? He was on summer break from his last year at college in Sacramento. He walked in for an ice cream one night and didn't leave until after closing."

"You two hit it off that fast? How did you know for sure he was interested in you?"

"Besides the fact that he wouldn't leave?" Steph laughed. "He came back at opening the very next day and asked me out to dinner."

"Oh, I see. What if I'm not sure if my time with him was a date or not?"

Steph leaned forward and lowered her voice. "Do you mean with Logan the other night when you were here for ice cream?"

Shelby nodded and then sipped her drink without making eye contact.

"Well, from my perspective, you two looked like you were having a pretty good time."

Shelby's heart fluttered, then wilted. "But I haven't heard from him in the last few days."

Because it had been Father's Day weekend, Logan had told her that his family never knew if his dad would make it home for the holiday. Maybe that was why Shelby hadn't seen Logan and his brother playing basketball in the street. Maybe his father had made it back for the holiday weekend after all. It was not a holiday Shelby had ever celebrated.

Shelby stared out at the inviting water. "I was thinking of going down to the lake today and kind of hanging out, reading near the lifeguard station."

"Hmmm, let me think," Steph said. "Always works to play a little hard to get. Sit near, but not too close."

"What if he doesn't talk to me?"

"Of course he will. Logan knows a pretty, and super nice, girl when he sees one. Josh came on a bit strong at first and I backed up. He took the hint and gave me a little space. Later he told me it was really difficult because he wanted to be with me every minute."

"That's so romantic," Shelby said. She thought about Logan leaving for college in September and how hard it would be to say goodbye. That is, if she was still there herself. "What happened when Josh left for college?"

"I won't kid you, it wasn't easy," Steph said. "My dad was ill by then, so I started managing the shop. We kept a long-distance relationship going somehow, even with both of us so busy. As soon as Josh graduated, he showed up on my doorstep, dropped to a knee, and proposed marriage."

"Really? What did you say?"

"I said, 'But you don't even live here yet.' He took me in his arms and said that was his next stop, renting a house."

Shelby laughed, imagining Logan on one knee. "A storybook romance, for sure."

Steph's smile faded. "Most of the time. My dad retired and now we own the shop and that takes up a lot of time. And I'd like to start having a family."

"That's great," Shelby said, then noticed a shadow cross her new friend's face. "Does Josh feel the same?"

Steph shook her head slowly. "Josh says we're not ready yet. But he doesn't have any idea when he will be." With that, Steph exhaled with a sigh, stood, and started clearing off their table. "All will work out, right?" she said with a shrug.

Shelby hoped Josh would come around soon. They were such a sweet couple.

"Let me help with that," Shelby said, starting to clear the table.

"You go," Steph said, waving her away. She winked at Shelby. "Have a good swim."

WHEN SHELBY GOT to the lake, the first thing she noticed was that Logan was supervising some kind of training out in the water. Another lifeguard was at his station. She was proud of herself that she kept her distance and enjoyed a swim. And of course, watched him covertly when he wasn't looking. Not surprising, he was a very strong swimmer. She checked in her bag to see if there were any calls on the new cell phone. None. She'd only given the number out to her clients so far. The afternoon was peaceful as she read her book for a while, and then closed her eyes to relax.

She felt a shadow block the sun from her body and opened her eyes to see Logan standing there, wet hair slicked back and water droplets glistening on his firm, bronze body.

"Hello," he said.

Shelby leaned up, balancing herself on her elbows. Logan perched down beside her. "Sorry I haven't had time to talk today," he said. "Training duty."

"Of course," she said.

"I only have a short break. But I wanted to come over and say hello."

"Hey, Logan, who's the cute girl?"

Logan's head snapped over to the two young guys smirking and eyeing Shelby. "Move on, boys," he said.

"Well, excuse us," one said. "We didn't know she was taken."

"Idiots," Logan said.

"Did they mean me?" Shelby asked.

"You don't even see all the guys looking at you, do you?"

Shelby shook her head. "Not really."

Logan smiled. "Another thing I like about you."

Did he really just say that? she wondered. About her?

"Glad you made it down to the lake today," Logan said. "I have to get back to work now."

"Right," she said.

He turned to go and then stopped. "Hey, why don't you text me your cell number so we can talk sometime?"

"Sure thing," she said. "But I don't know your number."

"It's an easy one," Logan said, rattling off some numbers.

Shelby repeated them over in her head several times as he walked back into the lake. Then she opened her beach bag, pulled out her new phone, and put in his contact number. Later, when she was alone tonight, she would figure out what to say in her text.

CHAPTER 14

Theo paced the living room, ruminating again about his idea. Cam's call had been the final kick in the butt he needed to focus. He'd done a lot of thinking since he'd last run into that sweet Shelby, and now he had a clear idea of how to proceed. If done right, it would make many people in the community happy. And several dogs. But first he needed to get the go-ahead from one person.

Under the hand-painted beagle magnet on his refrigerator, he had posted Shelby's landline and later her grandmother's cell phone scribbled beneath. He decided to call the landline first.

A sweet but older voice answered. "Hello. This is Alice, and also Shelby's Dog Walker Service."

Theo grinned. "Hello, Alice. Shelby might have mentioned me. I'm Theo. I met your granddaughter while I was walking my dog, Wally."

"Well, hello," Alice said. "I've heard all about you and used to see you around town. I'm afraid Shelby is at the lake swimming, but she'll be home soon if you'd like me to take a message."

Theo thought for a second. Perhaps it would be proper to discuss everything with Shelby's grandmother first. "I have an idea that I would like to run by you and Shelby regarding her dog walking clients."

"Why don't you come by the house about 3:00 today? We can all talk here. Do you know where we live?"

"I do," Theo said. "I'll see you then. And thank you."

"Thank you," Alice said before hanging up.

"We're going on an outing," Theo said to the dog. He buttoned up his freshly ironed blue shirt, a change from his usual rumpled one. Then he checked his hair in the mirror, what he had left of the silver-gray locks, one more time. He wanted to be sure he looked well put together today before he went and knocked on the door of Shelby's grandmother. After all, he wanted her to consider his good intentions. He was going to offer his backyard for the dogs to play in, and he wanted to get permission first. Nothing wrong with that.

He leashed up Wally and put on his sunhat, then headed toward Shelby's house. He was glad he had called ahead. He had mentioned stopping by the other day, and Shelby had said afternoons were best. Also, she had said Alice was almost always home.

When he got to the pale blue house with the white fence and red door, he knew he had arrived. He noticed colorful flowers blooming along the borders and a trimmed yard. It was obviously well tended by a woman's hand. "Come on, old guy," he said to Wally. "Let's go up and see what good we can do here."

Together they walked up the few steps to the front door and knocked politely.

"Just a moment," he heard a female voice say.

The door opened and he recognized the woman he knew to be Alice. "Good afternoon," he said. "I'm Theodore Rosen, or Theo, the one who just called, and this is Wally. I met your lovely granddaughter when she was out walking Scarlett." He knew he was repeating himself, but he was nervous.

"And here she is," Alice said as Scarlett raced out the front door barking.

Wally and the red poodle mix started sniffing each other, tails wagging wildly.

"They're old friends by now," Theo said.

Alice nodded. "I can see that. Come on in. I've heard all about you. Shelby will be home soon."

"I won't take much of your time," Theo said. "I was hoping that the three of us could have a short chat this afternoon."

Alice smiled. "Sure. No problem at all. Let me put on some coffee."

"That would be great," Theo said. "Something smells wonderful in here, like warm brown sugar."

"Oh, that's one of Shelby's favorites I just made. It's a rice crispy cookie." She pointed to the dining room table for Theo to take a seat. "Go ahead and let your dog off the leash," Alice said. "I'm sure they'd like to play."

Theo freed Wally and watched the two dogs race through the cozy living room. Scarlett would chase Wally and then turn around and hide under a chair and bark for him to play with her some more. Wally put his nose under the chair and Scarlett raced out, grabbing a toy in her mouth and squeaking it repeatedly.

"My," Alice said. "Wally sure perked up, didn't he?"

"A young pup can do that sometimes. Scarlett's brought him back to life." Theo thought about Shelby, the dogs, having a new purpose and how it had worked for him as well.

"Ah youth," Alice said. "Shelby's time here has certainly brightened my day." Pulling some cream out of the refrigerator, Alice asked what he would like in his coffee.

"Please don't go to any trouble. Black is fine," Theo said, taking a seat. The table was set for three, with a bouquet of mixed flowers in the middle. He had to admit, it was a nice contrast from his house.

The front door sprang open and Shelby entered, beach towel

in hand. "I thought I heard some barking and commotion in here." She smiled over at Theo. "Hey, I see you found the place."

"Yes, I did," he said. Then he remembered he still had his hat on and swiped it off his head before placing it down beside him. "How was your swim?" he said.

"Refreshing," Shelby said, shaking off her wet hair. "Went for an early dog walk this morning, and into vacation mode this afternoon."

Alice strolled over with a tray of coffee accompanied by a plate of cookies and a bowl of caramel mix. She placed everything on the table and took the chair next to Theo.

"They look delicious," Theo said.

Theo watched a smile surface on Alice's face. It was a pretty one. Her eyes were kind, but sadness lurked behind them. He sensed a bond of loss between them.

"Looks like I came home just in time," Shelby said, taking a seat next to her grandmother.

"So," Alice said, "what's this impromptu meeting about?"

Theo sipped the fresh-brewed coffee and took a deep breath before making his announcement. "Because we don't have a dog park in Moonwater Lake, and there certainly is a need for one, I have decided to offer your granddaughter my sizable, and completely fenced, backyard for the dogs to come and play."

"Really? That's amazing," Shelby said. "I've been hoping for a place I could take the dogs off leash and let them run free and play."

Alice smiled at Theo. "What a splendid idea, and the adults can meet up while their dogs play as well."

"Thanks," Theo said, relishing in the compliment. He cleared his throat. "Alice, I just wanted to make sure that it was okay with you and that you approve of the idea, and..." He was stumbling over his words.

Alice's eyes twinkled. "Thank you for your generous offer. I'm sure the dogs would love it. And it is certainly fine with me."

"Can I give you a hug?" Shelby said, rising from her chair.

Theo was stunned. "Well..." He looked at Alice, who was nodding.

Shelby threw her arms around his neck. "Thank you so much. This is going to be wonderful. Don't you think so, Grandma? You can bring Scarlett over and Eleanor can bring over her dogs and we can invite the Redds to bring Oscar!"

Theo piped in. "And I'll notify Trevor."

"Right," Shelby said. "I can let Mindy know. Karma would love to run and play. And Mindy can get out of the house and watch."

"Well, it sounds like a done deal to me," said Alice. She picked up the plate of chocolate chip cookies. "Would you like another one to celebrate?"

Theo was happy to oblige. It'd been a while since he'd had homemade baked goods. The soft, buttery cookie melted in his mouth. "Delicious. One of the best I've ever had."

"Grandma is an expert baker," Shelby said. "She used to win contests with her cookies."

Theo felt his mood lift. It might be the sugar, but he thought it was probably something else. Something he had not felt in a while...comfort, belonging. Something to look forward to. "Well then, it sounds like we're all in agreement."

"When can we start?" asked Shelby.

"Anytime you want," Theo said. "Why don't you and your grandmother start by coming over and taking a look at the yard?"

"That's perfect," Shelby said. "We can make a list of everything we might need."

"I'll contact Trevor about making sure the fence is secure," Theo said. He looked at Shelby. "Do you think you can pick out a few doggy toys with me? I was thinking Wally could use some new ones soon anyway."

"Of course! And we will need to come up with a schedule." Shelby looked to her grandmother. "What do you think, Grandma? Will you help us with this?"

Alice paused. Her eyes went from Shelby to Theo and back. "I guess I could bake some dog cookies for you all. Help with the shopping."

"That's a great start," Shelby said. "And will you bring Scarlett? I'll be there too, of course."

Theo watched as the two women looked at each other, one young, one older, but he knew something special was happening between them.

"Yes," said Alice. "I will bring Scarlett over."

"No time like the present to come by," said Theo. "Unless that doesn't work for you two?"

Alice nodded. "We'll clean up here and meet you at your house within the hour."

CHAPTER 15

*S*helby grabbed her old, but still functioning, laptop and the baggie of leftover cookies and put them in her backpack. They had tried to sneak out the front with Scarlett resting quietly in her bed. But the dog would have none of that. She wanted to add her input to the meeting, so she accompanied them as they proceeded down Seventh Street. They turned toward the lake when they reached Misty Meadow Lane where Theo lived. Alice held Scarlett's leash, and for the first time since Shelby had moved here, they were all taking a walk together. The trip had been the breakthrough Shelby had been hoping for, and now a walk and a project they could work on together might do the rest. Shelby was glad her grandmother's waist-expanding baking hobby gave Alice another way to be involved. And she'd noticed Alice had put on a little lipstick before they left the house.

Theo's presence at their house today, and his offer, had shifted things. A tiny glimmer of hope fluttered in Shelby's heart. Maybe, just for now, she could let herself feel it. As they reached the end of the quiet road, Theo's ranch-style home, surrounded by old growth blue oak and Pacific madrone, came into view. A stone walkway led to the front door, where Theo waved to them from behind a screen door. As he opened it, Wally trotted toward them with a tired, old woof to show them this was still his territory.

"I haven't seen my dog move that fast in a long time," Theo said. "But then I can't remember the last time we had three lovely ladies come to visit."

Shelby liked being called a "lovely lady," and from the look on Alice's face, she did too. "We brought the rest of the cookies from our meeting," Shelby said. "They're in my backpack."

"Thank you for that," Theo said. "Come on in."

The house was natural wood inside with exposed beam ceilings and picture windows facing the backyard and lake. They offered the only light coming in the room, as the other windows had curtains drawn. Wedding and family pictures hung in the entry hall, everything neat and in order, except for a stack of unopened mail on a table by the door. Shelby remembered stacks like that at home with her mother, when Dana couldn't face even opening them.

Shelby laid her backpack on the kitchen counter that looked like a large wood cutting board. She handed the cookies to Theo, who promptly put them out.

"These are definitely spoiling me from anything store-bought," he said.

"Plenty more where those came from," said Shelby, smiling at her grandmother.

Alice's blush reminded Shelby of a young schoolgirl's. Did she? Did he? Of course, she reminded herself, old people still had crushes too. She kind of liked the idea.

Theo guided them into the open concept living room, centered around a white-washed stone fireplace.

Alice walked over to the window. "What an amazing view you have."

Theo moved beside her and followed Alice's gaze across the lake. "My wife and I picked this spot several years ago," he said. "I had just retired as the director of a nonprofit in Oregon. We'd been living on a lake, but the winters were cold and the children long gone. When we visited Moonwater Lake, we knew we'd found our new home."

"We felt the same when we first came up here for a vacation," Alice said. "After working an orchard and farm for several years in central California, we were ready for a change."

Theo looked down at Alice. "It is a very special place."

She nodded and turned back to the outside scenery.

Shelby watched as her new friend, Theo, and her grand-mother talked easily. The dogs had curled up together in Wally's overstuffed bed by the fireplace. For a moment, Shelby felt like the only one without someone to be with. But then she realized that she had helped bring these two lonely people, and dogs, together, and that made her happy. And the dog park would do even more. Perhaps...her mind drifted to Logan. The full moon was coming up in a few days, and Logan had invited her over to his house. They were neighbors after all, she rationalized. Maybe he was just being friendly. But maybe...

"Shelby," Theo said, suddenly standing in front of her. "How about I get us some of my homemade Arnold Palmer iced tea and we go sit out on the deck and talk dog park?"

Back to Earth now, Shelby said, "I'll help."

"You two go sit outside. I'll be right there."

Shelby followed Alice out the glass door to the deck over-looking a completely fenced, grassy yard that sloped gently toward the water. They took a seat at the redwood table and chairs that sported a pine green umbrella to block the blistering sun.

"Theo's backyard is perfect for dogs," Shelby said. "All it needs is a few toys and balls."

Shelby let her mind roam across the spacious fenced portion of the yard. There were large grassy areas where the dogs could play and do their business, lush trees with shade for resting, and a sturdy fence that allowed for protection without blocking visibility to the lake.

Theo carried a small tray of treats and drinks to the table and placed it in the center. The dogs were at his heels, and Shelby could see why. On a small plate, arranged decoratively, were several varieties of dog cookies as well as Alice's chocolate chips on a separate one.

"Help yourselves, ladies," Theo said as he sat down to join them.

Shelby distributed dog treats evenly between Wally and Scarlett, who promptly gobbled them up before begging for more.

"Well," Theo said, "it looks like Wally's appetite has returned as well."

Shelby surprised herself by saying, "That's what happens when you're happy."

"And have a good buddy, too," Theo said.

There were a few moments of silence at the table after that as everyone registered his words. Shelby watched a bluebird land on a feeder hanging from a nearby branch and fill his little stomach. A boat with colorful sails glided through the water in the distance. She took a deep breath and let the moment sink in.

Theo cleared his throat. "Would you two like a tour of the yard?"

They started down the couple of steps to the grass, the dogs at their heels.

"What a perfect spot for a dog park," Shelby said. "You can easily fit up to eight dogs here, and they will love it!"

Theo smiled. "I thought the same myself. All the space can be put to good use." He pointed out areas that needed some work in the fence and showed them the storage shed with plenty of room for doggy items.

"It's perfect," Shelby said.

Theo looked over to Alice. "If we are all in agreement, why don't we write up a list of things we need and get started?"

Alice nodded. "It couldn't be better."

After exploring the yard for a while, Theo motioned to go back to the deck. "Let's get to business, then."

"Be right back," Shelby said. She went in the house and retrieved her laptop, then placed it on the table in front of her.

Theo raised a brow. "I see you are quite organized. Where shall we start?"

"First, I have some questions."

"I'm ready," Theo said with a chuckle.

Shelby caught the smile he threw toward Alice and for a moment she felt like she was back with her grandmother and wonderful grandfather again. "This all needs to be convenient and easy for you, Theo. I was thinking the dog park should be limited to only dogs we know and that all get along well."

"Agreed," Theo said. "And I think being open two days a week would be fine for me for now."

Shelby typed up the suggestions so they would have a record of their agreement. "You can set the hours and we can make a short set of rules, like all dogs must be current on vaccinations and the owners are responsible for all doggie cleanup."

"That is a must," Theo said. "I hadn't even thought of that."

Shelby felt a thread of worry creep in, but the smile on Theo's face chased it away. Many plans had gone astray in her life before and she'd learned not to get too excited about anything.

Alice lit up. "I think you will need a special aluminum trash receptacle with a lid. Everyone can take turns emptying it when the dog park closes for the day."

"Another good idea," Theo said.

"As my first donation pledge," Alice said, "I will buy and furnish you with a super-sized supply of doggie bags."

"Our first donation," Theo said. "Thanks to Alice, our practical donor. And of course, I will donate the space."

Shelby gave her grandmother a side hug. "You're the best." She turned quickly to Theo. "And you are too."

Theo sipped his tea. "I think we three can plan a little field trip to Pet Universe to get some things."

"Like what?" Shelby asked.

"We'll need a water station, some toys, and equipment," Theo said. "I'm pretty sure Trevor, who is very handy with building, can secure the fence and build a ramp for running on."

Shelby could hardly contain her delight. This was shaping up even better than she'd hoped. "I have another idea. For the grand opening, all members can donate a toy as a membership fee."

"And I'll bring fresh-baked doggie cookies," Alice said.

Scarlett barked at the word "cookie" and everyone laughed. Shelby couldn't remember the last time she'd seen her grandmother so relaxed, or for that matter, felt that way herself.

"If Scarlett agrees, then I think we have a deal," Theo said. He rose and started clearing off the table.

"I'll take care of it," Shelby said. "It's a work meeting after all." She carried the tray back to the kitchen and put the glasses in the oversized farm sink, and then joined Theo and Alice near the front door.

"A very productive meeting," Theo said. "I'll let you know when Trevor gets back to me, and we can schedule our shopping trip."

Shelby put the leash on Scarlett. "We'll be ready. I'll start spreading the word and we can set up a volunteer work party, while the dogs stay home, to help set things up."

Theo followed them outside, where Alice thanked him for his generous hospitality before they waved goodbye and started home again.

"What a nice man Theo is," Shelby said.

Alice nodded, a small smile turning up the corners of her mouth. "Not many like him around anymore," she said.

Shelby knew Alice was missing Grandpa Stan, but she was also sure she'd seen a spark between Alice and Theo. And sparks could turn into flames, couldn't they? She picked up her step. She was a bit of a hopeless romantic herself.

SHELBY WAS ALMOST home after taking Eleanor's dogs Dixie and Ruby for a walk. As the ex-mayor, she seemed to know everyone. Her bridge club was today, with a luncheon to follow. When Shelby had told Eleanor about the dog park meeting, Eleanor thought the idea was fabulous. "Just let me know what I can do," she'd said. "And thanks for including me."

She'd also stopped by and told Mindy, who seemed eager for the new space. Mindy would need a ride to Theo's, and Shelby had some ideas for that. All she had to do now, with the new cell phone her grandmother had bought her, was text Steph and everyone would know. Theo had told Trevor, and that made seven dogs, counting Scarlett. Of course, some days it may be less.

A warm shower and curling up with her latest book sounded perfect. As she entered the cul-de-sac, she saw Logan in gym shorts with his younger brother, who was not quite as tall, shooting hoops at the end of the street.

"Hey, come join us," Logan said, waving at Shelby.

Her fatigue drifted away at the sight of him and she jogged over to join them. "You'd better watch out," she said. "My hand-eye coordination is pretty good."

"Let's see it then," Logan said. He roughed up his brother's hair. "This is my little brother, Gabe. Gabe, Shelby."

Gabe squirmed away. "I'm not so little anymore," he said. "I'll be fourteen in a few months." He turned to Shelby, a bit shy as they made contact. "Aren't you the dog walker?"

Agile and quick, Logan dribbled the ball up and back as Shelby watched.

"That's me," she said to Gabe.

"That must be the best job ever. I love dogs."

"But our father says they're too much trouble," Logan added with a frown.

"Mom wouldn't mind one either, but…" Gabe said.

"Heads up." Logan threw Gabe the ball.

Gabe dribbled it down the street before shooting a perfect basket. Shelby clapped, "Great job."

"Don't encourage him," Logan warned. "He loves to show off, especially for girls."

"And what's wrong with that?" Shelby asked.

Logan rolled his eyes and stepped in closer. "He keeps hoping our father will notice him. Good luck with that. It'll never happen."

"Mine died when I was four years old." The words had just slipped out.

Logan's face drained of color. "I'm so sorry. I didn't know."

She held up her hand to stop him. "It's okay. I don't know why I said that."

Gabe darted around them, dribbling the ball. Shelby shifted from side to side, uneasy, and she wanted to change the subject. She didn't know anything about Logan's dad, but Logan seemed hurt by him.

"Your mom sounds nice," Shelby said.

"She is. You'll meet her tomorrow night when you come over to watch the full moon from our deck. She told me she bought stuff for us to all make s'mores in the fire pit."

"Love them. Can I bring anything?" she asked.

The dimples were back, and her heart skipped a beat as he said, "Just yourself."

Gabe circled back and tossed Shelby the ball. "Let's see what you got," he said.

Logan gave her a smile and stepped to the side to watch. Nothing like pressure, she thought. Shelby dribbled the ball a few times and gauged her distance and angles before starting forward. The shot was perfect. She watched as the ball barely touched the rim before dropping expertly through the basket.

Logan trotted after the ball. "Game on," he said.

The three of them took turns stealing the ball, blocking shots, and competing to get a basket. If they were keeping score, it would have been neck and neck. She dragged the back of her hand across her sweaty brow. This was not time to care about looking pretty. She was holding her own with the boys and thoroughly enjoying it. After a particularly long shot swished into the basket, Shelby turned to the boys. "Anyone think they can beat that?" she said with a smile.

Logan raised his hands in the air. "I give," he said, winking at her.

Shelby tossed the ball to Gabe. "I'm going to take a break."

"Quitting while you're ahead," Gabe said, teasing.

As Gabe continued taking shots, Logan and Shelby took a seat on the curb and watched for a while.

"How's the dog walking biz going?" Logan asked.

Shelby told him all the exciting news about a dog park and the work party she was organizing. He listened intently.

"Cool," he said. "Just let me know if I can help out. Good work, Shelby."

He lifted his right hand up to hers for a high five and she tapped his hand with hers. The chemistry between them was palpable. Their eyes locked and Shelby knew he meant every word he said.

Gabe circled back to them and tossed the ball to Logan, breaking the momentary trance. "C'mon, you guys, are we playing or not?"

As they stood to join him, a harsh male voice shouted, "Logan!"

Shelby turned to see a suit-and-tie-clad Mr. DeLuca, standing hands on hips at the end of the driveway. Beside him, Logan's mom was the complete opposite of her husband, in a light summer dress, her fair blonde hair loose around her pale shoulders. Mr. DeLuca had close-cut, dark hair, silver-streaked at his temples. His highly dignified and super polished demeanor was intimidating.

Logan, ball in hand, turned toward his father. "Yes?"

"I have to leave now, and your mother needs your help *inside.*"

Logan nodded and tossed the ball to Gabe. He exhaled, sadness washing over his face. "You two stay. As usual, our dad is leaving before the Fourth of July party."

"He'll make it home in time," Gabe said, looking hopeful.

"Sure he will," Logan said to his brother. But his voice was filled with doubt.

"I'll see you tomorrow night for the full moon viewing," Shelby said.

Logan gave her a thumbs up. "I'll come over and get you at 8:00."

Shelby watched him walk away. The droop of his shoulders made her heart ache. Maybe not having a dad wasn't so bad. But she wished she'd known hers. She turned to find Gabe sitting on the curb and took a seat beside him.

"You okay?" she asked.

Gabe shrugged. "Kind of." He looked down at the street and lowered his voice. "If I told you a secret, would you keep it?"

"Absolutely." Shelby reached out her little finger to him. "Pinky swear." After their pact was sealed, she waited to hear what Gabe had to say.

"With you being a dog walker and stuff, I thought maybe you could…" He stopped, looking around to make sure no one else was listening. "Help me with something."

"And what might that be?" she asked, lowering her voice as well. Not that anyone could hear them. Before he could speak, a black limo turned down their street and into the DeLucas' driveway. Mr. DeLuca came out, wheeling a black suitcase, which the driver promptly took from him and loaded into the trunk. He was on his cell phone and didn't so much as wave goodbye to Gabe as he left.

Gabe dropped his head and sniffed.

"You can tell me," Shelby said. "I know what it's like to have no one to talk to. When I'm not here with my grandmother, I'm alone most of the time. My mom is always out somewhere."

He looked up at her and nodded. "I need some dog advice."

"I thought..." she started to say.

"For someone else's dog," he clarified. "So, what if I was kind of helping someone take care of their dog?" He looked to her for reassurance and she gave it. "And this person is sort of sick?"

Shelby was concerned who that might be. "So, what is your question?"

"I want to make sure I'm doing it right," Gabe blurted out. "I take the dog out and play with it twice a day in her yard. She tells me what to feed it. Mutt is so happy when he sees me, but when I leave, he looks miserable."

"It sounds like you're doing it completely right," Shelby said.

Gabe shuffled his feet. "The thing is, the lady seems like she might be sick or something. Mrs. Williams lives in an old cabin by the lake in the trees behind our houses." He pointed to show Shelby the location. "She's all alone and doesn't have much. I've used some of my allowance to help buy the dog food, but I think Mutt needs more. Like a bath or shot or something? He's a good dog. You should see him."

Shelby thought for a moment. Spread around the lake were some senior citizens who had lived in the area a long time. If the woman was alone and possibly ill, this was probably more than Gabe should be handling. "You're a real sweetheart to help Mrs. Williams out. How would you feel about taking me to meet her and Mutt?"

"I don't know," he said. "She made me promise not to tell anyone. I found Mutt by our yard one day, really skinny and hungry. So I fed him. I sleep in the screened-in porch a lot and

Mutt kept coming back and whining for more. Then one night I followed him home and found his owner. She was surprised to see me and almost out of food. She gets some delivered once a week from a meals program, she told me, and shares it with the dog. I started bringing her some too. We have so much at our house."

This was definitely way more than a young boy should be handling. Even one with a big heart and the fortitude to try to right a wrong. "I don't think she'll mind if you take me with you. I think together we can really help them both."

"Okay," he said. "But you can't tell."

Gabe led her on a narrow deer path partially obscured from the shore by overgrown trees and blackberry bushes. In a clearing was an old summer cabin, its once red paint faded and its roof covered in pine needles. As they approached, a smallish white and tan dog with wiry hair rushed out from a doggy door barking. When he saw Gabe, he jumped into his arms and licked his face.

"Hi, boy, I told you I'd be back soon. I brought a friend this time."

Shelby petted the scruffy dog. His matted fur needed brushing, including the white-tipped ears, one sticking straight up, the other bent down. His deep brown eyes watched Shelby's every move. "Hello, Mutt," she said, reaching out her hand for him to sniff it.

She was rewarded with a quick lick before he clung back to Gabe.

"Let's go inside," Gabe said, leading them to the door. He rapped on the door. "Mrs. Williams, it's me, Gabe."

An elderly woman with white hair pulled back in a bun opened the door. Her pallid skin and faded clothes that hung loosely on her body worried Shelby.

The woman eyed Shelby suspiciously. "Who's this?"

"I'm Shelby. One of your neighbors and a dog walker. Gabe

told me about Mutt and I thought I would offer my services free of charge to walk your dog and help Gabe out sometimes."

"Why would you do that?" The woman narrowed her eyes.

Shelby put her arm across Gabe's shoulders. "Gabe and I are pals and we both love dogs. I don't mind helping at all." She'd hate to see this woman lose the dog, her only companion. But she could tell the woman was nervous about trusting anyone.

Mrs. Williams eyed Mutt. "He sure could use a little walking. And a bath. I don't seem to have the energy to do much for him these days."

"We'll take care of it," Shelby said. "No one will think anything of seeing me walk another dog."

The woman nodded. "All right, then." She hesitated, looking Shelby over. "Never seen you around before."

"I'm spending the summer with my Grandma Alice," Shelby said.

"Alice Meyer? Nice woman. We used to exchange cookies at Christmas."

Shelby smiled. "That's the one." She petted Mutt, who had relaxed into Gabe's arms now, and then motioned to Gabe to leave. "Nice to meet you. Before we go, do you have a phone?" Shelby asked. "If you give me your number, I'll call you and give you mine in case you need anything."

"Can't afford one," the woman answered.

"Oh, okay," Shelby said. "No problem."

Gabe kissed Mutt on top of his head and lowered him to the floor. "See you soon," he said.

Mutt barked in reply. There was definitely a strong bond there. Shelby took a few steps back. "We'll be going now."

At the edge of the yard they turned and waved again.

Mrs. Williams stood in the doorway watching them go, then called Mutt to her and shut the door.

On the way back through the woods, Shelby could see the resemblance to his brother Logan, but Gabe's temperament seemed more easygoing. She made plans with him to keep his secret and help with Mutt. She was also going to talk to her grandmother about Mrs. Williams and see if there were any other services to help her as well. She didn't seem sick, just isolated and alone. Perhaps they could bring by a batch of cookies sometime.

When they reached their cul-de-sac, Shelby winked at Gabe. "Bye, partner," she said.

His grin said it all.

CHAPTER 16

Shelby helped Theo unload all the fantastic dog items from their shopping trip to Pet Universe. They brought everything through the gate to the backyard. Trevor, in his usual jeans and t-shirt, was working on the fence, making sure it was escape-free. Even Theo and Alice were in jeans today.

"Hey," Trevor said. "What'd you do, buy the whole store? Here, let me help."

Once everything was unloaded to the deck, Alice brought out a knife and scissors for opening, cutting off tags, and getting things ready for the work party arrival at 1:00.

Theo pulled a red plastic fire hydrant out of a large box. "Look at this," he said, chuckling.

Shelby had a good laugh as she imagined the dogs lifting their legs around it.

"What will they think of next?" Trevor said.

As promised, Alice had bought a large stainless steel trash can as well as plenty of doggy bags and a dispenser.

"Here's the water station." Theo pulled out a wooden stand with four stainless steel bowls that fit in the base for water. "Let's put it near the hose in the shade, and that way it'll be easy to fill and refill."

Alice pulled out one of the raised dog beds. "This needs to be assembled," she said.

This was one of Shelby's favorites. It had plastic legs and a canvas top so the dogs could lie on it, and it was waterproof.

"Don't forget, I'm building a ramp so they can run and chase each other across," Trevor said. "It'll be ready by tomorrow."

Shelby watched as her dream became a reality, and was grateful for all the wonderful people making it possible. The dogs were going to adore coming here.

"Well," Alice said, "I think it looks pretty good. Don't forget that someone needs to go pick up Mindy."

"I'll do it," Trevor said. "Can you tell me where she lives?"

Alice gave directions to Trevor, then turned to Shelby. "We're all set."

At promptly 1:00, people started to arrive. Mindy, in her usual workout clothes and ponytail, leaned on Trevor's arm and balanced herself with a crutch on the other side, maneuvering carefully with the cast. Shelby put a chair down on the grass in the shade for her so she could watch and not have to walk up the steps to the deck.

Even Trevor had not brought his dog Buddy today and Wally was asleep in the house. They needed time to set everything up before the dogs ran wild in the yard.

"Hi, everyone," Mindy said.

Alice went over and gave her a hug. "You're looking much better. How much longer?"

Mindy frowned as she eyed her foot. "A few weeks and then I'll have a different brace with more mobility." She took a seat. "Trevor," she said motioning to him and the bag he carried in for her.

He pulled out a box of tennis balls and a couple handheld ball-throwers. "These are from Mindy," he said.

"Thanks, Mindy," Shelby said. "I'm so glad you made it."

"Me too. And thanks for sending Trevor over to get me."

"Yeah, he's a really nice guy," Shelby said, watching as Mindy nodded absently, her eyes roaming over to Trevor, where he was storing some of the toys in the shed.

"Look who's here," Theo said.

Everyone turned and there was Josh Redd, coming along with a dog toy in his hand, which appeared to be a multicolored rope, ball, and a pulley all in one.

"Hey," he said. "Need another pair of hands?"

Shelby almost didn't recognize him without his striped ice-cream-covered apron. In his swim shorts and baggy shirt he looked like a tourist from the beach.

Theo greeted him. "Welcome."

"What can I do? Put me to work."

Theo pointed over to an empty flower bed. "I was thinking we could clear out the bark and pat down the soil, to give the dogs another spot where they can rest. Sometimes dogs eat the bark. I had to break Wally of the habit."

"Sure thing, I'm on it. Got some garbage bags and a shovel?"

"Of course."

"It's great to see you, Josh," said Shelby. "Too bad Steph couldn't come too."

"Well, someone has to man or woman the store and scoop the joy. And besides, I never get out. This is fun for me. Where should I put the toy?"

Shelby pointed to the shed. "We have boxes in there for safe storage from chewing dogs."

"Hello," a friendly voice called from the gate.

Shelby turned to see Joann, carrying in a big stuffed dinosaur.

"I know I don't have a dog right now," she said, her eyes drifting to the ground.

"Perfectly fine, we're happy to have you," Shelby said.

"I thought I'd come and see if I could help. I brought a toy. It has squeakers everywhere, even in its legs."

"Oh, they're going to love that," Shelby said. "Thanks so much."

Joann continued. "If you'd like, I can check around for any hazards or plants that might not be healthy for the dogs. I'm a bit of an expert on that."

Shelby hadn't even thought of that. "Of course."

"Then I'll just see what I can get busy with."

Shelby looked around. She'd never lived anywhere long enough to get involved with others like this. It was wonderful to see everyone come together. Even Logan had sent her a text that he couldn't make it and was stuck covering an extra shift at work. He'd sent a picture of himself with a sad face leaning against the lifeguard station. But, he'd added, "Don't forget the full moon tonight at my house."

She was glad she was busy all day, otherwise she'd have thought of nothing else. Geese squawked overhead, seeming to watch the goings on below, adding to her excitement.

"Hello," Eleanor called out as she entered the yard dressed up as usual in a pale pink pantsuit with little pearls around her neck. Her hair was swept up beautifully, silver and glistening. It didn't look as if she would be getting her hands dirty in that outfit, but she was lending support and that was what mattered. "Well, look at all of you," said Eleanor. "A real team effort here." She pulled up a shopping bag and brought out a furry tree stump with squirrel faces sticking out of various holes.

"What is it?" Shelby asked.

"Isn't it darling? It's a little house for baby squirrels. You know how dogs love squirrels." She pulled out a stuffed squirrel and gave it a squeeze, producing a loud squeak. "Endless fun."

"Lemonade, everyone," Alice called from the deck.

Eleanor turned and waved. "Shall we go?" she said to the group.

Trevor helped Mindy up to the deck to join everyone. They sat on benches and chairs and enjoyed their icy cold beverages.

"Thanks for coming," Shelby said. "This is our first official meeting of the Dog Walkers Club."

"A great name," Eleanor said.

The others chimed in in agreement.

"Today we set up everything and we are almost ready to open. First, Theo has a few things to share."

"For starters," Theo said, "I'd like to be open about two days a week. During these hot days we might want to do mornings. Remember, the main thing is come have fun. Pick up after your dog and help clean up after we close the park and that's really about it."

"It's really nice of you," Josh said, "to offer this place to gather and let the dogs play."

"My pleasure," Theo said. "Now we just need to choose an opening date."

"How about a toast?" Alice held up her lemonade and others followed. "To the Dog Walkers Club," she said.

THEO WALKED BACK into the house after everyone had left for the day. Wally was curled up in his bed fast asleep, probably overwhelmed from all the recent activity. Theo took a seat on his leather recliner, put his head back, and closed his eyes. Empty silence. Now that he had ventured out again, being alone seemed that much more pronounced. He reflected on all the smiling faces and laughter that had filled his backyard. It would have made Jean so happy to see this, even though her raised vegetable garden beds, unattended and dormant now for so long, had been made into a resting area for dog beds. He could almost hear her chuckle at that.

On his next weekly Skype call with his son, Theo thought he'd leave out all the commotion going on here. Cam had his own way of seeing things. He was very fastidious, and all the mess and noise of a dog park would probably set him off on another lecture. If Cam had his way, Theo would be living in a sterile senior community somewhere where his needs would be cared for, and Cam would not have to worry about his busy schedule being disrupted if there was an emergency.

To be fair, Theo had given his son cause to worry these last several months. But Cam had first suggested they move to an active senior community a year or so before Jean died. Jean had laughed at Cam's suggestions. "We are very happy here in this small town," she would say. Even though Cam considered it the middle of nowhere, Jean would just make a face at Theo and they would laugh over being perceived as country bumpkins. The fact was, he and Jean had never been happier than at Moonwater Lake.

Until she'd gotten sick.

And even then Jean had worried more about how Theo would do after she was gone than her own declining health. Over and over Theo had promised her he would find a way to still enjoy life again. But he'd never believed it. Until now, he supposed. Glimmers of happiness had started to filter into his daily life. Shelby and Alice were starting to feel like family. Family of the heart, Jean had called it.

He reminded himself to count his blessings. Wally stirred in the corner, and he was surely one of them. Alice's warm smile came to mind, and he felt a flicker in his heart. It was too soon. And was it right to even let himself think about another woman?

"Be happy," he could almost hear Jean shouting out to him.

With a deep sigh, he closed his eyes and joined Wally in an afternoon nap.

CHAPTER 17

*A*fter a busy afternoon setting the dog park up, Shelby was looking forward to going to Logan's tonight and watching the full moon rise from their deck. Alice made sure she ate supper, and although she felt a bit too excited to eat, the fish and chips were very tempting.

After a long shower, she laid out a couple of her new shirts next to her skinny jeans on the bed, deciding which one would look the best. "I'll have to bring a sweatshirt for later," she said to herself, since it would get cool down by the lake. Logan told her the moonrise over the lake lasted until after 10:00 p.m., but he'd come get her about 8:00 p.m.

"This one," she said, holding up a soft turquoise shirt that went well with her blue zip-up jacket. Before leaving her room, she looked in the mirror one more time. It was a far different reflection than she was used to seeing. Rosy-cheeked and all smiles. "All right," she said, "here goes."

She walked out into the living room where Alice was watching TV with Scarlett nestled beside her on the couch. "Come and sit by me," Alice said, patting the couch next to her.

"What are you watching?" Shelby said.

"Some show on fixing up old homes to look like new. It makes me wonder if I should take on a project. Your grandpa and I talked about remodeling the kitchen sometime."

Shelby looked around. "I don't know. It looks pretty good. I love your house just the way it is."

"Well, thanks," Alice said. "You look lovely. Are you ready for tonight?"

Shelby took a deep breath. "I guess I am."

Her grandmother laughed. "Of course you are. I'll be right here across the street if you need anything."

At that, there was a knock at the door. Shelby, her eyes wide, looked over at her grandmother.

Alice nodded at the door. "What a gentleman, escorting you across the street. Go answer."

Shelby slowly opened the door, where, of course, Logan was waiting for her. For a moment she could hardly believe this was real.

"Good evening," Logan said. "All set?"

Shelby's breath caught at the sight of him. It was the first time she'd seen him in jeans and a white t-shirt that set off his deep tan. Her crush on Nick back in Las Vegas paled in comparison to the boy in front of her.

"I'm ready," she said.

"Can I come in a minute and say hi to your grandma?"

Shelby stood aside, waving him in. "Sure, of course. I should have invited you in."

Logan greeted Alice very politely, letting her know they would be a little late, but he would make sure Shelby got home safely.

Shelby's heart melted a little more. "I'm all set," she said.

"All right," Logan said, walking her to the door. "I hope you're ready for s'mores."

They waved goodbye to her grandmother and walked across the street. Shelby was curious to see inside Logan's sprawling house. The double front doors opened up into an entry displaying spacious, open rooms and peaked ceilings. Massive windows revealed their impressive view. A lit path curved down to their private dock. The darkening lake reflected traces of deep purple and magenta light lingering from the sunset. It felt like standing in the middle of the lake floating in their living room.

Logan's mother, an attractive but reserved woman with white blonde hair, walked over to greet them. "You must be Shelby. I'm Iris."

"Nice to meet you," Shelby said.

Gabe was right behind her. "Hey, good to see you, Shelby."

"You too," she answered. "How are you doing?"

For a moment he looked a little nervous that she might forget herself and say something about Mutt, but of course, she just gave him a sly wink.

Iris walked over to the massive granite island separating their kitchen from a formal dining area. "Everything is set," she said. "Are you up for making s'mores?"

Shelby eyed the tray of scrumptious-looking chocolate candy bars, marshmallows, and graham crackers. "Absolutely."

Logan took Shelby's arm and walked out the French doors. "The fire pit is warming out on the deck, and there are some sticks as well. I'm ready if you are," he said.

The group headed down to the redwood deck with a circular cement patio in the center. Ash hardwood Adirondack chairs and benches surrounded the grill with crackling firewood heating the coals. Iris carried the tray out with the chocolate and the other supplies and put it on a table beside them.

"Okay, grab a stick," she said.

"Me first," Gabe said. He slid a marshmallow on the top before roasting it over the flame. "I like mine crispy," he said.

"I do too," Shelby said as she placed her marshmallow over the fire. Gabe was amusing to watch. He was at the awkward, gangly stage and still had braces. But his light hair and delicate features like his mother promised he'd be quite handsome man in a few years.

Logan followed suit. "I like mine golden-brown."

"Oh, that's no good," Gabe said.

Iris laughed. "You can make them any way you want."

Shelby's first impression of Iris being a bit pale and withdrawn began to change. In the glow of the firelight, everyone joked, laughed, and seemed happy. If Logan had not hinted at conflict under the surface, she'd had thought them to be a fun, carefree family.

Soon the marshmallows were smoldering and ready to be placed on chocolate slabs sandwiched between graham crackers. With Shelby's first bite, chocolate and gooey marshmallow oozed down her chin.

"Oh, my," Iris said, reaching for the stack of napkins and handing them around.

Shelby quickly used hers. "These are delicious."

The boys echoed her response.

Gabe ate several more, but Shelby was content. The sky was fading to black and soon it would be time to walk out on the pier alone with Logan.

Iris stood and stretched. "It's getting late. You two better head down to the dock. According to news, the big moonrise should start soon."

"Can I go?" Gabe said.

Shelby watched Logan frown. "No, this is just for Shelby and me."

"Oh, right," Gabe said, turning around.

Iris put her arm around Gabe. "Come on, we'll go in and do some fun stuff together."

"But I want to see the moon," he said.

Iris handed Gabe the empty platter to carry and nodded for him to follow her back to the house. "We can see it from the deck."

Gabe attempted one more pleading look toward Logan but, with no response, turned, muttering, "All right."

Logan took Shelby's hand. "Come on, it's time. Make sure you grab your sweatshirt on the chair."

They walked the stone path that wove onto a T-shaped wooden dock. At the end where it was built over the water, Logan had placed some fluffy towels for them to sit on and rolled up others to use as pillows. "It's best if you lie down," he said. "You can see better."

He certainly had thought this out. There was even a folded blanket. He waited for Shelby to pick a side and then he lay down next to her only inches away. She propped up a towel under her head and looked up into the clearest sky she had ever seen.

"There must be a million stars out there," she said.

"Actually, there are billions," Logan replied. "The exact amount, of course, is unknown, but…"

Shelby turned and gave him a look. "So literal."

He broke into a dimpled smile. "I'm used to being in science classes and spouting out answers."

"Figures," she said and they both broke out laughing.

Logan propped up on his elbows and pointed to a grouping of stars. "That's Orion's Belt. See the straight row of stars? If you follow them, they point to the North Star."

"I see it," Shelby said.

When he lay back down, their arms touched. Sparks flew between them, like tiny stars shooting across the sky. Neither of them moved or said a word. A lone howl echoed in the distance.

The sound was clearly distinguishable, but trying to hide her grin, Shelby said, "Do you know what species that is?"

He started to answer and then mock frowned at her.

"Caught ya!" she said.

Logan shrugged. "What can I say. You know me too well."

Shelby liked the sound of that.

"It's so different at night," Logan said. "Peaceful. We can watch for shooting stars."

Shelby remembered her grandfather teaching her to make wishes when a star streaked across the evening sky. Right now, she had almost everything she could wish for.

A cool breeze blew up from the water and goosebumps covered her arms. She zipped her jacket all the way up.

He turned to face her. "Are you cold?"

"A little."

"Do you want to leave?"

"No," she said. "I don't want to miss the full moon." She sat up and wrapped her arms around herself.

Logan put his arm around her and pulled her to him. "Okay?" he said, looking into her eyes.

She could barely breathe. Her body tingled. Shelby rested her head on his shoulder and let her eyes drift shut. If she stayed real still, the night might never end. She could hear the water lapping over the legs of the dock.

A hooting owl cried out, as if announcing the moon's arrival over the hills. "Look," Logan said. "Wow."

Eyes open, Shelby watched as an orange-tinged moon drifted up into the sky. Long rays of light streamed across the water, reaching toward them on the dock. A fishing boat moved lazily across the golden reflection.

"It's enormous," she said.

"It appears that way this time of year," Logan said. "The light is amazing. I can see why the original Native Americans here had a legend about it."

Shelby tore her eyes from the water's surface and faced Logan. "You mentioned that."

He spoke softly. "They say, and I quote, 'Countless years ago, legend said a lover's kiss as the full moon reflects across the lake will connect two souls forever.'"

The moon's glow shone on Logan's face, making his eyes

glisten like gold stars. Logan's soft fingers caressed her cheek and slid down to her lips. A sigh escaped her. Never taking his eyes off of her, Logan leaned in and let his lips brush hers. Shelby swayed and drew a deep breath. Her eyes flickered open for a moment, the moon glow filling them. She wrapped her arms around his neck and pressed her lips to his. Even the stars faded away and there was only Logan and Shelby.

CHAPTER 18

*S*helby floated through the next few days, barely aware of what she was doing. Half the time her eyes were closed, remembering the full moon night on the dock with Logan. Her first kiss. She touched her lips with her fingers and sighed deeply. She couldn't wait to see him again. But she made herself be patient and let it come naturally. Luckily, she'd been distracted with dog walking and getting everything ready for the club. But, she didn't want him to think she was avoiding him either. This dating thing was complicated.

It was a hot afternoon and a swim sounded perfect to cool off. And natural, she reassured herself. She selected her pale yellow bathing suit with a cutout triangle over her stomach. It showed off her tan the best. She added a touch of lip gloss, brushed her hair, grabbed a towel and a t-shirt, and started out the door.

Alice called out to her from the kitchen. "See you later. Don't forget, I'm making your favorite for dinner tonight, the popcorn chicken."

"I won't. Be back soon." Shelby hurried down the steps toward the path to the beach. Maybe Logan would ask her out again tonight? She could wear her new sundress. Right before she reached the wooden steps to the sand, she slowed down. She didn't want Logan to see her rushing toward him. All of a sudden, as she got closer, she felt shy again and wondered if she should sit near him or not too near. "Oh, that's silly," she told herself. With a deep breath, she stood up tall, pulled off her t-shirt to show off her bathing suit, and walked across the sand toward the lifeguard station.

When she got a little closer, she froze in place. Was that Madison, hanging all over Logan? At first, he didn't seem too interested in her. Shelby stepped back in the shade and watched. Madison must have said something funny, because he started laughing.

Madison edged in closer to Logan, reminding Shelby of a cat stalking her prey. She put her hand on Logan's smooth, tanned arm and gazed up at him. Shelby watched Logan, not sure what he would do next. He looked down at Madison's hand, and before he could do anything, Madison reached over and planted a kiss right on Logan's lips.

"No," Shelby said, embarrassing herself by her volume.

"What's wrong, dear?" a lady passing said. "Are you okay?"

The woman's voice had attracted Logan's scrutiny. Then he saw Shelby standing there. She wanted to melt into the sand. Madison turned as well and gave Shelby a sly smile as if she'd known all along she was watching.

Logan couldn't leave his post. Shelby knew that. He waved her over, but she didn't want to know what he had to say. All she wanted to do was to get out of there as fast as she could.

"I'm fine, I'm fine," she said to the lady as she turned to run, almost tripping in the sand. She was glad she had sunglasses on because she could feel tears starting to roll.

"Wait."

Oh, gosh. Logan was coming after her.

"Wait," she heard again. "Shelby."

Shelby stood perfectly still with her back to him. "You shouldn't leave your post."

"John's watching it for me. I don't know what you saw, but I am absolutely not interested in Madison." He tried to put his hand on her shoulder to console her.

"Don't touch me," Shelby said, pushing it off.

"Please, Shelby. Turn around, look at me."

"I didn't see you exactly pushing her off."

"It's a touchy subject," Logan said.

She turned to face him now. "Yeah, it sure is. I'm going to go home now. You'd better go back."

"I'll call you later," Logan said. "This is nothing, believe me."

She turned and started walking away.

Logan called after her. "Shelby."

Shelby just kept walking. She wanted to believe him, she really did, but her heart was breaking.

Once she was far enough away, she stopped under a shade tree and dried her eyes.

"What's wrong? Are you okay?"

Not another one, Shelby thought. But this time, when she turned, it was sweet Joann out taking a walk and probably hoping to find some dogs to pet.

"I'm all right," Shelby said. "It's just...sometimes. You know how it is."

Joann shook her head. "Believe me, I know how it is, honey."

The grief mirrored in Joann's eyes resonated deeply with Shelby. Instinctively Joann seemed to understand how grief could wrap around your heart like a deadly vine and never let go.

"Sometimes we just have to pick ourselves up and keep going," Joann said.

Shelby nodded. "Know all about that too."

"Lots of good things happening for you too, like your new dog walking business."

Shelby was glad to change the subject. "Don't forget we're

going to have the grand opening of the dog park next week. I hope you'll come. You can never have too many people petting."

Joann smiled, but it did not reach her eyes. "Of course, I'll be there. Maybe someday I'll even bring my own dog."

"I hope so," Shelby said. "If you ever decide you want another dog, I'd be pleased to help look for one. Go to the shelter with you."

"I just might take you up on that soon," Joann said. "But for now," she put her hand over her chest, "my heart is still aching for my little one."

"I'm so sorry," Shelby said.

Joann nodded. "I'm going to head home now. You have a nice evening. I'll see you soon."

Shelby watched Joann go. Alice had said Joann never married and had taken care of her own mother with Alzheimer's disease for many years until she died last year. And then Joann had lost her precious dog Roxie. But Joann was still out there taking care of herself with a brisk walk, petting dogs, and trying to help Shelby. And that's what Shelby would do too. She didn't need to think about boys the rest of this summer. She was going to help her customers, build her business, and make the dog park the best Moonwater Lake had ever seen. After all, she was used to rising above disappointment.

When she got home, her grandmother was sitting on the porch in her rocker. "How was the lake? You're back so soon."

"Fine," Shelby said, trying to avoid elaborating.

"Your mother called while you were gone," Alice said.

Shelby froze. "And?"

"She was quite upset. Her and Gus had a fight and she wanted you to call her as soon as you got in."

One look at her grandmother's sympathetic face and Shelby burst into tears and ran into her room.

"I should have known it was all too good to be true," Shelby said, falling into bed. Why would a guy like Logan ever fall for a young girl like her? And there was no way she was calling her mother back. She could deal with her own troubles for once.

Her grandmother came in and sat gently on the bed beside her. She patted Shelby's shoulder. "Sometimes a good cry is just what we need," Alice said. "You rest now. I'm here if you need me."

FAR AWAY IN THE DISTANCE, Shelby heard the phone ringing. She struggled to come out of a deep sleep and finally opened her eyes to a black, dark room. She'd gone right to bed after dinner and had no idea what time it was. The ringing was coming from her grandmother's room down the hall. Panic fluttered cross her chest. Finally, the ringing stopped. Shelby peeked an eye out at the clock. "5:00 a.m.?" Too darn early. Maybe it was a wrong number.

She turned over to go back to sleep but was interrupted by a gentle knock at her bedroom door open. "It's your mother," Alice said.

Shelby groaned. "At this hour?"

With an apologetic look, Alice nodded.

Shelby sat up. There was probably no real emergency. Shelby had been too upset to return the call yesterday. Dana had probably been up all night, crying and drinking. Something Shelby had seen so many times before. She switched on the light by her bed.

Having been torn out of bed herself, her grandmother looked a bit disheveled. Her eyes drooped along with her shoulders as she handed Shelby the phone.

Shelby muted it for a moment. "Why don't you go back to sleep, Grandma? I'll handle this."

"Are you sure?" Alice asked.

"You go," Shelby said. "I'll be fine." She took a deep breath before answering. "Mom?"

Her mother's familiar slurred tone told her everything. Same old thing again. "He didn't come home all night," her mother said. "We had a little fight and then he just left." Shelby hated it when Dana cried, but she'd heard the same story so many times before, she had trouble feeling sympathetic anymore.

"What happened?" Shelby said, moving into her usual routine that seemed to help.

"I don't know. I don't even know. I was just talking about our family and being together and how I wish we could stay in Florida forever. And then he brought up getting married." She stammered a bit. "I—I got a little nervous and didn't know what to say. And then when he saw that I wasn't sure, he looked so hurt. What was I to say? Then he just walked right out the door and said, 'Well, let me know when you're sure.'"

This was a different twist from the typical stories Shelby was used to hearing. Usually the man had left Dana and never come back. This one wanted to marry her?

Her mother broke down again. "I've only been married once, and it was to your father. And look how that turned out. Maybe I'm just doomed in love."

Shelby flashed for the millionth time on how incredibly sad it must have been for Dana to learn her husband had died in a crash only a few years after getting married. But at some point, she had to move on. It was fourteen years ago. And Shelby had watched her mother make the same mistakes over and over.

"I know, Mom. It's okay. Everything will work out. He must really love you if he asked you to marry him."

Her mother continued to sniffle. Then it hit Shelby just what this could mean. Oh my gosh, what if they get married? What if they move to Florida permanently? There was no way Shelby wanted to move again. She was happy here. Well, pretty much happy until she'd seen Logan with Madison yesterday. And he was leaving for college in a few months anyway. Shelby was building her own life here and she could finally finish high school in one place. She was torn, wanting her mother to be happy, but also finally wanting herself to be, too.

"You're probably right," Dana said, "and I do love him. What do you think, Shelby?"

Shelby wanted to say, "I'm the daughter. You're the mother. I don't know what to think." But she said, instead, "Whatever your heart tells you." And she meant it.

Dana sighed. "I love him. I really do. I'm just so afraid."

"I know, Mom," Shelby said. "It's been hard. Maybe you should call him."

"I don't want to call him," Dana said. "Then he'll think... "

"What will he think?" Shelby asked. "That you care?"

"Wait, wait," Dana said, "I hear someone on the stairs. Oh, it's him. And he's standing at the front door with a bouquet of flowers." Her mother's voice lightened as she said, "Gus, I'm so glad you're here. Come in."

Shelby ran a hand through her bed head hair and stifled a yawn while she waited for Dana to come back to the call.

"Everything's fine now, Shelby," Dana whispered. "Bye."

Her mother hung up the phone. She hadn't asked a word about Shelby, how she was doing, or sorry for calling at five in the morning, not even realizing Shelby was on the West Coast. Not even an, "I love you, bye." It was always about Dana and some man.

Shelby laid the phone by the side of her bed. She contemplated bringing it back to her grandmother, but figured she didn't want to wake her, too. Dana had done enough damage. She turned off the light and tried to fall back to sleep and pretend the call never happened.

~

A FEW HOURS LATER, Shelby heard her grandmother bustling around the kitchen and could smell fresh coffee wafting into her room. When she sat up, her whole body felt heavy. Maybe she'd just stay here all day. She sure didn't want to go to the lake or see Logan. But then she remembered the club had scheduled a last-minute pull-everything-together meeting for the dog park opening later today. That made her smile. That was worth getting out of bed for.

After a quick shower, she threw on some shorts and a t-shirt and went into the kitchen to greet her grandmother. Faint music played in the background and there were fresh flowers on the table indicating Alice had been out gardening already today. A good sign.

"Coffee?" Alice asked. "I know your mother's call broke up your sleep."

Shelby rolled her eyes before taking a sip of the steaming coffee. It was so nice to have someone care about her. Dana really never cared that much about herself or those around her. She was like a young child that everyone didn't want to see hurt herself.

Alice brought some muffins and cut-up fresh fruit to the table and joined Shelby. "Thanks for the breakfast. You take such good care me," Shelby said. "I'll do the dishes after."

"It's a deal," Alice said. "Is your mother all right after the fight?"

"Gus came back with flowers and all is well again. And get this: He asked her to marry him."

Alice looked surprised. "Well, that is something new, isn't it?"

Shelby nodded. "Who knows? We might be getting another call late tonight saying it's off again." She needed to shake off her grumpy attitude this morning.

"That could be true," Alice said, "but you never know. Maybe this one is different."

"Well, if it's going to be anyone," Shelby said, "it'll be him. Gus really does seem to love her and he's a nice guy."

"I'm glad to hear that. He seemed polite and attentive to her."

Shelby took a fresh strawberry from the bowl and let its sweetness dissolve in her mouth. "I hope she doesn't expect me to go with her to Florida."

Alice looked up. "I was afraid of that myself."

"I love it here, Grandma. I really want to stay."

"And I really want you to," her grandmother said. "Your happiness is very important to me. For now, let's just let this call blow over and move on with our day. We have the dog park to look forward to."

"Right," Shelby said, thinking that was good advice. She reviewed in her head all they had to accomplish today.

A knock at the door sent Scarlett racing and barking toward it.

"Now what?" Shelby asked. Usually no one showed up this early in the morning. She hoped it wasn't... Oh no. She looked through the window and there was Logan standing with a bouquet of wild roses and white daisies with golden centers. For a moment, it was a little much for her. She had just talked to her mother, who had a man standing at her door with flowers, and now Shelby did, too. She opened the door and Logan gave her a sideways smile.

"For you," he said.

"They're beautiful," she said hesitantly.

"Can you come outside for a moment?" he asked. "I didn't want to go to work without talking to you first."

She glanced back at her grandmother, who waved her on. Shelby stepped out on the porch. They sat on the white wicker chairs with the comfy sky-blue cushions. The flowers lay between them on the glass table.

For a moment neither spoke, until Logan turned to face her. "Shelby, I want you to know there's nothing between Madison and me, and I'm very sorry you saw her make a move on me yesterday."

"Madison sure seems to think otherwise," Shelby said.

Logan frowned. "I can't say much, but I will tell you her parents and mine are friends. They know each other from the club in the Bay Area. Last summer my dad asked me to take Madison out once after she'd had some health issues. You don't say no to my dad."

"Oh," Shelby said. "If I'd known…"

"How could you?" he asked. "We went out. I was polite as I could be, but afterward I told her I'd like to be friends. She didn't take that well."

"I can see that," Shelby said.

"This summer she has been even pushier, trying to prove to herself and her friends that she could change my mind."

"And did she?" Shelby asked.

"Absolutely not. I don't want to hurt her, but to be anything more than friends would never work for me."

He was here, wanting her to understand. It meant a lot. Logan reached out his hand and Shelby put hers in his. The sweet scent of the flowers, coupled with the warmth of his fingers wrapped around hers, made everything else fall away, leaving only the beautiful sunny day before them.

CHAPTER 19

The final afternoon work party had been going on for a while when Shelby looked up and saw Logan. This was the second time today his appearance had been a surprise. He was still in his red trunks, but he'd added a shirt and flip-flops.

"John took over the rest of my shift today. I wanted to make sure I was here if you needed anything," he said.

"Thanks for coming," she said. "There's still plenty to do. Why don't you help Trevor with the fence?"

"Sure, whatever you need. I'm here to help."

Shelby returned to the deck, where her grandmother was refreshing the iced tea container.

"Well, that was nice of Logan to come help out. He's a good guy," Alice said. "Why don't you take a short break?"

"Caught you two lovely ladies resting on the job," Theo said with a smile as he joined them under the shade of the umbrella.

Alice laughed. "I've been inside baking dog cookies. It's hard work."

"Smells like the peanut butter kind in my kitchen. I thought they were for us."

Alice laughed. "I'll make you some too. The people kind."

Trevor turned toward the group and made an announcement. "Thanks to Logan's help today, the fence is totally dog-proof now."

"Trevor has been so helpful," Theo said. "And that boy Logan is a hard worker too." He looked right at Shelby. "A real standup kind of guy. One you can trust."

"That's what I thought," Alice said. "Glad to hear it."

Alice must have mentioned Shelby's date with Logan the other night and they were trying to reassure her.

Embarrassed, Shelby shrugged. But it was nice to hear. Things felt good with Logan for now, but she would still be cautious. If nothing else, her mother's failed relationships had taught her that.

"I'm going back to work," Shelby said.

"We'll join you soon," Theo said.

As Shelby walked away, she heard Theo mention something about a picnic to Alice. She was glad she had her back to them so they couldn't see the grin that brought to her face. She walked around helping where she could. Josh and Steph had both made it today and so had Eleanor. Mindy and Trevor were putting dog toys together. The laughter between them and steady glances made it pretty clear how well they were getting along. Perhaps, Shelby thought, they should call this venture the Lonely Hearts Dog Walkers Club. She laughed to herself. It wasn't so far from the truth. She'd have to remember to mention it to some of the others.

About an hour later, with everything completed and ready for the grand opening, people started to leave.

Eleanor waved from the gate. "See you all at the Fourth of July party."

That was coming up soon and Shelby had heard so much about it and what a grand event it was. Her grandmother had suggested several dishes they could make together and bring over for the occasion.

Logan moved in beside her. "The dogs are going to love this place."

"I think they will," Shelby said. "And thanks for all your help."

"A commendable project, for sure. And…by the way, I'm off tomorrow. When you finish your dog walking in the morning, would you like to go on a canoe ride with me? We keep one at our dock. I could pack snacks, my guitar, and we could paddle up the lake to a cool spot I like."

Shelby liked the sound of that, but she didn't want to sound overly eager. "I guess that would be all right."

"Well, don't sound too excited," Logan said with a big smile. "You know I've never asked anyone else to go there with me before."

She liked the sound of that too. "I'll meet you about 1:00. And, Logan, thanks. It sounds wonderful."

"I can walk you home if you'd like," he said.

"Let me check and see if my grandmother wants to walk back with us. Be right back."

Shelby found Alice inside petting Wally and slipping him another cookie. "Do you want to walk home with Logan and me?"

Alice winked at her. "You two go."

"I'll make sure Alice gets home just fine," Theo said.

Shelby was sure he would.

SHELBY FINISHED WALKING HER CLIENTS' dogs for the day and was looking forward to the canoe ride with Logan. She'd worn a bathing suit under her clothes and walked over to Logan's house.

"Come on in," he said. Waiting by the door was a small plastic cooler and his guitar. He handed Shelby a ball cap before putting one on himself. "The sun gets pretty hot out there on the water," he said. "I put towels in the canoe too."

"You are prepared," she said.

Logan led her to a hand-crafted wooden canoe waiting at the end of his dock.

"After you," he said, helping her in.

They each took an oar and paddled out into the glistening lake. They kept close to the shore, where the summer homes and boat docks cast long shadows across the water as they passed. A young boy ran down his deck, drew his knees tight to his chest, and splashed into the water, followed by his black lab.

"Looks fun," Logan said.

Shelby thought about how much Gabe wanted a dog and could see him doing the same antics if he had one. "It does."

Together they continued to paddle in sync as the canoe coasted along the east loop of the lake. Their peace was broken by a loud shriek overhead.

Logan pointed upward. "A red-tailed hawk." It soared down from a tall tree after its prey. "Time for a fish dinner," he said, laughing. "Plenty of them here. Did you know this lake has been here for almost ten thousand years?"

"Really?" Shelby wondered how much the area had changed after all that time. How wild it must have been before the tourists descended upon it. "And the flocks of white pelicans?"

"I'm not sure," Logan said. "Good question. I'll have to look it up."

They glided silently across the water, the sun beating on their shoulders.

"There's my spot up ahead," Logan said. "Let's paddle over." He pointed to a tree sheltered in a sandy cove. Tall reeds floated in the water as they glided around them toward their destination.

With the temperature rising, Shelby welcomed the shade. And the company. A few boats slipped by in the distance, but otherwise they were completely alone. Just her and Logan. Like a dream. Then her mind kicked in. Would she know what to talk about? What if he tried to kiss her again? Relax, she told herself.

Logan had been nothing but kind. She was a very good swimmer if she needed to dive for it...the thought made her laugh.

Logan, muscles springing into action, jumped out first into the shallow water and pulled the canoe the rest of the way to shore. He reached out his hand to help Shelby to the sand, and then grabbed the cooler.

"Nice place," Shelby said, wading ashore carrying the towels. She chose a cool spot and spread the towels out like a picnic blanket.

"How about a cool drink?" Logan asked, opening the cooler.

Shelby was impressed as she watched him pull out icy drinks and sandwiches. "Did you make these yourself?" she said.

"Well, I had a little help," he said. "I told my mom I was hoping to go canoeing later and she offered. You have your pick of assorted iced tea and flavored waters. My mother's favorites."

"Iced tea is great," Shelby said. She chose a chicken salad sandwich on a French roll and took a bite. "Delicious!"

"My mom is an excellent chef. She makes most things from scratch." He patted his firm stomach. "We never go hungry."

She knew Logan was joking, but there had been times Shelby had feared just that. Going hungry. Dana made very few attempts to cook. Leftovers from her waitress jobs when she was working sustained them many nights. And an occasional special trip to a fast food place. The contrast of her life and Logan's struck hard. A shadow crossed her heart at the glaring contrast of her life and Logan's.

"It's a relief to have the rest of the day off," Logan said. "I was glad I could arrange it so I could be there to help you too. I know how important the dog park is to you."

Shelby was impressed again. He was trying, and she could try, too.

"I appreciated you showing up. And of course, the flowers."

"I'm not done yet," he said with a wink.

Her heart flipped. He was going to all this trouble for her. There was no other reason than that he liked her.

After they finished lunch, Logan went back to the canoe and retrieved his guitar. "I'm not the best," he said, "but I can carry a tune. Maybe you'll join me."

Shelby smiled. "I can't wait to hear you. Me, not so much."

He tuned the strings and began to sing one of Shelby's favorite Bruno Mars songs, "Just the Way You Are." She could hardly look in his eyes, almost golden in the sun, staring at her as he strummed the guitar and sang lyrics about not wanting to change a thing about her. Logan had a beautiful melodic voice, and like everything else about him, it was amazing, like the song said.

Shelby hummed along, trying to act cool when she felt just the opposite. "You're really good," she said. "You could do that professionally."

"It's not something I want to do for work," Logan said. "It's for fun and for my friends. But thank you."

Logan laid down the guitar and put his arm around Shelby. "Are we okay?"

She melted into him. "More than okay."

He leaned in and kissed her gently on the lips. She responded back, allowing the kiss to linger.

"You're very special, Shelby," he whispered.

She wanted to say something back, but words wouldn't form. Instead, she snuggled in close. What a relief it was to have him back in her life. His body was sturdy and strong, and so was his heart, it seemed. At least for the summer, she reminded herself.

When the late day heat intensified to what felt like way over a hundred degrees, they decided to pack everything up and go back to the canoe. Logan tossed her some sunscreen from the rear of the canoe. Shelby slathered it on and tossed it back. His arms glistened in the sun as he covered them with lotion. Mind on the paddling, she told herself as they worked their way back to his dock.

After tying up the canoe at the DeLucas' they sat down at the edge of the dock, their feet dangling over the water.

"Don't forget," he said. "Our annual Fourth of July party is coming up. You'll be there, right?"

"Of course," she said. "I wouldn't miss it."

"I wonder if my dad will make it home for the party," Logan said despairingly.

"Why wouldn't he?" Shelby asked.

"He's a corporate partner with an international law firm in San Francisco. He's overseas more than he's in the States, and rarely home."

Shelby laid her head on his shoulder. "It must be hard on your family."

He sighed. "Yeah."

Shelby couldn't even remember her father. And they'd lost touch with his side of the family after he'd passed. She wasn't sure she was looking forward to officially meeting Mr. DeLuca either.

Logan gave her a quick hug. "Let's go," he said, pulling her up from the dock. Face to face, she wondered if he would kiss her again, but he turned back toward the house. On the way up, they ran into Gabe heading toward the path to Mutt's house.

"How was the ride?" Gabe asked.

"It was great," Shelby said.

Gabe looked from Shelby to Logan and back again. "I bet."

"Get going," Logan said teasingly.

He walked Shelby back to her house and watched as she walked up the stairs to the door. She turned to wave. "I'll text you later."

CHAPTER 20

"What do you think?" Alice asked when she emerged from her bedroom wearing a white cotton sundress with pale blue stripes and a V-neck.

"You look beautiful," Shelby said.

Her grandmother blushed. "At my age?"

"Why not?"

Alice's silky white-streaked curls framed her face, complimenting her rosy cheeks and sapphire eyes.

"Perfect for the Fourth of July party." Shelby looked down at her belted tan shorts and off-the-shoulder floral blouse. "Am I underdressed?"

"Oh no, dear," Alice said. "I stopped by last year briefly with Joann and some people even wore swimsuits and cover-ups. It was very well attended. They even have their own private fireworks off their deck."

Shelby raised an eyebrow. The DeLucas certainly seemed to have enough money to do whatever they wanted.

"Theo didn't know what to bring, so I suggested a fruit salad," Alice said. "You should have seen him yesterday at the Veterans

Center with his Photograph Your Dog Day. Scarlett and I went along to help."

"Did it go well?" Shelby asked.

"A lot of veterans showed up with their dogs in various scarves, hats, and even a few bows. Trying to get the dogs to hold still was our biggest challenge. Especially Wally, who was very naughty and stole some dog cookies off a table."

Shelby laughed. "I'd love to see some of those photos sometime. I hope Theo can take a group shot of our dog walkers club sometime."

"I'm sure he'd be delighted to." Alice looked at the clock. "We better get everything packed up. I told Theo we'd meet him over there by 7:00 p.m." Earlier they'd baked lemon blueberry cupcakes with red, white, and blue buttercream icing and put them in a large Tupperware container. "Can't have too many desserts," Alice said.

Logan told Shelby that the DeLucas always provided juicy burgers, oversize hotdogs, and BBQ ribs. She was a little anxious over meeting Logan's father, and wondered what he would think of her.

"Ready when you are," Alice said. She turned to Scarlett. "Sorry you can't come, little one. No dogs."

Shelby rolled her eyes. "What is Fourth of July without dogs?"

"I know," Alice said. "But Anthony DeLuca does not seem to be fond of them."

The sun was just starting to set as Alice and Shelby made their way across the street. Iris welcomed them at the door and directed them to the kitchen as she continued to greet guests arriving behind them.

"Hey, Shelby, nice to see you!" Gabe shouted as he flew by with a tray of hotdogs in his hand. She waved back, wondering how it was going for Gabe helping with Mrs. Williams and Mutt. Hopefully well.

The house, decorated with colorful flower arrangements and

lit candles, was buzzing with people and laughter, so different from the quiet night of the full moon. They placed the cupcakes down on the counter, and a couple of servers, obviously hired for the night, removed the lid and carried the cupcakes outside. Alice and Shelby followed. Tables of various sizes were set up across the lawn, and twinkling lights draped across the trees. On the buffet tables there were lavish spreads of salads, stacks of buns, both white and wheat, platters of appetizers, and a separate dessert table. The aroma of savory barbeque wafted through the air, making Shelby's stomach growl.

Standing by a brick outdoor oven and grill top was a familiar-looking, tall, dark-haired man in a white polo shirt with navy piping around the neck and sleeves and matching cargo shorts. His presence dominated the scene. Logan's father. He had made it for the party after all.

"Oh, there's Theo." Alice waved toward him. "I think I'll go over and see how he's doing."

"Great idea, I'll join you in a minute," Shelby said, looking around for Logan. She knew he had to be somewhere nearby. He was probably down on the dock, away from the commotion. But she couldn't see through the crowd to be sure.

She spotted the Redds near the dessert table. Happy to see a familiar face, Shelby walked over to see them placing a sheet-size cake with firework decorations on the table.

"Happy Fourth of July," she said.

"Greetings, Shelby," Josh said. "First time I've seen you without a dog."

Shelby laughed. "Yeah, all the dogs are at home."

"I guess it's not a dog-friendly affair," Steph said. "I'm sure Oscar is hoping for leftovers."

"Not enough food, either," Josh said, with a wink.

Steph gave him a light swat on the arm. "C'mon, you, let's go get some dinner."

Shelby wasn't ready to eat yet. The sky was darkening, and

outdoor lighting had come on along the paths and around the tables. She noticed Madison and her family speaking to Mr. DeLuca and hoped she could avoid running into them here. Shelby scanned the tables and found Eleanor and her husband sitting at one under a red umbrella. Her husband looked like he had just left the golf course, right down to the yellow and tan oxford shoes. But Eleanor looked as elegant as ever in a pale peach polished cotton pantsuit and her silver hair swept up into a French twist.

"Look who's here," Eleanor said as Shelby approached. "This is my husband, Charles." A handsome man, with salt and pepper hair and kind brown eyes, reached out to shake Shelby's hand. "I've heard wonderful things about you." He pulled out a chair. "Why don't you join us for a minute?"

"Yes, come sit with us," Eleanor said. "Make sure you taste my cinnamon apple roses I baked. They're on the dessert table."

"Sounds amazing," Shelby said.

Eleanor smiled. "You let me know what you think. Now tell us, how is your dog walking business coming along?"

"Excellent," Shelby said, raising her voice over the throng of people still arriving. In the distance, she could hear fireworks across the lake.

"We're all very excited about the new dog park. Aren't we, Charles?"

Eleanor's husband nodded. "Good job, Shelby. A real plus for our community."

Shelby's eyes wandered down toward the dock. Sure enough, sitting near the fire pit roasting hotdogs was Logan. Gabe, in a chef apron, had joined him. When she turned back to the table, Eleanor waved her away.

"Go on, be with the young ones. Have fun."

Shelby said her goodbyes and approached Logan. "Need some help?"

"Sure thing." Logan handed her some hotdogs to put on the sticks to roast over an open fire.

"Oh, that smells so good," Shelby said. As people came over, she used tongs to place hotdogs on their plates. At an adjacent table were buns and every kind of fixing possible, from onions, to chili and cheese, to sauerkraut.

When the crowd thinned, Logan asked Gabe to take over so he and Shelby could eat. They loaded a few hotdogs on their plates and wandered over to dress them.

"What do you like on your dog?" Logan asked.

"I like everything," Shelby said. "Mustard, ketchup, onions, relish, cheese. No sauerkraut please."

"Me too," he said as they moved down the table. "This is my mom's secret Fourth of July potato salad her friend Jude gave her. You have to try it. She even makes her own mayo for it."

"I will," she said, piling it on her plate. It was made with red potatoes, eggs, and plenty of mayo as promised.

They took a seat at a small table under some trees where it was a bit quieter. It had a clear view of the lake. The outdoor lights reflected across the dark water with a dreamlike quality.

"I see your dad made it," she said.

Logan nodded but said nothing.

Shelby dug into the creamy potato salad and was not disappointed. "There are so many people here," she said. "I've never seen most of them."

"My dad invites some of his important clients to entertain, and my parents' friends often drive or fly up from the Bay Area for this event. They're fairly easy to spot from the locals."

Shelby grinned. Many of the guests were quite well dressed, and champagne was being served on trays going by, as well as crab-stuffed appetizers and shrimp puffs. Not your usual Fourth of July party. She turned when she heard her grandmother's sweet laugh behind them. Theo, in a crisp button-down shirt, sat alongside Alice. Shoulder to shoulder, they were obviously enjoying each other's company. It looked like Theo had his hand over Alice's as they talked.

"Looks like they're falling for each other," Logan said with a wink.

Shelby's heart warmed seeing them both happy again. She looked around at the beautiful scene that she was lucky enough to be a part of. She was with Logan. The charcoal-colored sky indicated that the fireworks were going to start soon, and they'd already started in her heart. Happiness was no longer throwing its shadow over her; it was shining its light.

"You look lovely tonight," Theo said to Alice. She seemed to have a glow about her now, and he hoped he had a little to do with that.

"Well, thanks. You look pretty good yourself."

Theo could feel himself blush. It had been a long time since a woman had given him a compliment. When he'd first arrived tonight, he'd walked around and said hello to many of the other guests. But the party had really started when Alice arrived, and he was happy they could get some more alone time.

The fireworks across the lake were gaining volume and Theo heard dogs barking anxiously in the distance. "I'm a little worried about Wally tonight," Theo said. "He hates loud noises."

"Poor baby," she said. "We don't have to stay long. Scarlett isn't fazed by anything. But if you want to leave soon…"

"Wally will be all right for a couple hours. I put him in his cozy kennel where he feels safe and added a few of his favorite treats to tempt him. And I'm enjoying sitting right here with you."

A smile lit Alice's face. "Me too. Did Wally get his appetite back yet?"

"I don't want to worry anyone. Dogs can be fussy, but he's

hardly eaten at all the last few days but a few treats. Today even that didn't interest him."

"Have you thought about bringing him to the vet?" Alice asked.

Theo's heart dropped at the thought that anything might be wrong with Wally. "Some," he said. "It might be all the excitement around the house. I think I'll wait until after the grand opening party for the dog park. Sometimes he seems fine, and others not. I know he's an old man, like me," he said with a smile.

Alice laughed. "Well, you let me know. I'm happy to go with you if you want."

"Thanks for the offer," Theo said. "I hope Trevor is fairing all right tonight. I haven't seen Mindy either."

"I hadn't thought of that," Alice said. "The fireworks must be hard on veterans. Mindy told me she wasn't up to a big gathering either."

"Trevor told me he has a routine for times like this and some exceptional headphones. I offered to bring some food by, but he said he had it covered."

Suddenly, a shaggy brown and white dog with its tail between his legs galloped furiously up to the deck. A firework went off and the dog howled before cowering under a table. Theo rose to assist the dog, but before he could get to it, Gabe rushed in and pulled the dog into his arms. Shelby and Logan were not far behind and ran to Gabe's side. Theo and Alice joined them.

"I wonder who that dog belongs to?" Alice said. "Let's go see if we can help."

The crowd hushed, backing up to give space to Gabe. The poor dog was curled up in Gabe's arms with his head on the boy's shoulder. Anthony DeLuca walked over and stood in front of his son. "Where did this dog come from?" he said.

Gabe glared up at him. "He's scared."

"Well, he doesn't belong here," Anthony said. "You know our rule about dogs."

Theo was surprised when Shelby spoke up. "Mr. DeLuca, I'm your neighbor across the street, Shelby, Alice Meyer's grand-daughter."

"She's my friend too," Logan said, standing up to his father.

"Is this your dog?" Mr. DeLuca asked Shelby.

She shook her head. "No, but I know where he lives, and I would be happy to take him home right now."

"I'll go with her," Gabe said.

"And me," Logan echoed.

Theo wished he could intervene and help them out, but he had no idea what to say. Alice gripped his hand as they waited for Anthony DeLuca to make a decision.

Anthony looked around and forced a smile to his guests. "Everything is fine here. Enjoy yourselves."

People backed away and conversations echoed in the air.

"Logan can go," Anthony finally said. "But it's dark out there, so come right back."

"The dog feels safe with me," Gabe protested. "I'm going too."

Their father shook his head and sighed. "Just be quick. You boys are supposed to be helping at the party."

Logan opened his mouth to say something and then closed it. Theo had a pretty good idea what he wanted to say. There was more hired help at this party than Theo had seen in any restaurant in town. The dog looked terrified, which made Theo think about Wally again.

Anthony turned back to his guests as if nothing had happened. Theo was glad when Alice spoke up. "Shelby, please let us know as soon as you return, and if you need anything, we're here."

Theo nodded in agreement and was graced by a grateful smile from Shelby.

Logan held up his cell phone and turned on the flashlight app. "We'll be fine."

"And right back," Gabe said.

Theo and Alice watched them walk down to the footpath that led to summer homes along the lake.

"That was nice of them to take that dog home," Alice said.

Eleanor and her husband approached them. "Well, you've got quite the granddaughter there," Eleanor said. "She even knows the stray dogs in town!"

"Yes," said Alice. "I'm very proud of her."

"We both are," Theo chimed in.

"It's nice to have some family nearby, isn't it?" Eleanor said wistfully. She gazed up at her husband. "I sometimes miss ours, but we do love it here, don't we?"

Her husband nodded. "I think I could use a glass of wine about now."

"And one of those char-grilled burgers. The aroma is driving me crazy," Eleanor said.

"Well, what are we waiting for?" asked her husband.

"Getting hungry myself," Theo said. He looked to Alice. "Shall we join them?"

They walked over to the buffet table and picked up plates and buns. Anthony DeLuca was nearby flipping the burgers. He looked almost like a regular guy when he was in his shorts grilling.

"What kind would you like?" Anthony asked as they held up their plates. "I've got medium rare or well done."

"I'll have the well done," Theo said.

Alice groaned. "Medium rare for me."

They walked over and put all the fixings and sides on. At the end of the table was a punch bowl of sangria, with limes and fresh berries floating on the surface. Alice filled up her cup with the fragrant drink.

"I think I'll have a beer," Theo said, reaching into one of the many overstocked coolers.

Behind them, Eleanor and her husband had started a conversation with another couple. They seemed to know everyone in town, Theo thought. Probably because of her political experience and being quite the socialite.

Plates full, glasses in hand, Theo suggested they go back to their table under the trees. "It's a real treat to eat food that someone else cooks for a change, and homemade to boot," Theo said.

"Well, we can fix that," Alice said. "You can come over for dinner anytime. In fact, why don't you come over the night after we do the grand opening? The three of us, and the dogs, can celebrate with a special dinner."

"I'd love to," Theo said.

Alice held up her cup for a toast. "It's a date."

A barge containing fireworks floated a few hundred feet from the DeLucas' deck. After a quick announcement, the show began. Whistling fireworks shot up into the sky in an astounding array of colors. Theo looked over to Alice's joy-filled face, lit up by the lights overhead. For that moment, they were both like kids again, mesmerized by the dazzling Fourth of July display.

CHAPTER 21

*S*helby was awakened from a deep sleep by the sound of a car door slamming in the cul-de-sac. She got out of bed and walked over to the window. Carefully, she peeked out of the blinds. A low fog dimmed the early morning light, but she could still see the black limo in Logan's driveway across the way. Iris was standing in a nightgown and robe with her arms crossed over her chest as she watched the car speed away. Logan stood beside her. He wrapped his arm around his mother's shoulder and guided her back in the house.

Mr. DeLuca had just arrived at the lake only two nights ago for the Fourth of July party and was leaving already? Shelby had noticed a tension between him and the family, and it was not helped by Mutt showing up. She turned to go back to bed, but Scarlett was at her feet, whining to go outside for her morning ritual.

"It's a little early," Shelby said. "But all right, let's go."

After throwing on some jeans and a sweatshirt, she leashed the dog and grabbed her cell phone. Logan had looked pretty down. Maybe he would like to join them on the walk, so Shelby texted him.

Heading out with Scarlett for an early walk. Want to join us?

Shelby brushed her teeth and hair in the bathroom while waiting for a reply.

Yes. Meet you out front, he answered.

The birdsong was like a symphony overhead as they walked toward the water. The morning mist rose from the surface of the lake, warmed by the sun penetrating through the fog. Shelby waited for Logan to speak first, not wanting to pry.

They sat down on the damp sand and stared out over the water. Scarlett lay down beside Shelby and nudged into her leg.

"You're up early," Logan said. "Did we wake you?"

She knew exactly what he was referring to but tread lightly. "I was ready to get up soon anyway. It's the grand opening today for the dog park."

Logan kicked some sand with his foot. "Right, congrats. I wish I didn't have to work." He took a deep breath. "I'm sorry for the scene this morning."

"I didn't hear anything except the slamming of the limo door."

When he turned to her, his eyes were moist. "They fought after the guests left the party the other night, and again this morning as my dad packed to leave for another work trip. Gabe and I stayed in our rooms, but the argument was hard to miss. She was upset he was brokering deals during the party instead of being with the family. And he made such a big deal about Mutt showing up, then brought a quick end to the conversation when my mother tried to intervene. It doesn't take much anymore to get them started. My mother ran in the house crying when he left and will probably spend the rest of the day in bed. I wish I could do something for her."

"I'm so sorry," she said. "I wonder what your dad's deal is with dogs, anyway."

"Who knows?" Logan said. "My mom said once he'd been chased by a big black dog on his way to school as a young child. But it's hard to imagine my dad letting that faze him."

"Some things never cease to scare us," Shelby said.

Logan shrugged. "I guess."

"I'm glad we got Mutt home safe and sound that night," Shelby said. "Gabe is a quick thinker. You've got to hand it to him, snatching some food for Mrs. Williams and the dog from the party."

"He's a great kid," Logan said. "I just wish my dad would hang around long enough to notice it."

Shelby thought a moment, trying to figure out what to say. "It's hard to be happy when our parents are miserable."

Logan hugged her in close. "You always seem to understand."

"You can tell me anything," Shelby said.

He titled her chin up to meet his gaze. "Thank you. And you can always tell me anything, too."

Shelby thought about his offer. She'd never had anyone to really tell about her mother. The shame and fear of judgment had kept her holding that burden all to herself. "It's been hard living with my mother moving all the time, no money or friends. But I can see how it can be just as hard even with all those things."

Logan smiled. "So what is the secret to happiness do you think? Running away and leaving our parents far behind?"

"Oh no, I already tried that once. It lasted an hour!"

His laugh was contagious, and Shelby joined in. Logan ruffled her hair before kissing her on the forehead.

"We're lucky to have each other," he said.

Shelby's breath caught. And what about when he left at the end of summer?

"What's the frown about?" he asked.

"Sorry. I love what you said. It's just...sometimes I wonder why you like me when you could have any girl?"

"I don't want any girl, Shelby. I didn't think I could find a girl like you. Beautiful on the inside and outside. Honest, real, and truly caring about others."

"No one other than my grandmother has ever told me that before," Shelby said. "Especially a boy."

"Then they are all crazy and don't deserve you."

She reached up and stroked Logan's face. "I think I'm still dreaming."

His warm kiss sent her mind and heart spinning. She melted into his arms as the kiss lingered.

"Do you still think you're dreaming?" Logan asked.

"Now I know I am!"

IT WAS FINALLY the grand opening of the dog park. Shelby and her grandmother were on their way to Theo's, with Scarlett trotting along next to them.

"Scarlett," Alice said as they approached Theo's back gate, "you're going to get to see all your friends today."

"Morning," Theo said as they entered the backyard. "I thought I'd let Wally out alone a little before the crowd gets here. He's still not feeling that great, so he may want to just go in and sleep."

"Oh, I'm sorry to hear that," Alice said. "I hope he feels better soon."

Scarlett yanked toward Wally. Keeping her on the leash, Shelby let her sniff the tired-looking beagle, but Wally didn't respond in kind. He just waddled back up the steps and went inside.

Wally just didn't seem right. Scarlett was whining for her friend to come back out. Shelby was concerned, too. "It's okay, Scarlett, there'll be more dogs here soon." She let the dog off the leash and Scarlett launched for the ramp that Trevor had built. It was about three feet high in the middle with inclines at both ends, and Scarlett raced up and back on it many times.

"Well, she seems to love that," Alice said, "Maybe we need one of those."

"You can always ask Trevor to build you one," Theo said.

"Did I just hear my name?" Trevor came walking in with Buddy at his side. Mindy and Karma were with him.

"No more cast," Shelby said.

Mindy held up her leg. "Just a little brace now, but I still have to be careful." She released Karma, who ran straight to Shelby.

"Hi, girl," she said, petting the energetic black and white shepherd. Scarlett came racing over, barking at Karma to play with her. Off they went circling the yard, through the nylon tunnel, up the ramp, and then directly for the box of toys.

"I brought something," Mindy said. "A rope and ball chew toy I ordered online."

Trevor removed Buddy's vest and gave the sign for him to play. Mindy tossed the toy to the golden dog, who promptly caught it.

"Oh, Buddy, you've still got it," Trevor said. Buddy shook the toy and tossed it in the air before catching it again in his mouth.

"Impressive," Mindy said, smiling up at Trevor. Then she looked over at Shelby. "This park is fantastic. Thank you. I'm so glad Karma hasn't been locked in the house with me all this time. She would have gone completely crazy."

"So how can I help today?" Trevor asked Shelby.

Shelby looked around. Everything was ready and in its place. There was fresh water in the drinking station, plenty of doggy bags and toys. The yard had been freshly cut, probably by Trevor. Everything was perfect. The dog park of her dreams. She could feel tears pooling in her eyes.

Theo came over beside her and put his arm around her shoulder. He looked over to Trevor. "We couldn't have done it without you. So just enjoy."

"Aww," said Trevor, "it was nothing."

Mindy, in a bright-colored sundress and sandals, reached for Trevor's hand. "You made a real difference here. Now let's go throw some balls."

Trevor's smile was bright, and so was Mindy's. Shelby was happy to see it. The shadows from Trevor's face seemed gone, and his eyes brighter somehow.

"I haven't seen Trevor smile like that before," Theo said. "He was so sad when he moved here a few years back. I think Mindy's been good for him."

"I think they're good for each other," Shelby said.

"Agreed," Theo said. "I wonder how long Mindy will be here before heading back to the city."

Shelby shook her head. "I'm not sure. I know she'd rather stay here."

They watched Trevor throw balls and the dogs tear after them. For a quick break, they'd trot over to the water station and have a big, sloppy drink.

Joann arrived carrying a basket of tennis balls, which she placed on the grass next to them. "This should keep you all for a while."

Shelby reached over and picked one up with each hand and threw them out into the yard.

"Thanks for bringing them, Joann."

"Great idea, Joann," Mindy said as she joined them.

"Oh, I wouldn't miss this," she said. "A chance to pet dogs, and who knows, just maybe I'll get one soon."

Shelby gave Joann a little hug. "When you're ready."

"Right," Joann said. "It's really not fair to get another dog when my heart is still filled with Roxie." She stared out at the dogs, a faraway look on her face. "I'm so lonely for a furry companion. My home seems so empty without one."

"I understand," Mindy said. "I don't know what I'd do without Karma. If you need any help picking one out, let me know."

Joann sighed. "Thanks. I'll probably go to Friends for Life Rescue outside of town and look around to see if one calls to my heart."

"Count me in, if you want help too," Shelby said.

Suddenly there was loud yipping, and two little, white furballs came racing in the grassy yard with Eleanor trailing behind them.

"Those two have been barking the whole way," Eleanor said, fanning herself. "I don't know how you manage to walk them, Shelby. They pulled the entire time."

"I get it," Shelby said. "I can show you some ways to use a collar and some commands, if you'd like. My Grandpa Stan used to show me how to work with dogs when they still had the farm."

"That would be wonderful. They're wearing me out, those two. Look at them."

The pups were running up and down the ramp, followed by Scarlett, followed by Karma, followed by Buddy in the rear. All of the adults stood together watching.

"My yard has never been so full of happy dogs." Theo looked toward the house. "I wish Wally was up to coming out."

"Where is he?" Trevor asked.

"He's not feeling well today. I think I'm going to have to take him in to see the vet soon if he doesn't perk up."

"That's too bad," Mindy said. "Keep us posted."

Karma headed for the waste area and the others followed. The humans raced for doggy bags just in case.

"I don't know what it is about dogs," Eleanor said. "The minute one goes, they all have to."

Shelby had noticed that herself. She'd read some helpful books lately on canine companions to stay informed with her business. Dogs were pack animals who marked their territory. Other dogs who came upon the scent could discern a lot about fellow canines in the neighborhood.

Amidst the barking, Josh's voice called out, "Hi, everyone. Sorry we're late." Alongside him were Steph and little Oscar. "Steph's dad's holding down the shop, so we were both able to come for this special occasion."

Steph walked over and held a big box in front of her. "And

guess what we brought? A happy dog park grand opening ice cream cake."

Shelby lifted the pink lid to find cute faces of various breeds, plus polka dot marzipan dog bones along the buttercream border of the cake. Right in the center was Moonwater Lake. "You decorated this?"

Josh pointed to his wife. "She's the artistic one."

"Shall we retire to the deck and partake before it melts?" Theo said. Waiting for them there were paper plates and forks courtesy of Alice, who had been busy in the kitchen prepping. Alice cut and served the cake all around, while Shelby passed out homemade peanut butter apple dog treats to the canines before taking a seat next to Mindy. Everyone chatted around the table and ate their cake.

"This is delicious," Mindy said.

Shelby nodded. "How are you doing now that you can walk and get around more?"

Mindy shrugged. "Well, to be honest, now that I'm healing, my parents are starting to put pressure on me to come back to San Jose."

Shelby's stomach dropped at the thought of her mother doing something similar. And without any notice.

Mindy continued. "They think because I can get around some, I should be rushing home and get back to my office job in the city. My employer keeps emailing to find out when I can return too." She paused. "And you know what I finally figured out, Shelby? I don't want to go. I'm having a great time here, and so is Karma."

"Do you have to go back?" Shelby asked.

Mindy thought for a moment. "No, not really. With enough persuasion, I'm sure my job would let me work remote. Or, there are a million other companies that would hire me. I don't want my job taking over my life again."

"Good call," Theo said, joining in the conversation.

"I talk big," Mindy said, "but I'm a little afraid if I tell my parents, they might just drive up here and try to drag me home."

"Well, you're a little old for that," Theo kidded. "But honestly, we're here if you need us."

"You're right," she said. "I own my lake house, am a self-supporting adult, and it's my life."

Shelby considered what it would be like to be independent, to have her own job and her own house and not be controlled by the whims of her mother. She imagined it would feel darn good. The time would come for her, if she worked hard, stayed the course with school, and was true to herself like Mindy was doing.

A warm breeze drifted up from the lake and with it a flock of white pelicans appeared overhead, their wings spread wide. Shelby listened to the voices of her new friends and watched the dogs frolic in the yard. She'd been an intrinsic part of creating all of this, and it felt like home.

"I brought a little gift for everyone," Eleanor said from across the table. She opened her purse and brought out a small bag and took out a small art print. "Look at this," she said. The colorful picture had two dogs sitting near a lake. "I was in the city last week at an art festival and thought this artist's work was perfect for today's occasion. I just couldn't resist. I got one for each of you," she said, handing them out.

"I love it," Shelby said. "Thank you."

Alice leaned over for a look. "Delightful and so kind of you."

"You are all welcome," she said. "I remember when my husband used to buy me sweet little gifts like this. It's been a long time," Eleanor said wistfully. "All he does now is play golf. I hardly see him."

Eleanor chuckled but Shelby could see the sadness in her eyes. Eleanor always seemed so together, busy with a million friends. It was hard to imagine her being lonely too.

"It's always been obvious how much Charles adores you," Theo said.

Eleanor sighed. "Lately, we're just two ships passing in the night. Or day." She looked out at her dogs. "Thank goodness for my two fluffy babies."

Dogs really were best friends to so many people, and Shelby was glad bringing everyone here together would help too.

Alice retrieved another pitcher of frosty iced tea and placed it on the table. She took her seat next to Theo. "The carefree life of a dog," Alice said, pointing at the dogs who were spread out on the deck next to them napping in the sun.

Josh laughed. "Those lucky dogs. They sleep, they eat, they don't have to work."

Steph turned to him and playfully tapped him on the shoulder. "You enjoy your job and so do I."

"So true. It's just that all the tourists get to be a bit much sometimes. It's nice to have a break. "

"Don't forget it's those tourists that keep us going through the winter when we close for three months," Steph said.

"And a million little children," he answered.

"Oh, but they're so cute," Steph said.

Josh rolled his eyes. Shelby watched Steph's smile disappear. She hoped Josh and Steph would work this out soon. Steph really wanted kids. Shelby wondered if her own mother had wanted a child. Dana had been in her early twenties when the love of her life had died and left her with four-year-old Shelby. Back in her high school psychology class, Shelby had read about how sometimes when people have devastating loss, it stunts their emotional growth. Perhaps her mother was stuck at age twenty-two. At least there had not been any more frantic calls from Dana, and Shelby hoped that was a good thing. But her stomach knotted just thinking about it, so she pulled her thoughts back where they belonged on this wonderful day.

The temperature was rising and even the umbrella over the table was offering little shade. Shelby was glad they had met in the morning. Some of the dogs were lying under trees, panting. The water bowl had been replenished multiple times, and Trevor had kept a hose close by.

"I think the dogs are getting tired," Theo said, surveying the scene.

"Agreed," Mindy said, standing up and calling Karma to her. "What a wonderful idea this was. Thank you again, Theo, for having us over."

Steph and Josh called for Oscar, who paid absolutely no attention. "We better get back and relieve my dad. He's got Emily helping, but it's our busiest time of day," Steph said.

"Of course," Shelby said. "Let me walk you to the gate."

Eventually they caught Oscar, who was much more interested in chewing on one of the new toys than running and hiding with it. Slowly, everyone left, each person cleaning up, putting things away. Trevor made sure everything was in order before taking Mindy home.

Alice and Theo were still on the deck talking when Shelby returned from saying goodbye to everyone. As she walked up the steps, she heard Alice talking about the bathroom sink, how she needed to call a plumber. Theo promptly offered help.

"I'll make tonight's dinner extra special then," Alice said. "That's the least I can do." Theo smiled. "No need, I'm glad to help."

Awww, Shelby thought. Maybe I'll just conveniently be out during that dinner so they can have some time alone.

Theo smiled at Shelby. "I think we had quite the grand opening. Enjoyed by all, people and dogs alike."

"It was wonderful," she said.

Theo rose. "I'll walk you two ladies to the gate." When he eyed Scarlett, he added, "Sorry, three ladies."

"Are you sure you wouldn't rather rest tonight after this busy morning?" Alice asked.

"Oh no," Theo said. "I'm going to go take a nap with Wally, and I'll be good as new by tonight."

"See you at six," Alice said.

CHAPTER 22

*B*efore heading over to Alice's house for dinner, Theo offered Wally some of his favorite roast chicken treats. After Wally took a few bites, Theo breathed a sigh of relief. "Good boy." Wally rolled over and let Theo rub his belly. "My sweet boy, what would I do without you?"

He watched the dog pad over and drop in his bed by the fireplace. Wally kept one eye open, watching Theo brush off any dog hair from his khaki pants and gather his things before leaving. Theo had a pang of guilt that he was leaving the dog home, but he didn't think Wally was up for the outing.

"I'm going out for a little while," Theo said. The dog's ears perked up. "I know you won't mind, because you'll be sleeping. I won't be late." He petted the dog's head and looked into his beautiful brown eyes.

Theo had always loved beagles. So had his wife.

"Ah, Jean," he said, "our little furry boy's getting so old." He took a deep breath and continued. "I'm going over to Alice's tonight. Have a little dinner. I'll let you know how it goes." Theo laughed to himself. He could almost feel Jean's approval settle in his heart.

He waited until Wally had lowered his head, curled up in his bed, and shut his eyes. The dog's breathing was even and calm. Theo remembered to bring Alice's gift before locking the door behind him. Earlier today, after his nap, he'd gone to the Lakeview flower cart in town and bought a bouquet of colorful Gerbera daisies. He held them behind his back as he walked up the steps and knocked on the door.

"Right on time," Alice said as she opened the door. The fragrant aroma of herbs and spices greeted him as well.

Alice's silver-gray hair waved around her pretty heart-shaped face. She was slightly flushed, probably from cooking, but her smile was what took his breath away. "For you," he said, handing her the flowers.

"How sweet of you," she said, her blue eyes sparkling. "They're beautiful. Let me get a vase. Come on in."

"Where's Shelby?" he asked.

"She thought she'd try the new fish and chips place and hang out down by the water for a while."

"I see," Theo said. "I don't suppose our dinner plans had anything to do with that?"

Alice chuckled. "That's probably it. Or she's tired of hearing us old people talk."

"Anything I can do to help?" he asked.

"Just have a seat at the table. I hope you like what I made. One of my specialties, curried chicken over basmati rice, with a spinach salad and homemade green goddess dressing."

"A feast," Theo said. "I love curry and there's really nowhere in town that makes a good one."

"I'm delighted." Alice placed two ceramic plates steaming with the chicken dish on the table next to the matching bowls filled with salad. There was an iced mug at Theo's setting.

"Would you like a beer?" she asked.

Theo was flattered Alice remembered what he enjoyed. "Do you have any of that good amber ale?"

"I certainly do." Alice brought him the bottle and poured herself a little bit of a light peach-colored rosé before sitting down.

"You are quite the cook," he said.

"You haven't even tasted it yet," Alice said.

Theo lifted his mug for a toast. "To the wonderful people of Moonwater Lake and its new dog park."

Alice clinked. "And to good friends."

Theo enjoyed the malty flavor of the ale. Friends, Alice had said. Was that a message to him that he was in the "friend category" with her? Why was he even thinking about this? What did he really want from their relationship?

Theo wasted no more time digging into the wonderful meal. Their conversation flowed easily, from town politics to volunteer opportunities. He couldn't remember the last time he'd felt this comfortable and relaxed. It was as if they'd known each other for a very long time. He looked over at Alice and recognized a part of himself. This was a woman who had also known love, a soulmate relationship, and ultimately great loss. Was it possible to feel that way again?

"Penny for your thoughts," Alice said.

"Only a penny," Theo said.

Both of them laughed at the trite and overused phrase. How much was he willing to share? What did he have to lose at this point? "I was thinking how enjoyable and easy it is to spend time with you."

Alice hesitated and he hoped he hadn't said too much.

"Guilty," she said with a grin. "Me too."

Their eyes met and Theo's heart did a little jig.

After dinner was devoured, Alice offered dessert. Even though home-baked strawberry pie sounded incredible, Theo asked politely if they could have dessert later. Theo insisted he take a look at the problem faucet next. It would be an easy fix, he determined and asked if she had a wrench. Alice produced her husband's old tool kit, and Theo found replacement washers that allowed him to fix the leak right up.

"Shall we sit outside for a while?" Alice asked.

Out on the porch, they sat side by side in the wicker chairs. Theo reached over and took Alice's hand. Her soft, warm fingers gently squeezed back. Blazing through the branches of the manzanita trees were strands of indigo and burnt umber sky. Moments like this stirred hope in his heart and brightened the path of his future

They sat in silence for a little bit, enjoying the moment. Theo thought about how important each day was, especially later in life, when we had to count them. As the sun moved out of sight to another time and place, a splattering of stars welcomed the night sky. Perhaps he should leave soon and let Alice get some sleep.

"Thank you again for a wonderful dinner," Theo said.

"And thank you for fixing my faucet. I must admit," Alice said, "I am not used to having to deal with things like that myself. My husband took care of so many things. I've had to learn quite a bit since he passed."

"I'm sure you have," Theo said. "It's not easy."

"But it's good for me. It's helping me grow," Alice said. "I need to be more independent."

Theo squeezed her hand gently. "Well, it's also good to have friends and people who are there when you need them."

He basked in her gentle smile.

"You're right," she said. "It's been wonderful having Shelby here, too. I wish she could stay. I've never seen that girl so happy and confident, and we have wonderful schools at Moonwater Lake."

"Well, why can't she?" Theo said. "From what Shelby has confided in me briefly, her mother is off with a new boyfriend and may not return." He could feel Alice's hand stiffen in his and hoped he hadn't said anything to upset her.

"You don't know her mother," Alice said with a deep sigh.

"Dana has been unpredictable for a long time now. Shelby has had very little stability in her life because of it. I'm sorry to say that about my own daughter. Sometimes I blame myself and my husband. She was our only child and was very ill as a baby. We never stopped coddling her, giving in to her. And did she ever learn how to manipulate us. I fear Dana never grew up."

"Kids are hard sometimes," Theo said. "Believe me, I understand. I encouraged my son to get a good education, to travel, see the world. He sure did, and then he never came back. We Skype."

"I know what you mean," Alice said. "Families are all spread out now."

"My son thinks I should move to Seattle to be closer to him and his wife," Theo said. "Where they can more conveniently keep an eye on me. I told him I absolutely do not want to leave my home and my lake."

"I understand," Alice said. "Being in my own home is important to me. Getting older can be tough, but we also need to maintain our own lifestyle for as long as possible."

"I agree," Theo said. "Your granddaughter Shelby has helped breathe new life into our little town."

"She's helping out Mrs. Williams too," Alice said.

"Is Mrs. Williams still here?" he asked. "I thought her husband passed a few years ago. All alone out there, I'd assumed she'd gone to live with family."

"So did I," Alice said. "It seems she refused to leave her house. I understand from Eleanor, who is seeing what help is available, that there is a social worker who checks on her sometimes and she gets Meals on Wheels." Alice lowered her voice. "Shelby tells me, and this is top secret, that Mrs. Williams has a little dog, and she's trying to help out with it too."

"That's nice of her," Theo said. "Great girl that one. Big heart."

Alice nodded. "I was thinking I'd go check on Mrs. Williams soon too."

"Let me know if you want some company," Theo said.

The evening chill was setting in, and Theo didn't want to keep Alice up too late or Wally waiting too long. He stood and offered Alice his hand.

"It's getting late. I'd better be going now," he said reluctantly.

Alice stood facing him on the steps. "Whenever you're ready."

"To be honest," Theo said, "I'm quite worried about Wally."

"Of course," Alice said. "The vet in town is closed on the weekends. But if I remember correctly, the emergency one is open. But it's almost an hour away."

"Maybe I can get him through until Monday. Either way, its time."

"Let me know how he's doing," Alice said as she waved goodbye. "Wait. You forgot dessert."

Theo patted his very full stomach. "Maybe tomorrow?"

"I'll bring some by," Alice said.

Theo walked the six blocks to his house. The balmy night was clear, and a multitude of stars punctuated the sky. California weather could be wonderful. A lot better than Seattle, he thought to himself.

He opened his front door, feeling better than he had in a very long time. "Wally. Wally. Where are you?"

Turning to switch on the light, he tripped on the small rug on the hardwood. As he tried to break the fall with his hands, his knee hit the floor with a thud. Pain radiated through his body. It was shocking to flail through the air, in your own house no less. It was probably the one beer, an old rug, and the dark. Why hadn't he left on more lights?

When Theo could focus again, he looked around. Wally had not come to greet him. Tears threatened. It was times like this he wished he wasn't alone anymore. He caught his breath and felt around his body. Nothing was broken. He hoped he could stand. Carefully, he pushed himself up to a seated position and, as he did, noticed the picture of his wife on the end table.

"What was I thinking?" he said to her. "Jean, I'm too old for this stuff. Taking flowers to a woman, thinking I'm young again, and then falling right on my face."

He managed to pull himself up and leaned his weight against the couch. Across the room Wally lay motionless on his bed, even with all the commotion. Theo made his way slowly over and sat down on a chair next to him. "Oh, Wally," he said, petting the dog's soft head. Wally barely opened his eyes. "I know the feeling," Theo said. "I'll let you sleep."

Theo wished he could carry the dog to his bed, but it was just not possible. He placed a blanket over Wally and hobbled into his bedroom. He managed to peel off his clothes and climb under the covers. He really couldn't think anymore. He just wanted to sleep.

CHAPTER 23

*T*heo knew he should get up, but the effort it would take seemed overwhelming. Every muscle ached, but none more than the one in his chest. He imagined what a broken heart might look like. Did it actually have a jagged crack down the center? Were pieces falling off and drifting into his bloodstream? Sunlight pierced through the window blinds, reminding him the morning was slipping away. Had dinner with Alice last night been just a dream to remind him of what he couldn't have? It had felt so right.

Wally nudged in closer.

"I see you made it to the bed after all," Theo said to the dog.

Wally gave him the "please take me out" look with his irresistible brown eyes nestled in his white fur. Theo knew he had to get up and at least let the dog out. They had to stick to their routine: outside, breakfast, and then their daily constitutional walk along the lake path.

"Okay, boy, I get it," he said. Theo groaned as he sat up in bed. His knee throbbed, a painful reminder of last night's fall. He slid his legs over the side of the bed, rose, and stretched. When his wife, Jean, was alive, they would "rise and shine" each morning and Wally would leap in the air, excited to start their day. No one was leaping anymore. Theo wearily put on his slippers and a robe and let the dog out the sliding door. Theo watched Wally wander the grass, determining his perfect spot before doing his business. A dog's needs were quite simple. Food, a good place to pee, a walk, and love. For offering him those simple things, Wally gave his full heart in return. And for now, Theo would give what was left of his heart to his faithful, furry companion.

Once finished with his business, the dog shuffled sluggishly up the steps and through the open door toward the kitchen. Some things never changed. But all things changed eventually, Theo reminded himself. If he lost Wally...

"Don't even think about it," he said aloud.

After feeding Wally and watching him pick at his food, Theo contemplated his own breakfast. He wasn't hungry. A wave of fatigue washed over him. He'd worked enough in social work settings to know the signs and cycles of grief. "Make sure you eat," his doctor had told him.

Perhaps some coffee. While heating water for instant coffee, he thought about how his son Cameron in Seattle would cringe if he knew his dad did not use fresh-ground beans. A travesty. Theo snickered. He made himself a piece of wheat toast and sat down at the dining room table to watch the birds dive in and out of the feeder attached to his window. Due to the marshes and grasses around the lake, the variety of birds at the lake was plentiful. Jean had delighted in the parade of sparrows, finches, and wrens that came to visit. She would be happy to see the fresh seed he added every day, especially in winter.

A furry chin rested on Theo's foot. He bent down and patted the dog on the head. "Are you ready for your walk?" he asked. He stood and assessed his ability to walk. Limp was more like it. "It will have to be a short one," he said.

Wally headed to the door, where his leash dangled from a

hook. Routines were important to keep. Sometimes that was all you had any control of.

∽

THE AROMA of fresh-brewed coffee lured Shelby from her room. It definitely helped motivate her to get up early for dog walks. She walked out in her pajamas and heard her Grandma Alice humming in the kitchen. The scent of cinnamon and butter made her mouth water.

"Good morning." Shelby said.

Alice hummed as she moved around the kitchen, dressed and freshly made up. "Good morning. Did you sleep well?"

Shelby was surprised to see her grandmother so animated, and then she remembered Theo had come to dinner last night. And there were fresh flowers in a glass vase on the table.

Shelby smiled. "Someone's happy this morning."

Alice shrugged it off and reached for the coffee pot. "Would you like a cup?"

After pouring coffee for Shelby, Alice picked up a spatula on the counter by the stove. "I'm making you some French toast. You used to love it when you were a little girl."

This was going to be a wonderful morning, but a real sugar rush. "I have less than an hour until I have to pick up Mindy's dog. I've got to check my calendar; I think I have Dixie and Ruby today too."

"Have a seat," Alice said. "I've been soaking the bread in a vanilla, cinnamon, and egg mixture with a touch of cream, and it's ready for the frying pan. We used to call it railroad French toast when you were little, do you remember?"

"I think I do."

"Your grandpa and I took you and your mother on the Coast Starlight train all the way to Oregon for a vacation. All you could talk about after the trip was the choo choo French toast."

Shelby sipped her coffee. "How old was I?"

Alice placed the gooey bread in the buttered frying pan, letting it sizzle as it cooked. "You were about five. Your dad had passed away the year before, and your mom was grieving. Grandpa and I decided to take you both up to Oregon and try and get everybody's mind off things. Your mom spent the whole time looking out the window and sleeping, but we took you to the wonderful Portland zoo."

"I remember. Didn't you buy me a hat with a face on it and long braids hanging down?"

"That's right!" Alice dished up the French toast and topped it with a splash of powdered sugar. "There you go. Enjoy."

This is the life, Shelby thought. She took a bite out of the buttery breakfast and moaned. "No one can make it like you, Grandma."

"Well, thanks. I know it's a bit heavy for summer, but I'm happy to make it anytime."

"Where's your breakfast?" asked Shelby.

"I ate an hour ago. I've been up fussing, getting the first batch of cookies... Oh, the cookies! I ought to go check on them."

Alice was deftly creating magic in her kitchen, just like the old days. Change was possible under the right circumstances, Shelby thought. She was beginning to feel like a new person herself. She thought about Logan. He was so... She hated to use the word dreamy, but that summed it up pretty well.

"The cookies are done," Alice said. "I'll let them cool and we'll give them a try."

"So, what are you baking this morning?" Shelby said, finishing off her French toast.

"I thought we'd try some of the ginger cookie sandwiches that your Aunt Judy used to make. Do you remember them? They're very simple but delicious. Spicy, soft on the inside."

"What's the occasion?"

"Oh, nothing. I might just drop some over to Theo, kind of a good morning treat along with a piece of strawberry pie from last night. I baked some more dog cookies as well in hopes that they'll tempt poor Wally."

"I'm a little worried about him, too," Shelby said. "I know he's old, but hounds usually live to eat."

"I agree," Alice said. "Theo's afraid to find out what's wrong. I don't think he can deal with any more loss."

Shelby placed her fork down beside her almost-empty plate. "That would be awful. I don't even want to think about it." She looked down to see Scarlett sitting at her feet, waiting for any a morsel to drop. Shelby snuck her a tiny bite of French toast and Scarlett scarfed it up.

In the kitchen, Alice packaged up the sweets and treats. Her grandmother had barely ever used a computer and had been very excited when Shelby had shown her how to use Google to find a healthy pet recipe online. She'd been a willing student and learned fast.

Shelby rinsed off her plate in the sink. "If you wait for me to take a quick shower, I'll walk you to Theo's house," Shelby said. "It's on my way and I can cut through Misty Meadow Lane to get to Mindy's."

Alice had decided to leave Scarlett home, just in case Theo invited her in for awhile. Scarlett had so much energy and might disturb Wally. They walked a few blocks down the tree-lined path toward the lake, the morning sun driving the temperature up quickly. Soon Theo's house came into view through the trees. Shelby stood at the edge of the yard and watched Alice, packages in hand, walk up the steps and knock on the door. There was no barking that Shelby could hear, and a thread of worry gnawed at her stomach. If she didn't leave now, she was going to be late, so she turned to go. Alice would fill her in later when she got home.

CHAPTER 24

Theo peered out the window. Alice stood on the porch, packages in her hand. He wished he could turn around and ignore the knock. He'd come back from his walk and put his pajamas back on. He didn't feel like seeing anyone looking like this. Alice knocked again. He really didn't want to be rude; she'd done nothing wrong. He pulled his robe closed and cracked open the door. "Good morning," he said.

"I brought you something," Alice said, holding up the containers.

"Thanks." He reached out his hand through the small opening, and as he did, he saw the expression on Alice's face fall. He felt horrible.

"Everything okay?" she said.

He sighed and opened the door all the way. She gasped when she saw his full face. His own quick glance at the bruise in the mirror this morning had caused him the same response.

"What happened to you?" she said.

"Nothing, nothing. You know, just a little accident. I'm fine."

"Are you sure? Remember, I used to work as a nurse. If you need anything…"

"I'm fine," he snapped, taking a step back in the shadows of his living room.

There was an awkward silence when he didn't invite her in.

Alice handed him the containers. "I brought you a piece of strawberry pie and some dog cookies to tempt Wally."

"Very kind," he said, taking them from her. He felt guiltier by the minute for making her uncomfortable, but it was not the right time to invite anyone in. "I don't know if anything will tempt Wally. He won't even get out of bed."

"Let me know if there's anything I can do," she said.

The sympathy in her eyes made him feel worse. "There's nothing, but thanks. I just need to go lie down."

She nodded and turned to go.

Theo shut the door behind him and leaned against it for support. Alice probably thought he was trying to make her go away, which he was, but not because he didn't like her. It was because he did, and he really didn't know what to do with all these conflicting feelings today. And he just plain hurt all over. If she'd seen the multicolored bruise on his knee, she would have insisted on getting some help.

Wally was still lying in his bed by the fireplace. Just maybe, one of Alice's treats would get a response. But when Theo tried to interest him in one, Wally just turned his head away.

It was hard enough when Jean died, and now Wally. On top of that, he realized it was the morning of his weekly Skype call with his son. Another thing he didn't want to do. He went over to the computer in hopes that sending a message that he wasn't feeling well would delay the call. But the minute he logged in, the call was already ringing, and the video camera was turned on. He considered turning his side off, but his son would interrogate him even more.

"Good morning," Cam said, looking as chipper and clean-cut as ever in his designer tennis clothes.

Theo stepped back from the camera a little and dimmed the

light. At first, his son talked about his busy life and the trips they were planning. Theo found himself tuning it all out. He felt a bit woozy and dropped down into the computer chair. When there was no response from Cameron about his appearance, Theo wondered if his son even looked at the screen during these calls.

"Dad?"

Theo perked up. "Yes?"

"What happened to you? Is that a bruise?"

The lecture started and Theo wished he'd never answered the call.

"I told you, you need to come live with us," Cam said. "You're there all by yourself and it's not fair to make us worry like this."

Him worry! Theo thought. He figured his son just wanted him closer, so if anything happened it wouldn't inconvenience him. "Just stop," Theo said. "I'm fine. I have friends, I have my home, I have my dog." His voice quivered on that one. "You don't need to spend your valuable time worrying about me."

"That's not fair, Dad. We care about you. Maybe I need to come out there and check for myself."

For a moment Theo wavered. It might be nice to see his son. But then, he reconsidered. "Look, I might be old, but I'm not feeble. I can take care of myself and you don't need to make the trip."

"Fine," Cam answered. "Sorry to ask. But at least let me know if you need anything. Okay? And be more careful. I'll talk to you next week."

Theo turned off the camera and closed his computer. He really didn't want to talk to anyone. And he didn't need another worry like whether his son wanted to put him in some kind of care facility. And who knew where they'd put poor Wally? Theo sighed. If he was still alive.

He held his hands to his head, carefully avoiding the painful bruise. Jean would be angry with him for how he'd just treated

Alice and Cam. He wasn't a happy man at the moment. If he lost Wally, he couldn't bear it. And now he had probably lost Alice.

Theo wandered outside on the deck in hopes that the morning light would lift his spirits. The dog park structures in the yard waited for the next meeting. He hoped there would still be one. Negative thoughts poured in, threatening to overtake him.

"Oh, Jean," he said aloud. "I just don't know how much longer I can keep going."

CHAPTER 25

*J*ust as Shelby turned the corner on the way to Mindy's house, she received a text from Dana. She wished she hadn't given her mother her cell phone number, but Dana had insisted. "Besides," she'd said, "I want to send you pictures of Florida. It's so pretty." Ugh.

Urgent, must speak to you.

All she could think was, Not now. Dana had promised she'd only call Shelby's cell in an emergency, but here she was calling. Dana thought everything was an emergency. Before calling her mother, Shelby texted Mindy to say she might be a little late. Her appointment to walk Eleanor's dogs was scheduled for much later in the day, so she had enough time.

Works out perfectly for me, Mindy texted back. I didn't want to disrupt your morning, but if you could come in about an hour that would help a lot. My boss wants to do a conference call and it would be better if Karma was out then.

That did make it easier, Shelby thought. She was only a few blocks from home, so she decided to turn around and go back there and make the call to Dana in private. She texted her mother she'd call in a few minutes, but by the time she reached her grandmother's steps, her cell phone was already ringing.

"Hello, Mom," she said as she let herself in the door and greeted Scarlett. She sat down on a comfortable chair facing the front window, kicked off her shoes, and pulled her legs up under her.

"Hello, stranger," Dana answered.

Dana sounded perfectly fine, happy in fact. Shelby shook her head. "What's up? I'm kind of in a rush. I have my dog walking job soon." Scarlett must have heard the word "walk" because she started doing her "let's go" dance.

"Oh, really? That's nice," Dana said.

Now what? Shelby half listened until she heard her mother say the word "move." She could hear road noise in the background of the call.

"Are you calling from the car?" Shelby asked.

"Gus is driving. We couldn't wait to tell you something important."

"What did you say?" Shelby asked.

"You're going to love it here," Dana said louder. "I've never been happier. The ocean is actually warm, the sand pure white, and you can swim all year."

Shelby thought, Yeah, and there are hurricanes too, but she didn't say it. Her mother was enough of a storm. She didn't want to live somewhere where people had to be evacuated. She didn't want to live there, period.

When Shelby didn't answer, Dana continued. "And some exciting news."

"What is it?" Shelby said, trying to be patient as she put her shoes back on, hoping to leave soon.

"Gus has decided to relocate to Florida near his family, buy a nice big house where we can all three live together. And you could even get a dog."

"Oh," Shelby said. "And when is this supposed to happen?"

"Well, actually, Gus and I have already been looking with a realtor, and I think we've picked one out. It's a fancy, two-story house, and the high school is nearby."

Shelby thought about it for a minute. If the sale went through, and *if* was the important word here, did she want to go? There were so many more ifs: if Gus didn't kick them out, and if her mother didn't mess it up, they would have a more permanent home for her to finish high school.

"What do you think? Shelby, are you there?"

Shelby's breath was ragged, and her chest ached at the thought of leaving Moonwater Lake. "Let me think about it," she said.

"What do you mean, think about it?" Dana's voice started to rise. "I'm your mother. We're planning to come and get you in a few weeks, so you need to pack up and be ready."

Sunlight drifted through the windows. It filled the room and Shelby's heart with the familiar warmth of living here. "I don't think so," she said.

"Don't talk to me like that," Dana said.

Shelby took a deep breath. "I'm happy here. I have friends, I have a business, and I'd like to stay here with my grandmother."

"I knew you'd try to spoil it for me," Dana said. "You're still a minor, so what I say goes."

Shelby wanted to scream. Spoil it for Dana? What about for once her mother caring about what Shelby wanted? Dana and Gus were moving on with their lives. Let them stay there together. Shelby had never been happier than here at Moonwater Lake.

"I can emancipate now. I'm sixteen," Shelby said.

Dana's tone darkened. "Whose idea was this? Put your grandmother on the phone. Now!"

Just as Shelby said, "She's not home," she saw Alice coming through the front door, her face puffy, her eyes red. "I'll have her call you," Shelby said, moving toward the door to let Alice in.

"Make it soon," Dana said.

"Goodbye, Mother."

There was no reply.

Shelby hurried to her grandmother, Scarlett at her heels. "What's wrong?"

"It's nothing," Alice said, looking away.

"It doesn't look like nothing. Tell me," Shelby said. "Is Theo okay? Is it Wally?"

Alice dropped down into her recliner. Scarlett jumped into her lap and Alice hugged the dog tight to her chest. "It's both of them. And Theo wasn't his usual friendly self." A tear ran down Alice's cheek. "He had a big bruise on his forehead and said he'd just had a little fall."

"That's awful," Shelby said. "Should I go over there?"

Alice shook her head. "I don't think so. He made it clear he wanted to be alone."

Shelby was glad they didn't have a dog walkers club meeting for a few days, but she'd definitely check with Theo before scheduling another one. It would be a shame after all their efforts if it didn't work out now.

"Do you think the dog club is too much for him?" Shelby asked. "He says it's fine and he loves the company."

"It's not that," Alice said. "Don't take it on yourself. The dog park has made him very happy. He's concerned about Wally."

Shelby knew how much Wally meant to Theo, and he'd already been through so much losing his wife. Not now, she prayed.

Alice took a deep breath. "He's going to take him to the vet soon, and then we'll know more."

Shelby glanced at the clock on the wall. "I don't want to leave you like this," she said, "but Mindy is waiting for me."

Alice waved her away. "I'm fine. We can talk some more later."

As she headed for the door, Shelby remembered her own

dreaded call just minutes before. She turned back to her grand-mother. "There's more news. Dana just called."

"I'm not sure I want to hear it," Alice said.

Shelby agreed. Her grandmother's already stressful morning didn't need any more pressure. "It can wait until later."

"No, go ahead," Alice said. "I'd rather not worry about it all day."

"According to Dana, Gus is buying a fancy home in Florida and all three of us are going to live happily ever after there."

"Really?" Alice said. "And how do you feel about that?" Her grandmother's eyes looked weary. One minute everything seemed so happy again, and now it might all fall apart.

"I told her I didn't want to go."

"Good for you speaking up for yourself," Alice said.

"I'm tired of endless moves to satisfy my mother's whims. Who knows how long this one will last? And I'm so much happier here."

Alice stood and walked over to Shelby. "And I feel the same." She pulled Shelby into a warm hug. "There's nothing I'd like more."

Shelby wiped away a happy tear. "I better get going," she said, walking toward the door. "And by the way, Dana's last words were for you to call her."

Alice grimaced. "I think I'll wait a little while. Maybe have another cup of coffee, get myself together before I do."

Shelby laughed. "I'll see you later. Good luck with Dana."

CHAPTER 26

*A*fter the weekend, Wally seemed a bit more himself. Theo was relieved and had insisted the dog walkers club meet as planned. When he'd called, Shelby seemed distracted and mentioned something to him about problems with her mother.

The gathering of dogs and folks had gone well. Even Wally played a little bit. Theo wished he'd had more time to talk to Shelby. Maybe tomorrow. He hated seeing that lovely girl upset. He was relieved that Trevor had stayed behind to help with closing. Trevor's dog Buddy was sacked out under the graceful willow tree in a corner of the yard. Even he was tired. The heat didn't help.

"Go and sit down," Trevor said to Theo. "I'll clean everything up."

Theo was glad to do just that. He was still aching a bit from his fall a few days ago, but it would have broken Shelby's heart if he didn't have the second meeting of what Shelby had sweetly coined "The Lonely Hearts Dog Walkers Club." When she'd first told him the nickname, they'd had a good laugh.

He looked over to Wally, who was asleep on the deck. His tongue was peeking out the side of his mouth as he gently snored. He'd been a real trooper today, making an effort to play a little with the other dogs and eating one of Alice's dog-friendly cookies. Theo thought about Alice's absence at their meeting today. He hoped he hadn't scared her off with his previous behavior. The fall had really thrown him in more ways than one.

"Everything is picked up," Trevor said. He was holding a large trash bag in his hand and tying it up tight. "I left fresh water out for Wally and put most of the toys in the garden shed. Anything else?"

Theo scratched his head. "Don't think so."

"Be right back," Trevor said.

What a stand-up guy Trevor was. And from the looks of it, Trevor seemed interested in Mindy, too.

"Let's go, Wally," Theo said, loud enough to rouse him.

He led the way back in the air-conditioned house, where Wally plopped immediately on his bed. Theo sat on the couch and thought about what he'd cook tonight. He remembered the superb dinner with Alice and wondered how he might make up for his grumpy demeanor the other day.

After washing his hands in the kitchen, Trevor, followed by Buddy, joined Theo in the living room. "I think I'll be going now, get out of your hair."

Theo motioned for Trevor to have a seat. "Stay a while if you can, I'd love the company."

"Really? I thought you might be a bit burnt out after all the commotion."

"I must admit, I am," Theo said, "but it makes me happy too. I wish Jean could have been here to see it all. She would have been delighted."

Trevor took a seat opposite Theo, and Buddy sat on the floor next to him. "Jean sure loved Wally. And my Buddy."

"That she did," Theo said with a sigh. His mind jumped to Alice and Scarlett, and for a moment he felt guilty.

As if Trevor read his mind, he asked, "I hope Alice is feeling okay. I thought she'd be here today."

Now Theo felt doubly remorseful. "Probably my fault," he mumbled.

Trevor looked perplexed. "Your fault? How?"

Theo took a deep breath before looking over at Trevor. He trusted the man with his secrets more than he did his own son. "I told you about how I met up with Alice at the Fourth of July at the DeLucas' party."

Trevor grinned. "It sounded like you had a lot of fun, actually."

"That's the problem," Theo said.

"Why is that a problem?" Trevor tilted his head. "Seems like a good thing to me."

"You mean like you and Mindy?" Theo returned with a chuckle.

Now it was Trevor's time to stutter. "I, well…yes, I guess so."

Theo laughed. "We're both stumbling a bit with our hearts. You're young and have your life in front of you. And Mindy is a very special young woman."

"She is," Trevor said. "That's the problem."

Theo stretched to loosen his tense shoulders. "We both have big problems," he said with a smirk. "The good kind."

Trevor shrugged. "Things have been going pretty well between Mindy and me. Last week I brought her dinner and while the dogs played we got to know each other more. When I left, we kissed goodbye. At first I felt elated, but by the time I got home my mind was racing. Buddy paced the floor with me. I probably had him pretty confused."

Theo was concerned about his friend's PTSD being triggered. "Seems like you were confused, too."

Trevor's face was a canvas of racing feelings. "At first all I could think of was she was probably leaving soon, and I needed to protect myself. And then I realized, no guts no glory. So, for now, I am trying to stay in the moment and enjoy what we have."

"I'm proud of you," Theo said. "Darn good advice. Perhaps I should try it too. Guilt has been like a two-sided coin for me, both sides bad. One minute I feel awful that Jean has not been gone that long, and the next I feel bad that I hurt Alice's feelings. She is such an extraordinary woman."

Buddy put his head on Trevor's lap. "It's okay, boy," Trevor said. He looked up at Theo. "Why do you think you hurt her feelings?"

Theo squirmed in the chair. "The other night she had me over for dinner. We had a wonderful time together. The best I've felt in a long time. When I got home, I was a bit lightheaded and tripped on my own carpet." Theo pointed to his forehead. "Hence the fading bruise."

"I wondered about that," Trevor said.

"Along with the physical pain, it was a tortuous night of self-doubt. I felt like I had no right to care about another woman, or expect any happiness ever again. The next morning when Alice stopped by, I was afraid. In pain. And not kind to her."

Trevor walked over to Theo and put his arm around his shoulders. "You have every right to be happy," he said. "Jean would want that."

Theo wiped the telltale tears away with the back of his hand and sighed deeply. Buddy trotted over and laid at both of the men's feet, his body warm and reassuring. Theo looked over to Wally, whose breathing was labored, and the tears started fresh.

"I'm also worried about my dog."

"He did seem a bit off today," Trevor said. He wandered over to where Wally was lying and gently petted the dog's head. "You all right, boy?"

Wally opened one eye and coughed briefly before slipping back into his nap.

"Maybe he's just getting old," Trevor said with a shrug.

The cough was new and it frightened Theo even more. "We both are," he said.

"Come on," Trevor said. "You're quite the busy man now. You're teaching at the Veterans Center, you're hosting a dog park, and you have a new lady interested in you."

"No time to be feeling sorry for myself, I guess. But some days I just can't shake the sadness."

"Believe me, I know how you feel," Trevor said. "There is no right or wrong way to grieve or a timetable. The group counseling at the veterans center really helped me to understand how grief, guilt, and fear wait for us at every turn of the roller coaster of life. Especially after loss and trauma. I've come to believe the ones we have lost are not angry at us for still being here. Because I survived and others didn't, it does not mean I am supposed to be unhappy."

"It's kind of like Joann and her dog," Theo said. "She wears her grief on the outside. I wonder some days if seeing all the other dogs makes it worse. But Joann keeps showing up. There are so many dogs out there that need love. I have no doubt she will open her heart to one of them again soon." Theo looked over at Wally. "If I lost Wally, I don't think I could get another one." As he said that, he realized he'd been putting off taking Wally to the vet. "It's definitely time to take him in for a checkup."

Trevor nodded. "Probably a good idea. If he gets any worse, you just let me know. I'll drive you wherever you need to go."

Theo accompanied Trevor and Buddy to the front door and watched the golden dog and his human walk down the path to the sidewalk. He turned to go find his best friend and prepare for the night ahead. Theo hoped it wouldn't be a long one.

THEO TOSSED and turned in bed. Wally had not waddled up his doggie ramp and joined him. Instead, he lay curled up in a corner of the bedroom. His cough had become worse, and his breathing labored. Theo left the light on at his bedside, afraid to fall into a deep sleep in case the dog needed him. He got up to use the bath-room again, checked the dog and the clock. It was three o'clock in the morning. His mind raced out of control. Theo remem-bered the night Jean had woken him at precisely the same time and asked him to take her to the hospital. He had immediately called for an ambulance, not trusting himself to drive in the middle of the night in a complete panic.

He knelt down beside Wally and felt the dog's head. It felt like a fire under Theo's hand. "Wally," he said. But the dog remained listless, unresponsive to his touch or words. If he didn't act now, Wally could be gone by the morning.

It was pitch-black out, and the emergency pet hospital was an hour away. With his failing night vision, it would be impossible for Theo to attempt such a drive. His heart battered in his chest as he tried to slow his breathing and think clearly. The sun would start to rise in about three hours, but Theo feared that might be too late.

Sitting on the edge of his bed, Theo called the twenty-four-hour veterinary hospital and explained the symptoms. "Persistent cough, trouble breathing, and no appetite. His belly seems swollen, too."

As expected, they told him to rush the dog in as soon as possi-ble. Theo didn't want to think about what that could mean.

"Don't worry, I'll get you there somehow," he said to the dog. Wally barely opened one eye in a feeble attempt to respond.

Theo tried to get dressed but could barely button his own shirt. How did he think he could drive? Then he thought of Trevor. He hated to call him in the middle of the night, but one look at Wally and he knew he had no choice.

"It's Wally," Theo said to Trevor. "He's barely breathing, and he needs to go to emergency right now."

Trevor, stifling a yawn, still sounded clear and strong. "I'll be right there. Five minutes at most."

Theo could finally breathe a little easier. Trevor was used to urgent situations from being in the military, and he was someone Theo could rely on. He finished getting dressed, turned on the porch light, and waited at the door for Trevor.

Trevor raced up the driveway and jumped out of his car. "Where is he?" Trevor asked.

Theo led him to the bedroom and pointed. He watched Trevor gently slide the dog on a blanket and then scoop him up into his arms. "Let's go. My car," Trevor said.

Carefully seat belted, Theo held Wally in his lap for the drive that seemed to take forever. Buddy was asleep in the back seat and Theo took some comfort from that. At least there was almost no traffic, so they made good time and were there by 4:30 a.m. In the brightly lit waiting room, the familiar smell of antiseptic pervaded. Seeing them enter, a tech in blue scrubs rushed them into a room. Trevor took a seat with Buddy close at his side, while Theo paced the floor with Wally in his arms.

"The doctor will be right in," the tech said.

A woman wearing a white lab coat entered. "I'm Dr. Harris. And this little fellow must be Wally. Can you place him on the exam table for me?"

Theo nodded. The tech handed him some paperwork. He tried to fill it out but turned to Trevor for help, who took over the task, asking questions when needed.

Theo watched Dr. Harris examine his faithful companion, listening to his heart and checking his temperature. Theo felt faint when he saw the way the vet knitted her eyebrows in concern. He crumpled down on the wood bench next to Trevor and waited for the prognosis.

"We would like to take Wally in the back now," the vet said, nodding at the technician.

Dr. Harris walked over to Theo. "I think it's best we get him on some fluids and do some testing." She gave him a reassuring smile. "It will help us figure out how to get this boy feeling better. You can both wait here if you like."

Theo nodded in shock. "Please do whatever you can."

The vet carried Wally out of the room while the young female technician stayed behind. "Can I get you both something to drink?" she asked.

Theo shook his head.

"Dr. Harris will do everything she can for your dog. You are lucky to have one of our best doctors on duty tonight."

Her face was kind and Theo appreciated the reassurance.

"I'm Mary, if you have any questions."

"What kind of tests will they be doing?" Trevor asked.

The two men listened as the tech explained about chest X-rays, lab tests, and an EKG. Maybe they think it's Wally's heart, Theo reasoned. Thank goodness he hadn't waited any longer to bring him in.

Mary left the room and Trevor sighed. In quick response, Buddy sat up and put his head on Trevor's knee. Theo hadn't even thought about how this emergency situation might affect his friend.

"Are you okay?" Theo asked.

"I am," Trevor said. "It's just hard. There were so many special dogs in Afghanistan who helped save our lives. Sometimes we lost one and it was devastating. But a few dogs made it back with us to the U.S. One of my buddies was able to adopt one and bring him home." Trevor looked down at Buddy and ruffled his fur then looked up at Theo. "I'm glad we can be here for you."

Theo squeezed his eyes tight to hold back the tears and made himself take slow, deep breaths. The minutes ticked by as they waited silently for the results. It hadn't been that long ago he'd sat in an ambulance holding Jean's hand. She'd been on dialysis for stage 4 kidney failure, and in and out of pain. But then she would seem to bounce back and seem fine again. Regret circled him. After she was stabilized, he'd taken a cab home and promised to be right back with her things. As he'd walked in his front door, his phone rang, and his heart stopped. He wasn't sure it had ever really restarted after that. Jean was gone. That fast.

The door to the treatment room opened and jolted Theo back to the present. All eyes were on Dr. Harris as she gave them an encouraging smile. "He's resting more comfortably now. Wally was very dehydrated, but the fluids are helping. Has he always had a heart murmur?"

Theo nodded. "He has, but it never seemed to bother him before."

The vet continued. "It is common for beagles, especially at his age, to have some heart issues. That is what we suspected. It's a good thing you brought him right in."

"Can I take him home tonight?" Theo asked.

"We would like him to stay with us for a while so we can keep a close watch and possibly do more testing. We have him on some medication and we're hoping he will respond well to it."

Theo felt frozen to the spot. He did not want to leave. What if this was a repeat of the drive home after leaving Jean at the hospital?

"Can I stay and wait?" he asked.

"It's 5:00 a.m. now," Dr. Harris said. "I'll call you later this afternoon, and we can go over everything. There's a very good chance that Wally will be ready to go home with you then."

"I don't mind waiting," Theo said.

Dr. Harris offered him a sympathetic smile. "I know how you feel. But I'm afraid our accommodations are not that comfortable here. And besides, you look like you could use some rest yourself. You want to be refreshed for when Wally comes home so you can take the best care of him."

Theo knew she was right and felt that Wally was in good hands. Reluctantly, he followed Trevor and Buddy back to the car.

"They'll take good care of him," Trevor said. "They seem like pros. Right on top of things."

Theo could barely register Trevor's words. Everything seemed in a fog as they drove home. For quite a while Theo just stared out the window. Then he felt a furry nudge coming from the back seat. Buddy had pressed his head through the two front seats and was resting it on Theo's arm. Comfort spread through his body and he was finally able to breathe again as they made their way home.

When the sun tipped its head over the distant hills, his house came back in sight. Theo was desperate not to go back inside without Wally. Yet, if he didn't enter, the call would never come.

Trevor walked around to the passenger door and lent Theo a hand as he exited the car. "I'll walk you in," he said.

Theo shook his head. "No need. Go get some sleep and take care of Buddy."

Trevor hesitated. "Please call me the minute you hear or if I can do anything."

"There is one thing you could do," Theo said. "Please call Shelby and let her know what happened and that the dog park is closed for...now."

"Will do," Trevor said. "I'll just wait until you get inside."

Theo unlocked his front door and waved Trevor off. He walked slowly into the living room. It was so empty. No wife. No dog. He sat at the edge of his couch and rocked his trembling body back and forth. Wally's bed was empty. No sweet face and warm furry body greeting Theo this morning. How did anyone survive losing a dog? He would never, never get another one. He stood up and shakily walked to his bedroom and lay fully dressed on top of the covers. There was no way he could sleep. His eyes faced the phone on the nightstand as dread circled his heart.

CHAPTER 27

*S*helby, in jeans and a light sweatshirt, sat out on the cozy front porch of her grandmother's house and watched as the sun spread across the lake.

Meet me at the lake today? Logan texted.

I have a few dogs to walk and then I'll see you there, she answered.

For about a week now, they'd been texting early morning like this, before either of them had to go to work. Sometimes they'd go for a walk along the lake and watch the sunrise together and just talk. She'd learned so much about him and he was always attentive when she spoke. Although her life was radically different than his with all his family's travels, private schools, and charity functions, they both shared many of the same feelings on the inside. Shelby had always felt embarrassed for anyone to find out how little money they had, or to know about her homelife. Logan felt the same, but for opposite reasons. An embarrassment of riches, he had told her, when the world needed so much in so many places. The dichotomy between them was also what seemed to bond them closer. Shelby hadn't told Logan all about her mother's call a few days back and hoped she wouldn't have to. Across the street, he stepped out on his front porch and waved while they were texting. He always made her laugh.

Shelby rose and waved back. It was a beautiful morning for a walk. As she started down the porch stairs to meet him, the startling sound of the house phone ringing inside froze her in place. Another early morning call from her mother so soon? If she didn't run in and answer, it would probably wake Alice. She quickly texted Logan that she might not be able to meet him this morning and ran inside. Her grandmother stood in her nightgown, the phone in her hand, eyes wide, and all the color drained from her face.

"It's Trevor," Alice said, handing the phone to Shelby.

"Trevor. This is Shelby. What's wrong?"

As Trevor spoke, Shelby joined her grandmother on the sofa, where they huddled together with Scarlett in Alice's lap.

"I'll put you on speaker," Shelby said, switching it on so they both could hear. Trevor relayed all the details of his harrowing trip with Theo to the emergency vet and how Wally's status was still unknown.

"When will they know more?" Shelby asked.

Trevor's voice wavered. "Hopefully sometime today."

"Poor Theo," Alice said. "Is he with you, Trevor?"

"Theo insisted on going home and being alone. And to be honest, I'm a bit worried about him. The last thing he told me was to call you and let you know the dog park would be closed for a little while. I waited for the sun to come up to reach out to you."

Disappointment hit briefly, but it was nothing compared to the pain in Shelby's heart as she thought of poor Theo and Wally. "Thank you for calling us. I'll tell everyone. Please let me know if you hear anything."

"Of course."

Shelby hesitated. "Trevor, do you think Theo would mind if we gave him a call?"

"I think that would be a good idea. He may have fallen back to sleep, but I doubt it. He was too worked up. And if you don't mind, please let me know how he is."

Shelby hung up the phone and began to pace.

"I'll make us some coffee," Alice said. "And then we can figure out how to help."

Shelby nodded and took a seat at the breakfast bar. She watched Alice go through the motions of filling the pot with filtered water, grinding the beans, and laying out the mugs. The deep, rich aroma filled the air, just like any other morning, but it was not...at all. Shelby's happily constructed new world was caving in on her, just like it had so many times before.

Alice placed two china cups of coffee on the counter along with cream and sugar in matching rose-covered containers. The only sounds were the spoons clinking against the china as both women stirred and thought.

"Theo's been having a tough time lately and now this," Alice said.

"Wally has to be all right," Shelby said. "What would Theo do without him?" Alice sighed. "That's my fear. I think we should reach out to him, or at least you. I'm not sure he wants to see me right now."

Shelby shook her head. "Of course he does. He needs us both, now more than ever."

Almost an hour had passed, and daylight spilled through the front windows of the usually cheery front room. Shelby was pretty sure Theo would still be awake. He would certainly answer his phone, but he would think it was the vet and that might upset him more. She wondered if they should just show up instead. She made up her mind and turned to her grandmother.

"How about we bring Theo some breakfast? I doubt he's eaten."

Alice hesitated for a moment, doubt registering in her eyes. But then she stood and headed for the kitchen. "That's a good idea. You go take a shower and get dressed. I'll do the same, feed Scarlett, and then make a platter of deviled eggs and fruit and we can bring them over."

After showering and dressing, Shelby called the dog walkers club members and let them know what was happening and that she was taking the day off. She also texted Logan that she would not be able to meet him today and a short explanation. He wished her luck. Everyone she called offered their full support and hoped for the best for Wally. Shelby promised to let them know as soon as she heard any updates.

When she returned, Alice had breakfast all packed up in a basket, including a thermos of fresh coffee, and was ready to go. "Are you sure I should come too?" Alice asked.

"Absolutely," Shelby said. "I'll feel better with you there too, just in case."

Alice nodded and slipped on a light cardigan, and together they walked over to Theo's. The morning birdsong filled the air. It always seemed to, no matter what was happening, even if your world was collapsing, Shelby thought. When they reached the house, all the blinds were closed, not a sound coming from inside. Shelby knocked on the door and they waited. At first no one answered, so Shelby knocked again.

Theo cracked open the door and peered out at them. He looked confused at their presence.

"We brought you breakfast," Shelby said, holding up the basket.

Theo just stared at them, his face worn, eyes red.

"Trevor called and told us about Wally. We thought you could use some company."

"We won't stay long," Alice said. "Perhaps a little coffee might help."

He held open the door. "I'm sorry for my disheveled appearance. Please come in."

Theo pushed his graying hair back with his hands. He looked like he had slept in his clothes, and not well.

Alice deftly set everything up in the dining room and gestured for them to sit at the table that faced the lake.

Shelby opened some of the curtains to let in some light, before sitting down to join them. She watched Theo sip the coffee, but he didn't take a bite of the food. She was not sure what to say or do to make things better. The empty dog bed by the fireplace haunted the room.

"I called the dog walkers club," she finally said. "Everyone sends their love and prayers for you and Wally."

"That's very nice," Theo said. "He's such a special dog."

"Please let us know if there is anything we can do to help," Alice said. "We're always here for you."

"Thank you," he said, looking up at Alice. "That means a lot." Theo reached for an egg and took a few bites. "Wally loves eggs. I wish…" His voice broke.

"When he's home and better, I'll make sweet Wally anything he wants," Alice said.

A smile drifted across Theo's face at Alice's words. Shelby could see the difference it made when someone was really there for you. She finally felt that way herself since living with Alice and being friends with Theo. She thought of Logan and their times together and her heart felt full.

"I wish there was more we could do," she said to Theo. She watched his eyes gaze longingly toward the dog bed.

Theo sighed then buried his head in his hands.

Shelby looked over to Alice, hoping her grandmother could help.

"Would you like us to wait with you until the vet hospital calls?" Alice asked.

Theo nodded but did not make eye contact. "I remember when we first brought Wally home," he said. "One of Jean's friends had gotten a puppy on a whim, and it proved too much for her to handle. I almost said no when Jean suggested we take the pup. And he was a handful," he said wistfully. A sad smile crossed his face. "I've never been sorry we opened our home to him."

They sat in silence as the clock on the mantle ticked away the minutes. No one touched their plate again. Finally, Alice stood and started cleaning up.

Shelby hugged her legs to her chest and stared out the window. The running ramp and red fire hydrant looked lost in the yard without the dogs. The lake glistened like most summer mornings and she could see boats entering the water. Life went on no matter what happened. It didn't seem right sometimes.

The phone rang and everyone jumped. Shelby turned to Theo. "Do you want me to get it?"

Theo stood. "I'll do it." He hurried over to the counter and hesitated before picking it up and saying hello.

Shelby and Alice kept their eyes glued to him as they caught pieces of conversation, Wally's name, and a few questions. Theo grabbed a pen and paper, took notes, and then hung up. Shelby held her breath, waiting to find out the results.

"He's coming home in a few days. He's doing well," Theo said.

Shelby could see the relief visually wash over their friend. She jumped up from her chair and hugged him. "That's great news!"

Theo turned to Alice. She held out her arms and he fell into them. He laid his head on Alice's shoulder and she gently patted his back.

Shelby sniffed back happy tears and a good amount of relief. Everything would be fine, she told herself. Go back to normal. Her new normal she loved so much here.

"Let's sit back down," Theo said, "and I'll tell you what the vet said."

They gathered around Theo as he explained that Wally had

217

some heart issues causing fluid to build up in his lungs and cause the coughing and difficulty breathing. But the good news was that he was responding well to the two medications. If his progress continued today, Wally would be ready to go home after spending a couple more nights there.

"Dr. Harris was very hopeful," Theo continued. "She said Wally ate a good breakfast and was flirting with all the girls at the office."

"Of course," Shelby said. "He's such a cutie."

"Do you mind if I call Trevor and let him know," Alice asked.

"Go right ahead," Theo said.

After speaking with Trevor and making sure Theo was all right, Alice and Shelby packed up to go home. With all that was going on, Shelby had barely had time to think about her mother's call and the impending changes that might bring. She pushed the thought away. There was plenty of time to deal with her mother later. And there was a good chance Dana would change her mind anyway. She remembered to text Logan and briefly let him know what was going on.

"I'm leaving the thermos and eggs for you," Alice said. "Promise us you will go and get some rest."

Theo walked them to the door. "I promise."

Alice continued. "As soon as you know the pick-up time, Shelby and I will drive you over to get your boy."

"Are you sure?" Theo asked. "It's a long drive."

"We wouldn't have it any other way," Alice said.

A FEW DAYS LATER, they were on their way to pick up Wally. Trevor was teaching a class at Lakeside Veterans Center that morning and he had offered to cancel it and come along, but Alice had said she could handle it. Shelby was amazed to see her grandmother willing to drive such a long distance with no hesitation whatsoever. Alice's days of never leaving home were certainly behind her. Shelby had insisted Theo sit in the front on the way there. For the ride home, Wally's bed was waiting for him in the back seat and Theo would be at his side.

Shelby listened to her grandmother and Theo chat in the front seat. Theo kindly apologized to Alice for his impoliteness the other day when she'd brought him the pie. Alice insisted there was no need, and she totally understood. Shelby was relieved to see the two of them friends again. There was enough heartache going around. For a moment it was like the old days riding along with Grandma Alice and Grandpa Stan. They'd always seemed content and enjoyed being together. Shelby thought about Logan. He'd been concerned when she'd texted him about Wally and Theo and asked if she needed anything. Next time they spoke she was going to ask how he was doing too.

Once inside the animal hospital, they were brought into a private room. Alice and Shelby sat, but Theo insisted on standing. The air conditioner blew steadily on them, and the chill added to Shelby's nerves as they waited. When the door opened, the vet entered with a big smile on her face, carrying Wally. Theo rushed forward and Wally all but jumped into his waiting arms.

"As you can see," Dr. Harris said, "he's doing quite well." She scratched behind his ears. "We're going to miss this charming fellow."

Theo sat down in a chair next to Shelby, shifting Wally's weight in his lap. Alice stood behind him, her hand on his shoulder for reassurance.

"Hello there," Shelby said, giving the dog a kiss on top of his head. "You're looking very handsome today."

Her heart melted when the dog looked up with his chocolate brown eyes. All their prayers had been answered.

The vet took a seat across from Theo and discussed how heart disease was common in older dogs. She reassured Theo that Wally could still have a good quality of life and, with some diet and lifestyle changes, do well for quite a while. "We suggest you have him monitored at your local vet about every three months, and of course, we are always here if you need us," she said.

Shelby wondered what "quite a while" meant, but there was no denying Wally was an older dog and anything that would extend his life was a gift. For Theo's sake, she hoped it would be for a very long time.

Mary, the vet tech, entered carrying two bottles of medicine and some handouts. "All the instructions are on the sheets and the bottle," she said. "You can pick up his prescription low-salt diet at the front before you leave."

"Wally loves his treats," Alice said. "I'm happy to follow any protocol to make homemade ones within his special diet."

Dr. Harris looked impressed and wrote some recipe resources down for Alice. "In moderation, these should be fine." She turned back to Theo. "Just make sure he gets plenty of rest."

"What about his walks?" Shelby asked.

"That's fine as long as he seems up to it. Avoid hot temperatures or too much exertion."

Shelby thought about the dog park. "Can he play with other dogs still?"

"That depends a lot on Wally. Small dogs seem to do better with this condition. From what we've seen so far, he should be fine as long as you avoid activity that leads to excessive panting or weakness."

Theo spoke up. "That shouldn't be a problem. He mostly watches the other dogs anyway. We have our walk early in the morning, and neither of us are too fast."

The vet laughed. "I'm sure you will both do just fine."

Theo thanked the doctor and technician and put Wally down to walk out with them to the lobby. Wally pulled right toward the front door. "I see you're ready to go home, boy," Theo said. "Just one more minute."

Shelby held the leash and waited with Alice while Theo finished up at the front desk. Soon they were a happy crew starting their drive home. Within minutes Wally was fast asleep. And so was Theo. When the two snored in unison from the back seat, Alice and Shelby smiled at each other as they drove home.

CHAPTER 28

*T*he days had flown by and Shelby missed seeing Logan. She could think of nothing better to relieve the tension from the last few days than a long swim in the cooling lake. She put on one of her new bathing suits, grabbed a towel, and headed to the beach. Today she would sit right next to the lifeguard station.

When she reached the sand, she saw Logan standing at the water's edge, scanning the horizon. His tall, lean body and ever-darkening tan contrasted with the wisps of sun-bleached hair picked up in the breeze. She moved beside him and gently touched his arm.

"Hi," she said.

He glanced at her and nodded.

No "Good to see you." No smile. Logan kept staring out at the water. For a moment, the familiar feeling of rejection set in. They'd barely spent any time together lately and the texts were sparse. Had his feelings changed?

She started to turn away. "I'll see you later," she said.

"Wait," Logan said.

His eyes searched hers and the worry behind them was apparent.

"Sorry," he said. "Why don't you sit by my station today? August is the worst month. Crowds, partiers, and reckless people. I have to keep a very close look, but we can talk a little."

"You sure?" Shelby said, looking up at him. "I'm fine with going somewhere else."

"It's not you. Just not having a great day."

"I understand," she said. "Do what you need to. I'm fine."

She put her things down near the station amidst the crowded beach. She'd been so wrapped up in her own problems and Theo's, she'd not really taken the time to see how Logan was. He looked like he needed to talk, and she wanted to be there for him. Not everything needed to be taken personally, she reminded herself. Logan's mood was about what was happening with him, not her. She was of no use to herself or Logan if she forgot that. Trust was not something she was used to giving, but she was getting there with Logan.

The lake was overcrowded, so she dove in and swam out a ways to get away from the masses. She floated on the cool surface of the lake, letting the stress go as the water supported her. The sky above was brilliant blue. It was time to let go and relax. The sounds from the beach faded and her mind cleared as she drifted with the gentle current. Being in the water had always soothed her, a place she could escape, and just float.

From the distance, Shelby saw another lifeguard come to relieve Logan for a break. She swam back and toweled off while he stood waiting for her.

"Tell me something good," he said, his lopsided, dimpled smile back.

"The dog park is reopening tomorrow, and Wally's doing so much better."

"I'm happy to hear that," he said.

His smile was warm, but his eyes were still listless. The dark circles under them told of the sleepless nights he'd had, much like Shelby's.

"How's it been since your dad left?" she asked.

Logan sighed before meeting her gaze. "Not good."

"Do you want to talk about what's going on?"

Logan took her hand. "Let's take a walk where it's more private."

To avoid the crowds, they walked up the trail Logan had shown her before. The towering trees provided a shady retreat, and a large boulder provided a quiet place to sit.

"It's been tough at my house the last few weeks," Logan said.

Shelby squeezed his hand. "Tell me what's going on. I'm sorry I haven't been there for you much lately."

"No worries," he said. "You've had a pretty full plate yourself."

Shelby waited for Logan to open up to her.

"According to my mother, my dad won't be joining us much, if at all, the rest of this summer. He is, and I quote, 'On an extended business trip to the San Juan Islands near Seattle.' Some international clients are flying him out in a private plane for meetings. Like we're supposed to believe that? It's the middle of summer, and that's one of the most beautiful places on Earth to vacation. He said he might not always have reception. What's he going to be on, a yacht? Even they have reception."

"I'm sorry."

Hurt and anger had shattered Logan's usual lighthearted demeanor. He continued. "My mother has her doubts, too. She's been walking around in a daze, not eating, barely sleeping. I think she's worried that he's not coming back this time at all."

"Would he do that?" Shelby asked.

"Who knows what he would do? My birthday is coming up, and he didn't even remember that."

Logan looked disgusted. She felt terrible for him and for Iris. "Maybe I can help somehow," she said, putting her hand over his. "I know what it's like to have a parent that's difficult to deal with."

"Do you?" Logan said. "Your mother sounds fairly easy compared to my dad."

"Well, she's not," Shelby said. "Just because she's not a jet-setter running all over the world with big clients doesn't mean she's any easier to deal with. You have no idea what my life has been like."

Logan apologized profusely. "I didn't mean it like that. I'm sorry. I'm just worried about my mother. I can hear her crying through her bedroom door and I feel so helpless. And Gabe is constantly talking about wanting a dog as if it would replace having a father. Everything is so on edge and I feel powerless to fix it."

"It's not your job to fix it, believe me," Shelby said. "I've tried with my mom. They are the parents. Sometimes we have to put ourselves first."

He put his arm on her shoulder. "You are the wise one. Tell me about your mom."

Shelby told him about her mother, the dark times, and the pending demand for Shelby to join them in Florida.

Logan put his arm around her shoulders. "Will you go?"

"I don't want to," Shelby said. "I'm tired of leaving places. Do you have any idea how many times I've moved in my sixteen years?"

"No," he said. "I can't even imagine that. We've been in the Bay Area home since I was born."

"How could you possibly know how it felt after the way you grew up?" Shelby realized she was taking her anger and hurt out on him like he'd done to her earlier. "I'm sorry," she said. "These are sore topics."

"Believe me," he said, "if the family money were mine, I'd be doing things to save the planet. I'd live much more modestly. My dad could probably feed a small city just on what he spends on wining and dining each month."

Shelby shrugged. "It's so opposite with me. We never eat out. I don't even know how many schools I've gone to. About six elementary, multiple middle schools. And one high school so far. I've still got two more years and I hope to spend them in one place finally."

"It must be hard to make friends that way," Logan said.

"Impossible."

Logan turned Shelby to face him. He kissed her on the forehead. "But now you have me," he said.

In her mind she thought, Do I? Do I have you? He certainly had her heart.

"And you have me," she said back to him.

They gazed into each other's eyes, each other's hearts. Then he kissed her gently on the lips before taking her in his arms. Here with Logan, away from everything, nothing seemed like it could touch how they felt about each other.

The sound of motorboats speeding by broke the calm silence as the sun drifted overhead. "I'd better get back to the station soon," Logan said, breaking the spell.

Shelby brushed off the dirt from her shorts and stood up with him. "Are you feeling any better?" she asked as they walked.

"When I'm here with you, yes," Logan said. "When I'm with my mother, it's hard not to worry. She's talking about staying at the lake house instead of moving back to the city. I think everything at our city house reminds her of my father."

"Well, if I'm still here," Shelby said, "I'll keep an eye on your mother and Gabe."

"That's true," Logan said. "And it's not that far from Stanford. I got acceptances to other colleges, but my father insisted I go there. He's still hoping I'll do pre-law. I can come up on some weekends and holidays. And if there's a divorce, at least the lake house belongs to my mother's family."

They strolled toward the lifeguard station so Logan could relieve his replacement.

"Let's not talk about this anymore," he said. "It's a beautiful, sunny day. I have to work, but at least I can watch you swim."

"I'll swim for both of us," she said, with a wink.

Shelby sauntered down to the water, turning a few times to make sure he was still watching before diving into the delightfully cool water. Her body tingled as the heat sizzled off her. She swam out to the floating dock where people were hanging out fishing and cannon-balling into the water. She pulled herself up, dripping wet, and sat on the edge with her feet dangling over. Logan had binoculars in his hands and they were facing right at her. With what she hoped was a seductive smile, Shelby waved, wishing he was sitting beside her. Hopefully there would be another chance for them to enjoy the lake together soon.

CHAPTER 29

Shelby allowed herself a leisurely morning shower. The relief after Wally's recovery had kept Shelby's mind off her mother's threat about moving to Florida for the last week. But the latest text from Dana stating they would be coming to get her soon, and the links to pictures of cookie cutter homes in Florida, had set Shelby on edge. She hoped Dana was just having another one of her highs, which tended to drop quickly to another low, then the plan would be abandoned. She highly doubted if Gus was ready to buy a house already after only a few months and move Dana and her teenage daughter in too.

By the time she toweled off and dressed, the pit of Shelby's stomach felt like a triple-tied knot straining to break. There was so much at stake. In these last couple of months at Moonwater Lake, she'd felt happy, laughed more than she could have ever thought possible. She felt normal, and that she mostly fit in. And, of course, there was Logan, and Theo, and all of the adorable dogs. Shelby wondered if she stayed living with her grand-mother, would she let her get her own dog. It didn't matter. They could share Scarlett. She was more than enough.

Shelby reminded herself that Wally was doing so much better

after a week on the medication. Theo was elated when the vet told him that, judging from the way Wally responded to the medicine, he'd probably have lots of walks with friends to come. Theo had even agreed to have a short dog walking park gathering today. Everyone who could attend would bring their dogs briefly. Shelby hoped it went well.

In the kitchen, not only was Alice up and dressed, she'd also taken Scarlett for her morning walk and baked fresh dog treats to bring.

"You've had a busy morning," Shelby said.

Alice laughed. "And it feels good."

Shelby looked at the clock. "Yikes, I never sleep this late," she said. "We've got less than an hour to get over to Theo's."

"You needed the rest," Alice said. "I saved you a slice of bacon cheddar quiche, and there's still hot coffee in the pot. We'll make it in plenty of time."

"I'll just have a bite, and off we'll go."

Not long later they were out the door. Scarlett knew right where they were going and led the way. The dog leapt in circles as they approached Theo's house. Posted on the entry gate to the yard was a new sign someone had made. It said, "Shelby's Dog Walking Club."

"How sweet," Alice said.

Shelby traced the hand-carved letters with her finger. The people here cared enough about her to make her feel welcome and appreciated. It meant the world to her.

They opened the gate to find everything set up and ready. Mindy was there with Karma. Trevor and Buddy were, of course, nearby. Scarlett ran off to greet her friends.

"Well, hello there, little girl," Trevor said to Scarlett, who ran over to Mindy for a quick greeting before charging for Karma. She chased Karma up the ramp and through the tunnel, Buddy not far behind them.

"Morning," Theo said, his eyes going right to Alice. "I'm glad we could have this meeting today." He pointed to Wally. "My little man is still up on the porch, but he's at the steps, watching."

Alice handed Theo the box of dog treats. "How's he doing?" she asked.

"So much better. Thanks to you all."

Everyone's eyes were on Wally now as he took a few hesitant steps down toward the grassy yard.

"You can do it," Trevor said.

Next thing they knew, Wally rambled over to greet Shelby, his thick tail wagging.

She scratched behind Wally's ears. He looked up at her and barked expectantly. "I'm happy to see you too," she said.

"I think he wants a cookie," Theo said, smiling. He fumbled to open the Tupperware box and pulled out a bone-shaped treat. The dog gobbled it up. "I guess he's back to his old self," Theo said.

Scarlett raced over, wanting to join in. "Scarlett, sit. Be gentle with Wally," Alice said. Scarlett sat and was rewarded with a treat, after which the two dogs exchanged sniffs.

"Well, that was a great start," Theo said.

While waiting for the others to arrive, Shelby sat on one of the benches to watch the dogs play.

Mindy and Trevor stood next to her. "Dogs are so easy to please," Mindy said. "Food, friends, fun. I wish my life was as simple."

"Is everything okay? Your leg looks almost completely healed," Shelby said.

Mindy held her cast-less leg in the air. "Yes, it's good news, but it's also part of the problem."

The dogs raced by, Scarlett in the lead with a rope toy hanging from her mouth that both Karma and Buddy wanted for themselves.

"Anything I can do to help?" Trevor asked.

"I wish," Mindy said. "Unless you want to call my parents and tell them to stop guilt tripping me into coming back home, I'm afraid there is nothing."

"Guess not," said Trevor. "So, you have a decision to make."

Shelby held her breath and listened. She knew those two had grown close. There was still a good month of summer yet, but change was biting at everyone's heels.

"My parents are very conventional, first generation from India. They think I can't be happy without getting married and having children. Soon. They don't understand that I think differently and am able to make my own choices."

"Right," Trevor said. "Lots to think about."

Mindy sighed. "That is not the life I want. The slower pace here and the fresh air are much more to my liking."

"Mine too. It's a good life here," Trevor said. "But you'll have to let me know what you decide."

Shelby watched Trevor's shoulders drop. Briefly he squeezed his eyes shut.

"Got to go," he said. Then he turned and walked up toward the porch.

"Trevor sure took off fast," Mindy said. "I hope I didn't upset him."

"I saw that," Shelby said. She wondered the same thing. Perhaps he just couldn't handle all the emotions coming at him at the thought of Mindy possibly leaving. Shelby knew what that was like. "I'm sure, like all of us, Trevor just wants you to be happy. And he'd miss you if you go."

The gate sprang open and Steph with her corgi Oscar arrived. His fluffy coat shone in the sun and he was wearing a checkered bow tie. Right behind them, Eleanor entered with her two barky girls. The puffballs had matching pink bows in their hair today.

"Hello, everyone," Eleanor called out as her girls raced across the yard.

Joann was right behind them, a big smile on her face as Scarlett rushed over to greet her. Shelby appreciated her show of support.

Shelby greeted each dog and then watched them take off to play. Their antics never ceased to amuse her as she watched their owners diligently follow their pups around with plastic bags, cleaning up and laughing. Even Wally got up for a while and chased a ball for Joann.

It was almost back to normal now. Almost, Shelby thought. Her mother's words echoed in her mind. She looked from person to person, from dog to dog. She did not want to lose all of this. She remembered her teacher, Mrs. Warren, telling her about choices, that she always had one, and this time she was going to make the best one possible.

CHAPTER 30

It had been a few days since Shelby had spent time with Logan at the lake. Every time she thought of their conversation, it reminded her of the instability of her own life. Her grandmother had long since gone to sleep, and she was reading in bed trying to sleep, when suddenly there was a knock on her bedroom window. Her heart raced. She tiptoed over to the window and opened the blinds, and there stood Gabe, his face barely visible in the light from the front porch. Tears ran down his cheeks. In his arms was Mutt. He held up the ragged dog, who was panting heavily.

Shelby motioned for Gabe to come around to the front door. She quietly opened the door so as to not wake her grandmother.

"Come in, come in," Shelby whispered. The night air was cold and misty. It was hard to imagine how hot it would be later in the day.

Gabe started to explain.

"Shh." She held her finger to her lips, motioning for Gabe to be quiet as they crept back into her room. She shut the door and turned on the light.

Gabe plopped on her bed, cuddling Mutt to his chest. Shelby

sat beside them.

The dog was quivering. Shelby took her blanket and wrapped it around the dog and Gabe. "Poor little, Mutt. It's okay. You're safe," she said. "What happened?"

"I was sleeping outside in the screened-in porch," Gabe said, "when I heard Mutt crying and scratching on the door. I let him in right away. He looked awful. All shaky. I snuck in the house and got him some food and he gobbled it up. I don't know how long he'd been out there or when he last ate."

"Oh no," Shelby said. "We probably need to check on Mrs. Williams too." It was after two in the morning and she hated to wake her grandmother and it was so dark out. The minutes ticked by while her mind raced. Perhaps the dog had just escaped again.

She checked Mutt thoroughly. Nothing was broken, it seemed. There was no blood. He laid his nose down on the covers and his eyes drifted shut. They sat for a while warming up while Shelby tried to figure out what to do.

"Leave him here," Shelby said. "You go home, I'll watch you from the door. In a few hours when people are awake, my grand-mother and I can go check on Mrs. Williams. We'll let you know right away when we return."

"Are you sure?" Gabe asked.

"I'm sure. My grandmother won't mind. Scarlett's locked in the room with her right now. Scarlett loves everyone. It will be fine."

"But what if Mutt—?"

"Don't worry," she whispered. Mutt was asleep now. Leaving the dog on her bed, Shelby pulled on a robe and walked Gabe quietly to the front door. She left the porch light on so he could see better as she watched him cross the street and slip around the back of the house to the screened-in porch. Shelby closed the door and shut off the light. She could hear Scarlett barking softly from her grandmother's room and hoped Alice wouldn't wake up. In the kitchen she filled bowls with dog food and water and brought them to her room in case Mutt woke up.

It was too dark to wander down the lake path to Mrs. Williams' home, and the mist would make the walk slippery. The dog had probably escaped again, looking for food. She knew her grandmother would be up in a few more hours and would know what to do. Shelby went back into her bed and set her phone alarm, hoping to get a little more sleep. Mutt was curled up at her feet, lightly snoring. He seemed content, Shelby assured herself. Warm covers, full belly, and thanks to Gabe he was safe.

She slept for a few hours then checked on Mutt again. The dog was bundled up against her and in a deep sleep. It almost looked like there was a smile on his face. She propped up in bed and watched the early morning sun trickle through her blinds. There was no sleeping now. What if Mrs. Williams...? She tried not to let her mind go there. And what about poor Mutt? Gabe had looked heartbroken. Dried tears had stained his face. He must have wiped them with a dirty hand; they looked permanently embedded in his cheek. Finally, she heard her grandmother's door open and the familiar sound of letting Scarlett out for her morning routine in the yard.

Shelby threw some clothes on, then made sure Mutt was still asleep before shutting the bedroom door behind her. She didn't want Mutt coming out, just in case he and Scarlett didn't get along.

"What are you doing up?" Alice said when she opened the front door. "And dressed?"

"Something happened," Shelby said. "Do you remember when I told you about Mrs. Williams and her dog Mutt? The one that showed up the Fourth of July?"

"Yes, I do. I mentioned it to Eleanor because she is still involved with social services. She said Meals on Wheels were delivering to her and she would put in a request for a wellness check as well." Alice paused. "Why, what happened?"

"A few hours ago, Gabe showed up at my window holding a pretty ragged-looking Mutt. Gabe was worried when the dog woke him, crying outside their screened-in porch."

"How did the dog know to go there?" Alice asked. She let Scarlett off the leash and took a seat in her recliner.

"Gabe likes to sleep out there," she said. Of course he would, Shelby thought. That way he can spend more time with Mutt when he shows up looking for food. "Actually, he'd been sneaking Mutt food for a while as well as helping Mrs. Williams out."

Alice frowned. "Where is Gabe now?"

"Gabe was pretty worried, but I made him go back to bed. I told him we'd check on Mrs. Williams as soon as you woke up. I wasn't sure what to do. Should we call 911?"

Shelby's stomach growled. A hot cup of coffee would be welcome, but it could wait until they figured this out.

Alice shook her head. "That's probably panicking. I think what we should do is put Mutt on a leash and walk him back to Mrs. Williams' house and check on her before we make any decisions."

"Agreed," Shelby said. "I'll get the dog and my cell phone." When she got into the room, Mutt was awake. Tail wagging, he was munching food and looked happy to see her. A small wet spot on her floor alerted her that he'd probably needed to be let out. He was used to having a doggy door. She did a quick clean up while Mutt finished his breakfast.

Shelby was elated her grandmother was there to help figure this out. She put the dog on the leash, and he scrambled into the living room to meet Scarlett. They sniffed and circled, then seemed satisfied to ignore each other after. At the door, Scarlett barked after them, hoping to come too. But it was best to leave her behind for now.

"Thanks for coming," Shelby said.

"Of course. You could have woken me last night," Alice said.

Shelby wasn't used to having someone who was truly there

for her day and night, especially in a crisis situation like this. It was usually her mother waking Shelby up because she needed help. And once, when living in Las Vegas, her mother hadn't come home at all one night. Shelby had frantically looked for her the next day and even called the police. No one had been there to help her when her world was crumbling. Fear had gripped her heart as she wondered if she'd been abandoned, or worse yet, her mother was dead. Police found her at a poker machine in a casino. She'd been playing all night and lost track of time. Dana laughed about it when the police showed up. Shelby had been both furious and relieved. Here with her grandmother she felt safe and loved and wasn't going to let that go.

The morning birdsong lightened Shelby's heart as they walked briskly along the dirt footpath, mindful of rocks and branches. It was not a well-worn area, full of twists and turns as it led them through the trees to Mrs. Williams' home. When they got close enough, Shelby released Mutt from the leash, and he tore across the yard to the door. There were no lights on as they cautiously approached the front door and knocked. At first they didn't hear anything. Then Shelby put her ear to the door and thought she heard some moaning.

"I think something's wrong," Shelby said.

Alice tried the door and it opened right up. "Not even locked?"

Her grandmother's expression did nothing to comfort Shelby's mounting anxiety.

"I'll go first," Alice said.

She opened the door and reached for the light switch. When she turned it on, Mrs. Williams was lying on the floor. One of her legs didn't look right and she was shivering all over. Mutt went over and lay beside her.

Mrs. Williams reached out her hand. "Help me," she pleaded.

Alice dropped to the floor, taking the woman's hand. "We're

here now. Everything will be all right." In the calm voice of an experienced nurse, Alice said, "Shelby, call 911."

Shelby's fingers could barely punch the three numbers in. The first thing the operator asked was for a location. "I don't know the address here," Shelby said, trying to keep the panic out of her voice.

With Alice's help, Mrs. Williams was able to mumble the address to them.

While Alice comforted Mrs. Williams and put a pillow under her head, Shelby filled the operator in on the details of the situation. She sat down and wrapped her arms around Mutt, who was quivering too. The house was so cold and damp. Shelby wondered how long Mrs. Williams had lain on the floor by herself. Thank goodness Gabe hadn't come here by himself last night. It really would have scared the boy. Shelby hoped she'd made the right call last night by waiting.

Alice found a tattered blanket on the sofa and placed it over Mrs. Williams, careful not to move her in case there was an injury.

The sound of a siren racing up the drive, and a howl from Mutt, alerted them to the help that was thankfully arriving. The EMTs rushed in, wheeling a stretcher and supplies. A tall man seemed to be in charge and immediately approached Mrs. Williams.

"How long has she been there?" he asked, kneeling on the floor.

"We don't know," Alice said. "We just got here about a half hour ago, but I think it's been a while."

They watched as the EMTs checked her pulse and blood pressure. "I'm a retired nurse," Alice said. "I've been monitoring Mrs. Williams' vitals the best I could. Her pulse is slow and irregular, and her extremities are quite cold. I think she may have broken her hip."

The medic nodded. "Mrs. Williams, nod if you can hear me."

Mrs. Williams groaned. "Pain," she said.

"We'll take care of you," the medic assured her. He turned to Alice. "Did you notice any medications nearby or emergency contacts listed?"

Alice shook her head. "We'll look around and let you know right away what we find. She's a widow."

Very carefully they slid Mrs. Williams onto a stretcher. "We are taking her to Lake County Hospital."

As they reached the door, Mrs. Williams cried out, "My dog!" Mutt barked as if in response. "Please take care of him."

Shelby took Mrs. Williams' hand as they walked her out. "Don't worry about anything. We'll take Mutt home with us. He'll be well cared for until you come home again."

"Thank you," she managed in a raspy voice.

Alice and Shelby watched as they put Mrs. Williams in the ambulance. Shelby held Mutt in her arms so he wouldn't follow.

"Thank the heavens for that dog," Alice said as they walked back inside. "I don't know how long she would have lain there before somebody found her."

It made Shelby queasy to think about that vulnerable woman alone out here in the woods by herself. She took a quick look in the fridge and there was almost no food. She'd had no idea how bad Mrs. Williams' situation was or she would have done more to help her.

After checking the house for medications or contact information and finding nothing of help, they walked back to Alice's house. Gabe was sitting on the front porch waiting for them, his fists under his chin.

He jumped up when he saw them and pulled Mutt into his arms. "You still have him."

"You're a hero, you know that, Gabe?" Shelby said.

He looked up, bewildered. "What do you mean?"

"If it wasn't for you and Mutt, Mrs. Williams may not have been found," Alice said. "She'd had a fall and needed help. We did what we could and then an ambulance came and took her to the hospital. You did well. She'll be fine."

"Are you sure?" Gabe asked, catching his breath.

Shelby put her arm around Gabe's shoulder. "Don't worry, they'll take good care of her. And we'll take good care of Mutt until she's better."

"But," Gabe said, "what if she doesn't come home from the hospital?" He held the dog up to his face, and Mutt promptly kissed Gabe's cheek. "I wish I could keep him. He wants to be my dog."

"I know," Shelby said. "Why don't we ask your mother if Mutt can stay with you for just a few days until we know more?"

"Okay. I guess you never know. With my dad gone for a few days she might say yes."

Shelby remembered Logan telling her his dad might be gone for the rest of the summer. Maybe they had not told Gabe. "Let's go ask, then," Shelby said.

They walked across the street and Gabe let them in.

"Hello," Shelby said, wanting to let his mother know they were there.

Iris, hair in a low bun, was in a robe drinking coffee at the kitchen island. She laid her cup on the granite counter and stood when she saw them. "Gabe, what are you doing outside? I thought you were..." She glanced at Shelby and Alice. "Is everything okay?" Then she looked down at Mutt. "Why is that dog back? Who does it belong to?"

"It could be mine," said Gabe hopefully. He put his palms together in prayer fashion. "Please."

Iris stared at her son, obviously confused. "I don't know."

"Do you have any more coffee?" Alice asked. "We have a bit of a story to tell you."

"Sure, sure. Have a seat. You just caught me off guard." She pointed to the kitchen table, her gaze going back to the dog.

"Mutt can stay on my lap," Gabe said.

Iris let out a deep breath and shrugged. "I guess so." A few minutes later she brought coffee and cream and placed them on the table. "Are you all hungry?" she said.

"We're fine. No need to put you to any trouble," Shelby said. The warm coffee was a welcome comfort after a grueling night.

Iris took a seat and turned to Alice, who filled her in on all the details leading up to Gabe helping to rescue Mrs. Williams and Mutt. Iris sipped her coffee and listened, her eyes going from Gabe to Mutt and back to Alice as the story unfolded.

Gabe lowered his eyes. "I actually have been helping with the dog for a while now," he confessed to his mother.

"I see," Iris said. "So before Fourth of July even?"

Gabe looked up and nodded. "I've been feeding him some-times and petting and taking him for walks. Mrs. Williams is all alone out there, so she let me help. And plus, Mutt and I get along so well." Mutt nestled his head against Gabe's shoulder. "Just think how sad he's going to be now with Mrs. Williams in the hospital."

Iris smiled and her eyes softened. "He does look pretty content in your arms."

"Do you think we could keep Mutt just for a couple days?" Gabe begged.

Iris looked at her son and then around the table at the rest of them. "Well, he is kind of cute," she said, a smile slipping out. "But you'll have to give him a bath."

"I'll give him the best bath ever."

"I can help with that," Shelby said. "We can wash him at our house and bring him back to you clean as new."

Iris thought for a moment. "He could sleep on the screened-in porch with you," she said. "Now I know why that's your favorite spot."

"That would be great," Gabe said, grinning.

"We have plenty of dog food," Alice volunteered. "We'll bring some over."

Gabe jumped up and down, the dog's ears flapping in the wind. "Do you hear that, Mutt? You can stay."

At that moment, Logan walked in, basketball shorts and no shirt, wiping sleep from his eyes. Shelby felt her breath catch.

"What's all this? Is that Mutt?" He walked over and petted the dog.

"So you knew about him too," Iris said.

Logan shrugged. "Guilty."

"He gets to stay with me." Gabe looked back at this mother. "At least for now."

"Welcome to the family, Mutt," Logan said. He smiled at Shelby. "Good morning. I wondered what was going on so early out here this morning."

"Well, you can thank your brother for that," Iris said.

"Looks like I missed out on all the details," Logan said.

"You did," Shelby said. "I'll tell you the whole story. Coffee first?"

Logan followed Shelby into the kitchen. "What the heck happened?" he asked.

They stood drinking their coffee while Shelby relayed all the details of the night before, trying not to be distracted by Logan's closeness. His hair drifted across his forehead, and she wanted to reach up and brush it out of his eyes.

"Thanks," he said. "But tell me something. How long have you known about Mutt?"

"A while. And what about you?" she asked Logan.

"Me too. Gabe didn't know, but I saw him sneaking food and disappearing in the woods before the Fourth of July party. That night when we brought Mutt home, I knew it wasn't for the first time."

Shelby lowered her voice. "When Gabe first told me about Mutt, he asked me to keep it a secret. I didn't want to break his confidence by saying more. I figured he would tell you all soon. And Mutt needed some care."

"Gabe must really trust you, if he confided in you," Logan said. "He's pretty reserved, usually. He could have come to me."

"He's such a sweet kid," Shelby said, touching Logan's hand lightly with her fingertips.

Logan looked back toward his mother and Alice, then took her hand in his. "I'm sure glad my father isn't here. I'd hate to think what would be happening instead. Gabe loves that dog so much already."

Alice stood and called over to Shelby, "Let's get home now. Scarlett will want breakfast, and probably feels like we deserted her."

Shelby took the scruffy dog from Gabe's arms. She could feel his ribs under her fingers. Just in time, she thought, holding him close. "We have all the supplies at our house. He'll be in good hands."

At the door, Iris thanked them for taking such good care of Gabe.

"See you later at the beach," Shelby called to Logan.

If she had the energy, she thought.

∾

WHEN SHE GOT HOME from the DeLucas' house, Scarlett was whining in the kitchen.

Alice called the dog to her. "We're back," she said, "and your food is coming." She put the dog bowl down in the kitchen and Scarlett scarfed up her breakfast, her dog tag clinking on the stainless steel food bowl.

After bathing and brushing out Mutt, Shelby was exhausted. "I think I might take a little nap," she told her grandmother

"Are you sure you don't want to eat first?" Alice asked.

"Maybe later."

Alice nodded. "Of course. I'll check on Mrs. Williams later today. I'll give the hospital a call and see if they will give me any information on visiting times. I'll also let Eleanor know what happened."

"That would be great." Shelby yawned. "I don't know if I can sleep. I'm so...I don't know, restless."

"Why don't you just curl up on the couch? I'll be quiet in the kitchen."

"You don't need to be quiet," Shelby said. Watching Alice puttering around the kitchen was a comforting sight. Stretching out on the couch, she rested her head on the pillow. Scarlett jumped up and lay next to her, then gave her slobbery kisses all over Shelby's face. "Sweet girl," Shelby said, running her fingers through the curly red hair on top of her head.

She loved this dog and never wanted to leave her. Shelby never wanted to leave her grandmother, either. It was the first time she felt like she could breathe, exhale, and nothing was going to fall apart if she didn't stay on guard every minute antici-pating...anticipating and being prepared.

Shelby tried to fall asleep, but the adrenaline still pumping through her body made it impossible. Insomnia was not an unfamiliar pattern for her. Maybe once things were settled she would sleep better. She thought about Logan. He'd been so sweet this morning, and she'd loved seeing him all ruffled just out of bed. He would be leaving for college in a few weeks. Would she really see him again after that? Would he text her? Would he come back on the weekends? Or he might meet some older college girl and forget all about Shelby. That didn't make her happy at all. She thought about Logan's mother, Iris. She had a soft heart and had let Mutt stay. If Mr. DeLuca returned, Shelby was sure her grandma would take Mutt if Mrs. Williams wasn't able. There was no way they were going to let that dog be homeless.

"Just a small snack," Alice said, laying a tray of peanut butter toast for two and hot tea on the coffee table. She took a seat next to Shelby and poured the tea.

Suddenly starving, Shelby pushed herself upright and joined her grandmother for a bite.

"It's been quite an eventful morning," Alice said, warming her hands on the cup. "Are you okay?"

"I am," Shelby said. She nibbled on the toast smothered in crunchy peanut butter that had melted slightly into the warm bread. "But everything's moving so fast. Pretty soon the summer's going to be over." Suddenly Dana's last phone call resonated in her ears. There'd been so many distractions. "Have you heard any more from Dana?"

"Oh my gosh," Alice said. She put her cup down on the table. "I completely forgot. She asked for us to call her today."

"Wait. Before we do, I've been thinking."

"So have I," Alice said.

Shelby sat up straight. "I don't want to leave you and Moonwater Lake. I've made up my mind. Is it really all right with you if I stay here until I finish high school?"

Alice smiled. "Nothing would make me happier. But we do need to talk to your mother. She's the one with full legal custody."

Shelby's shoulders dropped. She reminded herself she had options. "I'm sixteen now and I know there are legal ways to make this work. Maybe if we try to reason with Dana, and show her our side, she'll understand."

Alice didn't say a word. Shelby knew why. It would be a stretch of the imagination to think that Dana would put Shelby's needs first.

Alice stood and retrieved her cell phone from the kitchen counter. "I think we'd better call Dana before discussing this any further."

Shelby agreed. She stood next to Alice, watched as she punched in the numbers and then put it on speaker. When it kept ringing, Shelby felt a wave of relief that they could avoid it until another day. But it was not to be.

"Hello, Dana. I hope we haven't disturbed you," Alice said.

Shelby listened as her mother gushed over the new house purchase. Alice barely got a word in.

"Yes, that is great news," Alice said. "When is it going to close?"

When Dana told them the date, Shelby felt her stomach cave in like a sinkhole with nothing to grasp onto.

"That soon? I see," Alice said. "You probably want to talk to Shelby now."

Shelby closed her eyes, praying the answer was no, but when she opened them, Alice was handing her the phone.

After saying hello, her mother jumped right in with all the details. Dana was in one of her highs about the house being in escrow.

"Just think," Dana said, "you'll live in a palatial house, have your own room and bathroom. And you can swim in the ocean anytime you want. I miss you. You know how much I depend on my little girl."

There was a time when Shelby would've loved the idea. A family, a house, her own room. But now she had everything she wanted here in Moonwater Lake.

"I'm very happy for you, Mom," Shelby said. It was now or never, she told herself. "But I still feel the same about staying here."

There was a tense silence before Dana answered. "That's not possible, Shelby. Gus and I have already made plans to drive out in a couple of days. We'll pick you up and have a few days for a little vacation before we need to get back and sign the final papers on the house. So you'd better start packing."

Shelby was stunned. She didn't know what else to say except no, no, no, no! Obviously "no" was not a word Dana understood when it came from her daughter. She had Gus to rely on now, and Shelby wanted her own life.

"When exactly will you be here?" she asked. After Dana answered, Shelby counted the days. It left a little over a week to make her plans and set her strategy in motion. Now was not the best time to argue with her mother.

"Fine. I hear you," Shelby said, ending the conversation before it went any further. She put down the phone and looked at Alice. "I'm not going. Please don't let her take me, Grandma."

"If that's what you want, I'm here for you all the way," Alice said. "And I have some ideas. We'll work together on this. You're not alone. You've got me and Theo. You've got Eleanor, who knows the local laws backward and forward. And Joann, who worked at the high school. You've got Logan. Perhaps his dad will even help you with the legal issues."

Shelby threw her arms around her grandmother. "You're the best."

Her emotions were all over the place, with fear threatening any peace of mind. "Do you think there is a force great enough to stop Dana when she's determined?"

"Absolutely," Alice said. "We are just as determined. I think we both could use a nap to clear our heads before we put our plans in place."

Exhaustion swept over her. Tears were threatening, and she didn't want her grandmother to see her cry. She wiped her eyes. "I'm sure I can get some sleep now. You have a good nap too."

She went to her bedroom and shut the door behind her. Dana's words echoed through her brain. She was so used to giving in and not fighting back. The minute her head hit the pillow, she burst into tears. It felt like things were falling apart brick by brick, like the earthquake they'd been in once when they'd lived briefly in Southern California. Everything had shaken, fallen, and broken, and it seemed like it would never stop. As usual, her mother was the central force. The fault line running through Shelby's life. She had to stop thinking like this. This was her old self, the lost and doomed self, and that was no longer her. She was liked and respected here. Loved. And no one was going to take that away from her. Not even her mother.

CHAPTER 31

Theo discussed the types of cameras available, including using their cell phone if they had one, with the veterans attending his session today at LCV. Eight brave souls had signed up for his afternoon workshop, and he was surprised how easily he'd slipped back into a teaching role. Alice, in a pretty summer dress, sat at the back of the room offering moral support. The small classroom offered privacy, several old tables that could be pushed together, and back wall windows emitting natural light.

Theo went around the table asking students what type of camera they would be using. Some of the older folks like him, nearing three quarters of a century in age, went for the easy-to-use old standby cameras. One of the women in the class, who was probably closer to Trevor's age, preferred her phone. Before closing, the group discussed where they would go for their first shoot and decided on an easy access part of the lake where the white pelicans tended to gather.

After the last student left, Theo packed up his cameras and notes and joined Alice, who was waiting for him near the door.

He had convinced her to sign up to offer a special Saturday afternoon skills class on cookie baking.

"You are an exceptionally good instructor," Alice said. "And so patient."

"Thanks," Theo said. "As a master cookie baker, you will be too."

Alice shook her head. "I'm not so sure. I don't even follow a recipe most of the time."

"Just think of it this way," he said. "Who wouldn't be excited to spend an afternoon mixing dough and eating warm-from-the-oven chocolate chip cookies?"

"When you put it that way, how can I go wrong?"

After filling out a form to offer a baking workshop at the front desk, Alice put on her straw sun hat before they left. When they stepped outside, Alice's mood seemed to drop. Theo saw worry in her eyes, and her smile had turned to a frown.

"I have something I'd like to discuss with you," she said.

Theo's heart plunged.

Alice took his hand and squeezed it. "It's about Shelby."

"Oh...I see," Theo said. "I could use some refreshments after that long class. How about I take us to Redd's and you can tell me all about it?"

Alice looked pleased and Theo's heart returned to normal functioning.

"I've become a regular there," Theo said. "One of my fondest memories as a young lad dating was splitting a tall chocolate soda."

"I'm game," Alice said.

They walked down the sidewalk, past the Moonlake bookstore and its colorful window display of local authors' books in the window. Lying outside the door, sprawled out in the sun, was the town's charcoal gray cat with the turquoise eyes. He allowed the locals an occasional pet, but mostly avoided the tourists.

"How are you doing today, Mr. Cat?" Alice asked.

Recognizing a friendly voice, the feline stretched leisurely and then rubbed up against Alice's leg. Theo watched her charm him into rolling over on his back. Obviously content, the cat's purr rose another decibel.

"You certainly have a way with animals," Theo said. "Shelby too. It must run in the family."

Mr. Cat was used to roaming the town at will and followed them a few blocks until they turned on to Main Street. An oncoming rather large dog heading toward them prompted Mr. Cat to take a detour toward the town museum.

Theo was happy to see there was no line outside Redd's Ice Cream Parlor. The rising temperature was making him a bit woozy and he longed for a cool place to sit. The comforting smell of waffle cones greeted them as they entered. They sat in one of the old-fashioned booths with comfortable vinyl seating, right under an A/C vent. It was also in a private back corner where they could talk.

"Nice to see you both," Steph said with a smile. "Menus, or are you ready to order?"

Theo looked over to Alice. "We would like a chocolate soda and two straws," he said.

Steph grinned. "Just one?"

Alice nodded shyly.

"Whipped cream?" Steph asked.

"Of course," Theo said. "And a cherry on top."

"Coming right up."

A young child ran by with his ice cream cone in hand and toppled to the ground in his haste. The ice cream landed on the floor and the boy began to cry.

"It's okay," Steph said. "We'll just get you another one."

The boy's mother gave Steph a grateful smile.

"Steph is such a nice person," Theo said, "just like her dad."

Theo watched Alice fidget in her seat. It was not like her and obviously something was bothering her.

"Do you want to tell me what happened?" he asked.

"Shelby's mother, Dana, called yesterday and it was..." Alice hesitated. "I don't know how to say this."

Theo felt his shoulders tightening. Shelby had become like family to him, and she deserved the best.

Alice took a deep breath. "Dana's boyfriend Gus is buying a house in Florida. They want Shelby to move in with them and will be here to pick her up within two weeks at the most."

The sound of the milkshake machine whirred in the distance. A line was forming at the counter and orders were being taken. The voices in the room were drowning out their conversation, so Theo leaned forward to be heard. "And how does Shelby feel about that?" he asked.

"Very unhappy," Alice said.

"Unhappy?" Steph asked. She was standing at their table with an icy chocolate soda, piled high with whipped cream with two straws protruding through. "This will fix anything." She placed the soda in the middle of the table. "Enjoy."

"Shall we?" Theo said. Like two high school sweethearts, they sipped their soda. It was heartening to see Alice's eyes light up as the drink worked its magic.

Alice clanked the spoon against the glass as she stirred the soda water and ice cream mixture. After the last, noisy sip, Alice sat back in the booth. "Thanks," she said. "Just what I needed."

"Always a good pick-me-up," Theo said. She still looked a bit down and maybe he could help. "Do you want to share what else happened?"

"I don't know what to do. Shelby is very shaken and absolutely does not want to go. I've tried to talk to Dana, but she won't listen. I feel like it's my fault."

"Your fault?" Theo said. "How can that be?"

Alice lowered her gaze and clenched her fists. "I could have done better raising Dana. Remember I told you she was sick growing up? I had her a bit late, at thirty years old. We almost lost our only child to pneumonia before she was two years old. It scared us both. Our life centered around her and she got away with so much. If I had been stronger and set better limits, maybe she would have turned out differently." She looked up at Theo and sighed. "Then after Dana's husband was killed, we tried to help her, but everything we did only pushed her further away."

"Don't blame yourself," Theo said. "You loved her and did the best you could. Our children have to grow up to make their own choices. And the hardest thing to do is let them, especially when a grandchild's welfare is at stake."

"Watching the way she treated Shelby, all the men coming and going and the constant moving, it broke my heart. And if I said anything, Dana would avoid us for months. Then when my husband, Stan, died, Dana made a brief appearance at her father's funeral and left the next day. I was devastated."

Theo hated to see Alice hurting like this. "I understand. And I am here for you and Shelby, no matter what."

"Thank you," she said.

"I think all parents, or at least the good ones, worry about the same thing. I've had plenty of days I wonder what I could have done differently or better with mine."

"You too?" Alice said.

"I wonder with my Cam if I put too much pressure on him to do well in school and to succeed. And now look at him. He lives in Seattle and all he does is work. But I realize, that's his choice for now. As parents, we have to step back and let them learn their own lessons."

Alice nodded. "I guess so. It's hard when you want to help, save them the pain and lessons we've already gone through."

"We survived," Theo said with a smile. "They will, too."

"I agree," Alice said. "It's Shelby who concerns me most. She wants to spend her last two years of high school in a stable environment and I think that would be best for her. But I've never been good at standing up to my own daughter."

Theo agreed. He didn't want to interfere, but there was something to be said about helping those in need.

"Sounds like we need to call out the reserves," Theo said. "I'm in."

Alice laughed. "You have no idea the battle we will be facing."

"I'm sure all the members of Shelby's dog walking club will do what they can to help. Shelby is sixteen now, right? Legally she's able to make her own choice of where and who to live with."

Alice sighed. "That's true, if Dana will let her."

Steph wandered back to their table. "Anything else I can get you two?"

"Excellent, as always," Theo said. "Just the check please."

Theo paid the bill and escorted Alice outside. On their way home, they kept under the shade of the tall trees as much as possible. There were few other walkers on the path, mostly young people, and a family rode by on bikes of various sizes in the street. Heat waves rose off the lake below, but the beach was as crowded as ever with colorful umbrellas making the sand look like an old fashioned painting.

When they reached Alice's porch, Theo gave Alice a reassuring hug. "I hope you know I'm here for you."

Alice looked up into his eyes. "I feel so lucky that we've found each other, even so late in life. I never thought…"

Theo smiled. "And I never dreamed."

"And yet here we are," Alice said. "Mature enough to finally realize love is a gift, no matter when it graces us."

"And wise enough to know we have to say 'yes' to it while we still can."

Alice smiled. "Yes," she said.

Theo smiled back. "Definitely, yes."

CHAPTER 32

$\mathcal{S}$ helby had an appointment to walk Karma today and Mindy would be joining them. Mindy had requested for Shelby to continue walking with them as she recovered. Shelby was keeping her dog walking schedule reliable no matter what, and wasn't going to let her worries change that.

Before she left, she texted Logan to see how Mutt was doing and let his family know the latest progress on Mrs. Williams. Shelby had been relieved to hear Alice and Eleanor had visited the hospital yesterday. Mrs. Williams was recovering. Even though she had been alone the night they'd found her, Mrs. Williams said she could not remember a thing about it. Sometimes, Shelby thought, that was a good thing.

Mrs. Williams' daughter had arrived and was making arrangements to transfer her mother to a care facility. Shelby thought about her own grandmother. How alone Alice had been since Grandpa died, and how much better she seemed to be with Shelby here. She hoped Mrs. Williams would end up living with someone who loved her. And of course, Mutt too.

With a minute to spare, she slipped on her tennis shoes and assured Scarlett she'd be back soon. When she reached the walkway to Mindy's house, Karma must have heard her coming. She could hear her whining behind the door.

Mindy opened the door looking refreshed and ready to go in her jogging clothes and her hair in a neat braid. "You can see how anxious Karma is to go for a W-A-L-K," Mindy said.

"Come here, sweetheart," Shelby said, leaning down to pet Karma, who was panting with excitement. "We'll take you. Don't worry."

"I really don't know what I'd do without her. She's the best companion ever." Mindy strolled across the living room floor. "Look at this, me walking. Next thing you know, I'll be running again."

"Today we'll take it slow," Shelby said with a smile.

"Whatever you say," Mindy said. She closed the door behind them as they stepped outside.

Shelby put a leash on Karma and helped Mindy down the steps of the front porch. They walked toward the park overlooking the lake. Mindy was slow, and Karma was anxious to get going. She sniffed the ground and checked the trees for squirrels.

The town was buzzing with people. August was their biggest tourist month and every type of lodging was filled to capacity. Shelby had heard Steph talking about hiring another person just until after Labor Day.

"Let's walk over to the park," Shelby said. "A bit more shade and quiet."

Mindy nodded. "I heard the sirens the other day and asked my neighbor what had happened. She told me about Mrs. Williams. Do you know how she is?"

"Sadly, she fell and broke her hip," Shelby said.

"That's going to be a long recovery," Mindy said. "I feel bad for her."

"If it wasn't for her dog, who knows when she would have been found."

"She has a dog?" Mindy asked.

"Remember the dog that came to the Delucas' on Fourth of July? That was Mutt, Mrs. Williams' dog. She was living all alone out there except for Mutt. Gabe is taking care of the dog for now."

Mindy put one foot slowly in front of the other. "A dog by your side can make all the difference," she said. "I wish my parents would understand that. They never let us have a pet when we were growing up." Mindy sighed. "It's hard to stand up to my parents, but that's what I've been doing. Sometimes you have to risk everything to get what you really want."

Shelby gasped. "That's exactly what I've been thinking."

They walked in silence for a few minutes until they reached a bench. "Short rest," Shelby said. It felt strange sitting on what she thought of as "Theo's bench." They looked out at the bright turquoise water. Karma curled up at Mindy's feet, but her eyes kept watch on every passerby.

"And how have you been doing?" Mindy asked.

Shelby felt confident confiding in Mindy, and told her the story of her mother calling and the possibility of having to move to Florida soon.

"Sounds like your mother is trying to include you and make a better life."

She hesitated, not sure she wanted Mindy to know the full extent of her difficult and unstable life. No one here knew much about Shelby's past besides her grandmother and Logan.

"That's one way to look at it," Shelby said. "My mother has a history of moving us relentlessly from place to place. Only once was I allowed to have a dog. We had a little house with a small fenced backyard, and my mother's job was finally going well, so she told me I could have one. We went to the Humane Society and I picked out an older dog that no one else seemed to want. She had big droopy ears, sad brown eyes, and her muzzle was mostly white. But she was my very best friend and I loved her. It wasn't a month later when my mother met a new man, quit her job, and we moved again."

"And the dog?" Mindy asked.

Shelby sniffled. "She went to the pound. I was so heartbroken. I prayed as hard as I could that someone else would take her. But she was old. And even now when I think about it..."

Mindy put her arms around Shelby. "I understand. I'm so sorry."

"I want to stay here at Moonwater Lake," Shelby said. "Even if I'm only sixteen, I know what I want and what's best for me."

"Of course you do. I want to stay here too," Mindy said. "And I'm a full-grown adult still fighting with my parents!"

"We are quite a pair," Shelby said.

Mindy laughed. "I've thought long and hard about it, and the people I've come to know here. And then there's Trevor. He's a very special man."

"He is. And so helpful," Shelby said.

"My parents would never approve of him, but to me, he's everything I've ever wanted. He's kind and gentle and funny."

"And Buddy and Karma love playing together, too," Shelby said.

"They do, so cute together." Mindy turned her scrutiny to Shelby. "I've seen you and Logan together. And you both look so happy."

"Logan is my first real love."

"Aww," Mindy said. "What a summer. I guess we both have some choices to make. I made the decision to stay regardless of my feelings for Trevor. And I'm unsure how he feels about me."

"I see the way he looks at you," Shelby said. "He really cares."

Mindy's eyes brightened. "The first time he volunteered to pick me up for the dog park, I knew he was special. Not only did sparks fly between us, but he was so caring the way he helped me down the stairs and into the car and he didn't even know me. But he also hasn't been around in days. I don't want him to feel pressured that I'm staying just for him. I like my easygoing lifestyle here. I like working from home. And the people and pace are much more relaxed here. Once I'm better, Karma and I can run the paths around the lake."

"I feel welcomed here," Shelby said. "Like I can be myself and fit in. And I love my clients."

"And we love you too," Mindy said. "But...I have something to confess. You're probably not going to like it."

"What? I could never be angry at you."

"Well, maybe not angry, but disappointed." Mindy squirmed on the bench. "I was getting stir-crazy at home, so I went for a walk with Karma by myself a few days ago. We went down the trail to the lake. I really thought I was steady enough on my feet, but... "

"Oh no," Shelby said. "Did you hurt yourself?"

Mindy seemed fine, but the sheepish tone of her voice worried Shelby.

"I'm good now. But I wasn't as ready as I thought." Mindy pointed toward the path. "You know that part that gets kind of rocky right before you reach the lake?"

Shelby nodded, trying not to imagine the worst.

"I tripped and fell, then slid down a few feet. I was more stunned than hurt, but I just sat there and cried. I used to be so independent, running miles on mountain trails near San Jose."

"Oh no. You could have called me," Shelby said. "I would have come to help you. Anytime."

"Thanks, Shelby. It was very early morning. I was glad no one was around to see me, but I wasn't sure that I could stand up. Karma seemed to know just what to do. She came right over and lay beside me, just like I'd seen Buddy do when Trevor was having a hard time. Then she licked the tears off my face. I looked in that dog's eyes and realized that she'd love me no matter what. It didn't matter if I could walk or run. Or even stand. Karma loved me, and that's the kind of love I want in my life. And that's when I decided to stay here at the lake and follow my own heart."

"That's beautiful," Shelby said, reaching down to snuggle Karma. "But you are okay now?"

"I'm more than okay." Mindy grimaced. "But you should have seen us. I leaned on Karma and gradually stood up. Together we hobbled back home. I cleaned myself up and then we had breakfast. At one point I just started to laugh and couldn't stop. I think I learned my lesson. Sometimes things have to be taken slowly. I don't have to try to be perfect, for myself or anyone else."

Shelby thought about how much she pressured herself to do well in school, to take care of her mother, to make sure their life didn't fall apart. "In the past, I'm not sure I've listened to my own heart," Shelby said. "What does it feel like?"

Mindy laughed. "Well, you know how you feel when you see a cute dog and your heart leaps open?"

"Yes," Shelby said. "I want to hug all the dogs."

"That's the feeling," Mindy said. "Close your eyes a minute, and think about what it is that you really, really desire in your life. Tell your mind to be quiet for a moment and just listen."

Shelby could hear a voice whispering to her, "Stay where you are loved." She opened her eyes and could feel the tears forming. But they were happy tears.

"I've been afraid to really hope I'd get to stay here at the lake." Shelby wiped away tears. "Choosing what brought me joy never felt right before. I do love my mother, but this time it's different."

"Let's make a pact," Mindy said. "I'll help you and you'll help me. I'm going to call my parents tonight and tell them. I can only imagine what they're going to say. Then I'll email my boss and tell him I'll work remotely. If that's not acceptable, I'll train my replacement."

"Good for you," Shelby said. "I'm working on a plan for my grandmother to get temporary legal custody so I can go to school here. We'll do whatever it takes."

"We deserve to be happy," Mindy said, giving Shelby a high five. "On that note, I think I'd like to go back home and rest awhile." She pushed herself up from the bench. "When we get back, you can take Karma on a long run and wear her out."

"I hope you'll be joining us for that sometime soon," Shelby said.

After she brought Mindy home, Shelby and Karma took to the lake path, picking up their pace as they went. Colorful wildflowers releasing their sweet smell were sprinkled alongside the trail. Overhead, leaves danced in the breeze as it whipped through Shelby's hair. Karma panted, her head high to catch the wind as they traversed the wooden bridge into the denser woods that wound behind the lake. Without a doubt, this was home.

CHAPTER 33

*T*heo woke up thinking about his wonderful time with Alice when they'd volunteered together a few days ago. He'd loved having her there watching him instruct the photo class. Sharing the soda after was the cherry on top. He laughed to himself at the pun.

As he went through his morning routine, his mind drifted to Trevor. The last time he'd seen him, he'd seemed a little withdrawn, and Trevor hadn't been to the last dog park meeting a few days ago. Eleanor had given Mindy a ride that day. Theo hadn't seen him around lately, not for an ice cream meet-up or even walking Buddy. Over the years since they'd first met, Theo had watched that young man plunge in and climb out of his PTSD symptoms. Something in his gut didn't feel right.

"Come on, Wally. Let's go and take a little walk over and visit your pal Buddy."

He leashed up the dog and they walked the five blocks down to Trevor's cabin. Theo knocked on the door and waited. When no one answered, his stomach knotted. Everything had been going so well. Then, the door creaked open. Trevor, unshaven and blurry-eyed, stood at the opening.

"Did I wake you?" Theo said.

Trevor pushed his mussed hair back from his forehead. "I've not been sleeping well." Buddy joined Trevor at the door and Wally's tail wagged furiously. "Do you want to come in?"

"If you don't mind."

"No problem," Trevor said.

Inside, dishes were splayed across the coffee table and clothes crumpled over a chair. Buddy's eyes never left Trevor as he wandered a bit aimlessly through the living room and then turned toward the kitchen.

"You want something to drink?" Trevor said. "I could probably use some coffee."

"I'll just have water," Theo said. "I've had my morning coffee."

"Hope you don't mind if I make myself a cup."

"Of course," Theo said. He took a seat on one of the comfortable leather sofas. Wally lay at his feet. Buddy followed Trevor around the kitchen as he made coffee, never leaving his side. When Trevor handed him the glass of water, Theo noticed the man's hands shaking and he didn't make eye contact. It was obvious Trevor wasn't doing well, and Theo was glad he'd come over.

Trevor tossed some clothes aside, took a seat, and sipped his coffee. Buddy kept by his side.

"So what's going on?" Theo said, trying to sound casual.

"Not much. Working. Been busy with a new website design client."

"We haven't seen you around lately. Eleanor went over to pick Mindy up last time for the dog park gathering." At the sound of Mindy's name, he noticed Trevor twitch. "You and Mindy still doing okay?"

"What do you mean, doing okay?" Trevor snapped. "We were never really doing anything."

"Sorry. You two seemed to get along so well, and she's a great woman."

"That she is," Trevor said, "but she's probably leaving soon. Her family has different goals for her, and I'm not one of them."

So that was it, Theo thought. Trevor was trying to protect his heart by rejecting himself first before Mindy could.

Theo leaned forward. "That's not what Mindy said when she was over last time. She's pretty convinced she's going to stay at the lake."

"Really?" Buddy nudged in closer and put his head down on Trevor's foot. "That doesn't mean she's interested in someone like me."

"Someone just like you from what I can tell," Theo said. "Someone with a big heart who helps out the community any way he can."

Shoulders hunched, Trevor stared at the floor. It tore at Theo's heart to see his friend in this state.

"Mindy speaks fondly about you and Buddy all the time. And when you two are together, the sparks are visible."

Trevor looked up, his face pale. "I just can't bear another loss. I lost so many buddies in war and it's an uphill battle just to function sometimes."

"It's normal to be afraid and shy away from something or someone that might hurt you," Theo said. "I totally understand. My heart goes pitter-patter when I see Alice. And an old heart like mine shouldn't be doing too much of that."

Trevor laughed and Theo felt a wave of relief.

"Don't you think I felt that way at first with Alice? She lost a loving husband."

"Oh, come on," Trevor said. "You're the best man I've ever met."

"I'm old, and grumpy, and moody…"

"And a wonderful human being," Trevor said. "If there were more kind-spirited people like you in this world, it would be a better place."

Theo was taken aback by Trevor's words. He'd been so closed

off in his own grief, he hadn't noticed the people around him he could still be present for. And love. "That doesn't mean I don't feel afraid," Theo said, "and still think of Jean and possibly risking my heart again."

"I bet Jean would want you to be happy," Trevor said. "She was one of the most amazing women I ever met. Always smiling with a kind word of encouragement to offer. The last thing she'd want is for you to be miserable. And face it," Trevor said, "we've both been pretty sad guys lately."

Now it was Theo's turn to laugh. Wally stirred at his feet, his head popping up to see if he was missing anything.

"How about this?" Theo said. "You reach out to Mindy and be brave, and I'll reach out to Alice and be brave, and together, we'll see where all this bravery leads us."

Trevor put his thumbs up. "It's a deal."

"Now that that's settled," Theo said, "I think I'll take my lazy dog and go home for lunch." He stood up and Wally followed him to the door. "I also have my Skype call with my son later today. Something else to look forward to."

Trevor chuckled. "Oh, come on. Is he still trying to get you to move back there?"

"Yes. As if I would ever want to live in cold and rainy Seattle. The noise, crowds, and traffic…how does anyone ever get around in a city?"

"I get it. I wouldn't last five minutes. And besides, you have lots of friends here looking out for you."

At the door, Buddy finally left Trevor's side and circled around Wally, saying a quick dog hello and goodbye.

"One other thing," Theo said. "Shelby's going through a tough time. Her mother is insisting she move to Florida with her. Shelby absolutely does not want to go. I am organizing a meeting at my house to lend her support."

"Count me in," Trevor said. "And thanks for coming by. I feel much better now."

"Any time," Theo said. "You and me both."

CHAPTER 34

*S*helby was wearing her favorite pink and yellow bathing suit. Her tanned skin glowed as she applied the sunscreen. She loved her new sun-tipped highlights in her hair. She laughed at herself when she remembered how she had resisted coming here. Summer at the lake was the best ever. From her spot on the beach, pretending to read, she peeked from behind her sunglasses at Logan sitting at the lifeguard station.

When Madison had walked by earlier, she'd given Shelby a condescending look. Shelby was sure those girls couldn't understand what in the world Logan saw in her. When she saw herself through their eyes, Shelby sometimes wondered the same thing herself. But Logan had reassured Shelby that what he saw in her was something he really liked. Even being such a cute and smart guy, he also had a big heart. Not like some of the other popular boys Shelby had met at school who kept their distance from her. Logan was different. He looked inside the person for who they were too.

She looked closely at Madison standing at the water's edge. Her bathing suit hung loosely on her bone-thin body. And even with a tan, Madison looked pale. Shelby felt a pang of sympathy for the girl. Madison was beautiful and rich; she could have just about any boy or friend she wanted. It must have stung when Logan wasn't interested. After seeing Madison that day when her mother was yelling at her at the ice cream place, Shelby wondered if Madison's meanness might come from a place of desperate unhappiness.

Shelby heard her name called and looked up. Logan waved her over. The warm sand seeped between her toes as she strolled over. Logan's bright smile made the day even better.

"I wish we could go for a swim together," he said.

"The life of leisure?" Shelby said with a grin.

"Well, some of us have to work," Logan teased. "But I'll be happy to watch."

His words made her smile. She waded out a few feet and then dove head first in the turquoise water to swim. There was nothing better to melt stress away than your arms, legs, and body gliding through the cool, clear lake water. She put her head up to the sun and let it dance on her face as her wet hair clung around her shoulders. A fishing boat motored by beyond the swimming buoys, causing a ripple in the water. She let herself float with it.

She flipped on her back. Above, the blue canvas of sky was punctuated with white, puffy clouds in all shapes and sizes. Some even looked like a string of little pink hearts. Everything looked like hearts to her these days with Logan. If only she could float here forever, and these days would never end. The moment she started thinking about her mother's call, the old feeling of powerlessness returned. If she couldn't secure living with her grandmother, she'd be ripped away from all of this. Her body felt heavy, the water cold, and everything seemed wrong.

As if nature mimicked her, a gust of chilling wind blew in, bringing with it a dark gray cloud that momentarily blocked the sun. Shelby decided to get out of the water and dry off. The happy mood she entered the water with did not exit with her. And then she saw Logan wave. She hesitated to go speak to him until she pulled herself together. Worry pressed on her chest, making it hard to breathe.

She turned away from Logan and wrapped herself in her towel before plopping down on the sand. Maybe she should just go home. Before she could decide, she saw Logan being relieved for his break. Logan, eyes masked in dark sunglasses, his whistle still around his neck, approached her. It figured. As much as she wanted to talk to him, she could feel tears forming in her eyes and flipped her sunglasses on before he got any closer.

He sat down and put her cold hands in his. "You looked like a graceful dolphin out there propelling yourself through the water."

Before she could stop it, she started to cry. Of course at that moment, Madison and her friends had to be passing by on their way to the stairs. Shelby turned her back away from the group and put her head on Logan's shoulder. She was sure those girls were probably thinking, "Yeah! Good. Logan's breaking up with her," which made Shelby cry harder.

Logan put his arm around her and held her close. "What's wrong? You know you can tell me."

"Everything," Shelby said. The closeness of his body and comforting sound of his voice began to relax her. "It's my mother," Shelby said. "She's really coming this time to take me to Florida with her."

"I see." Logan didn't sound too happy about it either.

She looked up at him. "And I don't want to go." Tears started all over again. "And now everyone on the beach is seeing me cry."

"So what? No one else matters," Logan said, wiping a tear from her cheek.

Those words snapped Shelby out of her pity party. She took a deep breath. "You're right. My grandmother and I are trying to work out a way so I can live with her now. Feeling so happy in the water reminded me just how much I have to lose if my mother won't agree."

"I'm with you," Logan said. "Let's just sit awhile until you're ready to go home. How about this? I'll take you out for a special dinner tonight at the seafood place on the pier. Get your mind off things."

"I'd love that," Shelby said. She wiped her tears with the back of her hand. "I'm such a mess."

"You're not a mess," Logan said. "You're having a hard time and have every right to be upset from what you've told me. I'll talk to my dad. His firm does pro bono work sometimes. Either way, we'll get this figured out together and we'll celebrate later. Okay?"

"Definitely." She looked around and no eyes were on them. She kissed Logan softly on the lips. "You are the best."

Playfully he ruffled her hair. "I'm going back to work now and tell John I'll be leaving a little early today. I'll pick you up about six." Logan stood and helped Shelby to her feet and they walked together to his station.

"See you later," she said. "I'm going to go stand in the shower, get all this sand off, and scream for a while."

Logan chuckled. "Now, that's a good idea."

"Maybe I'll do a little pounding on the bed, too," she said with a grin.

"Go for it. Do whatever you need to. And tonight, we'll have fun and solidify some plans."

Shelby purposely didn't look over at Madison and her posse, who were huddled at the base of the stairs. She could feel their eyes on her but reminded herself she didn't care what they thought and walked right on by without a glance their way.

SHELBY OPENED the front door eager to tell her grandmother about her dinner date. Alice was on the phone, nodding and repeatedly saying, "I see." Alice mouthed to Shelby to hold on just a second and pointed over to the couch. Just great, Shelby thought. She hoped it wasn't Dana again.

Shelby sat down and waited until Alice hung up the phone.

"What's up?" she asked hesitantly.

"It's mostly good news about Mrs. Williams," Alice said.

"How is she?"

Alice sat down in her recliner and Scarlett leapt up on her lap. "She's doing fine, resting peacefully. She will be going to a private rehabilitation hospital while she recovers. It's got lovely views of the lake, just north of here, and maybe they'll even let us bring Mutt in for a visit. After that, her daughter is going to bring her home to live with her in Arizona."

"It must have been so hard for Mrs. Williams living out there alone after her husband died," Shelby said.

Alice nodded. "I can imagine. Now she'll get all the care she needs."

"What about her house?" Shelby asked.

"I guess the daughter will be selling that, too."

Shelby was afraid to ask. "And the dog?"

"They won't allow dogs in the care home. And from what I've heard, Mrs. Williams is telling everyone what a comfort it is to know that Gabe is taking good care of her Mutt now."

"Fingers crossed he gets to keep him."

"Either way," Alice said, "Gabe always has us as a backup. The dog will not be homeless."

"Gabe really loves Mutt," Shelby said. She hoped Iris wouldn't have to tell her son that his father wouldn't let him keep the dog

"Miracles happen," Alice said with a smile. "Meanwhile, let's think good thoughts and try not to worry."

DRESSED and ready for her date, Shelby took one last look in the mirror. She'd trimmed her bangs a little and loosely curled the

bottom of her hair. The style, along with some light makeup, definitely made her look a bit older.

She went into the living room in search of her grandmother to say goodbye before she left, and found Alice was in bed reading. By the look of the front cover, it was a summer romance novel. Scarlett had her head on Alice's lap and opened one eye when Shelby entered.

"I'm ready to leave for my dinner out with Logan," Shelby said.

"The food there is the best in town," Alice said. "Your grandpa and I used to go there. Wonderful memories." A smile drifted across her grandmother's face. "It's easy to live in those memories, but I've come to realize and be grateful that I still have today."

Shelby kissed her grandmother on the cheek. "I'm so glad to hear that."

"And by the way," Alice said shyly, "Theo asked me on a date. We're going to the Movies in the Park in a few days."

"Very fun," Shelby said. "I guess I better be going now. You and Scarlett have a cozy night."

"Don't be too late," Alice said kiddingly.

Shelby decided to walk over to Logan's house so she could let them all know how Mrs. Williams was. Before she could knock on the door, Logan opened it and stepped out. His hair was combed back, and he looked dazzling in khaki pants with a neatly tucked-in, crisp, cream-colored, button-up shirt. Shelby was glad she'd worn her new pale blue maxi dress with the V neckline. The small-heeled sandals dressed it up a bit too.

"Hey," Logan said, "I was just coming over to get you."

"You look like a model in one of those teen magazines," Shelby said, hoping she didn't sound like an idiot.

He raised an eyebrow and smiled. "You look pretty dazzling yourself."

Shelby could feel herself blush and wished she could fan

herself off. "I have a little message for Gabe and your mom," she said, "so I thought I'd come by a little early."

Logan motioned for her to come inside.

"Nice to see you, Shelby," Iris said. "You look lovely. I hear you two are going out for dinner at the Seafood Cafe tonight."

"Yes. I'm looking forward to it," Shelby said.

Iris smiled. "It's one of our favorite places. Their crab cakes are divine. You two will love it."

"Sounds yummy," Shelby said. "Before we leave, is Gabe here? I have some news about Mrs. Williams."

"Gabe!" Iris yelled toward the back room. "Come on out here, and bring Mutt."

Gabe straggled out with Mutt at his heels. The dog was almost unrecognizably clean with a checked bandana tied around his neck and his head held high. Mutt's face was trimmed to reveal a narrow snout and to allow him clearer vision around his eyes.

"Hi, Gabe," Shelby said. Mutt heard her voice and raced over. She petted his now silky coat. "He's had another trim, I see."

"We took him to the groomer for the works," Iris said. "Doesn't he look adorable?"

They're definitely warming up to him, Shelby thought.

"He's not as skinny anymore, either," Gabe said.

Logan laughed. "You've made sure of that," he said to his brother.

"Mutt looks like a new dog," Shelby said. "You are taking such good care of him." Shelby paused. "I thought I'd let you all know that Mrs. Williams is recovering well from her broken hip."

"Ouch," said Gabe. "She must be in so much pain."

"My grandmother said they're managing it very well at the hospital. Mrs. Williams' daughter is here now taking care of her."

"That's comforting to know," Iris said. "What about when she goes home?"

"She won't be going home. She'll be going to a rehab hospital in the Valley and then moving to Arizona with her daughter."

"Oh," said Gabe. "What about Mutt?"

Shelby smiled at him. "Mrs. Williams is telling everyone how happy she is you are taking care of her dog. I'm sure she'd be relieved if you could keep Mutt permanently. She seems to really want you to have him."

"I really want him. Come here, Mutt!" He hugged the dog and looked at his mom. "Can we keep him, Mom? Please? You like him, too."

"If it were up to me..." Iris shrugged.

Logan stepped in. "Mom, it's up to you just as much as anyone. We all need to stand up to Dad sometimes. We're allowed to be happy and have a normal life."

Iris sighed. "I know, Logan. Let me talk to him. For now, Mutt is staying with us, and I will do my very best to make sure we can keep him."

"I hope that Mutt won't miss Mrs. Williams too much," Gabe said, kissing the dog on top of his head.

"With all of us around? Mutt's going to be very happy," Shelby said.

Iris came over and gave Shelby a hug. "Thank you so much, Shelby, for everything you've done for Mrs. Williams, and for Gabe, and for Mutt. Please tell your grandmother thank you, too."

"I will," Shelby said.

Iris glanced at Logan, who had gone into the kitchen for a glass of water. Then she leaned in close and whispered to Shelby, "If you'd like, please come the night after next for a surprise pizza party for Logan's eighteenth birthday. I'll text you the time."

"I'd love to," she murmured back.

"Hey, what are you two whispering about?" Logan said as he strolled back beside them.

Shelby smiled. "Oh, nothing."

Logan narrowed his eyes in suspicion, then smiled. "I think we should be off now. Are you ready?"

Shelby tossed her sweater over her shoulders and turned to Logan. His smile, dimples in each cheek, melted her as usual.

~

THEY STROLLED ALONG MAIN STREET, hand in hand, under the town's twinkling lights past the little shops and cafes. The balmy evening was perfect, with the slightest of breezes ruffling through the flower baskets hanging from the old-fashioned streetlights. The Seafood Café, with its well-lit "open" sign, was a short walk out to the wooden pier, where boats docked when coming in to town. The lights from the boats reflected off the darkening water in reds, blues, and yellows.

Logan held the door open for her. "After you," he said.

The hostess seated them by the window, where they could watch the first tangerine rays of the sunset spill over the lake.

Shelby watched out the window as the sun began to drop behind the low purple mountains. "The view is beautiful from here," she said. "Thanks for inviting me."

"My view is quite beautiful too," he said, staring at her.

Butterflies flapped their wings in her stomach. He always knew what to say. He looked particularly handsome with the candlelight from the table reflected off his face. Classical music played overhead, setting the perfect romantic mood.

Logan smiled. "And besides, I think we both needed cheering up, and being with you always works for me."

"Hello there," a familiar voice said.

They looked up to see Eleanor and her husband walking by to be seated. "I see you have exceptional taste in food," Eleanor's husband said.

Eleanor winked at Shelby. "And men. Enjoy your dinner."

As they passed, Shelby noticed the lavish bouquet of flowers in Eleanor's husband's hand. Eleanor was beaming.

"Things were a little rocky with them, but it looks like they worked things out," Shelby said. "Eleanor told us the two of them are even playing golf together now."

"Sometimes you just need to spend time together, I guess," Logan said, looking over at the couple. "And sometimes you need to think about what really matters. I wish my dad would. If he'd realize how much he works, how alone my mother is, and how rarely he spends time with us, maybe my parents would smile like that again."

"I'm sorry your dad is so out of it," Shelby said. "It seems like sometimes people get so wrapped up in other things that they lose perspective."

"That's my dad, all right," Logan said, "but let's not spoil the night talking about him." Logan pulled out the menu. "I want you to order whatever your heart desires."

Of course, Shelby ordered the specialty crab cakes with three homemade sauces. They ordered a Caesar salad with shrimp to share. Logan ordered the trout and a bottle of sparkling water with lime.

The waitress carried over a basket of the fragrant-smelling crusty sourdough bread with warm, creamy butter and the sparkling water.

Logan poured them both a glass and then held his up for a toast. "To a wonderful summer," he said.

Shelby clinked her glass to his. "The best ever." She hadn't known this kind of happiness existed, and to be sitting here across from this amazing guy, in this special place, she felt so lucky.

"Try this bread," Logan said, passing the basket to her.

"Oh my gosh," said Shelby, taking a bite. "Amazing."

Their entrees arrived, decorated with flowers and fresh herbs, and Shelby could see why everyone raved about this place. Logan might be accustomed to meals like this, but it was a first for Shelby. Outside, a lone sailboat crossed the blackening lake approaching back to the pier.

"Moonwater Lake is so special," she said.

"Sure is," he said. "Ever since we started spending summers here, I've always looked forward to coming back. I wonder if my mother will really make the lake house her home now. It would mean a lot of changes."

They were both facing possible upheaval, Shelby thought.

She took another bite of a crab cake with a different sauce and sighed. "This meal is incredible."

"You haven't even had dessert yet."

"Did I hear dessert?" the waitress asked. She rolled a cart over to the table with several delectable-looking confections. Shelby wondered how she'd ever decide. "This is our homemade strawberry torte topped with chocolate meringue, and this is our key lime cheesecake, made fresh daily. We also have peach praline pie, and last but not least, our sampler of homemade ice cream with our special caramel and hot fudge sauce."

Logan looked over at Shelby.

"I can't make up my mind," she said. "You choose. They all look wonderful."

Logan assessed the offerings. "I think we'll need two."

"Really?" Shelby said.

"Definitely. What would you suggest?" he asked the waitress in a formal way of someone used to fine dining.

"I can suggest our key lime cheesecake. It is very popular, as is our ice cream."

Shelby nodded. "Absolutely."

"Would you like any coffee or tea?" the waitress asked.

Logan looked to Shelby, who shook her head no.

"Not right now," he said. "Thank you."

The waitress brought the desserts with two spoons and they dug right in. The cheesecake was the perfect combination of tart and sweet. Shelby could eat this forever, lost in the comfort of its creamy texture. The thick rich chocolate and caramel sauce clung to the ice cream and melted in her mouth. After several more bites of each, she put down her spoon. "I just can't eat any more."

"Me neither," Logan said. "We'll have the rest of the pie packed up, and you can take it home. Maybe your grandmother would like some."

"I'm sure she would," Shelby said.

When the waitress appeared and presented them with their check, Logan asked for a box as well.

Shelby knew it had to be incredibly expensive. Logan pulled out a credit card and laid it down on the tray. "Totally my treat," he said. "I hope you enjoyed it, Shelby."

"It was the best dinner of my life," she said honestly.

Logan reached for her hand across the table and held it in his. "I hope there will be many more in the future."

She hardly knew what to say. She didn't think he was the type of person who would say that kind of thing lightly or make promises and not keep them. But he was still going away to college, she reminded herself.

On the way home, Logan suggested they find somewhere to talk. "We can look at the stars and discuss our dysfunctional families and see what we can figure out together."

They walked down the quiet sidewalk leading out of town toward the empty park, where they had their pick of the benches facing out to the lake. They chose the one with the best view and snuggled up together. A few early stars lit the sky, and a sliver of moon peeked from the night sky.

"You first," Logan said. "Tell me everything about your situation with your mom."

"Everything?" she asked.

He nodded.

Shelby found the words flowing out to him, the whole moving story. Her voice lowered, "My mother...I don't know how to put this, but my mother has never stayed with a man more than six months since I've been old enough to count. I don't know if this one will be any different. I have two years left of high school. I want to spend them in one place, here with people I love, where I feel safe and happy. I have my own business now and can help support myself."

"I get it," Logan said, "and you should have that. You're sixteen. You're old enough to start making your own decisions. I'll remind my father and let him know you need advice now. He knows a lot of people, and it would probably be quite easy for him to make a few calls."

"You would do that?" Shelby asked.

"For you, yes," Logan said. "I know if I request it, he'll do it. He does try to reach out to me sometimes. Usually I just push him away."

"Why?" said Shelby. "If he's reaching out..."

"There have been so many issues between us," Logan said, "starting with the way he treats my mother." He waved his hands in the air in frustration. "He's disappointed with my wildlife biology major and insists I go to law school and follow in his footsteps. It is so opposite of who I am, and he can't see that. Some of his clients have questionable values, especially about the environment, but he doesn't seem to care where the money comes from. We barely see him. It's like he doesn't even care about us."

"I get it," Shelby said. "It's really painful when parents aren't what we hoped they'd be and can't give us what we need." She raised her head and kissed his cheek. "It's all right to be angry and it's all right to be sad. You'll be going to college soon and start a new life there."

"I hope so," Logan said. "I don't know what's going to happen. My parents seem to be leaning toward a divorce. It's going to be really hard on Gabe. Sometimes I think maybe my dad's got another family he's hiding somewhere."

"Oh, no," Shelby said. "Do you really think that?"

"Probably not," said Logan. "I don't think he has the time." Logan tilted up Shelby's chin and kissed her gently on the lips. "Enough about them. We have each other now," he whispered.

Stars glistened above, but Shelby didn't notice them. The night faded away in his arms, along with all her worries. When she was with him, it was like time stopped and it was only the two of them in the world.

Logan pulled back, his eyes staring into hers. "I want you to know this is not just a summer fling for me. I really care about you, Shelby. And I don't want to date anyone else."

Shelby's breath caught. "I really care about you too, Logan. You fill my heart."

"Aww," he said, "that's a sweet way to put it. I didn't know that girls like you existed. Authentic people with genuine feelings, who really care about others. You are one of the few people I feel like I can relax and be myself with."

"Always," Shelby said. "I wish..." She stopped herself, not wanting to put any more pressure on Logan.

"What?" Logan said. "That the summer didn't have to end soon and me leave for college? I feel the same."

"But you'll be back, right?"

"Every chance I get, every break. If my mother stays here, that'll be even easier. If not, I'll just stay at our lake house. And we always spend Christmas here. Have you ever been here at Christmas?"

"Once, when I was a little girl. I remember it was incredible," Shelby said. "There was a parade in town and colorful lights around the shops and carolers singing from boats."

"That's it," he said. "We build a warm fire and put lights and ornaments on an enormous tree, all the while drinking hot cocoa. This year, you can decorate with us."

"I can't think of anything that would make me happier,"

Shelby said. "I just...I worry about my mother. She usually gets what she wants."

"Well, not this time," said Logan. "What you need, and what you want, counts too."

Shelby realized she was probably falling in love with Logan. She was only sixteen years old, but the feelings were real. She remembered when her mother told her how she had fallen in love for the first time at seventeen with Keith, the man who was to become Shelby's father. Dana had said he was the love of her life, and at the time, Shelby hadn't really understood the depth of her mother's words. Now she could. The thought of possibly losing Logan ripped Shelby's heart to pieces. No wonder Dana was always looking for another man to fill what must be an enormous hole in her heart from the loss. Shelby really hoped Gus would finally be the man her mother was looking for. And maybe it would be the right thing for Dana and Gus to live alone for now, like a honeymoon period. Best for them and best for Shelby.

She lifted her head up to Logan and he leaned over and kissed her again. She put her arms around his neck, and as he deepened the kiss, she melted into him. Wrapped in each other's arms, she felt like they were floating over the lake and out to the stars.

CHAPTER 35

*T*heo had called a special meeting at his house, hoping the old saying, that there was strength in numbers, would come through for Shelby. When Alice had confided in him about Shelby's experience growing up, his heart had ached for her. Shelby seemed so content here, and he wanted to see her stay that way. He would do his best to see that they came up with a solution that would benefit everyone. Wally raced to the door as Shelby and Alice knocked once and entered. Shelby was putting on a brave face, but she did not seem her old perky self.

"Come on in," Theo said. "No one's here yet. I thought we could have a little chat before." He looked at Shelby and winked. "I have Coca-Cola." He knew she loved the drink. "And I have iced tea and some lemonade. What would you like?"

Alice opted for the iced tea.

"I'll have a Coke," Shelby said. "A tall one, with lots of ice."

Theo handed them each a drink, then they proceeded out to the deck. They sat at the table where he had recently installed a new extra-large red striped umbrella to block the sun. He'd bought comfortable matching chairs with vinyl cushions to brighten up the place. Much more enjoyable now to watch the sun drift across the water and the moon rise over the trees.

"Any more word from your mother?" Theo asked.

"Not since the last call a few days ago," Shelby said.

"I see." He glanced at Alice, who was frowning.

"Let me put it this way," Shelby said. "Dana is very upset because I'm ruining *her* plans."

"And what exactly did she mean by that?" Theo tried to contain his anger and stay calm.

"It appears that Gus enjoys the idea of a nice little family, just the three of us in the new house. Don't get me wrong, I love the idea the two of them being happy together. But I'm not a little girl anymore, he's not my father, and I don't trust Dana." Shelby looked at her grandmother.

"I understand," Alice said sadly. "I do, but you know, everyone deserves another chance, and I hope both you and your mother can get one."

Theo patted Shelby gently on the back. "This is a tough one. Maybe your mother will be happy this time. But that doesn't mean that moving there is best for you."

"Thank you," Shelby said.

She sniffled, and Theo felt terrible. He was glad he'd put tissues out on the table as a precaution. A fallback to his old days in social work.

"Honey," Alice said, "it'll be fine. We're all here. Everyone's coming today to help you get what you want."

"I want friends," she said. "A normal life. I want to graduate and go to the prom. What happens if I move to Florida and Dana and Gus have a fight? Dana will pack me up and move again. Who knows where we'd end up, or how many more schools I'd have to go to? I'll be applying for college scholarships and it won't look good on my transcripts."

"It makes perfect sense for you to stay. We'll talk to your

mother, try to reason with her," Alice said. "We'll offer to fly you out at Christmas, and during other breaks, for a start."

Shelby took a few Kleenex and dried her eyes. "That's a good compromise, I guess. But if it's awful there, and they're fighting and..."

"No one's going to force you to stay there, if you don't want to," Theo said. "You're old enough now to legally make many of your own choices."

"We can hope it will work out for Dana and Gus," Alice said. "She could use some happiness too."

"I agree," Shelby said. "But her happiness isn't necessarily mine."

They heard a knock at the gate as people began to arrive for the special meeting of the troops, dog-free as requested. The group today was comprised of many people with various resources that could surely be of help.

"Come on in, come on in," Theo said.

Walking through the gate was Eleanor wearing a wide brim summer hat and sunglasses. Behind her was Trevor with Buddy and Mindy by his side. Theo had left Wally inside to rest in the coolness of the air-conditioned house.

"I didn't want to leave Buddy home, but he has his vest on today, so he'll stay right by me. Hope that's all right," Trevor said.

"No problem," Theo said.

Joann was quick to follow, a smile on her face as she greeted them. Something was different about her today, and Theo hoped it meant good news.

"Come on in, everyone. There are drinks on the table."

Steph carried over a familiar pink box from the shop in her hands. "I brought some treats," she said. "We've started making chocolate chip cookies, and I thought I'd give each of you one to sample. They're for our new cookie crumble hot fudge sundae."

"Sounds amazing," Shelby said. "I could use one right now."

"Anytime," Steph said. "You come over later and I'll make you the first official new sundae on the house."

Everyone assembled around the table, under the welcome umbrella, with a cold drink in hand. Theo wished a breeze would come up from the lake. If it got any hotter, he'd suggest they go inside.

"Let's get to work here," Eleanor said. "What is Shelby's current status?"

Theo laughed to himself. Eleanor may have retired from the position of mayor not that long ago, but she was still quick to take the role of leader.

Theo filled them in a bit more on everything that had happened over the last several days, including all the details of Dana's call and plans to move Shelby. "I thought we could go around and everyone share their input and ideas on how we might be of help to Shelby."

"Great idea," said Eleanor, "and I'd be happy to go first."

"Before anyone starts, I'd like to say something," Shelby said. "I've come to love it here and being with all of you, and of course the dogs." She looked over at Alice. "I have the most wonderful grandmother in the world. Theo, I cannot thank you enough for everything. And I want you all to know I'm ready to do whatever it takes to stay."

"And we love you," Joann said. "I used to work at the high school in the counseling office. I can help you get registered. There are a few legal issues we'll have to take care of since your mother is your current guardian, but there are plenty of ways to work around that."

"We should talk about getting some legal help as well," Eleanor said, "and see, if emancipation is needed eventually, what would be involved."

"Anthony DeLuca might help," Shelby said. "Logan mentioned he does some pro bono work."

"Top attorney, that one," Eleanor said. "I'll do what I can with my contacts, and I have quite a few."

"And I can do online research as needed," Mindy said.

"And I'll help Mindy," Trevor said.

Theo watched as Shelby's face became more animated with each offer of assistance. There was certainly a good amount of hope floating around the table.

"I'm always here if you need to talk," Steph said. "I can offer moral support and free ice cream for the next month."

"I'll definitely take you up on that," Shelby said, chuckling. She looked around the table, making eye contact with everyone. "I can't thank you enough. One more thing. My mother said she's leaving Florida soon, so we do need to move fast."

"We will. No problem," Theo said. "I think we have a strong plan to get started with."

"All right then," Steph said. "It's time for cookies." She held up the plate and Theo could see the chocolate chips were slightly melted and glistening in the sun.

"Sustenance for the soul," Mindy said as she reached for a cookie. "These are amazing."

Shelby took a napkin and patted her lips. "I'd really like to hear how all of you are doing too."

"Well, I have some news," Steph said.

Theo thought Steph had a bit of a glow about her today. He couldn't have been happier to see how well that young couple were thriving since they'd taken over Redd's Ice Cream Parlor.

"Josh and I might be pregnant," Steph said. "He agreed a few weeks ago to start trying."

Clapping resounded in the air. Congratulations offered all around. Another resident of Moonwater Lake might be joining them soon, Theo thought. A tiny little one. Next to him, Theo noticed the way Mindy and Trevor smiled at each other after the news. And they were holding hands under the table. Trevor must have gone to talk to Mindy, and it had obviously worked out well.

"I have an announcement, too," Joann said.

A smile crept up her face. Her eyes sparkled. This was the way Theo remembered Joann before the grief of losing her dog had cast a shadow over her these last months.

"You all know I've been combing the shelters for the right dog, and I think I found him. His name is Fritz and he desperately needs a home after his owner passed away. I put in my application and I'm waiting to see if it gets approved."

"Of course it'll be approved," Shelby said. "What better owner could there be than you?"

"What does he look like?" Eleanor asked.

"He is the cutest thing you ever saw. He's pretty tiny. Probably a mix of Chihuahua and maybe terrier. His black and tan ears stick straight up, and he looks almost like an elf. And his eyes are so soulful, almost human."

"It sounds like you're in love already," Alice said. "I bet Scarlett will love playing with him."

"He'll be a great addition to the dog park," Theo chimed in.

Eleanor cleared her throat. "While we are all sharing news, you will be surprised to hear I'm actually enjoying playing golf with my husband."

"I am surprised," Alice said. "That's one thing I never thought I'd see."

"What can I say?" Eleanor shrugged. "I know I complained a lot that my husband was hardly home. I realized it takes two to make a relationship work. And my husband pointed out that I've been a little stubborn, particularly around the golf. I guess even I have to admit that I'm not perfect either."

Everyone laughed. Who is? Theo thought, reaching for another cookie. Eleanor was always so well put together and confident. She was a force to be reckoned with. Everyone was capable of change if they really wanted to, he guessed. Even him.

"It makes me happy to see how well things are working out for each of you," Shelby said.

"You'll be next," Theo said. "Don't you fret."

Around the table, everyone nodded and assured Shelby that all would be well, and soon. Theo stood, adjourned the meeting, and thanked everyone for their input. Then he turned to Shelby and Alice and offered to walk them home. Mission complete.

CHAPTER 36

$\mathcal{T}$he next few days were filled with paperwork, deciphering the computer research Mindy had done for her, and meeting with the registrar at the high school. Tonight was Logan's surprise party. He hadn't even told Shelby it was his birthday. He probably didn't want to make a big deal of it. Shelby was glad she had some notice so she could buy him a present. She'd texted Iris that she would bring a birthday cake.

Perfect, Iris texted back. *My husband Anthony is going to try to be home tonight. He called yesterday. Logan spoke to him about your situation and said he will help.*

Great news! Shelby texted back.

Shelby and her grandmother had spent the morning baking a beautiful triple-layer chocolate cake with ganache filling and caramel buttercream frosting. It said "Happy Birthday, Logan" piped in dark chocolate icing on top. Then Alice had spent the afternoon cooking fried chicken and cutting up a fruit salad to fill the picnic basket for her movie date in the park tonight with Theo.

They'd both retired to shower and dress, which was taking

Shelby a little longer than usual. She wanted to look her best for Logan and if Mr. DeLuca turned up as well.

Alice walked into Shelby's bedroom and twirled in a circle, showing off her embroidered jacket set over a rose-colored shirt. "What do you think?" she asked. "I've tried on several things trying to figure out what would look nice and still keep me warm in the park tonight."

Her grandmother looked like a flushed schoolgirl getting ready for a first date.

"You look very pretty, and so does the new lipstick we picked out. I'm sure Theo will agree."

Alice grinned. "I hope so. And look at you, gorgeous. Now, you better be off and go surprise that boy of yours."

"Right," Shelby said. She retrieved the cake and present but realized it wouldn't be a surprise if she just walked in with it through the front door. She wasn't sure what to do, so she texted Iris. *Should I carry in the cake and say "surprise?"*

That works, Iris wrote. *Logan thinks we're ordering pizza. He probably thinks we're all being pretty mean forgetting his birthday.*

Shelby sent a smiley face back and turned off the phone. She took one more glance in the hall mirror to make sure her white capris and lacey blouse worked. Her dark hair cascaded over her tanned shoulders. She'd put on some Pretty-In-Pink lip gloss and a touch of mascara. Content with her appearance, she headed out across the street.

When she knocked on the DeLucas' front door, no one answered at first. Probably Iris and Gabe were hiding so the birthday boy would answer.

"Surprise! Happy birthday!" Shelby said as Logan opened the door.

Shock registered on his face and then a huge grin. "Thanks. I think you're the only one who even remembered."

"That's not true," Iris said as she, Gabe, and Mutt bounded out from the back room. "Happy eighteenth birthday."

"You guys," Logan said. "You had me wondering all day if you forgot."

Gabe grinned. "That was the idea."

Mutt barked in affirmation.

"Thanks, everyone." Logan ran his fingers through his hair and glanced down at his old t-shirt and gym shorts. "You could have given me a little warning."

"That would spoil all the fun," Gabe said. "We ordered three different kinds of pizza. They'll be here soon."

They moved into the kitchen and Shelby put the three-tiered cake on the granite island and the gift box next to it. Everyone grabbed a bar stool while Iris made up some drinks, handed them out, then took a seat beside them.

"The pizza's not going to be here for about half an hour," Iris said. "I wanted to make sure we had a little time to talk." She winked over at Shelby, and Shelby figured it out. They probably put a delay on the pizza hoping that Mr. DeLuca would arrive.

"That's fine," Logan said. "I'm not that hungry yet. But that cake looks amazing."

"Later," Shelby said. She held up the sea green envelope with a sea turtle engraved on it. "Why don't you open your gift while we're waiting?"

Logan took the box in his hands and examined it. "Something to do with turtles, I gather."

"Just open it," Gabe said.

Logan slipped off the ribbon and lifted the lid. He held up an imprinted certificate and took a moment to read it before turning his gaze to Shelby. "You couldn't have gotten me a better gift. Thank you."

Shelby nodded, pleased how much he liked it. "The donation to help save endangered sea turtles is in your name. The organization will follow up with you as new statistics come in too."

"What a thoughtful gift," Iris said. "You'll have to wait until later for our gift."

Mutt whined to be picked up. Gabe brought him up on his lap. "Look at this dog. He's the best."

Logan scratched behind the dog's ears. "Totally."

As the minutes passed by, Shelby noticed Iris kept glancing discreetly toward the front door.

"Honey," Iris said to Gabe, "I think you might want to put Mutt in your room for the night. With all the pizza and the cake, you don't want him getting sick."

Gabe nodded. "Right, he is kind of a beggar. I'll put him away."

Just as Gabe joined them back in the kitchen, the doorbell rang. Shelby didn't think his father would be ringing the bell, so it had to be the pizza.

Iris answered the door. "Thank you very much," she said, taking the three boxes from the delivery woman and placing them on the dining table where plates and forks awaited. "Pizza, anyone?"

"Let's eat!" Logan said.

Iris caught Shelby's eye before answering with a shrug. "I don't see why not."

Her disappointment was apparent. Shelby hoped Logan's dad would make it home for everyone's sake. Meanwhile, she enjoyed trying the different pizzas and watching Logan and his family laugh and joke during dinner. So unlike her own birthday back in May.

Suddenly, the front door sprang open. All eyes followed as Mr. DeLuca, not to the surprise of anyone but Logan, stumbled in.

It was obvious that something was wrong. Anthony looked pale and was wearing ill-fitting clothes. He seemed surprised to see everyone gathered, and didn't make eye contact or wish Logan a happy birthday. Iris stood and hurried over to him.

"Anthony," she said, getting his attention. "Is everything okay?"

There was dead silence in the room.

Anthony braced himself against the wall. His voice quivered. "Not really."

"Do you need to sit down?" Iris asked. She guided him over to a wingchair in the living area adjacent to the dining room.

Logan, Gabe, and Shelby stayed seated, watching the scene unfold. Shelby felt incredibly out of place and wished she could politely leave.

"What happened?" Iris asked.

Anthony took his wife's hand. "Our small plane went down," he said. "In the water."

"What?" Iris said. "Why weren't we notified? I could have come."

"I'm fine," he reassured her. "I've just left Harborview Hospital." He put his head in his hands.

It was shocking for Shelby to imagine what Anthony had just gone through. Logan and Gabe listened wide-eyed, seemingly frozen in their seats. Shelby wished she could do something to help.

"Why didn't you call?" Iris asked. "When did this happen?"

When Anthony looked up, Shelby barely recognized the man she'd seen here on the Fourth of July. "I wanted to be the one to tell you." He looked over at his sons. "All of you. Only yesterday I was on a short flight for my last meeting before heading home for Logan's birthday. And then..." He shook his head back and forth as if in disbelief. "The fog was so thick. We crashed into the water, had to get out and float in the freezing water. The pilot was injured. Oh my God," he said. "I'm lucky to be here. I love you all."

Iris threw her arms around him. "Come and lie down and I'll call a doctor."

"The hospital released me," Anthony said.

"Come on now," Iris said, helping him stand. "I'll get you a cup of hot tea and prop you up in bed."

"Thank you," he said. He grasped Iris's hand as she walked him toward the bedroom.

Iris glanced back to where they were all still sitting at the table and put her palm up for them to stay right where they were.

This is horrible, Shelby thought. Not only is it Logan's birthday, but his father could have died. "I'm so sorry this happened," she said to both the brothers.

Gabe sniffled. "I want to go see him."

"We will," Logan said. "Let Mom get him settled first."

A low bark from the back room reminded Shelby that Mutt was still there in Gabe's bedroom. With all that had happened, she hoped the dog's presence wouldn't make things worse.

As soon as Iris returned, Shelby stood and said, "I think I should leave."

"Probably so," Iris said, looking a bit dazed herself. "I'll pack up one of the pizzas. Please take it home and have it with your grandmother."

"Thank you for having me over." Shelby hesitated. "Under the circumstances, would you like me to take Mutt to our house for a few days?"

"No," Gabe said.

Iris turned to Gabe. "Just for a day or two," she said. "It would be best if you went and got him."

Gabe looked like he was going to burst out in tears, but he went and retrieved Mutt and brought him to Shelby. "He's still my dog," Gabe said.

Shelby cradled Mutt in her arms. "Of course. I'll bring him back real soon."

Logan walked Shelby to the door. "I'm so sorry this happened," she said, taking his hand. "Call me anytime."

"I'm going to walk Shelby home, Mom. I'll be right back."

Shelby knew she didn't need him to accompany her across the street, but he probably wanted to get out of the house, and she wanted to be there for him.

When they reached her front porch, Shelby hugged him. She could feel him shaking in her arms. "I'm so, so sorry, Logan," she said. "Please let me know if everything's okay as soon as you can."

Logan nodded.

"And happy birthday," she said.

"Right," Logan said. "And thanks for the cake and all."

Logan turned, shoulders stooped, and walked slowly back home. Shelby's heart went out to him and his family. It was going to be a hard night for them all. For a second, it crossed her mind there wouldn't be any legal help for her tonight, which was of no importance at this point. Logan's father was alive and safe. That was the most important thing. She slipped into the house with Mutt and remembered her grandmother was out with Theo tonight. There was no one home for her to confide in. Scarlett raced out of the bedroom. Shelby put Mutt down and Scarlett greeted him with a sniff. At least she had her furry comfort. And Scarlett was a very good listener too.

$\mathcal{I}$t had been a challenging year for Theo. Too many times he thought grief would win in the battle to keep his head above water. But in the midst of summer, as he dressed to go to the movies with Alice, he felt almost young again. If someone had told him that at the age of seventy-five, he would be getting a second chance at love, he would have never believed them. He laughed to himself as he buttoned his shirt, then pulled on a light blue sweater to keep the chill out tonight.

"Look at me getting all spiffed up to go on a date," he said to his faithful beagle, whose eyes had followed his every move, probably hoping for a walk or a snack.

Wally cocked his head to one side.

"You're surprised too," Theo said to the dog. "Look at us both. You've perked up since we met Scarlett. Ah, there's nothing like a girl, right?"

He finished getting dressed and tossed a couple lawn chairs in the back of his Toyota Prius, then drove over to pick up his date. The summer movies in the park were just two miles away on a well-lit road in Oak Grove Park. Alice was bringing a blanket and picnic basket of treats. To Theo's delight, *Grease,* an old favorite for both of them, was playing tonight.

When Alice opened the door, Theo took in a breath. "You look radiant tonight," he said.

Alice blushed. "I never noticed just how blue your eyes are. That sweater really brings them out," she said.

Feeling rather suave, Theo beamed. "Shall we go?"

The picnic basket and folded blanket were by the door. Theo picked them up, offering Alice his other arm as he escorted her down the porch steps.

"What a lovely night," Alice said, looking up at the sky. "Not too warm, just right."

"And plenty of stars," Theo said. He opened the trunk and put the basket in. "I also packed some of the folding chairs from the dog park so we won't have to sit on the ground."

"Very smart," Alice. "Not as easy as it used to be."

"My Toyota awaits you," he said, opening the car door and helping her in. "Not exactly greased lightnin'."

Alice chuckled at the reference to the movie they were going to see. "But I'm hopelessly devoted to you anyway," she said grinning.

Theo's heart skipped a beat...in a good way.

On the way there, Alice shared her concerns. "I'm still a little worried about Shelby."

"Everyone's got her back, including me," Theo said. "I'm sure we can help work this out. I hope her mother will be reasonable."

"So do I," said Alice. "So do I."

"Speaking of kids," Theo said, "I was thinking, if it's all right with you, I'm going to tell my son and his wife about you."

"More than all right with me," Alice said. "I'd love to meet them."

The park was crowded when they arrived, and it took a little while to find a parking space. They walked across the grass toward the stage, where the screen was already set up. People were settling and talking among themselves. Kids ran around playing in front of the stage.

"How close do you want to sit?" Theo asked.

"Not too far back," Alice, "but not way up front either."

"I agree."

The smell of food and buzz of excitement lingered in the air. Off to the side of the crowd, they found a spot under an oak tree where they could have a slight amount of privacy. Alice set down the basket as Theo set up the chairs.

"What do we have in the basket?" he asked.

"How does fried chicken and fruit salad sound?" Alice asked.

"Sounds delicious."

"And I have homemade potato chips, thick and crisp and salty."

Theo's stomach rumbled. Alice was a talented cook and baker. He appreciated all the time she'd spent preparing this feast.

"And for dessert, guess what I baked? Lemon raspberry cookies." She drew out checkered napkins and a tablecloth and laid out the spread.

70s music played in the background, piped in through the speakers, as they began to eat.

"Look at all the families," said Alice. "So many young ones in the summer."

"That's the way it is here," Theo agreed, wiping his hands on a napkin. "And then in the winter it gets a little less crowded, but not so much anymore."

"Right," Alice said. "But the tourists keep all the businesses going, so we're happy for that." Some kids were throwing a Frisbee for their dog. "We could have brought Scarlett and Wally."

"But sometimes it's nice to be alone," he said. "Besides, those dogs would be begging for food, barking, and trying to chase the squirrels."

"You're right. But they would have loved it."

"Next time," Theo said. And he hoped there would be many more next times.

When the host for the evening announced that the movie was ready to start, Alice cleared away the food. Once they were comfortable in their chairs, she covered their knees with the blanket. The excitement of the movie, the songs, the drama, and holding Alice's hand brought him deep contentment. The song, "You're the One That I Want" began and Theo squeezed Alice's hand. On the inside, for a moment, he was a teenager again, no matter how old he looked on the outside. Alice laid her head on his shoulder and Theo put his arm around her. How lucky he was. John Travolta, larger than life on screen, flipped up his collar and asked Olivia Newton-John to dance with him. From characters jumping on cars to falling in love, the movie was everything he remembered. The audience started clapping along with the music, and Alice and Theo joined in.

Alice's smile reached from ear to ear. They could still have fun. Be happy again. When the finale concluded, everyone stood and cheered. Theo turned Alice to face him and mustered up the courage to kiss her tenderly on the lips. She looked surprised at first, but then stood up on her toes and kissed him back.

Alice took a deep breath. "We're two lucky people, aren't we?"

"We are," Theo said.

They walked to the parking lot. After loading the car, they hopped inside and Theo turned on the heat. For a moment they sat together, looking out at the stars as the parking lot emptied.

"What a great movie," Alice said. "Just as good as when I first saw it."

"I agree," Theo said. "And even better watching it with you." He turned the radio on softly as they drove back.

Theo pulled up to the curb in front of Alice's house and escorted her to the porch. His palms were sweaty, and he felt like a teenager on a first date again as he decided whether to kiss her at the front door. His heart won out.

CHAPTER 38

A few days had passed since Logan's eighteenth birthday party and so much had happened since. The night Shelby had come home early, she had waited up for Alice to get home from the movies with Theo. Her grandmother had seemed so happy, she hated to tell her about Anthony DeLuca's harrowing experience. Alice and Shelby had stayed up talking into the night and finally gone to sleep. Mutt whined at the front door but eventually curled up with Scarlett and went to sleep. But Shelby hadn't heard anything or seen anyone leave Logan's house. She'd been working a lot, so she hadn't been home every minute to watch. It would be good to know.

There had been no word from Logan. Finally she received a text from him.

Done working at 3:00. Can pick you up. Let's go for a drive and I'll fill you in on everything.

Shelby felt a wave of relief wash over her. She hadn't wanted to interfere, but of course, Logan's lack of communication had made her worry more. At least there hadn't been any more calls from her mother, either. Joann had contacted the high school and all was clear for Shelby to enroll as soon as she had a signed document from Dana.

At three o'clock, she walked outside to meet Logan in front of her house. He pulled up in his parent's silver Lexus LX SUV and stepped out to open the passenger door for her. His face looked pale despite his tan, but his smile was still there when he saw her.

The car was more luxurious than anything Shelby had ever ridden in before. The seats were a blue-gray leather that still smelled new. The steering wheel and part of the dashboard were a deep red, setting off all the dials and buttons. A map of the lake was displayed on a screen in front of them.

"You ready?" he asked after they fastened their seatbelts.

Logan turned on the A/C and drove through town, passing the Coffee Magic shop and town grocery store until they reached the road that circled the lake to the north. To their left were oaks and madrone trees scattered across the hills that were now covered in wild poppies. The lake shimmered to their right and was dotted with boats.

"It's been a long couple of days," he said. "I'm sorry I didn't contact you sooner."

"No problem," Shelby said. "I didn't expect you to, but I have been worried."

"Everything was crazy. My dad is physically fine, but he was emotionally traumatized. I've never seen him that way."

She waited for him to elaborate when he was ready. The road before them began to climb in altitude. The trees were changing to fir and lush ferns that grew in the shade. SUMMIT LOOKOUT 2 MILES, a sign said.

"I'm going to pull over here," Logan said. "The view is awesome."

They were the only car in the small parking lot. Together they walked over to the edge of the viewing area. Forests in all shades of green and rolling mountains surrounded the massive lake below. "Breathtaking," Shelby said. "You can see everything."

"I've been wanting to bring you up here. I'm glad we made it."

They took a seat on a bench and sat in silence as the sun worked its way across the sky. Perched on a cliff in the higher altitude, the lake valley looked like a painting in the distance. For a moment Shelby felt vertigo as she looked below, and it underlined the terror Logan's father must have felt as the plane went down.

Logan seemed in a trance as he told the story. "I still can't believe it happened. They were on their way to the San Juan Islands in Washington State. My dad said the pilot was experienced and when they'd left Seattle the skies were clear. But thick fog rolled in as they crossed the Sound. Zero visibility, the pilot said."

"How scary," Shelby said.

Logan nodded. "Are you sure you want to hear this?"

"Of course," she said, moving closer to him for support.

Logan continued in a low voice. "My dad noticed the pilot panicking and knew they were in trouble. Their air speed was over a hundred knots. Then a pocket opened up and my dad saw the water about forty feet below them. The impact was brutal," he said. "But the worst thing was the cabin started filling with water."

Shelby could imagine the horrifying scene. She could hardly believe anyone survived.

"He must have been in shock," Shelby said. "I would be."

"For sure," Logan said. "My dad sprang into action and pushed a window out. Him and the pilot managed to climb out on the wing carrying life jackets. My dad said his whole life flashed before him during those twenty or thirty minutes sitting there in the freezing fog watching the plane sink right out from underneath them." Logan let up a deep sigh. "My fight with him before he left could have been the last thing we ever said to each other."

"But it wasn't," Shelby said, reassuring him. "He's home and he's safe. He survived."

Logan shook his head. "It's a miracle, and I don't say that lightly. They ended up floating in freezing currents. My dad couldn't feel his arms or legs. Just as he was about to give up, a small yacht approached. Those people saved them and contacted the Coast Guard. My dad was wrapped in blankets, shivering like crazy. The couple's black lab pressed itself between my dad's legs. He hugged its body, absorbing the dog's warmth and comfort."

Shelby felt tears coming down her cheeks. "Dogs always know where they are needed."

Logan looked at her. "He finally told us he'd been afraid of dogs since he was a kid and was chased by one on his way to school. Not anymore, he said."

"Was he injured?"

"His sternum was bruised from the impact and he had a few minor injuries." His voice quivered as he spoke. "He told us his computer, his papers, everything that he thought was important to him were in that plane as it sank. And yet, he realized when he hit that freezing cold water and feared he might die, he realized that none of that meant anything." Logan's voice caught in his throat "He told us his love for my mother and me and my brother Gabe was all that really mattered."

Shelby pulled him into her arms. "I'm here for you," she said. He trembled in her arms and she stroked his hair.

People were coming and going from the lookout, speaking loudly, and Shelby suggested they go back to the car for some privacy.

Logan stared out the front window. "I've always wanted my dad to care. I've always wanted us to be a priority, but before I didn't think it was possible. It's like he's a different person, one I never knew." He turned and smiled at her. "Not only that, he's told Gabe to bring Mutt back to our house and he's letting Gabe keep him."

"Gabe must be so happy," Shelby said.

Logan nodded. "I also talked to my dad about you."

"Really? Thank you."

"Of course," he said, stroking her cheek.

Shelby realized this was a pivotal turning point for Logan and his family. She wondered if it would affect where they would live, how Logan would feel about her, and if everything would change. But most of all, she was so happy for Logan, his mother, his brother, and little Mutt.

"My dad has agreed to help you with your mother. He said you have legal rights, and if you want to come to the house, he'll go over them with you. My mother said you can come by later today if you'd like. She's making a special dinner for my dad and invited you. Afterwards you and my dad can talk."

"Are you sure everyone is up to a visitor? I can wait," she said.

"I'm sure," said Logan. "We're all sure. My dad knows how important you are to me."

It was a relief to hear Logan say that.

His eyes met hers. "Thank you for listening."

"Anytime," she said. "I'm happy to." By the look of the sun waning in the sky, Shelby encouraged Logan to turn around and get back for the important dinner tonight.

On the way home, he relayed some of the family's plans, easing Shelby's mind even more.

"You won't believe this," Logan said, "but my dad has agreed for us to live up at the lake, and let Gabe go to school here. We'll use the city home more for short trips and special occasions. He said he can work anywhere and he's going to tell his firm he's going to do a lot less travel, if any. I think he's in no hurry to get on a plane again."

"I bet," Shelby said.

"Enough about me," Logan said. "Any more word from your mom?"

"Not yet, but everybody's been helping me figure things out. Mindy sent me information on emancipation, and I'm hoping your dad can tell me more about temporary custody. Joann said we'll just need to establish my legal guardian and I can enroll in school."

"I'm sure my dad will do all he can to clear this up tonight. He knows time is short."

Short it was, Shelby thought. She wondered just how much time she had left before Dana descended.

~

ALICE HAD BEEN INVITED to join the DeLucas for dinner too, but she'd already made plans for an early dinner with Theo, so Shelby headed over to Logan's house alone. Mutt had leapt with joy when she'd returned him to Gabe earlier that day. Iris, in a gauzy summer dress, opened the door for her. The aromatic smell of garlic, tomato, and herbs made Shelby's mouth water.

"You're just in time," Iris said. "You remember Logan's dad, my husband, Anthony."

Shelby put her hand out. "Glad to see you, Mr. DeLuca."

"Call me Anthony," he said with a smile. "I'm so glad you could join us."

Relief washed over Shelby at his warm greeting. She barely recognized this Anthony, wearing a loose t-shirt and jeans, as the same man she'd briefly met Fourth of July.

Mutt came racing in from the screened in porch, followed by Gabe.

"You have to see Mutt's new stuff," Gabe said.

Mutt was wearing a fancy new collar with bones circling it.

"And look," he said, "the leash matches." Gabe looked at his dad adoringly. "My dad bought it for him. And even took him for a walk."

"Well, it's about time that dog had something that befit his new stature," said Anthony, and everybody laughed.

Shelby bent down and petted Mutt. "You certainly have landed in a good home." Mutt kissed her cheek. Shelby looked back at Gabe. "Don't forget, you can bring him to the next dog park club meeting."

"Can't wait," Gabe said.

Everyone took a seat at the lavishly set table with candles burning in the center. Shelby sat between Logan and Gabe. From the sound of his tail drumming the wood floor, she was sure Mutt was at their feet.

"Our first course is an antipasto," Iris said, passing around the platter. She smiled at her husband. "Everything I cooked tonight I learned from your mother."

"Happy mangia," Anthony said. "Or in English for our guest, 'Let's eat!'"

Iris explained each dish to Shelby as she served them. The crispy bruschetta with roasted caramelized cherry tomatoes and basil was next, followed by pasta carbonara topped with fresh-grated parmesan cheese.

Shelby reflected on the stark difference from the dinners she'd had with her mother. Dana never cooked. She'd either bring home fast food or leftovers sometimes from her jobs.

"This pasta is delicious," Shelby said to Iris.

"My wife makes excellent pasta from scratch," Anthony said between bites.

Iris smiled at Shelby. "I'd be happy to show you how sometime. The other ingredients you are tasting are pancetta, fresh eggs, Parmigianino and pecorino, cheese and a lot of coarse ground black pepper."

"I've never heard of pancetta," Shelby said.

"It's like ham," Gabe piped up. "But just wait till you taste her gnocchi."

Shelby had no idea what gnocchi was, but she sure wanted to try it.

The conversation flowed just like Shelby imagined it would in any normal family. There was lighthearted teasing and banter. Iris told anecdotes about when the boys were young, and both

Logan and Gabe moaned. In every way Shelby felt comfortable and part of the family.

She didn't think she could eat another bite when Iris carried out a large pan of tiramisu covered in chocolate shavings. "I've always wanted to try that."

"I hope you like it," Iris said. "This recipe has cocoa, espresso, wine, and mascarpone cheese layered with ladyfinger biscuits."

The rich, creamy dessert did not disappoint.

After dinner, Logan's father suggested that he, Shelby, and Logan go to his home office and get down to business. Gabe trailed off to his room to play video games. Shelby offered to help Iris clean up first, but Iris waved her along, assuring her she had it covered.

Logan sat beside her for support in the perfectly organized office.

Anthony took a seat at his sleek glass desk that faced French doors opening to a full lake view. She watched him shift into professional mode as he opened his laptop and began.

"Let's start with you telling me whether there is any more news from your mother that I'm not already aware of."

"Only that she's determined," Shelby said. "But I'm pretty determined myself."

"Have you thought about your options?" Anthony asked. "Emancipation or temporary custody with your grandmother as a legal guardian?"

"Yes, I've hardly been able to think of anything else," Shelby said. "I'm really hoping my mother will be reasonable after she hears me out. If I can talk her into letting me stay, what do I need in place to secure that my grandmother, Alice Meyer, will be my legal guardian until I turn eighteen?"

"Your best and fastest solution would be for your mother to sign a temporary custody agreement appointing Alice as your legal guardian. I've drawn up a preliminary draft for you to look at. I presumed that might be your optimum recourse. I'll print a copy and you can take it home to review."

"And what if her mother says no?" Logan asked.

"Shelby could petition for emancipation," Anthony said. "But that is up to her."

Shelby squirmed. "I'm hopeful I won't have to go that far. It feels so...I don't know, hurtful. She's still my mother. But I believe it would be better for both of us if I finish high school here."

"All right," Anthony said. He retrieved her copy of the document from the printer and placed it before Shelby. "Take it home and look it over with your grandmother. Then let me know if your mother agrees. Once she signs, I'll get it processed for you."

Shelby stood. "I can't thank you enough."

Anthony looked over at his son before answering her. "I'm happy to do it."

After Anthony left the room, Logan looked at Shelby. "How are you doing?"

"Surprisingly okay. Your dad's great."

Logan blinked twice in surprise. "I don't think anyone's ever told me that before. I'm grateful he's willing to help."

"Me, too. I'd better get home and go over this with Alice before she goes to sleep

tonight."

"I'll walk you home," Logan said, following her toward the front of the house.

"Okay. But first I'd like to say thanks to your mom." Shelby put her head in the kitchen. "Are you sure you don't want any help, Iris?"

"I'm just about done here, and tonight you are our guest."

"Dinner was incredible," Shelby said.

"Well, I hope it will be the first of many more to come. Perhaps you'd like to help cook the next one? Learn some of the family recipes?"

"Definitely," Shelby said. Another reason to add to her long list of why she wanted to stay at Moonwater Lake. Now more than ever.

"Good luck with your mother," Iris said. "And please let us know if we can assist in any way."

Once everyone waved goodbye, Logan walked her across the street.

"You have a wonderful family," she said. "Thank you for including me tonight."

"I wouldn't have it any other way." He gave her a hug and whispered in her ear, "I'll see you in the morning."

Shelby watched longingly as he walked back. Halfway there, Logan turned and waved and she returned it before entering her house and closing the door behind her. Leaning against it, she let the waves of happiness wash over her as memories of the night lingered.

"Shelby, is that you?" her grandmother called from the bedroom.

Shelby found Alice sitting up and watching TV in bed with Scarlett lightly snoring beside her.

"I had the absolutely best night," Shelby said.

"I'm so glad to hear it," Alice said. "Theo and I had a lovely dinner as well."

Her grandmother's voice seemed flat. Perhaps she was just tired.

"I see you're holding some papers," Alice said.

Shelby had forgotten they were still in her hands. "Logan's father drew up a temporary custody agreement with you as my guardian for us to review. We can let him know in the morning if we want him to formalize it."

"We'd better get right to it," Alice said. "Your mother called. She'll be here in two days."

CHAPTER 39

Shelby woke early the day of her mother's arrival to go for a long walk alone by the lake and try to clear her head. She'd hardly slept the night before in anticipation. Yesterday had been frantically busy after everyone on "Team Shelby" had been alerted to the new timeline and had shown up at Alice's to help Shelby prepare. She was as ready as she could ever be. Theo had offered to join them for lunch today, so that he would be there when Dana arrived.

Sweat rolled down her neck and back as she raced around the last bend of the path before turning for home. She stopped and took a deep breath to absorb the calm and stillness of morning on the lake. Familiar birdsongs echoed between the trees. She was prepared. Logan's father had brought over the final temporary custody and legal guardianship agreement yesterday. It clearly specified she would live with her grandmother until Shelby turned eighteen. Now all she needed was her mother's signature. A feeling of dread pitted in her stomach at the thought of having to file for emancipation if Dana wouldn't sign it. She shook off her worries and walked briskly home.

"Morning," Alice said when Shelby returned. "Are you hungry? I'll make whatever you like."

"Not quite yet," Shelby said. "But thanks. I'm going to take a quick shower and get dressed."

The morning seemed to drag on as the time drew closer to her mother's arrival. Shelby moved around the house looking for things to distract her racing mind.

As the day progressed and she knew her mother was due any time, Shelby's nerves started to take over. The what ifs were racing through her mind faster than she could catch them. She'd never really been able to say no to her mother before, and she was anxious about saying it now. Theo had talked to her about setting healthy boundaries, something she'd never learned about before, and it made sense.

Theo arrived just before noon to join them for a light lunch. Shelby picked at her salad, her stomach rebelling at the thought of eating.

Alice busied herself clearing away the dishes and making a fresh pot of coffee. Scarlett followed her around hoping for a scrap. Almost three months ago she had been apprehensive to come here, but now she never wanted to leave. Shelby kept checking out the front window. Theo stayed steady at Shelby's side and she gave him a grateful smile.

"Don't worry," Theo said in his reassuring voice. "Your grandmother and I are here to help in any way we can."

Her grandmother had just sat back down to join them when Gus's truck pulled along the curb outside. Shelby watched as they walked up the path to the house.

"I'll get it," Alice said, standing.

As Alice opened the door, Shelby immediately noticed how tanned and healthy they both looked. Her mother's hair was blonder than ever, trailing down her barebacked sundress. And Gus looked trimmer as well. She kept her seat, waiting to see how things unfolded.

"Hello, Mother," Dana said, stepping inside. "You remember Gus?"

"Of course I do. Gus, how are you?" Alice said.

"Very good. I hope you are too."

"Just fine," Alice said. "Come on in. I made some fresh coffee."

Gus waved Dana in before him. "Just a quick cup for me," he said. "I thought I'd leave you ladies alone." As he said that, his eyes darted to Theo.

Theo stood, introduced himself, and shook Gus's hand. "Nice to meet you. I'm Theo, one of the neighbors here at the lake. You may have heard Shelby started a dog walking business. The club meets at my house."

"I've heard about that," Gus said, turning to Shelby. "What a great summer job for you."

"There you are," Dana said. "Come over and give me a hug."

Shelby hesitantly walked over and leaned in for a hug. She patted her mother's back, keeping some distance between them before pulling back.

"You look great," Dana said. "Getting a lot of sun and fun?"

"Yes," Shelby said, "and dog walking."

Dana nodded. "Oh, right, right. I'm glad to hear that."

There was an awkward moment while everyone stood silently in place. Even Scarlett had retreated to her bed and was watching with one eye open.

"Why don't we all go sit at the table?" Alice said. "I'll bring the coffee."

The minute they sat down, Dana launched into a gushing description of the house: the upgraded kitchen with a massive marble eating bar, four bedrooms, and their own swimming pool. Shelby listened, all the while tracking Dana's expressions and Gus's reactions. The two of them acted like happy newlyweds. At that moment, her mother reached out for the coffee creamer, and Shelby saw an engagement ring on her finger.

Flashing her hand around, Dana said, "We have even more news." She beamed up at Gus. "We're engaged."

"Oh my," Alice said. "Congratulations."

"Yes, congratulations," Theo echoed.

Shelby felt numb. Everything appeared to be stacking against what she hoped to accomplish today. When Dana looked to her for approval, Shelby forced a smile.

"Is there to be a wedding soon?" Alice asked, her voice sounding thin.

Gus placed Dana's hand in his. "It's in the works. We'll let you know the date."

The conversation lulled as people sipped their coffee. Shelby tried to compose her thoughts and figure out what to do next.

Gus took a last sip of coffee and laid down his cup. "Nice to see you all," he said standing. "I'm going to go make myself scarce now. I know you ladies have a lot to talk about." He glanced over to Shelby. "We have plenty of room for your things in the truck. Whenever you're ready, we'll take off."

Shelby felt frozen to her seat.

Gus looked concerned when she didn't respond, but Dana didn't even seem to notice. "Thanks, honey," Dana said. "I'll text you when we're ready."

After Gus left, Theo turned to Shelby. "Can I talk to you for a moment in private?"

Shelby followed him to the back hall where they were out of listening range. Scarlett trailed behind them and scampered toward her bed in Alice's room. Lucky dog, Shelby thought.

"Do you want me to stay?" Theo asked. "Or would you prefer this time alone with your family? I'm just a few blocks away. You can call me if you need anything."

Shelby looked back toward the living room with dread. "I think it would be best if you left. I don't want my mother putting on an act in front of you, or me feeling like I can't say exactly what I mean. You're the most wonderful friend. Thank you for being here. I'll call you as soon as it's over."

At the front door, Theo turned and said, "Well, I'll be seeing you ladies." He smiled at Alice. "Thanks for the lunch. And you let me know if you need anything."

The three generations of women sat at the table alone, Dana staring at her ring like a child with a new toy. Her mother had barely asked Shelby anything about herself. Dana glanced at the clock on the kitchen wall. Probably timing her visit, Shelby thought.

"So," Dana said to Shelby, "where is your suitcase? I thought we'd spend a few minutes chatting and then head out. Gus mapped out a bit of sightseeing on our way back before school starts, and then—"

"Stop, Mother," Shelby said. "I am not packed, and I'm not going with you. I told you that before you decided to come."

Dana swerved toward Alice. "Is this your doing?"

"Of course not," Alice said. "Shelby's old enough to make up her own mind. I'm here for her, whatever she decides."

"Yeah, right. You've both been plotting against me, haven't you?"

Shelby bolted up. "It's not always about you, Mom. Just this once, it's about me." She took some deep breaths and moved over to a seat in the living room. Dana, her arms crossed, sat facing her. Alice took the couch.

"I don't understand," Dana said, her tone rising. "I told you about the house and everything. Why aren't you coming?"

"If you'd ever listen—"

"Stop," Alice said. "Arguing isn't going to fix anything. Let's talk calmly and see what decision is best for everyone."

Dana glared back at Alice, her face a pout.

Not a productive start, Shelby thought, trying to focus herself again. "You seem happy," Shelby said to her mother. "But so am I, living here at Moonwater Lake."

"I'm sure you can be happy in Florida too," Dana said. "Maybe even better."

Shelby's head throbbed and she rubbed her temples. "You're not listening, Mother." Any clear communication with her mother seemed impossible, but she tried again. "This is a better place for me for now. I have a good, stable, normal life for once. Real friends. My own business making my own money. And for your information, a boyfriend."

Dana's eyes narrowed. "Oh, is that it? You want to stay for some boy?"

Shelby glared at her mother. If she could only hear herself. The room felt suddenly cold and Shelby shuddered.

Alice spoke up. "This is not just some boy. This is a wonderful young man who will be leaving for Stanford in a few weeks. So no, Shelby wants to stay because there's an excellent high school where she can complete her education and apply for scholarships to college."

Dana looked at Alice and then back to Shelby. "An older boy. What's been going on here?"

It took everything in Shelby not to strangle her mother. With all the men her mother had been with, she had a lot of nerve. "The only thing that's been going on," said Shelby, "is somebody being kind to me and understanding. We really care about each other."

"Oh, I see, "Dana said. "And I don't care? Is that it?" Her mother's eyes narrowed. "What is it you actually want, then? And why did you wait until we got all the way here to tell me?"

Shelby steadied herself. There was no reasoning with her mother. She needed to simply state what she wanted. "I want you to sign over my guardianship to Grandma Alice until I'm eighteen and officially an adult. I want to finish my last two years of high school here."

Dana leaned forward, her face blotched and red. "I can't believe that you two are doing this to me."

Shelby threw up her hands in frustration. "How are we doing this to *you*?"

Dana slumped back in the recliner, her face morphing back to a dejected child. "What am I supposed to tell Gus?" she whined. "My own daughter doesn't want to live with us? I've been trying so hard to make this work. For you too."

"If you were doing this for me too," Shelby said, "you would have talked to me first. Listened to what I want and need."

"But...but..." Dana stammered. "We drove all the way across country and bought that house with the extra bedroom and—"

"Dana," Alice said, her voice firm, "be honest. Would you have bought that house anyway?"

"That's not the point," Dana said. "Gus wants a nice little family."

For a moment, the room spun. Shelby grasped the arms of her chair. The familiar ache in her heart threatened to engulf her. Did her mother ever love her? Was she even capable of it? Either way, she needed to say her words the way Dana would hear them.

"So this is really about Gus," Shelby said, "and what Gus wants."

"No, you're getting it all wrong," Dana said.

"Maybe, maybe not," Shelby said. "You finally found a good-seeming man. Maybe it would be best if you started your new life together just the two of you in your new home."

Dana bristled. "And what if that's not what I want?"

Shelby stood tall and remained strong. "Maybe you need some time to think about it." She reached over and retrieved the paperwork on the end table. "I have the guardianship document here. It would be a lot easier if you would sign it before you leave the lake."

Dana leapt off the chair, hands on hips. "Or what? You're still a minor."

"Legally at sixteen I can make my own decision on who I want to live with. I've spoken to my attorney and I can apply for emancipation if that becomes necessary."

Dana twisted her engagement ring anxiously around her finger. "I see you two have everything all planned out." She turned to Alice. "You're my mother, but you've never been on my side."

"That's not fair," Alice said. "I've always loved you and done my best."

"Well, maybe it wasn't enough," Dana said. "Don't you think I try to do my best too?"

Shelby cringed, knowing how much those words must have hurt her grandmother. "It's no one's fault," Shelby said. "We just need to get it settled so we can both move on."

Dana paced the room and stopped in front of Shelby. "You could have saved us this wasted and expensive trip."

"I tried to," Shelby said, "but you wouldn't listen."

Alice rose from the couch and confronted her daughter. "Dana, you need to listen to Shelby. You're an adult now and need to start taking responsibility for your own child's welfare. Take some time to think about what you're doing and how it's going to impact everyone, not just yourself."

Dana was speechless. She kept opening her mouth and nothing came out. "I—I—" she said. Then she turned her back to them and tramped to the door. "We'll just have to stay in town tonight, I guess. More costs. I'll speak to Gus and let you know our plans."

Dana pulled out her cell phone and called Gus to come pick her up. Then she strode out the door and slammed it forcefully behind her. Scarlett zoomed out, barking as the noise reverberated through the house, to protect them from any perceived danger. If only she could, Shelby thought.

"So," Shelby said to her grandmother, "I guess that didn't go so well." At least it was over, she thought.

"An understatement," Alice said. "Do you think I was too

harsh with your mother? I've let so many things go with Dana in the past. It felt right to speak up and tell the truth this time."

"You were brave," Shelby said. "But I'm not sure she heard a word either of us said."

Alice shook her head. "Give your mom some time to cool off. I know she loves you. Let's just hope she'll make the right decision in the end."

"I think I'll call Theo," Shelby said. "He'll want to know what happened."

"Good idea. We could use a stabling presence."

A few minutes later, Theo showed up carrying a pink box, with Wally at his side. Scarlett raced over to greet them, her tail wagging briskly.

"So how did everything go?" he asked. "It didn't last very long. I barely made it to Redd's and back before I got your message."

Alice took the box from his hand. "What did you bring us?"

"Steph and Josh thought you might need a little cheering up. They gifted you a box of cookie ice cream sandwiches."

Shelby peeked inside. "Perfect timing. Let's take them to the table."

Between bites, Shelby relayed to Theo what had happened, leaving out some of the gritty details. The dogs lay on the kitchen floor, content to munch on some of Alice's doggie treats.

"Would you like me to try to talk to Dana? Or Gus?" Theo asked.

Shelby shook her head. "Thanks, Theo. You're a good friend. But I don't think that's a very good idea." She wasn't sure anything would help at this point. And she didn't want to put Theo in the line of fire. Her mind raced, along with her heart. "If you don't mind," she said, "I'm going to go to my room to lie down for a while."

"Of course," Alice said.

Shelby's bed was a welcome sight. She plopped down, curled up on her side, and stared out the window. This was her very own room and she felt safe here. She wished she could speak to Logan in person, but she knew he was working late and had a family commitment tonight. Instead, she texted him. *It was rough. My mom is staying in town tonight to think things over. Should know more tomorrow.*

I'm sorry, Logan texted. *Let me know as soon as you know more. Miss you.*

It was going to be a long night ahead waiting to hear back from her mother. But for now, she burrowed under the covers and wanted nothing more than a long nap.

CHAPTER 40

*B*y nine in the morning, there had been no word yet from Dana when and if they would be coming back over today. Shelby continued her regular routine and covered her dog walking clients. Everyone had asked her how she was doing, and the dogs had been extra affectionate with their kisses and snuggles. Logan had texted early to see if she'd heard anything yet and offered to come over if she needed him. When she returned home a few hours later, her grandmother offered to make something to eat, but Shelby's stomach was still in knots.

"Have you heard anything yet?" Shelby asked.

Alice shook her head. "Not a word."

"I wish she would at least let us know if they're still in town," Shelby said.

At Shelby's feet, Scarlett rolled over for a belly rub.

"You sweetie." She stooped to the floor and ran her fingers through the curly, soft poodle hair. She couldn't stand the thought of not seeing all her furry friends again.

Dana's comments about Logan had really gotten to her, and even made Shelby doubt him for a minute. But she knew in her heart that what she had with him was real. No one knew how long anything would last, but it did not affect her decision. She was staying no matter what Dana did or said. She didn't think her mother would resort to physically kidnapping her and causing a scene, but she couldn't be entirely sure.

Without notice, the sound of a car pulling up in front of the house jolted Shelby from the floor to the window. It was Dana. Gus walked over to open the door for Dana and reached out his hand to help her out. Dana stood for a moment and looked toward the house. With a swift motion she tried to get back in the truck, but Gus took her in his arms. They spoke for a moment before Gus nodded toward the front door. Dana turned and walked up the path, her hand in his.

Alice was already up to answer the door. "You ready?" she asked.

Shelby nodded and her grandmother escorted them into the house.

Her mother's eyes were red-rimmed with dark circles under them. And for once, Dana wasn't in full makeup and perfect hair. It had not been a great night for all of them, it seemed. Dana seemed glued in place and didn't move.

Alice, her face lined with concern, suggested they all sit down in the living room. Shelby stayed standing with a clear view of the door and her mother. At first no one spoke. Then Dana glanced up at Shelby. "I can't say it was an easy night. Thank goodness for Gus," she said, looking over to him. "He helped me to see that..." Before she could finish her sentence, Dana began to weep.

Alice picked up a box of tissues and sat beside Dana on the couch. "We love you, Dana," she said, placing the box before her. "You know that."

That only made Dana cry harder. Gus patted her hand but stayed quiet.

"Sometimes I'm not sure why, but Gus loves me too," she said, clutching a tissue and blotting her face. "Gus has shown me what love really is, and that when you love someone, you want the best for them." Dana looked up, seeking reassurance from her family.

Shelby's heart glowed hearing the words coming from her mother. Maybe Gus was the one for her mother after all, and things would get better for all of them.

"That's right," Alice said. "That's how I love you too."

Dana sighed. "I know how difficult I was as a teenager," she said to Alice. "I was pretty wild and put you through a lot, but you and Dad were always there for me. I'm sorry for what I said yesterday."

Alice took Dana's hand. "We always loved you and were so desperately sad for you when your husband passed at such a young age. But now, it sounds like you've found a wonderful man."

"I have," Dana said, smiling at Gus. She stood and walked over to Shelby. "It's hard for me to say. I know I haven't been the best mother, but I do love you, Shelby."

"I love you too, Mom."

They hugged briefly, neither quite comfortable yet with the closeness.

Dana pulled back and took a step toward the door. "As sad as it makes me, Shelby, I understand your decision to stay here with your grandmother and finish high school at the lake."

"Thank you, Mom," Shelby said. "I'll visit you whenever I can."

"We'll look forward to seeing you," Dana said. She pulled Shelby in for another hug and whispered, "I'm sorry."

Shelby tightened the hug and whispered back. "Me too. But we'll be okay," she said.

Dana stepped back and Gus moved beside her, putting an arm around her shoulder. She leaned her head on his shoulder briefly before addressing Shelby again. "I know you'll be happy here and your grandmother will take good care of you."

"The very best," Alice said, joining them.

"And one more thing," she said to Shelby. "I'm proud of you.

321

Don't think I haven't noticed your good grades, hard work, starting a business, all of it."

Her mother's words were a healing balm soothing Shelby's heart. "Thank you. One last request," Shelby said, retrieving the custody agreement and a pen. She didn't want to break the spell by asking Dana to sign the papers, but she couldn't enroll in school without them.

For a split second, Dana hesitated before taking the papers and signing them quickly. "Some distance might help us all have a closer relationship. And that's what I want more than anything."

"Me too," Shelby said. Hope fluttered in her heart. Something she'd all but given up on years ago. And here it was returning like the blossoms in spring offering her another chance.

Dana glanced out the window toward the truck. "We'd better go now, right, Gus?"

"If you're ready," he said gently. "Shelby, I want you and your grandmother to know you're always welcome in our home in Florida. Even if I have to come pick you up to get there." He turned and kissed Dana on the cheek. "And of course, we'll let you know when the wedding is."

"And we'll be there. Both of us," Alice said. "How about a group hug?"

The three generations of women came together, maybe for the first time. Gus joined them. As the love moved between them, Shelby heard Alice whisper into Dana's ear, "I'm proud of you, too."

The moment of closeness lingered afterwards, before Gus walked them to the front door.

This time, saying goodbye was real and Shelby was not sure when she'd see her mother again. "I'd like to walk with you out to the car," she said.

Dana beamed. "Of course."

Before getting in the truck, Gus turned to Shelby. "I'm so glad it all worked out," he said. "I know it's going to take some time, but I hope we can be friends."

"Me too," she said looking up at his kind face. Why had she not noticed his caring eyes and genuine smile before?

Gus helped Dana into the truck, but before he could shut the door, Alice said. "I almost forgot. Congratulations on your new home!"

"Thanks, Mom," Dana said. "Don't forget, we'd love to see you both at Christmas."

"Good chance," Alice said. "And if you'd rather come here, the lake is enchanting at Christmas."

Shelby and Alice stood on the sidewalk and watched the couple drive off.

Alice put her arm around Shelby. "See? Sometimes things do work out."

"Thank you for everything, Grandma," she said. "It would never have happened without you."

"You did most of the work yourself, Shelby. Never forget that. Now let's get out of this heat and call Theo with the good news."

"You go ahead. I'm going to walk across the street and tell Logan and his family what happened."

Shelby stood on the sidewalk for a few minutes, arms wrapped around herself, hardly able to believe how everything had worked out. The ground beneath her feet felt stable at last. No tremors or aftershocks.

"Yes!" she yelled aloud to the sky above. Her eyes wandered to the house across the street. It beckoned her, as did the boy inside.

She all but skipped over and knocked on the door. Both Logan's father and mother answered.

"How did it go?" Iris asked. "I have to admit we peeked through the window. The hugs looked promising."

"They were," Shelby said, still feeling the shock wear off. "My mother signed the papers before she left. As soon as they are filed, I am officially under the guardianship of my grandmother."

"All right," Logan said, coming up beside his dad with Gabe. "Come on in."

"The sooner you get me that paperwork, the better," Anthony said. "I'll file it immediately and follow up on its progress."

"I can't thank all of you enough," she said. "I'll always be grateful."

"I'm so glad it all worked out so you can stay," Iris said.

Right on cue, Mutt scrambled over and rubbed his head against Shelby's leg.

"Looks like Mutt's pretty happy too," Gabe said. "Hey, let's all take Mutt for a walk."

Iris turned to Anthony. "How about you and I and Gabe take Mutt? We could use a little exercise."

Anthony shrugged, and then a smile crossed his face and he agreed. "Sure, let's go."

It was obvious Iris was making sure Shelby and Logan got some alone time, and Shelby was grateful for that. Once his parents left the house, Logan suggested they go outside. They walked down the path to the private dock where they'd watched the full moon the night of their first kiss. Water lapped against the dock, creating a gentle rocking motion. Logan took her hand and listened intently as Shelby shared the story.

"It's like a miracle how my mother came around," Shelby said.

Logan grinned. "There's been a lot of those going around lately. First my dad, now your mom."

"A perfect end to a perfect summer," she said. Shelby scanned the crystal blue lake stretching before them. A few of the trees lining the shore were already displaying some yellow leaves. It would be fall soon and she would still be here after all. She'd start school. But then she realized, Logan would be gone. A sadness crossed her heart and she sighed.

Logan lifted her chin and met her gaze. "I know. I'll be leaving right after Labor Day for college. But you and I have almost two weeks left until then. And I won't be that far away."

Shelby willed herself to stay positive for both of them. So much good had happened and it still would, no matter what. And Logan needed her support too. "How are you getting down to Stanford?" Shelby asked, trying to keep her voice even.

"My dad and I are going to make the drive together. He said we'll have more bonding time. Can't remember the last time we've done that." Logan grinned. "And he managed to drop in how the law is a very powerful tool and, in the right hands, it can accomplish wonderful things. Just in case I change my mind."

Shelby laughed. "There is some truth to that. He sure helped me. But it seems like he's behind you now, whatever direction you decide to follow."

"It does seem that way," Logan said. "And your mother's actions speak of the same support for you."

Everything was changing so fast; Shelby could hardly catch her breath. So many things she'd always dreamed of were right before her. But then there was Logan, who might be drifting away. "I'll miss you," she said.

Logan pulled her into his arms. "This is not the end, Shelby. Don't think that for a minute."

Shelby held Logan tight, his heart beating with hers. It was hard to trust his words, risk her heart. But perhaps that was the cost of happiness. And with Logan, it was worth it all.

CHAPTER 41

*I*t had been almost two weeks since Shelby's mother had left town and the happiness that followed from her decisions had touched them all. And now it was time, not for a goodbye, but for another chance.

Theo sat down on what he called "Jean's bench." Wally, in his fleece sweater, sat at his feet. It was just past dawn and the early morning chill reminded him that fall was just around the corner. Yellow and gold leaves dotted the grass. A hazy mist floated above the surface of the lake. Usually they'd still be tucked in bed, but he wanted to make sure he'd be alone and undisturbed.

"Jean," he said, "I haven't been here in a little while. Wherever you are, you are near to me. As you probably know, I've fallen for Alice. I've decided to give it a try. I still miss you, my love. I know you'd want me to be happy, and I am, in a different kind of way. I have two new ladies now. I have Alice and her granddaughter Shelby. And if you count their sweet little dog, Scarlett, I have three." Theo looked down his aging dog. "Wally's doing fine for now. They say he could live a couple more years."

Wally's tail thumped at the sound of his name. A chorus of

birdsong greeted the rising sun. This was home. Moonwater Lake, the blessed place he and Jean had chosen.

"Jean, you'll always, always be in my heart. I know you're watching over me, and that someday, you and I, and everyone we love, will be together again."

A flash of heat spread through his body despite the chilly air. It was as if Jean were answering him with a warm hug. Emotions moved through him like waves. Sadness, happiness, and everything in between. When they slowed, what was left was excitement for his life ahead. He was one lucky man. With a deep breath, Theo stood up and rested his hand on the back of the bench. Memories would never leave him, but there were many more to make.

"Come on, Wally, let's get back and prep for the dog park."

Wally was still a little bit slow on the walk back, but he was doing fine. He ate and slept well. He played some with the other dogs. He was loved. What more could a dog, or anyone for that matter, want?

A FEW HOURS LATER, after a warm breakfast and short rest, Theo was ready for the dog park play date. Mindy, Trevor, and their two dogs arrived to help set up. It was the last club meeting for now. Since they weren't sure how often they would meet after Shelby started high school in a week, everyone had confirmed they'd be there today with their dogs. Theo chuckled; it would be the whole Not-So-Lonely Hearts Dog Walkers Club now.

"Hello," Alice said as she walked in with Shelby and Scarlett. She held up a tray. "Special treats for all the little furry ones."

The news had spread that Shelby would be staying in town, and Alice had secretly dropped a cake off yesterday for the occasion and left it in Theo's kitchen.

"You did it, Shelby," Eleanor said as she walked in with Dixie and Ruby. "I knew you would."

Behind Eleanor were Josh and Steph, and short-legged little Oscar in his bow tie. Everyone gathered around Shelby, congratulating her again.

"Thank you all for coming today and for all of your help," Shelby said. "It sure feels great to be an official resident of Moonwater Lake now."

There was clapping all around and more than a few hugs. Theo had made one of the best decisions of his life when he'd opened his home to this dog park, he thought.

Steph and Josh were holding hands, grins on both of their faces. "We have some news too," Steph said. She placed one hand over her stomach. "We are expecting next spring."

"I'm so excited for you both," Shelby said.

Congratulations continued and Theo was pleased to see so many happy faces here today. It wasn't that long ago, he'd not been sure they'd be able to meet anymore.

"Hello," a familiar voice called out. "Here he is, my new boy, Fritz, who will be joining us today."

"He's adorable," Shelby said. "And those ears."

"I know," Joann said. "He looks like a little elf the way they stick straight up. I waited a long time, but I finally realized my heart is large enough to include another dog. And he is it."

Everyone gathered around and petted him. Fritz seemed to love the attention, holding his chin up for a scratch and giving a few kisses back. Joann clipped off his leash and put him on the grass.

"Let's see how this goes," she said.

Theo watched while the other dogs trotted over, sniffed the new member, and officially welcomed him in dog language. At that moment, Mutt came running through the gate, followed by Gabe and Logan. Mutt shot right over to the new dog, Fritz, and the two seemed to recognize each other. Perhaps Mutt had once been a rescue as well, Theo thought. He certainly was one now. And a very clean and groomed one at that.

While the dogs played, Theo invited everyone to join him at the table on the deck.

"I'll be right back," Alice said, heading inside.

After a few minutes, Alice carried out a homemade sheet cake. Theo watched Shelby's face glow as she read the words piped across it: *Welcome Home Shelby*. That girl's arrival had certainly set off a positive chain of events for so many people and dogs. And, of course, for himself.

While the dogs pranced, chewed, and frolicked, the group talked about how much they loved these gatherings. Everyone was in agreement that as long as the weather permitted, they would keep meeting and plan them around Shelby's school schedule. Theo assured Shelby he was flexible too.

"Since we're all catching up…" Mindy said. She looked over at Trevor and he nodded. "I wanted to let you all know I have decided to move up and live at the lake year-round now."

"Wonderful," Alice and Theo said in unison.

"You see that dog out there?" Mindy pointed to Karma. "She taught me about unconditional love. And all of you are so special. It may take my parents awhile to come around, and my boss isn't the happiest I'll be working remote, but I've learned to listen to my own heart. Right, Shelby?" she said, smiling over at her.

"So right," Shelby answered.

Theo glanced over to Shelby and Logan. There was still one more hurdle for Shelby to face. Logan would be leaving in a couple of days. Ah, first love. Theo remembered the summer so long ago he'd fallen in love with Jean. School had separated them too for a while. But their love was strong. His leaving might be a little rocky for Shelby at first, but she had good friends who would support her now. And Logan would come up during breaks now that his family was going to be living in their lake house most of the year. Moonwater Lake was certainly getting a population boom.

Noticing the iced tea pitcher was empty, and so were many of their glasses, Theo headed into the kitchen to refresh it. Trevor followed him in.

"Can I help with anything?" Trevor asked.

"I got it," Theo said, holding the bucket under the automatic ice maker before pouring more in.

"I want to thank you," Trevor said.

Theo looked up. "For what?"

"For our talk and encouraging me with Mindy. I realized there's no joy possible without risking pain, and by shutting myself off to pain, I'd shut all the doors."

Theo nodded. "It's a tough one, isn't it?"

"It's worth it, though," Trevor said. "She's worth it."

Theo patted Trevor on the back. "Good work."

"Here," Trevor said, picking up the pitcher. "Let me help you with that."

Back outside, Theo took a seat next to Alice. Her sweet smile in his direction made him feel a bit giddy. The dogs were running up ramps, tossing toys, barking, and chasing balls. Who would have thought a few months back, when he could barely get out of bed that dark morning, that all of this joy would come into his life? Thank goodness he had not given up.

"Don't forget," Joann said, "tomorrow starts Labor Day weekend, and you know how busy it's going to get here. Everyone keep your dogs safe."

"There'll be fireworks too," Theo said. "I know my boy doesn't like them at all."

"Oscar, either," Steph said. "But his thunder shirt does help some."

"Best to keep the dogs home," Logan said. "It'll be crazy down by the lake. We have a couple of extra lifeguards coming in just in case." He looked over at Shelby. "You might be needed, you never know."

She laughed. "Just let me know."

"All right, everyone," Alice said. "Let's clean up and we can finish arranging the new schedule after the holiday."

After everyone had left, Theo walked back to the deck, where Wally lay asleep under one of the chairs. He petted the old boy. "I guess I better call Cam before it gets too late," he said.

Theo opened his computer and sent a message to Cam that he was ready to talk. Within minutes his Skype call was ringing through.

"What's going on, Dad?" Cam asked. "We usually talk in the morning."

Theo gathered his thoughts. "I wanted to share a few things with you."

Cam's face dropped. "Are you sick? Anything wrong?"

"Actually, quite the opposite," Theo said.

Now Cam really looked perplexed. His wife, Judy, leaned into view of the screen to say hello. "Hi, Theo," she said. "Cam's working at home today, so you have both of us."

She was a good woman, and Theo thought Cam was darn lucky to have her. "Good, good," he said. "I know you two have been worrying about me being alone here and all, and I appreciate your concern."

"We've gone over this, Dad," Cam said.

Theo continued despite his son's tone. "Please, just listen. You know how much I loved your mother, and she'll always be in my heart. I didn't want to tell you about Alice until I was sure."

"Who's Alice?" his son asked.

His wife tapped him on the shoulder and smiled. "Did you meet someone?" she asked.

"Actually, yes. Alice, a widow here at the lake, a former nurse. A wonderful, kind woman. I knew her husband before he passed."

Cam looked stunned. "But you're seventy-five. You have to be realistic."

Judy shook her head. "There is no age limit on love," she said. "I am so happy for you both. Perhaps we can visit later in the year and meet her."

"You'll love her," Theo said. "And I'd love to see you both."

Cam just kept shaking his head like he was trying to digest the new information and it wouldn't compute. Then something seemed to click. He slowly nodded and his face softened. He looked directly at Theo. "Good for you, Dad. Good for you."

They said their goodbyes, promising to visit soon. Wally stood before him giving his let's-go-for-a-walk bark. Things were looking pretty good now all around. He thought about how summer was passing swiftly, soon fall would descend, and the stark, cold winter to follow. But this year, he wouldn't be alone.

CHAPTER 42

*I*t had been a crazy, busy Labor Day weekend. Shelby knew Logan had to work extra-long shifts Saturday and Sunday. Monday was still busy, but people were starting to go home. She'd avoided the crowds and stayed away from the lake all weekend. Logan and his father were leaving very early the next morning. He had texted her early this morning he was finishing up his packing, and with most of the tourists gone by 5:00 p.m., it would be a perfect time for him and Shelby to meet later today.

At five o'clock she went to meet him so they could take a walk together. He said they would find somewhere quiet to swim, so she'd worn a bathing suit under her shorts. It was hard for Shelby to imagine that today was the last time they would be together for a while.

When she reached the sand, she saw Logan and Madison standing face to face by the lifeguard station. For a moment her breath caught as she stood watching. After they finished speaking, Logan walked down to the water's edge. Madison turned to go and, noticing Shelby, walked over in her direction. And then, to Shelby's surprise, Madison smiled at her. "See you," she said with an amiable wave before walking away.

Shelby let out a breath she did not realize she'd been holding.

Unaware of what had just transpired behind him, Logan had waded into the water. Shelby admired his tanned silhouette, his hair glowing in the afternoon sun. She wanted to imprint this memory into her brain, before time moved on. Then she walked down to join him.

"Logan," she said.

Hearing his name, he turned toward her, his smile welcoming. He stepped out of the blue-green water. "Let's get out of here," he said. "We're going to take the back trail." Logan retrieved two towels and a small backpack from the lifeguard station. "Madison just stopped by."

Shelby was glad he'd brought it up. "I saw."

"She came to say goodbye, and say she was sorry if she gave me a hard time this summer. And then she thanked me," Logan said.

"For what?" Shelby asked, completely confused now.

Logan shrugged. "She said I inspired her by choosing my own college major despite my father's wishes. She's enrolled in art school, and her parents are freaking out."

Shelby could only imagine how much guts that had taken for Madison to make that choice. "Good for her."

"Let's walk," Logan said, leading the way.

They hiked up a narrow path that looked like more of a deer trail curving through a tree-lined hill. From the higher viewpoint, she could see a few stragglers lingering on the beach below. Eventually the path opened, revealing a small cove below that she recognized as Turtle Pond.

"I know this place," Shelby said as they scrambled down.

Logan shook out the towels and laid them on the sand and put his pack on top. He pulled off his t-shirt and tossed it down as well. "Let's have a swim," he said.

Shelby peeled the shorts off from over her suit, and they raced each other into the water. They swam along the shore, matching each other's pace like two dolphins popping up, smiling at each other, then diving deep again. Logan made a turn to swim back and Shelby reluctantly followed. She wished they could go on like this forever...splashing, laughing, not a care. When they reached the shallow area, Shelby stepped out. Suddenly flailing, she lost her footing on a slippery rock beneath the surface.

Logan threw out his arms and she fell into them. "I've got you," he said, pulling her close. Wrapped in each other's arms, her body melded into his. She lifted her head and his lips met hers. She swayed with the intensity of the kiss that they both knew might be their last.

"I'm going to miss you," he whispered in her ear.

"I'll miss you so much," she said.

They clung to each other for several moments, the silky water dancing at their ankles. Shelby knew she had to let go. It was time.

"Race you back to the towels," she said, breaking the poignant moment.

Logan ran through the sand and snatched the towels. "I beat you," he said, tossing one to her.

Shelby grinned. "I let you."

"We'll have to have a rematch when I get back," he said, drying off. "At the latest, it'll be Christmas."

The thought of four months without seeing Logan seemed unbearable. And there was her mother wanting her to come to Florida for the holiday. She wouldn't think of it now. They lay back down on the towels to dry off in the sun. Shelby shook out her hair, water droplets scattering everywhere.

"Hey," Logan said kiddingly.

"You can handle it," Shelby said.

Logan picked up his backpack and reached inside. "I got you something," he said, holding up a small box.

Shelby lifted the lid and pulled out a blue, black, and silver beaded bracelet. A flat turquoise center stone had a turtle etched into it. "It's beautiful," she said. A lump formed in her throat. It would forever remind her of their time together at Turtle Pond.

"I saw it at the craft fair last week and thought of you. Turtles do seem to be a totem for us, don't they?"

She slipped the delicately crafted bracelet on her wrist and held it up for him to admire. "It's a perfect fit," she said. Shelby doubted she would ever take it off.

A cooling breeze rustled through the trees, reminding them the afternoon was turning toward evening.

"You'll be starting school soon too," Logan said.

"Next week," Shelby said. "I'll start looking into colleges and scholarships and what requirements I need to finish. Are you excited for college?"

"I am," he said. "I know it's going to be tough, but it's one of the best programs in my field. I'll be studying day and night, but just know I'll be I thinking about you all the time."

"Me too. I mean thinking of you."

Logan laughed. "I wish we didn't have to, but we better start back now."

She knew Logan had a lot to do before he left tomorrow. And her grandmother was waiting with dinner for her. They navigated the trail back, lingering as they walked, stopping to glimpse the colors of dusk spreading across the lake. When they reached Shelby's house, Logan accompanied her to the porch. The day was waning and the street darkening.

Shelby forced herself not to cry. She hated partings. There'd been far too many in her life. "I'm not going to say goodbye," she said.

"Why would you, when it's only 'see you soon'?" Logan said, flashing her a smile.

Logan's eyes held sadness, but he was trying, and she would too.

"Right," Shelby said. "See you soon."

Shelby stood on the porch and watched him walk home. Everything in her wanted to run over and hug him one more time. But she stayed strong. If they were meant to be together, they would. She let herself feel what was truly in her heart, and for now that was enough.

CHAPTER 43

$\mathcal{I}$t was Shelby's first day at her new high school. Hands shaking with nervous excitement, she reached for her JanSport backpack. The school was just over a mile up the hill, but there was some early morning rain and Alice insisted on driving her. Theo was coming along, and afterwards the two of them were going out to breakfast. She'd run into Emily, Eleanor's niece, who she'd often seen when she'd dropped off Oscar. They had a few classes together, so at least she'd know one person at school.

As she finished getting ready, Shelby's thoughts drifted to Logan. It had been over a week since he'd left for college. He'd sent her pictures of the road trip with his dad and some of his new dorm room. They emailed or texted every day, and even though she missed him, she kept busy working and getting ready for her new life.

Some days she'd gone down to the lake, but it seemed so empty without him. Doubt crept in, wondering if he would really come back to her. But then she'd look around the amazing place she now called home and be flooded with grati-tude. She'd come a long way from that dejected girl sitting on the curb in Las Vegas with nowhere to go. And she knew that no matter what happened, she needed to trust that things would work out.

"Are you ready?" Alice called out from the living room.

Shelby took one last glance in the mirror to check her hair and new outfit. She was starting high school, where she would spend two full years, probably go to prom, and do all the normal things that she'd always longed for. Iris had invited Shelby's whole family and Theo over for Thanksgiving. Logan would be there, too. She was being given a second chance, and she was going to make the most of it.

Alice and Theo were waiting when she entered the living room.

"The rain just stopped," Theo said. "It looks like the sun is working its way out."

Shelby shrugged. "It's no big deal. I can walk."

"I know," Alice said. "But we really want to take you."

Then she understood. Alice and Theo didn't think she really needed a ride; they wanted to be there and watch her walk in for her first day. She smiled at the two of them, looking like expectant parents eager to be a part of her life.

"I'd love a ride," Shelby said.

"Let's go," Theo said. "It's no trouble. Besides, we wanted to try that new cafe near the high school. They're supposed to have an incredible breakfast."

"Let me know," Shelby said. "I'll probably be stopping over there some mornings myself."

When they arrived at the high school, Theo pulled the car over by the curb rather than the drive-through area. "I remember when I was in high school," he said, chuckling. "I didn't want to be seen with my parents dropping me off."

Shelby laughed. She had never had that luxury before now. "Thanks. I'll see you both later. And don't worry, I can walk home."

"All right," Alice said. "You've got your cell phone, if you need anything."

"I'll be fine."

"You'll be more than fine," Theo said.

Shelby exited the car and walked the last half a block to Lakeview High. A light drizzle filled the sunlit air. Clouds drifted by, revealing a faint rainbow in the distance. Emily stood on the brick steps in front of the school and waved to her. Shelby took a deep breath and moved forward to start her new life.

Shelby turned back to face her beloved groom. His eyes still glistened from tearing up when she'd walked down the aisle to him. So many smiling faces watched her as she'd floated by the chairs decorated with ribbons to match her dazzling blush and white lace gown. Steph and Josh were there with their nine-year-old daughter, Kristen, between them. Mindy and Trevor waved when she passed. In the front row, Alice sat hand in hand with Theo, who had just walked Shelby down the aisle. Next to them was Shelby's mother, crying into Gus's shoulder. She knew they were happy tears. On the groom's side were Anthony and Iris DeLuca and their family.

They stood on the dock overlooking the sundrenched lake. It held so many memories and would hold so many more. A light breeze rustled through the overhanging trees, carrying the sweet scent of peach roses woven into baby's breath and ivy in the arbor above. Before her, in his pale suit and matching boutonniere, was not the teenage boy she'd met ten years ago, but the handsome and kind man Shelby was about to marry. Her fingers touched the precious turtle bracelet on her wrist that he'd given her. Her "something blue."

Flute music floated softly in the background as the minister, in a dark suit and tie, moved into place between them. Cradled in Gabe's, the best man's, arms, Scarlett barked in approval. Around the dog's neck was a floral collar with silk bows, and their wedding rings rested on a satin pillow on the dog's back. Scarlett's curly red hair was threaded with white, but she was still the spunky dog that had helped bring them all together.

Shelby handed her bouquet to Emily, her maid of honor, and the minister began.

"On behalf of Shelby and Logan, I would like to welcome everyone here. Moonwater Lake holds a special place in the hearts of the bride and groom."

As they exchanged rings, Logan and Shelby recited the vows of love and gratitude they had written. "From this moment on, I take you as my best friend for life. I will love, encourage, and support you throughout our life together. I promise to stand by you always, so that through our union we can realize all our dreams together."

As Logan said, "I do," and Shelby repeated it in turn, she thought back to that summer so long ago that had led them here today, to share their love forever.

RECIPES FROM SUMMER OF SECOND CHANCES

SUMMER COOKIES

CINNAMON APPLE ROSES

BY JONATHON PROSSER

I shared these with my friends and family, and they all loved them. Wonderful for special occasions. Eleanor brought them to the Fourth of July picnic!

Preheat oven to 375 degrees. Bake for 40-45 minutes.

- ½ cup sugar
- 3 tablespoons cinnamon
- 2 eggs
- 2 tablespoons heavy cream
- 1 teaspoon vanilla extract
- 6 apples
- Sprinkle of Coconut flour
- 3 crescent dough rolls

Mix ½ cup of sugar and 3 tablespoons cinnamon. Mix 2 eggs with 2 tablespoons heavy cream and a teaspoon vanilla extract. Cut the apples in half, then thinly slice and core them. Microwave about 45 seconds, or until limp. Spread coconut flour on a clean surface and spread out on a sheet of crescent roll dough. Flip the sheet, stretching the sheet a little. Cut into 8ths.

Take the first strip and spread the egg wash over the top. Sprinkle cinnamon sugar mix onto the egg wash, to taste, perhaps a few pinches. Place apple slices on top of the strip then split the strip. Cover with a little cinnamon sugar and fold the strip over the bottom of the apple. Roll from the top toward you, keeping the roll tight and tucking apple slices in, if need be. Place in cupcake pan/liner. Repeat this for the other strips and the second dough sheet. Brush egg wash on top of the roses and sprinkle cinnamon sugar over the top of the roses. Good to top with chocolate syrup, caramel syrup, or powdered sugar.

JUMBO BROWNIE COOKIES

BY CAROL KLABUNDE

*T*hese deeply fudgy cookies are a great way to make a friend. A little espresso powder in the dough makes them even more over-the-top.

Makes about 12-18 dozen cookies.

- 2- 2 $^2/_3$ (16 ounces) 60% cacao bittersweet chocolate baking chips
- ½ cup unsalted butter, cubed
- 4 large eggs, room temperature
- ½ cups sugar
- 4 teaspoon vanilla extract
- 2 teaspoon instant espresso powder, optional
- $^2/_3$ cup all-purpose flour
- ½ teaspoon baking powder
- ¼ teaspoon salt
- 1 package (11.5 ounces) semisweet chocolate chunks

Preheat oven to 350 degrees. In a large saucepan, melt chocolate chips and butter over low heat, stirring until smooth. Remove from the heat; cool until mixture is warm.

In a small bowl, whisk the eggs, sugar, vanilla, and if desired, espresso powder until blended. Whisk into chocolate mixture. In another bowl, mix the flour, baking powder, and salt. Add to chocolate mixture, mixing well. Fold in chocolate chunks. Let stand until mixture thickens slightly, about 10 minutes.

Drop by ¼ cupfuls 3 inches apart onto parchment-paper-lined baking sheets. Bake until set, 12-14 minutes. Cool on pans 1-2 minutes. Remove to wire racks to cool.

JUDY'S GINGERSNAPS COOKIE SANDWICHES

BY JUDY LECESSE

Makes about 4 dozen.

- 2 cups flour
- 2 teaspoon baking soda
- ½ teaspoon salt
- ½ teaspoon cinnamon
- ¼ teaspoon cloves
- ¼ teaspoon ginger
- 1 cup sugar
- ¾ cups shortening
- ¼ cup molasses
- 1 egg

Filling:

- 6 oz cream cheese
- 7 tablespoons soft butter
- 1 teaspoon vanilla
- 3 to 3 1/2 cups powdered sugar

Preheat oven to 350 degrees. Mix flour, soda, salt, cinnamon, cloves, and ginger. In a separate bowl, gradually add sugar to creamed shortening. Cream until light and fluffy. Add molasses and egg. Beat well. Stir in dry ingredients $1/3$ at a time. Shape into small balls and roll in sugar. Grease cookie sheet and bake 5-7 minutes until tops start to crack.

Allow the cookies to chill for 5-10 minutes

For the filling, first mix cream cheese, butter, and vanilla in a small mixing bowl until smooth. Slowly beat in powdered sugar until light and fluffy. Once mixed, spread a small amount of icing onto a cookie. Take another cookie and place it on top. You now have your cookie sandwich! Be sure to put your cookie sandwiches in the refrigerator for about 30 minutes before eating.

CRISP SUGAR COOKIES

BY JEANNE CREA

*T*his is my Grandma Margaret's sugar cookie recipe, and this sugar cookie always fondly reminds me of her.

Makes about 4-6 dozen cookies.

- 3 cups flour
- ½ teaspoon soda
- ½ teaspoon salt
- 1 ½ cups of sugar
- ½ cup of shortening
- ½ cup butter
- 2 eggs, unbeaten
- 3 tablespoons milk
- 1 teaspoon vanilla
- ½ teaspoon lemon extract

Mix dry ingredients (flour, soda, salt) together. In a separate bowl, add sugar, shortening, and butter together, and beat in eggs, one at a time. Add milk and flavoring. Stir in the soda, salt, and flour. Mix well and chill. Preheat oven to 400 degrees. Roll into balls and roll in sugar. We use a greased glass with decorative bottom to flatten the ball and leave an imprint. For cut-outs, roll out small amount, very thin, on lightly floured board. Cut with cookie cutters, place on ungreased cookie sheet, sprinkle with sugar or candy. Bake at 400 degrees for 6-9 minutes.

CRANBERRY BLISS COOKIES

BY JULIA TRACHSEL

Makes about 4 dozen cookies.

Cookies:

- 3 cups flour
- 1 teaspoon baking soda
- 1 teaspoon salt
- 1 cup (2 sticks) butter, softened
- 1 cup granulated sugar
- 1 cup packed brown sugar
- 2 eggs
- 2 teaspoon vanilla extract, store-bought
- 1 cup white chocolate chips
- 1 cup dried cranberries

Frosting:

- 1 (8 oz) bar cream cheese, room temperature
- ½ cup white chocolate chips, melted in the microwave or double-boiler

- 1 teaspoon vanilla extract, store-bought or homemade
- 2 cups powdered sugar

Topping:

- 1 cup dried cranberries, roughly chopped
- ¼ cup white chocolate chips, melted in the microwave or double-boiler

In a separate bowl, whisk together flour, baking soda, and salt until well-blended. Set aside.

Using an electric mixer on medium-high speed, beat the butter and sugars together until light and fluffy, about 2 minutes. Add in the eggs one at a time, beating in between to incorporate. Add the vanilla, then reduce the speed to low and slowly add in the dry ingredients. Increase the speed to medium and continue beating until well-combined. Use a spoon to fold in the white chocolate chips and cranberries, and mix until just-combined. Do not over-mix.

Cover and refrigerate dough for at least 1 hour. Preheat oven to 350 degrees. Place dough by rounded tablespoonfuls onto a baking sheet that has been prepared with parchment paper, at least 2 $^1/_2$ inches apart. Bake for 10-12 minutes or until the cookies are lightly golden around the edges. Remove pan and transfer the cookies to a cooling rack until cool. Repeat with remaining dough until all cookies are baked. Wait until cookies reach room temperature before adding frosting and toppings.

Frosting:

Using an electric mixer on medium speed, beat together the room-temperature cream cheese and melted white chocolate until combined. (Be sure your cream cheese *really* is at room temperature before adding the white chocolate, otherwise the chocolate could seize up.) Add in the vanilla and mix until combined. Then reduce speed to low and add the powdered sugar. Mix until incorporated. Then use a rubber spatula to scrape down the sides of the bowl and beat for 1 minute more on medium speed until the frosting is smooth. You can add more powdered sugar for a thicker frosting.

Set some aside to drizzle over finished cookies. You may want to add a little water to help it drizzle easily, as it should be runnier than the base frosting.

Spread the original, thicker frosting on the cooled cookies. Immediately sprinkle the frosted cookies with the chopped dried cranberries. Use a fork to drizzle on the runnier frosting you have set aside, swishing it back and forth over the cookies to create a pretty pattern.

Pack carefully in a can or other container to keep fresh.

SOUR CREAM SUGAR COOKIE

BY JEANNIE DANIEL

*T*his cookie recipe was originally my grandma's, and one of my favorite aunts made her own touches. She added cinnamon and, using the raspberry bushes in her yard, she made raspberry frosting. I was with her that day and we made the cookies. It's a very fond memory of mine.

- 1 cup butter, softened
- 2 eggs
- 1 cup sour cream
- 1 teaspoon vanilla
- 3 cups all-purpose flour
- 1-1 ½ cups sugar 1 teaspoon baking powder
- ½ teaspoon baking soda
- ½ teaspoon salt 1 teaspoon cinnamon

Beat the butter and eggs with the salt until fluffy. Add the sour cream and vanilla. In another bowl, mix the flour, baking powder, and baking soda. Mix the flour slowly to the sugar mix until well-blended. Refrigerate for an hour or so until the dough is easy to handle. Preheat oven to 375 degrees. Drop by teaspoon onto a greased baking sheet and bake for 10 minutes. Let cool.

Raspberry Buttercream Frosting:

- 5 ounces of raspberries
- ½ cup of butter, softened
- 3 ½ cups powdered (confectioners') sugar
- 1 teaspoon lemon juice
- Milk (for consistency)

Put raspberries in a small sauce pan and cook over medium heat. Stir with spoon until they sauce. Put in a strainer to strain out the juice. Let cool. In a bowl, cream the butter, then add 2 cups of the confectioners' sugar. Add the raspberry juice and the lemon juice, and add another 1 ½ cup of the confectioners' sugar. Mix until smooth. Add a small amount of milk to make it the right consistency to spread. Spread on a cooled cookie. You can also take two cookies and put the frosting in between to make a sandwich cookie.

PLANTATION COOKIES

BY LETHA ARMSTRONG

*T*his is an old Southern recipe I've made for years now.

- 18 ounces of almond bark (I prefer the white, but can use either white or chocolate)
- ½ cup peanut butter
- 1 ½ cups mini marshmallows
- 1 ½ cups dry-roasted peanuts
- 1 ½ cups Rice Krispies

Put bark and peanut butter in microwave for 1 ½ minutes, or until melted. Stir at 30 second intervals. Add mini marshmallows, dry-roasted peanuts, and Rice Krispies. Mix well and drop by teaspoon onto waxed or parchment paper. Let harden and enjoy.

GRANDMA'S SOUR CREAM SUGAR COOKIES

BY ASHLEY FEHR

Total time: 40 minutes. Prep time: 30 minutes. Cook time: 10 minutes
Makes 24 cookies
Preheat oven to 350 degrees

- ½ cup unsalted butter
- 2 cups granulated sugar
- 4 eggs
- 1 teaspoon vanilla
- ²/₃ cup sour cream
- ½ teaspoon baking soda
- 3 teaspoon baking powder
- 4 cups all-purpose flour, fluffed and leveled

Frosting:

- ½ cup butter
- 2 ½ cups powdered icing sugar

- 1 teaspoon vanilla
- 2 tablespoons milk

In a large bowl with electric mixer, beat butter and sugar on high until creamy. Add eggs, vanilla, and sour cream and beat until smooth. Add baking soda, baking powder, and flour and beat on low until combined. Dough will be soft, almost like cake batter—this is fine. Preheat oven to 350 degrees and line baking sheets with parchment paper. Drop by heaping tablespoonfuls onto baking sheets 2-3 inches apart, bake for 10-12 minutes, until edges are golden and centers are set.

For frosting:

With an electric mixer, beat butter until smooth. Add sugar, vanilla, and milk and beat until smooth, adding additional sugar or milk to reach desired consistency. You don't want it too thin.

Color if desired and spread on cooled cookies.

CHRISTMAS COOKIES

RUGELACH

BY DEBBIE WASSERMAN

When I was a junior in high school, I would frequently visit my grandparents after they moved to Florida, as most New York grandparents did after reaching retirement. My grandma's friend knew I loved to bake and she gave me her family recipe for two rugelach doughs, one with sour cream and one with cream cheese. Although I never made the sour cream dough, when I made the cream cheese, I added in the filling of sugar, fragrant cinnamon, fruit preserves, and raisins, which was well-received. I've continued to send these to my cousins in Florida and my brother in Philadelphia, and they are included in every holiday and dessert tray throughout the year.

Makes 8 dough patties, or about 8 dozen pastries

DOUGH:

- 1 pound brick cream cheese, softened
- 1 pound sweet butter, softened

- 4 cups all-purpose unbleached flour

Filling—the amounts are approximate:

- 1½ cups light brown sugar
- $^3/_4$ cups white sugar
- 1-1½ tablespoon cinnamon
- Raisins
- Pecans, chopped (omit if allergic)
- Raspberry or apricot preserves (Any will do, your choice)

Cream butter and cream cheese until well-blended. Add ½ of the flour, mix on low. Mix in remaining 2 cups of flour with your hands. When dough holds together, make into 8 balls. Gently make into patties and wrap in plastic wrap. Do not overwork dough, and it will become tough. Each patty makes 12 rugelach. Refrigerate dough for about 30 minutes. Roll out a patty to approximately 10-12 inches. Cut into 12 triangles. Swipe each triangle with preserves. Sprinkle each triangle with sugar-cinnamon mixture. Place raisins and nuts on each triangle. Roll each crescent from wide side to point. Pinch and press sides down to hold in filling. Place point-side down on cookie sheet lined with parchment. Bake at 375 degrees until just starting to turn golden, approximately 15 minutes. Be sure to keep an eye on it. Take off pan before any sugar that may have oozed out hardens. Wrapped patties can be frozen for up to 4 weeks without tasting stale. Wrap tightly in a plastic bag; they freeze well for about 4-6 weeks.

LIGHT FRUIT COOKIES

BY VALERIE HILDEBRAND

My family and I come from Flin Flon, a northern Manitoba town. Before they both passed on, this was my grandma and mom's favorite cookie. It's also my favorite and it wouldn't be Christmas without it. At the age of 10, my mom handed me this recipe and said, "Valerie, from now on, you are the official Christmas cookie baker," and I took the prestigious role with honor and pride. I store the cookies in my mom's old cookie tin that was passed on to me.

Makes about 6 dozen.

- ½ cup butter
- ½ soft softening
- ½ cup brown sugar
- ½ cup white sugar
- 1 egg
- 1 cup all-purpose flour
- ½ teaspoon baking soda
- ½ teaspoon salt

- 1 cup coconut
- ½ cup chopped dates
- ¼ cup chopped red maraschino cherries
- ¼ cup chopped green maraschino cherries
- 1 teaspoon vanilla
- 2 cup quick oats

PREHEAT OVEN TO 325 DEGREES. Grease baking sheet.

Cream the butter and shortening until fluffy. Add brown and white sugars and cream together well. Add vanilla. Beat egg lightly and add to the sugar and shortening. Blend well. Add flour, sifted with the baking soda and salt. Mix in coconut, dates, and cherries. Add oats and blend with other ingredients. Drop by spoonfuls or roll into balls, flatten, and place on baking sheet. Bake at 325 degrees for approximately 23 minutes. Yields approximately 6 dozen, but I always double this recipe since they freeze well.

CHURCH WINDOWS COOKIES

BY DAWN SMITH

This is a recipe my grandmother made every Christmas and was known for making many delicious treats. She and my aunt would spend a few days at my house for the holidays when I was growing up. On Christmas Eve, we set up the card table to display all her goodies, with her Church Window Cookies taking center stage. My brother, sister, and I loved them so much she would be sure to make an extra-large batch for us. This was the beginning of our big Christmas Eve celebration tradition, when we would eat the delicious cookies while watching Christmas movies on the television and had our Family Game Night. A few years later, Grandma became ill and was not able to do much anymore and sadly passed away. Our Christmas tradition wasn't the same without her. After sharing with my son about the tradition, he talked me into making the Church Windows Cookies for Christmas. Now we make them together for the holidays and can share stories and memories about my grandmother.

- ½ cup unsalted butter
- 1 (12 ounce package) semisweet chocolate chips

- 1 (14 ounce package) coconut flakes
- 1 cup chopped walnuts
- 1 (10.5 ounce) bag colored miniature marshmallows

Melt butter and chocolate chips in a saucepan over low heat, stirring frequently to avoid burning. Once the chocolate is melted, let it cool slightly before adding in the marshmallows and walnuts. Once the marshmallows and walnuts are mixed into the chocolate, let the mixture cool. On a piece of wax paper, shape the chocolate into one long roll or shorter rolls, depending upon preference. Cover the roll (or rolls) with coconut. Wrap in wax paper and refrigerate until firm. Slice into ½ inch slices.

DATE COOKIES

BY ROSELYN STINGLEY

*M*y mom always made date cookies for Christmas. She did all the mixing of the cookies and cooking the date filling down. My job was cutting the dough with coffee cups and making a small hole for the date filling with a smaller cutter. I know my mom would have been proud years later when I made date cookies.

- 2 cups brown sugar
- 4 cups flour
- 1 cup butter
- 1 teaspoon baking soda
- ¼ teaspoon salt
- 3 eggs

Mix together and set in fridge overnight. Roll cookie dough on lightly floured surface. Cut dough with coffee cup into two pieces, one for the top and one for the bottom layer. Make a small hole on the top layer for the date filling to show through.

Date Filling:

- 1 cup dates
- 1 ½ cups brown sugar
- 1 ½ cups water
- 2 teaspoon flour

Cook mixture until thick, stirring occasionally. Cool. Preheat oven to 400 degrees. Spread date filling on bottom half of cookie, then place the top piece of cookie on top of the filling. Press together to seal the cookie. Put on a nonstick baking sheet and bake on 400 degrees for 10-15 minutes.

Acknowledgments

Writing this book has been a work from my heart. I want to thank all of the people who have supported and encouraged me and help bring this book to life.

Stephanie Mesa has been working closely with me since I began this writing journey. From plotting assistance to editing, from brainstorming to her incredible focus and diligence, I owe a big thanks to her. She also created the touching and beautiful book trailer for this project.

To my editorial team who I rely on for their expertise: Cate Perry, Audrey Mackaman, Cameron Chandler, Diane Lander-Simon and all of my incredible beta readers including: Harriet Horowitz, Judy Lecesse, Anne Wolters, Debra Ice, Pam Jennings Lyons, Amy Newman Connolley, Tina Giakoumis, Tracey Doerrer, Michelle Frey, and Paula Williams. To my ARC team a special call out to you, and to Terra Hix and Tracie Barton-Barrett

To my invaluable team for all their assistance and for always being there:
• Lectio Virtual Assistance for Authors including Geneva Agnos and Kristen Franzke
• Sean Fletcher for technical support and author backup
• Kate Rock LitChick

Several readers contributed their family recipes that are in the back of the book including: Jonathon Prosser, Carol Klabunde, Jeanne Crea, Judy Lecesse, Julia Trachsel, Jeannie Daniel, Letha Armstrong, Ashley Fehr, Debbie Wasserman, Valerie Hildebrand, Dawn Smith and Roselyn Stingley.

I want to acknowledge the wonderful people and organizations that offered me assistance with my research on this book including:

• K9s for Warriors an amazing organization that helps rescue dogs and train them for veterans with PTSD

• Old Dog Haven and all the great work they do to care for senior dogs

• Kimberly Lytle at Happy Swimmers for assistance with the drowning scene

Alan Ayers created the cover art on this book, and I was incredibly happy with the outcome. He was a pleasure to work with and an incredible artist.

Thank you to my friends and fellow authors for their endorsements Bette Lee Crosby, Judy Keim, and Dete Meserve.

To all of my family and friends, and of course, my beloved canine companion, Ellie.

Author swag: Littlemoon's Sunflowers by April Washington https://www.facebook.com/littlemoonssunflowers/ and

Todd Young at ToddYoungArt.etsy.com

www.andreahurst-author.com Website Design: Axiom Internet Solutions - Murray Fins

If you enjoyed reading this book, please leave a review on Amazon, they are truly appreciated.

Also, be sure to read ahead for an excerpt of the first full-length book in the Madrona Island Series, *The Guestbook*, and continue the journey to Madrona Island with the other books in the series, including:

Book One – The Guestbook

Everyone remembers their first love...But sometimes it's the second love that lasts

Fleeing her picture-perfect marriage among the privileged set of Brentwood and the wreckage of a failed marriage, Lily Parkins decides to move to the only place that still holds happy memories, her grandmother's old farmhouse. The lush and majestic setting of the Pacific Northwest calls to her and offers a place of refuge and perhaps renewal. Her grandmother has passed away, leaving the Madrona Island Bed & Breakfast Inn to Lily. Left with only an old guestbook as her guide–a curious book full of letters, recipes, and glimpses into her family history–Lily is determined to embrace her newfound independence and recreate herself, one page at a time. With the help of the quirky island residents she has befriended, she slowly finds the strength to seek out happiness on her own terms. But as soon as she has sworn off men and is standing on her own two feet, Lily meets Ian, the alluring artist who lives next door, and her new life is suddenly thrown off course. The last thing she wants to do right now is to open her heart to another man. Ultimately, Lily must decide if it's worth giving up her soul for security or risking everything to follow her heart in this romantic love story.

Book Two – Tea & Comfort

This second volume features the puzzling yet sensuous, Kyla Nolan. The story unravels the mystery behind her hasty departure from her glamorous New York life as a top model and her transformation to shop proprietor, herbalist, and local tea leaf reader on Madrona Island. Follow her battle with a reoccurring illness and the return of Lucas, the wealthy winery owner and former fiancé whom she left behind. Can a love that was so based on outside trappings survive illness and loss? With a touch of the paranormal, and her island friends, Kyla comes to terms with her fears and her heart's longings.

Book Three – Island Thyme Café

The third book features the vivacious and loving, Jude Simon, owner of the popular Island Thyme Café. After Lily's wedding festivities are over, Jude must face the dark secret from her past. Years ago, she'd found out her husband was cheating on her in an article in the local paper. Left a single mother of an infant daughter, Jude went on to make a success of her café, but still hides her broken heart behind her radiant smile. At almost 40 years old, she finds herself falling hard for her new chef, Ryan. Her feelings are returned, and just when she thinks she has found love at last, Ryan's own dark secret returns in the form of a seductive ex-lover who is determined to have him back. With the help of Kyla and Lily, Jude decides to fight for what she wants most and find the happy ending she has always longed for.

Web: www.andreahurst-author.com

ABOUT THE AUTHOR

 When not writing, visiting local farmer's markets, or indulging her love for dark chocolate, Andrea enjoys meeting fans at signings and working as an editor for other authors. She writes hopeful books in charming settings that take readers on uplifting journeys and leaves them with lasting impressions. She lives with her rescue poodle, Ellie, near Raleigh, North Carolina.

Click here to become more involved and join the Lavender Lane community on Facebook

Click here to sign up for my newsletter, and receive a free copy of Madrona Island B&B

Connect With Andrea
www.andreahurst-author.com
author@andreahurst.com

 facebook.com/andreahurstauthor
 twitter.com/AndreaHurst_
 pinterest.com/andreahurst7
 bookbub.com/authors/andrea-hurst

Made in the USA
Middletown, DE
15 July 2020